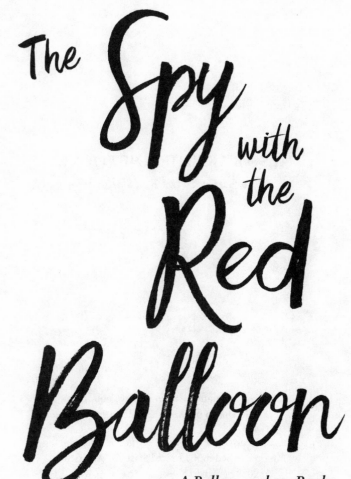

The Spy with the Red Balloon

A Balloonmakers Book

KATHERINE LOCKE

Albert Whitman & Company
Chicago, Illinois

ALSO BY KATHERINE LOCKE
The Girl with the Red Balloon

Library of Congress Cataloging-in-Publication
data is on file with the publisher.

Text copyright © 2018 by Katherine Locke
First published in the United States of America
in 2018 by Albert Whitman & Company
ISBN 978-0-8075-2934-8

Printed in the United States of America
10 9 8 7 6 5 4 3 2 1 LB 22 21 20 19 18

Cover design by Nina Simoneaux

For more information about Albert Whitman & Company,
visit our website at www.albertwhitman.com.

For my grandmothers,
and for my siblings, Jacob and Hannah

OP-1-5   OFFICE OF STRATEGIC SERVICES   4 April 1943
SPECIAL PROJECTS BUREAU
Memorandum for the Director
SUBJECT: Request to Recruit Persons with Unusual Gifts in the War Effort

The Special Projects Bureau requests immediate funds and personnel to begin identifying persons capable of using magic, a space for them to work, and the authorization to end their tenure at any time and by any means necessary to maintain the secrecy of the Manhattan Project and of magic. Colonel Mann of the Special Projects Bureau will assume responsibility immediately for this effort.

Andrew Mann
_____
Authorizing Signature

CHAPTER ONE

NEW YORK CITY, NEW YORK
AUGUST 15, 1943

ILSE

Sometimes, I thought I might drown in all the marvels of this world. Usually this happened when I saw planes flying and thought about all the engineering work and experimentation that had turned metal cylinders into modes of transportations and weapons of war. Sometimes this happened when I turned on the faucet and water flowed out, having been plumbed through a network of pipes designed by teams who'd thought about the past, present, and future needs of the city's residents.

Or, when I experienced the changing seasons, caused by the tilt of the earth. The idea that something off-kilter could cause anything as beautiful as the seasons regularly astonished me. Imagine how dull our lives would be if the earth had an upright axis, like a chandelier hung from the ceiling.

Today, the drowning happened because the sky was a wild sort of blue. The type of blue you could fall into, and when you tipped your head back, you'd see only blue in every direction. It was dizzying.

"Ilse," said Wolf, ever patient.

"Do you know *why* the sky's blue?" I asked him, squinting upward, even though Mama would have yelled at me about how my face would wrinkle and I'd never find a husband.

"You're going to tell me anyway."

He wasn't wrong. I suppose that's the thing about siblings. They know you like no one else does.

"Light," I said. "The blue light scatters farther from the sun's rays than red light."

"I'm going to pretend to understand that for the purposes of this experiment," Wolf said. "Do you think that light affects it?"

The last word pulled me out of my reverie, and I looked down at him, blinking rapidly as spots splashed across my vision and the cone cells in the back of my eyes adjusted to the rapid change in light. Wolf came into focus in front of me, a frown crossing his face. He never used to frown this much, but he'd lost his sense of humor the day the Japanese bombed Pearl Harbor. So far, neither Hitler nor the Emperor nor Wolf's frown seemed likely to surrender.

"Magic doesn't appear to be affected by light." I thought about our prior experiments, the ones done in our rooms late at night after Papa went to bed. "But to verify that, we'd have to test under multiple weather conditions throughout multiple times of day, or expose something with activated magic to—"

"Shhh, Ilse. Keep it down." Wolf huffed, looking around with a scowl as if we weren't at least a hundred yards from the nearest person. "I still don't think we should be here. But since you insist, please stop saying *that word* so loudly."

I continued. "Different wavelengths. It's not a bad idea. We can add it to the list."

"We don't have a list," Wolf said, but slowly, as if he wasn't sure he was telling the truth or was trying to reassure himself we didn't have one.

But we did. Or rather, I did. I pulled the red notebook from my schoolbag triumphantly and tossed it to him. He caught it and flipped it open to the first page, where it said at the top, List of Things I'd Like to Test with Regards to Blood and Physics.

"Are you *mad*?" my brother hissed. "You're going to get caught."

"It doesn't say 'magic,'" I protested.

"It says everything but!" He shoved the notebook back into my bag. "You're going to be the death of me. Look, I promised you I'd help, and I'm not going to renege on that. But you promised to be done before dinner. Let's get this started."

Between the two of us, I was the scientist. Wolf was in the park with me because he didn't trust me not to get into trouble. I didn't mind because I wanted to use samples of both of our blood. I didn't know if there was a difference between how they acted on the magic, or maybe the magic in the blood acted on the equations. Either way, there were so many variables between us that it seemed silly to conduct an experiment by myself when he could help.

Wolf didn't like to talk about what our blood could do.

I could barely keep myself from telling everyone.

Magic. Even the word itself felt otherworldly, rolling around on my tongue. Some of the earliest uses of the word weren't about the creation, but about the act of creating. Magic. Creating something out of what appeared to be nothing. But matter could not be created or destroyed. Magic only acted on what already existed and what could exist given the right circumstances.

It'd been an accident, discovering the magic. But once I'd discovered it existed, it was hard to stop asking questions. Where did it come from? What could it do? Why did we have it? Who else had it? Were we the only ones?

"Ilse," Wolf repeated again, sighing, fingers snapping in front of my face.

"I know, I know," I said, even though I didn't know, and that was the part that had me distracted. My mind felt like a tornado. It spun up with all the questions I had.

Wolf sat down on a rock, rolling up his sleeves and setting objects next to us: a kite, two apples, a handkerchief.

I sat down next to him, unpacking our little kit. It'd taken awhile to assemble. We'd spent most of the last three years figuring out what we needed. I mean I spent most of the last three years figuring out what we needed; Wolf was happy to ignore everything. But he didn't bleed once a month, so this was less of an issue for him. He just needed to avoid blood loss.

And by blood loss, I mean he needed to avoid the war.

The only reason Wolf was at university was to get a deferment. Papa didn't speak to him for a week after he enrolled. He couldn't imagine why Wolf was avoiding the war—or running away from the family business. Wolf had come up with some sort of excuse that hadn't really mattered, but he'd suffered. It'd been the first time he was the child who stepped outside the carefully drawn paths of our lives. Our parents had given up on me when I did calculus in third grade.

"I know I've figured this out," I said.

"You said that last time," Wolf replied dryly. "Let's try not to let everyone see that we're drawing blood in the middle of the park, shall we?"

I glared at him, even as I drew the syringe and needle from the case that held them down. Our unclotted blood made things float, so little leather straps designed for pens kept the syringes in place. I'd taken a thoroughly unappetizing first aid class for girls interested in serving as nurses in the Pacific and in Italy, and while I'd managed not to puke *directly* on the instructor's shoes when he'd shown us a photograph of necrotic flesh, I'd managed to acquire the one skill I needed: how to do a blood draw.

One of my earliest experiments had shown that clotted blood was practically useless. I'd love to know *how* it got that way—was magic a particle interrupted by coagulation?—but I hadn't figured out how to study that in the laboratory at school yet. They were not fans of students experimenting on themselves for some reason, and it wasn't like I could explain why I *had* to use my blood and not the blood of a rat.

Unless rats had magic. I hadn't thought of that possibility.

Wolf opened his mouth, and I could feel my name forming on the air, even though that wasn't possible, according to science, and I said hurriedly, "Your blood or mine first?"

He wasn't going to tolerate many more distractions.

"Mine," Wolf said after a beat. "I don't want you to be light-headed during this."

He held out his arm, fist turned toward the sky, and I readied the syringe, pressing down above his elbow so his vein filled up. I really didn't like this part, but it wasn't as though I had a choice. I slipped the needle into his vein, watching the blood fill to the top. Every now and then I missed, and the vein would blow, so I was always careful to see blood filling the tip of the needle before I drew back on the syringe. Dark-red blood flowed into the syringe, and when it had filled, I slipped the needle out of his vein, and he pressed his finger down hard on the crook of his elbow to close it off.

"Perfect," I murmured.

It'd taken me awhile to figure it out, but I had learned how to af-fix a paintbrush tip to a syringe, and I'd made a whole set of them. I screwed off the needle, screwed on the paintbrush tip, and bent over the kite, double-checking the equations I'd written down in my notebook.

"Got it?" asked Wolf, leaning over.

"You're blocking my light," I retorted. "Don't distract me."

"Fine, fine," he grumbled, sitting back. "I'm just trying to block the view of anyone watching."

"I think it's a form of narcissism to think anyone in this park cares what we're doing," I told him, painting slowly and carefully.

I didn't want to make a mistake. It wasn't like I could erase easily. "They think I'm fixing a kite."

"Ilse..." Wolf began to say, his voice light and casual.

"We're just two teenagers in a park," I insisted. "There's a war, but people can still have lives, you know."

"Ilse," Wolf repeated, but this time I noticed the difference. He kept his tone airy in a way that it never was. "Someone's watching us."

I nearly rolled my eyes, but I needed to concentrate on the equation. He was so paranoid. "Call out to them. Say we're part of a cult, and invite them to join our ritual."

"*Ilse.*"

If I had a penny for every time he said my name like that, I'd be rich. I glanced up, paintbrush hovering. "Fine. Where?"

Wolf shifted, leaning back on his elbows casually as if surveillance was something he always did. "Two o'clock. With the hat."

I twisted, looking over my shoulder. Wolf snapped, "Not my two o'clock, *your* two o'clock."

"How was I supposed to know you'd already adjusted for my perspective?" I grumbled, turning back around for my two o'clock. I stopped grumbling when I saw the man in the tan suit lighting a cigarette beneath a tree, his hat resting on top of his head like he'd just set it there. He wasn't looking at us, but he still looked out of place. The other men in suits weren't wearing their coats. This man was. How he didn't notice the heat was beyond me. Sweat trickled down my brow.

I turned back to the kite. "Ignore him. He's just some stranger from uptown."

"*We* are strangers from uptown," Wolf reminded me.

We'd chosen to come over the Brooklyn Bridge to avoid running into anyone we might know, but to stay in a neighborhood still predominantly Jewish. Where people with our coloring and our hair and our builds wouldn't be bothered. It'd been Wolf's idea.

"I'm almost done," I said quietly, bending over the equation again, my hand moving precisely and swiftly. "I can't stop, or the blood will clot in the syringe."

"You have to stop," Wolf said out of the side of his mouth. "The *result* of this experiment will be the kite flying. It's not like he won't notice that."

"Yes, Wolf," I retorted. "Because kites are definitely not known for *flying*. How out of place that'll look!"

"There's no wind," he snapped back. "Ilse, he's definitely looking at us."

"How could he *possibly* know what we're doing?" I asked.

"I don't know, but it doesn't matter."

"We could be part of a Satanic cult."

"That's not really helpful right now. Ilse, put the paintbrush away. I'm taking it away from you."

"You wouldn't," I said, just before I saw the shadow of his hand cross over my equation. I yanked my hand away with a yelp, and the tip of the paintbrush, blood dripping off it, slid right through the equation on the underside of the kite. I saw the flames just before the kite ignited, the searing gash across the fabric curling with embers and then bursting into flames. The cotton caught quickly—Damn fabrics and their low flash points! Had the magic done that?—and in a second, all forty-six square inches of the kite were a blazing fire in my hands.

A hand on my shoulder ripped me backward, and I tumbled with a yelp down the small hill. I shoved myself upright and looked up to see Wolf dumping a thermos of water on the kite and stomping at it with his feet. For a brief moment, I wondered if the flames were magical, and if there was something I ought to be doing or writing with blood. But then smoke curled around his shoes as he stomped and the kite burned up, the flames dying down because there was nothing left to ignite.

The people in the park who had ignored us before stared at us, and the weight of their gazes made my stomach turn in on itself. Wolf was breathing heavily as he shoved his hand through his hair and then planted his hands on his hips, staring down at the kite and all the smashed parts of our kit on the ground. He'd be furious with me, and that knowledge made my heart hurt. I hated when he was mad at me.

I needed a moment to summon the courage to start back up the hill toward my brother and the wreckage. And I wanted to find the cause of the accident. I turned around slowly, scanning the park.

But the man in the tan suit was gone.

CHAPTER TWO

NEW YORK CITY, NEW YORK
AUGUST 15, 1943

ILSE

"I know you're mad at me," I said for the sixth time as we walked back across the Brooklyn Bridge, lifting my voice a little over the wind and the sound of cars below us.

"I'm not mad at you," Wolf said for the sixth time, but his shoulders were tense and he had his hands shoved into his pockets. He didn't even stop to linger over the ships passing below us, moving from the ocean to the navy yard and back out again.

"You are," I insisted.

He sighed, slowing and taking a hand out of one pocket to scrub at his face. "I'm worried, Ilse. That's different than being mad at you."

"About the guy watching us?" I asked. We hadn't seen him when we left the park, nor anyone else who seemed to be paying us any attention. Not that that seemed to matter to Wolf.

"Him," Wolf admitted. "And everyone else in that park who saw the fire. Ilse, I don't know what we're playing with here."

"I know," I said quietly, because this I did understand. I knew what we didn't know. Sometimes I thought that was the hardest thing about living in this world: knowing that I didn't even know what I didn't know. How could I find the right questions to ask to get the answers I needed to move forward, if I didn't know that information? How could I...I didn't know why I wanted to move forward.

Why there seemed to be a destination, a place to go, questions to be answered, but it felt like a new science. Something just beyond my fingertips. But maybe magic was like science. It was a horizon we'd chase and never reach.

Wolf elbowed me lightly, and I looked over at him, shading my eyes against the setting sun. "What?"

"We'll try again another night," he promised me, his voice all gentle, like he thought I might cry.

"We don't have to," I said, even though the words made my throat tighten.

"I don't need to know more than I know now," Wolf said. "But you do."

"It's just once a month," I said.

He shot me a dark look, his mouth twisting a bit. "I wasn't talking about that. I meant, you have an insatiable curiosity."

Sometimes Wolf had a way of complimenting me that made me feel small, even when he didn't mean it. Most of the time, he felt like my only ally, the only person who didn't act as though I was assembled wrong—too smart for a girl, big mouth, no manners, too short, too loud—and other times, he sounded just like our parents, like I was a burden. At university, they thought it odd that I was a girl with such curiosity, but they treated my girlness as if it was the wrong part, not my curiosity. My parents treated my curiosity as if it was my fatal flaw. And Wolf's words made me wince.

The thing was, I thought Wolf might have been insatiably curious once upon a time. I remembered him taking things apart as a kid, just to see how he could put them back together, and he used to read everything he could get his hands on, anything from instruction manuals to classics to philosophy books. But something in the last two years had changed him. Maybe it was the war. Maybe that's what happened when boys grew up.

I missed the brother who didn't see my questions as a burden. I didn't want him to protect me from myself. I wanted him to be curious alongside me. But I didn't know how to say that without sounding childish and idealistic. And he still thought of me as a child, like there weren't a scant two years between us. Years that didn't used to matter.

"You can't always protect me," I told him. I aimed for flippant and fell short, my tone tripping into petulant and hurt. I swallowed hard against the tears and the things I didn't say—couldn't say—to him.

"No, I can't," he said as we walked down the steps of the bridge. And suddenly, inexplicably, I wanted to stay in a world where he tried. Even if I didn't want his protection. Even if I didn't need it. I wanted him to try, like he had an hour ago, somewhere back across the river in Brooklyn, in a park, with fire in my hands.

We crossed the city in relative silence, Wolf's hands back in the pockets of his trousers and my arms crossed over my chest while my bag, and the ruined kite and the discarded needles, banged against my side with every step. As Manhattan rose around us, the tension between my brother and me drifted away like a tide pulled back out to sea.

"Your face is going to get stuck like that," I told him when he frowned at a particularly long traffic light.

He rolled his eyes at me. "Have you ever tried being quiet?"

"Once," I said. "It was *terrible* so I vowed never to try it again."

He snorted, but I got the corner of his mouth to tip up again.

"Still thinking about the man in the park?" I asked.

"No," he said, sounding surprised. "Something else. It's nothing."

"You can't think about nothing," I said. "That's impossible."

"You're so annoying sometimes," muttered Wolf.

"You can tell me what you're thinking about, or I can talk about why I think the balloon caught fire when the equation was all about lift," I offered slyly.

Just as I'd hoped, Wolf scowled. "You can't talk about that out here on the streets. Ilse, be serious."

I grinned. "So I'm thinking that there's a concentrated amount of ma—"

He clapped a hand over my mouth. "Fine. Fine. It's Max's nineteenth birthday today. I was just..."

My face fell, and his hand dropped off my mouth. Guilt turned my stomach. I shouldn't have pushed, but I couldn't help it. My brother's best friend, Max Egan, had enlisted a year ago, and as far as I was aware, he hadn't written to Wolf. And Wolf hadn't written to him. I didn't know if boys didn't write letters to each other the way girls did, or whether something had happened between them—like they'd fought or Max had kissed a girl Wolf liked or something. I couldn't read what Wolf's emotions were now, his face like stone, set and solid next to me.

"You could write to him," I ventured.

He shook his head as we walked up the steps of our apartment building. "No, I think some things are best left until after the war."

But how do you know he'll come home? I wanted to ask. I didn't get a chance though, because as soon as we entered the lobby, our doorman, Ernest, said, "Oh Miss Ilse and Mr. Wolf, good evening. I bet you're excited to see that fancy visitor you have."

Wolf and I blinked at each other. *Fancy visitor?*

Then Ernest added, "Looked like a general to me."

Wolf swore a bit under his breath, making Ernest's eyes go wide, and I smiled to placate him. We didn't need him telling Mama about Wolf's salty mouth. But my mind was already flying up the stairs to our apartment.

Someone knew about what had happened in the park.

And that was my fault.

The elevator doors shut behind us, and I closed my eyes, doing the math in my head of force equals mass times acceleration. Acceleration equals delta velocity over delta time. If I knew how to use the magic in my blood, I'd be flying away from here as fast as I could.

Maybe it wasn't about what had happened in the park. Maybe the military man was here for Wolf. They usually sent a letter, but maybe this was an unusual situation. If he was being drafted despite attending university, I'd figure out the magic to save him.

I didn't care if everyone in the world saw me do magic. If it'd save Wolf from fighting in a war, I'd do it. It'd be my fault if he went to war. And a very small voice in the back of my mind whispered, *It'll be your fault if he doesn't come home.*

"We don't know what he wants," Wolf said finally.

"Where do we say we were?"

"In the park. We should only lie if we have to. You hadn't been to Prospect Park before, and you wanted to go. Okay?"

"Okay."

"Okay."

"If he's here for you…"

"Then I'll deal with it. It will be fine."

"You know that's not true," I snapped.

He smiled a little, despite the tension furrowing his brow. He spoke to our reflections in the elevator door. "Now you're protecting me. Let me guide this conversation. We'll face whatever it is."

"Even if you're drafted?" I said, keeping my voice low.

He looked down at his shoes. "We're in a war, Ilse. It isn't a choice."

"I don't like it," I said.

"I didn't say I did," he replied.

"Then tell them no!" I hissed.

"You can't tell them *no*, Ilse," he said in such a condescending tone that I wanted to slap him.

But the elevator doors opened, and I stomped down the hallway to our apartment. I didn't care what Wolf said. I'd meet with this general, or whoever was in our sitting room, but I wasn't going to make it easy for them to take my brother from me.

With a deep breath, I opened our door, tossed down my bag, and called out, "We're *home!*"

If I pretended everything was fine, maybe everything would be fine.

Our housekeeper, Myrtle, pushed through the double doors from the kitchen with a tray in her hands loaded with little sandwiches, cups, and a pot of coffee. She pursed her lips at my coat on the stairs as I snatched a little sandwich and stuffed it in my mouth. I hated cucumber sandwiches, but I was starving, and I wasn't facing someone here to draft my brother or arrest us for magic arson on an empty stomach.

I paused and said with my mouth full, "That's the *good* silver."

This was not a good sign. On the list of things that happened in the house, good silver came out for Rosh Hashanah and for breaking the fast on Yom Kippur. Pesach, if we did the second seder here. Shiva, after one of my grandparents died. But never any other time of the year had Mama broken out the good silver. Who *was* our visitor? What *did* he want?

"Miss Ilse, Master Wolf," Myrtle said severely. "Mind your manners. Your mama wants you in the sitting room."

"We know," said Wolf, dropping his bag in the hall next to mine. "Ernest told us."

Myrtle smiled at him, charmed as always by Wolf's good-and-obedient-son act. Then she turned to me, her face knotting into a frown. "Try to look like a young lady and not a hurricane."

"I despise hurricanes. I'd rather be a tornado." I couldn't help myself.

She sighed. "I suppose it's too much to ask you to watch your tongue."

I raised my eyebrows. "How can I watch something I can't see?"

Myrtle said something about my smart mouth and being a spoiled brat before she pushed open the doors to the sitting room and led us in there, with my hurricane hair and wind-whipped cheeks and all.

CHAPTER THREE

WOLF

Our sitting room faced west, and this late in the afternoon, the light was warm, sliding over the rugs and the settee where my mother sat, wringing her hands in her lap. With its floor-to-ceiling bookcases and the ornate lamps my father had collected from Turkey, it was Ilse's favorite place in our apartment, and I wasn't used to seeing other people in here, occupying her normal reading chair.

The man sitting in the olive-green armchair nearly blended into the chair with his uniform. I could have missed him if not for his balding head and sharp, angular face pointed in our direction. He studied us with his mouth set in a firm line, as if he were determined not to let any emotion play out on his face.

"Wolf, Ilse," said Papa, rising. His German accent trembled on his tongue. "This is Colonel Andrew Mann. He came to speak with you about your studies. Colonel Mann, my children."

He wasn't here for our studies. He was here to execute us. *No.* I took a deep breath. If he'd wanted to kill us, if what we did or could do was illegal, he would have made it look like an accident. A fire. A car accident. A fall from the bridge. He wasn't here to kill us. That was illogical. The only option was to play nicely and see how this played out.

I nodded to him. "Pleasure to meet you, sir."

Next to me, Ilse scowled slightly. "I didn't realize our studies were of interest to the American military. Don't you have a war to fight?"

"*Ilse*," hissed my mother, her face going white with shock, while my father and I winced for different reasons. My father, likely because he could never teach Ilse to hold her tongue. Or maybe he was afraid of being labeled an enemy combatant because of his German accent and his ill-mannered daughter. Me, I held my tongue because I'd forgotten that Ilse was a wild card. She'd tried to play it casual in the hallway, but that could only last so long. Most of the time, she said what came to her mind, and she didn't like the idea that her work—magic or university—might be cause for censure.

"I work for the military's Special Projects Bureau," said the colonel stiffly, and the delivery of the office snagged a bit. I turned the words and his tone over in my mind and then trusted my instincts. Not a lie. Not the whole truth.

He looked at my parents. "I'd like to speak to your children alone, if you don't mind."

Papa stood up, nodding like he'd expected this moment to come. He looked...proud, almost. Like he was grateful someone was here to tell me that university deferment didn't matter anymore and I'd be forced into war. His expression stung me. I'd known he thought me a coward, but not that he'd be pleased that I'd be in harm's way.

But Mama didn't move. "You won't talk to my children without me here. Ilse's still sixteen."

"I know," said Colonel Mann calmly.

Mama glared at him. "Wolf has a student's deferment."

"I am aware," the colonel said in the same patient voice.

Mama still didn't move. I'd never seen her stand her ground against male authority like this before, but I supposed that Ilse must have gotten it from somewhere. No one came between my mother and her children.

"Edie," said my father, his voice gentle instead of stern for once. "They'll be fine. Ilse can't go anywhere without our say-so. We'll be right here. Let them hear what the colonel says. They'll tell us everything, right, children?"

"Yes," I said immediately.

"Yes," Ilse agreed after a beat.

Mama shot her a look, her frown deepening, and then slowly rose to her feet, a hand wrapped around the pearls at her throat. She walked toward Ilse and me at the doorway and paused, letting go of her pearls to touch each of our cheeks, and then she brushed by us into the hall.

Papa followed her, and as the door clicked, I heard him ask Myrtle to get him something strong to drink. It was the only sign that he was as worried as Mama.

The room felt empty without my parents, and part of me wanted to reach out to them and say, *Wait, I don't know how to negotiate this.* But I was left alone in there with my little sister and someone who knew we could do magic. Someone who wanted to send us to war.

"Sit," said the colonel.

I moved first, sitting on the settee where my parents had just been. Ilse came and sat on the arm next to me, close to the books and non-committal, as if she thought she could run from this if need be.

"My name is Colonel Mann," he said again. "And more specifically, I work for the Office of Strategic Service's Special Projects Bureau. We've been monitoring both of you for some time, but I was moved to act today because I received a report this afternoon regarding an incident in the park."

"We don't know what you're talking about," I said calmly.

"Don't you?" Colonel Mann asked. "There are photos being developed now. Would you like me to have them delivered? I can wait."

Photographs. They had taken photographs of us. I hadn't even *thought* of that possibility, and secretly I cursed myself, struggling not to look sideways at Ilse. It didn't matter though, because for all that Ilse was, she wasn't a mind reader.

"We didn't do anything wrong," she said in a low, sulky voice.

The colonel's face twitched. *Victory.* He had us. "You caused a large autoignition event in the middle of a public park."

"It shouldn't have caused an autoignition event," Ilse said, her mind pouncing on the science and the magic and, apparently, leaving sense behind. "There's nothing in the equation that should have lowered the ignition point of cotton that far."

"And yet..." Colonel Mann said.

"Ilse." I elbowed her a bit. *Control yourself.*

He leaned forward. "How did you stumble upon equations?"

"Do not answer him," I told her, my voice firm.

I didn't need to look at her to know she was struggling with that. He'd asked her a question, and she had an answer. It must have been like torture, but Ilse managed to let out only a small, pained whimper, and then she fell silent, her shoulders slumped and her foot kicking at high speed next to me on the sofa.

I addressed Colonel Mann. "We won't let it happen again. If you need us to sign something to that effect, that's fine. But that's all we can offer."

"Unfortunately, Mr. Klein," he said, "you are not in a position to negotiate."

He reached down and I flinched, rising to step in front of Ilse, and then paused when I realized he was only reaching for a briefcase. He glanced at me with knowing eyes and unsnapped the briefcase.

"As I said, we've been monitoring you for some time. Wolf, hospitalized at age fifteen after an ice-skating accident. You had a head injury in which you spoke of levitating. Your parents made a large donation to the hospital, and that incident was removed from your medical record. Ilse, you were referred to psychiatric care when you were thirteen after—"

"Enough," I cut him off. I swore silently in my mind. He knew everything. "What do you want with us?"

"There's something we're working on," said Colonel Mann simply. "And I have need of people with your special talents."

I glanced up at Ilse for the first time. She was chewing on her fingernails, a dark curl wound in her other hand. Anxious, and trying to understand what was being played here. "Both of us? Ilse's only sixteen."

"I know," said he. "Both of you. Ilse is unusual. Ilse, you're highly educated, apparently brilliant, and you have a gift."

"Magic," said Ilse around her fingernails. "Just say it."

Colonel Mann almost smiled. "Magic."

"Wolf, you're astute and pragmatic. You're being wasted in university. We need you in this war." He spoke as if he didn't know exactly why I'd gone to university and sought a deferment. He continued placidly, "And you have a gift as well, even if you aren't as familiar with it as Ilse is."

"What Ilse knows, I know," I said, even though it wasn't true.

"Of course," he said, and his tone was almost pitying. He took folders out of the briefcase and closed it with a click. "Hitler's building a weapon. And if we don't stop him, he'll succeed. If he succeeds, he wins the war."

"What kind of weapon?" asked Ilse.

"What does this have to do with us?" I asked. One of us had to stay focused here.

Colonel Mann spoke carefully, as if he had a mouthful of marbles. "The weapon uses a certain controlled release of energy to do an immense amount of damage, bigger than anything we've ever seen before."

Ilse's head jerked up, and her hands fell from her face to her lap. "You're…He's splitting the atom."

The colonel glanced at the door as if our parents might be eavesdropping. "Christ, they weren't kidding about your mind. Quiet, girl. Yes. We fear he's trying to build an atom bomb, and that he's ahead of us. We know that he was working on it from the scientists who defected—"

"Escaped," I corrected. So many of them were Jewish. It wasn't defection if it was escaping death.

"Escaped," he acknowledged with a nod. "And we're working on a two-pronged approach to the problem. Three-pronged, if you think about it."

"Ilse, don't ask," I started to say, but she had already leaned forward and asked, "What are the prongs?"

"He would have told us anyway," I muttered to her. "You don't have to play nice with him."

"That was a completely respectable question," she hissed back at me.

The colonel, to his credit, pretended that he couldn't hear us. He cleared his throat and continued as if we weren't bickering. "The first prong is to win the war."

"Excellent strategy," I said, keeping my voice smooth.

"*Wolf*," said Ilse.

"The second prong is that we are pursuing our own atomic program." Here, the colonel broke eye contact with me and looked straight at Ilse. And good thing too, because I had to catch her wrist as she leapt to her feet off the arm of the sofa.

"Are you out of your mind?" Her voice squeaked, it hit such a pitch.

"You've never wondered if it's possible?" asked the colonel.

I glared at him. That wasn't playing fair, and he knew it. You couldn't put a question in front of Ilse and not expect her to answer it, or to explore it as far as she could. He was manipulating her, and I wanted him to know that I knew exactly what he was doing. I'd done the same thing as a child, but with smaller stakes. *Ilse, don't you want to figure out the most efficient way to organize the bookshelves?* had bought me a precious afternoon of silence.

Ilse predictably faltered, but only for a moment before she drew herself up, squared her shoulders, and shook off my hand around her wrist. "No. Because I won't have a part in killing people."

I blinked. "Wait, what? Who's killing people?"

"We are at war, Miss Klein." Colonel Mann raised an eyebrow. "It is kill or be killed."

"The theory behind the atomic bomb," Ilse said carefully, as if she was reciting from a book, and maybe she was, "is that a sustained chain reaction would split atoms and release colossal amounts of energy. The effects of this would be devastating. How devastating, we don't know, because no one's done this."

He surveyed her with a cool, glittering glare. "Hitler is building one. We must stop him from building it."

"Stopping him from building one cannot be done by building another," snapped Ilse. "Do you not see how there's a chain effect? You obtain one because he has one, and someone else will want one because we have one, and someone else will need one because that country has one. This is a line of dominoes you cannot reset, colonel. There is some science we should not touch."

"Thankfully," said the colonel, "I'm not here to ask your permission."

Ilse scowled. I looked back and forth between her and the colonel. Time to head off this fight. "Tell us what our role is, colonel."

"Once we have the bomb, we'll need a way to deliver it. And I believe that we can best do that by magic. Ilse, we'd like you to work on that side of the project." The colonel leaned back in the armchair, turning his attention back to me while Ilse sputtered and said something to the effect of *over her dead body.*

"Wolf, you're part of the third prong to stop Hitler from obtaining this deadly weapon. We need a team to steal whatever information they can find and destroy whatever they can't take with them."

"In Germany," I said. For years, thousands of Jews had tried to flee Hitler's Germany. Now the military was sending us right back into the heart of enemy territory.

"Yes," he said. "You'd go to England first. But I believe you're well equipped for this challenge. You're observant, smart, and practical. You aren't rash or hasty. You speak German."

"What does that have to do with magic?" I asked, ignoring the part where he apparently had analyzed my character. How long had we been under surveillance?

"You'll find out," he said.

Helpful, I thought, but I kept my mouth shut. A flicker of satisfaction appeared and disappeared on Colonel Mann's face. In a flash, I realized I was playing right into his hand and what game he was trying to play. He knew I was holding back. That was what he liked about me. That I held my tongue. That where my sister was rash, impulsive, prone to following her curiosity instead of fostering pragmatism, I was cautious, careful, self-aware.

"You're not separating us," Ilse said.

I sucked in a breath. She was my little sister, and she was loud and she was obnoxious and she was always in my business, and yes, I was jealous of her. But, she was my little sister, and we were in this together. We protected each other. We had each other's backs. I didn't want her to be in harm's way, but I had to admit, if I could have chosen anyone to have at my side, I would have chosen her.

"You are working on separate parts of the same project and will be stationed at different bases." Colonel Mann didn't seem perturbed by our shock.

"Ilse is only sixteen," I repeated, desperate.

"*Almost* seventeen," Ilse interjected, unable to stop herself.

I ignored her. "You can't just send her off by herself."

"I am aware of your sister's age," he said, his tone increasingly crisp and certain.

"I'm right here," Ilse reminded both of us.

The colonel studied me. "She won't be alone, and she won't be leaving the country."

"I still don't understand why you need magic," Ilse repeated.

"War," he said, "is terrible, Miss Klein. Magic is effective, difficult to detect, leaves no discernible residue, and allows us to act from considerable distance, saving American lives."

"I won't kill people," Ilse repeated. "And neither will Wolf. He has a deferment. I'm still in university. You cannot make us do anything. Not even if you have photographs of what happened in the park."

I had to admire her chutzpah, but I didn't know how to tell her that it wouldn't matter. They knew something about us that they shouldn't know. That was the only explanation for why Colonel Mann had shared such sensitive information with us. We didn't have an option to refuse. If we did, we'd be shot, or worse. There were, after all, things worse than death in this world.

His smile was thin again, no teeth. "Miss Klein, you are extraordinary. You know that. You've discovered magic and explored its uses without any guidance or support. Of course, you didn't get into NYU based on your magic. You got in because your capacity to understand physics is beyond that of any sixteen-year-old we've ever had in the United States. I'm not asking you to use one of your extraordinary talents or the other. I need you to use both. I need someone who understands the science and who can do the magic. And you're going to help us win this war. With magic. With dynamite. With sabotage. With deceit. Any way you can."

I sensed that his next move, if we didn't accept, was blackmail, but I didn't want to put Ilse in that position. If he backed her into that corner, she'd make a decision that couldn't be undone. I couldn't talk us out of every predicament my sister got us into. And this was one of them.

"Ilse," I said quietly. "Once we're in, you can guide decisions, right? You can't be a decision-maker from the outside."

"I don't understand," she replied, turning her wide eyes to me. "You want to do this?"

"No, but if we don't…He knows about our magic. They know about the magic. You think they'll really let us just walk out of here?" Colonel Mann said nothing, confirming my suspicions. The government wouldn't let us set more fires in Prospect Park. Ilse didn't look convinced however, and I didn't feel convinced. I lowered my voice and added, "Maybe it's the right thing to do."

Ilse studied me for a moment, her frown deepening. Then she turned back to the colonel and took a deep breath. "Okay. How big is it?"

I assumed she was talking about the bomb, but I couldn't be quite sure.

He shrugged. "I don't know."

"How much does it weigh?"

"I don't know."

"What is the target?"

"I don't know."

"And now I know you're lying," Ilse said with a grimace.

"I am not lying, Miss Klein," he said simply. "We don't know these things because it doesn't exist yet."

And a Nazi one might exist before ours did. The fate of the world would depend on me being able to destroy their ability to create the bomb. But with magic. So their other spies had failed. Something like that. My mind spun.

Ilse flopped backward very dramatically. "You want me to figure out how to use magic to deliver something that doesn't exist to a target you don't know."

Colonel Mann exhaled, his eyes sharpening with amusement. "Yes."

Ilse pressed her hands into her legs. "I want to serve my country, but I will not have a part in *killing people*. Or in my brother going to war because I accidentally set something on fire! And I resent the choice that's been placed before us."

The tension in the room splintered, fracturing like light refracting off shattered glass and bouncing across our faces. His stern, impassive face with his quiet even tones, Ilse's face, flushed red, her voice shaking harder than her fingers, steadier than her resolve, my bewilderment sliding through the newly formed spaces, the information I held in my hands that I didn't understand.

I thought of the reports we had, of what had happened to our family still living in Germany, of the boys who had died at Pearl Harbor. Ilse was right. I didn't want to be a part of killing people. But someone else had made that choice already. People were dying in this war, and they'd been dying for years, and that wasn't because of us. But we could end it.

They were building a bomb, a bomb that in the wrong hands could be the end of the world, and they wanted my little sister to help them deliver it.

And they wanted my help making sure they were the only ones building that weapon. I didn't know what I had to do to ensure that, but it was clear they expected that mission to be completed at any cost.

The weapon itself went against everything I'd learned. Everything I believed in. But if I didn't help, and Hitler won, or he got the bomb first, how would I feel? And if we said no—if I said no, or she said no—what did Colonel Mann do next, now that we knew this secret? I didn't like the options.

"I'm in," I said quietly, ignoring my unsure heart.

"Wolf." Ilse's voice cracked, like ice splitting beneath the weight of my words.

I couldn't look at her, but I bumped my shoulder against hers as an apology. "It's a war, Ilse. I was going to end up serving at some point or another, and I might as well do it with the magic out in the open. You'll be here. You'll be safe."

"But you…" she said and didn't finish her sentence.

I didn't know what to tell her.

The colonel leaned forward in his chair. "Now you must decide, Ilse. Are you in too?"

I took a deep breath, my hands smoothing down my thighs, leaving streaks of sweat on my pants. I looked over at Ilse who looked pale, but resolved. I knew what her answer would be.

"Yes," she said, and her voice trembled only a tiny bit.

CHAPTER FOUR

NEW YORK CITY, NEW YORK
AUGUST 15, 1943

ILSE

At half past ten, Papa went to sleep, just like he always did. His study was on the other side of my bedroom, and I could hear everything through these walls. I heard when he closed his cigarette tin and pushed his chair back, even on the plush Persian rug Mama had bought for the study to keep the room warmer in the winter—Papa hated to be cold—and I heard him set his empty glass on the coaster I'd knit him the year before last, when Mama had last tried to teach me something ladylike. I heard him close the department stores' heavy red books with a soft clomp. Everything he did to mark the end of the day.

I waited until I heard the door open, close, and his footsteps retreat down the hallway. Then I slid out from beneath my covers, wrapping a blanket around myself. Like Papa, I hated the chill at night, but not as much as I hated how stuffy the apartment was without the windows open. I pushed the pile of school notebooks off my small red notebook. I tucked it under my arm, protected from view by the blanket, and stepped over the floorboard that creaked at the start of summer when the humidity made the wood swell. I turned the doorknob and pulled gently, peeking around the corner into the hallway to be sure Papa hadn't gotten distracted at the end of the hall reading something before he made his way to my parents' room on the other side of the apartment.

The hall was empty.

I crept down the hallway, two doors on the left, and knocked lightly, pressing my ear against the door.

It was yanked open, and I nearly toppled right into Wolf's room.

"Shhh," he hissed as if I'd been the one to open the door without a care in the world. I made a face at him and marched past him, blanket dragging on the floor. I sat down on the chair at his desk, and he shut the door, clicking on the light on the bedside table. "It took you long enough."

"Papa was working late," I said, frowning. "Why are you so cranky?"

"I don't know, Ilse," snapped Wolf. "Maybe it's because I'm being sent abroad into a war I've worked very hard to avoid."

I bit my lip so hard that I could taste blood on my tongue. Everything that had happened today had been my fault. My fault that we'd gone to the park in the first place, my fault that the magic had gone wrong, my fault we'd been caught. My fault we'd been blackmailed. I didn't want to drop bombs. Not on anyone. Bombs weren't like bullets. They weren't precise. If they dropped a bomb I made or helped deliver on Hitler's house, it'd kill Hitler, but it'd kill innocent people too—if there were any innocent people left in Germany. There had to be, didn't there? There had to be people who resisted him, didn't there? I didn't want to have a part in killing innocent people.

But at least I'd be safe, here in the United States, working from wherever Colonel Mann told me I'd work.

Wolf would be in danger. Every day, for however long it took.

"I'm sorry," I said, my voice sounding small even to myself.

Wolf sighed, sitting on the end of his bed. "I know. It's not your fault."

"It is—" I began to say.

"It's not."

"If I had listened to you—"

"It's not your fault."

"I shouldn't have said 'magic' aloud. I shouldn't have been a brat. I shouldn't have done magic in public. I shouldn't have messed up that equation," I insisted, speaking swiftly over his interruptions. "And now it's my fault that they're sending you to Europe."

"We had a choice," said Wolf after a beat. "What's with the notebook?"

I recognized that he was trying to distract me, and this time I let him. I flipped it open to a page I'd dog-eared and passed it to him. "I have a theory. I haven't tried it yet, but I think it's a good theory. I think we can send letters to each other, letters that travel very quickly and get around other prying eyes."

"I'm not going to pretend to understand this," said Wolf, his eyes skimming over the equations. "How does it work? Explain it to me like I'm five. Nothing about air speeds."

I leaned forward, pointing at the equation. "If you write the equation that gets something to float—"

"And be careful, because if it goes wrong, things catch fire," Wolf said dryly.

"And you add a piece of hair," I said, raising my voice slightly over him until he hushed me, "then I think it'll 'find' me. It's like a magical homing pigeon."

"So if I write you a letter and tie it with your hair?" Wolf scrunched up his nose. "That doesn't sound feasible."

"I think if you just put a piece of hair under the seal it'll work, as long as the hair and the blood equation touch," I said. "We'll have to test it before we go. But that's the idea."

"It sounds flammable." Wolf handed me back my notebook.

I rolled my eyes. "Don't be such a Luddite."

"You know," Wolf said, "Luddites were on to something. Mechanization of industry has cost jobs, especially for a certain class of people who have struggled to replace that line of work with—"

"When you say things like that, my brain goes *la-la-la-la-la*," I whispered as loudly as I dared.

"That's how science sounds to me," he retorted.

"Science affects your life, even when you don't understand it." I tossed the notebook, and it landed softly next to him on the bed. "Ta-da! Gravity."

"Class and economic theory explain why you have a bed to toss that onto, and why you can read and write, and how you're going to university," he pointed out.

I stuck out my tongue at him.

He grinned. "I win."

"I did not say you won."

"You stuck out your tongue! Winners don't stick out their tongues."

"They don't gloat either!"

"Oooh." He laughed. "Fine. It was a draw."

"Science will always win," I said with a deliberately dramatic sniff. "It's the basis for everything. You can't have theories without neurons."

Wolf laughed and then clapped a hand over his mouth as I kicked at him, listening for our parents to open their door and come see why we were awake and making a fuss at such a late hour. He kicked back at me, and for a moment, it felt normal again, as if we were just two kids and the world wasn't at war and everything was fine. As if there wasn't magic.

But it'd been five years since there wasn't magic, and I almost couldn't remember my life without it. First it'd been Wolf, a paper cut when he was thirteen making the paper float. Then the sliced calf when he was fifteen, the ice-skating accident that'd landed him in the hospital, where he was speaking about levitating, too delirious with the blood loss to keep his secret. When I bled for the first time a few months later, I knew what was happening.

I'd never been good at secrets though. Too curious, too eager to share discovery, too earnest, too quick to speak instead of to think.

And now, after five years of hush money from my parents to the nurses who cared for Wolf and to the teachers who had heard my boast about flying, I'd broken the unspoken vow and revealed our secret.

I'd ruined everything.

"You look like you're going to cry." Wolf stood up, moving across the room without looking at me. I looked around for the first time since I'd entered and realized that he was already packing. Two bags were open on his floor, stuffed with sweaters and pants, a few button-down shirts, a photo of our parents and me at the zoo a few years ago. His room was simple—books and two lamps and his bed, everything neat and organized in a way my room never was. And soon it'd be empty, because he'd be overseas and we'd be apart for the first time since I'd been born.

I didn't even know *how* to be apart from Wolf.

"Now you *are* crying," Wolf said, appearing in front of me, blurry and indistinct.

I turned my face from him and wiped at my eyes with my blanket-covered sleeves.

"It's going to be weird," he said, moving a pile of books from the armchair in the corner to the floor so he could pull the chair closer to where I sat. "Who's going to explain long scientific processes to me for hours on end? I'm going to be so bored."

I sniffled into my shoulder, mumbling. "You don't have to make fun of me."

There was a soft knock at the door, and then someone opened it, making us scramble out of our chairs. Mama stood in the doorway, her dressing gown wrapped around her, and Papa stood right behind her. Mama's hair was down, long and dark, and she managed to look no less fierce here, in her nightgown, than she had staring down Colonel Mann earlier today.

"I told you," Mama said over her shoulder to Papa. "I knew they were awake."

Dinner had been an awful, silent affair. Neither of them understood why their children had been recruited, and we hadn't offered any explanations. They knew, at least in part, that their children had experienced supernatural things. But we never spoke of that. Not in this house, and not with them, not even when I knew that Papa wrote monthly checks to people in hospitals and schools to buy their silence.

"What's the point of knocking if you're just going to walk in?" I asked.

"My house. My doors. My doorways. My doorknobs," said Mama simply. "My rules, *bubbeleh*."

Papa opened his mouth and then shut it, knowing better than to argue about whose house it was. Papa's business and this apartment had been bought with Mama's family's money. He'd been a poor immigrant who had wooed and won over the beloved only daughter of a wealthy German-Jewish businessman of the Upper East Side. When I'd been younger, I used to make him tell me all the time about the first time he saw Mama and he'd thought she was an actual princess because he'd never seen someone as beautiful as her dressed in such nice clothing.

"Now," Mama said, walking into the room. I could still see that elegant girl in the way she carried herself. "It's time you two gave us some answers."

"We know," Papa said heavily, remaining in the doorway. "We

know it's because of your...unusual talents. We guessed, but it seems obvious now."

We stood, four silent people for a long moment, and then Wolf said, "I'm sorry."

Why was *he* apologizing? I was the one who'd gotten us into this mess and couldn't get us out of it. I was the one who'd caused the disturbance at the park. I was the one who'd ruined everything.

Dramatic, yes.

True, also yes.

"Where will you go?" Mama asked, trying to keep her chin up. But it trembled, and that hurt almost as much as knowing this was all my fault.

"We don't know," I admitted. "But I'll be in the United States. I'm working for the army somewhere."

"Doing what?" asked Papa.

"I can't tell you," I said, feeling the apology fill the words.

He nodded slowly, rubbing at his balding head. Wolf added, "I'll be abroad. And I can't tell you what I'm doing either. But I'll try to write when I can."

Mama's chin trembled. "We all know what's happening over there."

We did. When I was young, Mama and Papa had sponsored Papa's sister and her children to come over from Germany. Others chose to stay or only sent over their children. Mama's aunt and uncle in Hamburg had written regularly about everything happening, and then their letters had grown terser, sparse with details, bearing a swastika stamp on them when they'd arrived. Papa said that was because the Nazis had censors reading letters. But the letters had stopped a few years ago, and the newspaper articles had begun. Reports of ghettos and labor camps, of extermination and mass deaths. Jews were dying, and there was nothing we could do about it.

Except, maybe now. Maybe that was the upside of us getting involved. Maybe this was the only way we could stop Hitler from killing all the Jews in Europe. President Roosevelt wasn't in the war to save the Jews. But maybe we were.

"Listen to me," Mama said, advancing on Wolf. "Do not get caught. Do not tell them you are Jewish."

"My name..." Wolf began.

"Your name is not Zev," Mama said firmly, sharing the Hebrew version of Wolf's name. "You have a good German name. Use it. You will serve, and you will do your duty, and you will come home. Do you understand?"

Wolf's eyes shone with tears. "Yes, Mama."

She wrapped her arms around him and then reached out, pulling me into the hug. I closed my eyes, reveling in the embrace. I wanted to tell her I was sorry for sending her only son to war. I wanted to tell her I was sorry for being born with magic in my veins. But I could only cry into her shoulder.

CHAPTER FIVE

WOLF

Sometimes, when I wanted to be alone, I went down to Coney Island before the crowds descended on it, around sunrise when it was just the delivery trucks, the sign painters, and the sound of storefronts being rolled up, when it was just the people who made the experience and the sound of the ocean crashing against the sea. I didn't go down onto the sand, just stayed on the boardwalk, leaning on the railing and watching the sun rise over the ocean. It was strange to think that wherever that sun was, there were other people who had already been fighting and dying for hours. Our day hadn't yet begun, and for some, their day, their *lives* had already ended.

And soon I'd be one of them. Fighting, and maybe dying.

I wasn't ready to die.

How could I want to serve and not want to die? Wasn't that part of serving? A willingness to die?

I couldn't talk to my parents about this—my father had called me "a son he could be proud of" for the first time. I didn't want to disappoint him. And my mother. My poor mother was terrified, maybe even more than me, though she'd done a good job of hiding it. She had both me and Ilse to worry about. And Ilse. I couldn't tell her either. The army was going to drop me out of an airplane into enemy territory, if we even got that far, if we weren't shot down by the time we crossed the English Channel. And after that, my magic and I were going to do what—run around Germany blowing up their bomb factories? Their physics labs? Hope for the best? What did they even want me to do?

I didn't want Hitler to get this fancy, deadly bomb before we did. And if they were recruiting teenagers like Ilse and me, they must have been desperate. That's how I saw it anyway. Still, if Colonel Mann had just offered me the choice of stopping Hitler's bomb by staying home, would I have said yes?

A cowardly part of my heart said I would.

And yet, next week, I'd be on a ship, crossing the ocean. An ocean crawling with U-boats, to a land that'd chased away my family. And somewhere over there was Max. I didn't know exactly where he had ended up, but I knew he was in Europe, not in the Pacific Theater. Part of me was grateful for that because the news from the Pacific was brutal. Every day, I bought a newspaper and scanned the list of dead for his name. Just because it wasn't listed didn't mean I didn't worry, didn't spend half my nights staring at the ceiling, thinking of all the things I should have said before he shipped out.

Max had been excited to go. He was going to be a pilot, and he was so excited I thought he'd won the lottery or something when he told me. Max approached everything with an enthusiasm and confidence I hadn't found in my life yet. He and Ilse were alike in that way. They took what life gave them and saw something good and hopeful every time. I didn't have that gift. Or anything close to it.

In front of me, the waves crashed repeatedly against the beach as if to remind me that the rhythms of life would go on, with or without me.

That should have relieved me, but it just depressed me.

"Did you know," said a familiar voice, appearing at my elbow, "that sand is shorthand for the space between sea and land? Get it? Sea and land together make sand."

"That's not even remotely true," I said, shooting my sister a glance. She smiled, leaning on the rail next to me. The pink of her dress reflected the rising sun and the flush of her cheeks. She must have run from the subway station here.

"No, it isn't. It's from a Greek word, I think," she agreed. "But it's a good line. You should try it on some English girl."

"I don't think I'll be picking up any girls at soda counters," I said dryly.

"Maybe you will. Maybe you'll need to make contacts in the French resistance," she said dreamily, dangling her arms over the bar.

I looked out at the sea again. "Did it ever occur to you that I came here to be alone?"

"It did," said Ilse. "But just because you want to be alone doesn't mean you should be."

My throat felt tight suddenly. I didn't want to give myself away, though, because as close as Ilse and I were, she didn't need to have all my secrets. I didn't want to resent her for knowing everything more than I already did. I took a deep, slow breath, letting it out slowly through my mouth, while watching the water recede, curl into a new wave, and return right back to the same beach. There was a rubber-band effect to the waves, and I was sure that Ilse could explain it to me.

Part of me was glad to be getting out of New York City, glad for an excuse not to be Ilse Klein's older brother, the smart but *not-as-smart* Klein child, glad for an excuse to do something that didn't have to do with the family business. Before, I'd felt like a wave in slow motion. I'd always end up back on these shores, with the same people I'd always known my entire life, managing the department stores my father had grown while I was a child, marrying a German-Jewish girl, just like he'd done.

The feeling of inevitability exhausted me.

"Are you afraid?" asked Ilse.

I blinked, tearing my eyes from the horizon. "No. Maybe. A little. Are you?"

"Yes," she said in that shockingly honest way she had. "I know who I am here. I'm the girl genius. I'm the smartest one. But just because I'm the smartest here doesn't mean I'll be the smartest wherever I'm going."

"You're more than a smart person," I said, glancing sideways at her. Her brow was knotted in frustration. Sometimes I thought that it'd be easier to be Ilse than it was to be Ilse's brother, but sometimes I thought it was easier to be me, with my capable, intelligent mind just shy of genius. The future was a problem she couldn't solve. She didn't know all the variables. She didn't know what she didn't know, and she knew enough to know that.

"Am I?" she murmured, her voice so low that it was almost lost to the sea.

I tried to think of something to say, but she shook her head, her expression clearing again, like a swift summer storm that had rolled through and left as quickly as it arrived. "Do you know where Max is stationed?"

I looked down at our feet on the weathered boards. "No."

"Are you going to find out?"

"It doesn't matter," I said. "If he's not where I'm going, then it's not like I can change my plans."

"But you could write him. He's a pilot, isn't he? He could take leave wherever you're going," Ilse insisted. "You've been best friends for your entire lives. Mr. Egan's at the Upper East Side store today, isn't he? You could ask him!"

"What if he's dead? Max, I mean," I said suddenly. Ilse fell quiet, and then I snorted. "Never mind. Ignore me."

"No," she said fiercely. "I'm not going to ignore you. He's not dead. I won't believe that. We'd know. We'd find out. You'd feel it."

"That's not how real life works, Ilse," I told her, bitterness creeping into my voice.

"You'd know," she repeated stubbornly. Then she bumped her shoulder against mine. "I don't think it's stupid to be afraid though."

"I'm not afraid for me," I said with a sigh. "I'm afraid to find out that he's dead. I'm afraid to know, so I don't want to ask. It's stupid. If he's dead, he's dead regardless of whether I ask or not."

"Do you want me to ask for you?" Ilse asked after a pause.

I smiled a little bit, nudging her shoulder back. "No, but thank you. That's sweet."

"Don't tell anyone," she said coyly. "They mustn't know I have a heart."

"Your secret is mine," I replied, smiling.

She tilted her head until it rested on my shoulder, warm and scratchy. "I'm going to miss you."

"I'll miss you too," I said softly. How could I ever have wanted to leave her shadow? All she's ever wanted to do was stand in mine. For all her genius, Ilse was still my little sister. She still looked up to me, without ever realizing how she outshone me. I lifted my arm free of her head and threw it around her shoulders. "Come on. Let's go find breakfast. My treat."

CHAPTER SIX

ILSE

Papa lifted my trunk out of the back of the car and slammed the door closed. I tried to take it from him, but he shook his head, his mouth in a thin, flat line as Mama and I followed him into the train station. Chewing on my bottom lip, I glanced at Mama. She sighed, exasperated, and offered me her lipstick. I reapplied it even though there was no point. I'd chew it off from the nerves in a little bit anyway. But Mama's rule was that a lady should always look the best she could at any given moment. I didn't often live up to it, but for the next few minutes until the train arrived, I didn't mind her fussing over me. Soon I'd have to leave her here, and there'd be no one else to fuss over me.

Wolf slid out of the back seat, his hands in his trouser pockets, his gaze downcast. He'd been quiet since the day out on the boardwalk, but I knew that he wasn't thrilled about what had happened with Colonel Mann. He was leaving tomorrow for England aboard a Navy cruiser. I'd read all about the U-boats and insisted that Wolf send me a letter as soon as he arrived in England so I'd know he'd arrived safely. We'd tested the message system carefully in our hallway last night. It seemed to work, but that was in such a small space. Crossing an ocean introduced more variables.

I didn't tell him about my worries. He didn't need any more on his shoulders.

"Someone's going to see me writing on a letter with blood," he'd said, packing his own little magic kit of syringes and needle brushes now that we couldn't share one.

"I don't care," I'd snapped back at him.

He'd looked all soft, reaching over to lightly tap my cheek with his fist, the way we used to wrestle when we were little. "Oh, it'll be all right. They've ways to protect the ships. That's the least dangerous part of all this."

"Not helpful," I'd muttered.

Yesterday when I should have been packing, I'd written him a small notebook of all my equations for the magic and all of my tidbits—*drawing blood on the right side of the body seemed to be less efficient than the left side; proximity to the heart might increase the magical properties in the blood: oxygenation?*—because he didn't know the science the way I did. I'd always been the one leading the way with magic, and now he'd be on his own.

I could see the top of the notebook from his breast pocket now. I hoped I'd written everything down. What if I hadn't? What if I forgot one thing that I knew, and it was the thing he needed to know to survive?

I blinked as Mama kissed my cheek suddenly and said, "You and your brother, you make me proud."

She almost never said I made her proud. I wasn't the type of girl Mama had wanted, and I wasn't the type of girl Mama had expected. I was loud where she was quiet, I demanded where she acquiesced, and while she'd dropped out of university to marry Papa and have babies, I showed no such inclination. She didn't know what to do with a daughter like me.

We'd never talked about the magic, not after they'd paid people to keep our secret, and they hadn't mentioned it since the night after the colonel's visit. So, few people knew, and two of them refused to talk about it. Sometimes the secret burned inside me, like swallowing a hot coal.

Was she proud of me despite my magic?

Or because of it?

Did it matter?

The station platform where I'd been told to go was closed to all except *authorized personnel*, but as soon as I showed the guard my ticket and gave him my name, he lifted the barrier for me.

"No one else," he said, holding up his hands to my parents and Wolf.

"She's just sixteen," Papa said gruffly. "I think we ought to stand with her."

The guard scowled at Papa's accent, then glanced at me as if he didn't believe I was sixteen. Or didn't care. "Rules are rules. This platform is for the army train. Ticketed passengers only. And no Germans."

Mama held me firmly by the elbow and said, "Frank, we'll have to say goodbye out here."

I couldn't believe she was being the voice of reason, but here we were, and now I had to say goodbye to them. Tears stung my eyes, and I held on to Mama for a little too long. It hadn't felt real until now, but I was leaving them for the first time in my life. There'd be no Mama to tell me when I was talking too much science. There'd be no Papa to fix whatever was broken. There'd be no Mama to hold my hand or soothe away my nightmares. Papa wouldn't pat the top of my head in that affectionate, patronizing way of his, and Mama wouldn't be there, handing over her lipstick so I'd always be ready for whatever came next. Wolf was right. I'd have to grow up.

Papa kissed the side of my head and said, "Be good, Ilse. Listen to what they tell you."

"Brush your hair, and don't forget your stockings. Don't run around with bare legs and bare feet as if you weren't raised right," Mama said. "And go to sleep at a good time. God only knows what they'll be doing out there, throwing parties and riots until the late evening, but sleep is important."

I made a face. "Mama."

She added, "Brains need sleep, Ilse. Even brilliant ones."

I did *not* say, "I'm inventing a new kind of magic to deliver a yet-unproven science, Mama. I'm not sure I'll be getting any sleep." Instead, I sighed and said, "I know, Mama."

"Mind that attitude," Papa said. "Write us when you get there safely."

"I will," I said.

"*B'ezrat HaShem*," said Mama, "this war will be over soon, and you will both be home."

"Yes, Mama," I kissed her cheek again, then turned to Wolf.

He shoved his hands deeper into his pockets, I think so he wouldn't hug me. "Do good work, Ilse."

I smiled through my tears. "What if I can't?"

"You will," he said reassuringly. He tipped his head so our parents couldn't hear him. "You know science like you know magic, and you know magic like you know science. They aren't separate parts of you. Don't forget that."

"I'll see you at New Year's," I said, my bottom lip wobbling as we stepped apart.

"I promise," said my brother.

He handed me my trunk, and I wrapped my hands around the handle, leaning back against the weight. I wasn't as strong as Papa or Wolf were. "Will you write me too?"

"Of course," Mama said. She kissed my cheek. "Go. You'll miss your train."

I walked through the barrier and up the stairs, and I stopped only once to turn around and wave to them. Sunset light blinded me as I walked along the platform by the farthest set of tracks. I suspected this was so no other trains could pull up alongside our train. Three other girls stood underneath the overhang. I lugged my trunk to a bench and dropped it there so I could walk over to them.

One of the girls had big, stylized brown curls pinned on top of her head and bright-red lipstick. She looked me up and down, and for a moment, I thought her gaze was dismissive, but then a brilliant smile parted on her face, and she looked bright. "You must be the fourth girl. The good colonel told me your name, but I can't remember it for the life of me."

"Ilse Klein," I said, extending a hand. She shook it with a big, exaggerated gesture. I couldn't tell if she was making fun of me or she really did move like that.

"German," she said, raising her eyebrows.

"Jewish," I corrected. "You don't sound like you're from New York."

"No, Princeton. Worked at the university. Next thing I knew, they wanted me to interview for a job up here. I took the train up, and turns out they knew everything about me. Not the kind of job you say no to." She dropped my hand and lifted a cigarette to her mouth. "I'm Dolores Chester, but everyone calls me Lola. I thought you'd never make it. This is Polly Delaney. She's from Charlotte. We've been rooming together for the interviews."

She gestured to the tall, thin girl with short-cropped blond hair so light it almost looked white. She gave me a shy smile. She wasn't wearing any lipstick, but she had the kind of mouth I couldn't help but stare at anyway—pastel pink and perfectly shaped, as if she were a doll and her lips had been painted on. She shook my hand timidly and lightly, like a bird. The opposite of Lola. I gave her a weak smile.

"Nice to meet you," I said, still shaking her hand.

She laughed a little. My stomach tightened. "Nice to meet you too. Can I have my hand back?"

"Oh," I said, feeling my cheeks turn bright red. I dropped her hand. "I'm so sorry. Yes. Sorry."

"If you say it that many times, it starts to lose its meaning," said the third girl. She was African American and taller than me, though that didn't take much, and she wore a beautiful navy-blue dress with a wide, white belt. Her gaze was all caution and curiosity.

I held out my hand. "Ilse."

"Stella Montgomery," she said, shaking my hand. "We were going to be interviewed together, but I heard you set something on fire."

I flushed again, feeling like I couldn't find my footing in this conversation. "By accident."

Stella tipped her head to the side, the curiosity winning over the caution. "What do you think happened?"

"I think that mistakes in equations can lower the autoignition point for certain materials," I said truthfully. "I'm not certain why."

"Interesting," she mused. "I wonder if we can use that for the project. You discovered the equations too, I see. It took me years to figure them out."

"I don't think we should talk about that here," said Polly nervously, but I'd skipped right past that and caught on the content of Stella's words.

She was talking about the project. She wanted to use magic as a way to detonate the bomb, not just as a way to deliver the bomb. *She knew about the bomb.* I didn't know how to ask her about it—or if the other girls knew—so I could only sputter, "You know physics. Or chemistry."

"Chemistry," she said. "I'm a junior at Spelman. Or rather I was, until I was selected for this project."

"Like we had a choice," Lola said, flicking off her cigarette.

"We always have a choice," I said, thinking of what Wolf had told me. "Choosing not to make a choice is unto itself a choice."

"Oooh, she talks like a little professor," Lola teased, but my cheeks heated up anyway.

"Oh, leave her alone, Lola," chided Polly, giving me a sympathetic look. I hated feeling like I needed to work my way into the group, but I didn't have any other choice. This was my team. I wished I'd been interviewed like everyone else, whatever that'd been, and not recruited in a rush.

"So, Professor," Lola said. "What'd they tell you? They didn't tell us anything, did they, Polly?"

Polly shook her head, but I noticed Stella didn't reply. Just the two of us. Why just the two of us? I hesitated at Lola's question, wondering if this was a setup. *If this is my group, I need to trust them.* But I couldn't tell them everything, not if it was more top secret than our magic, and maybe if I answered, Stella would follow my lead. "We're trying to use magic to deliver a bomb."

As long as they didn't know what *kind* of bomb, I was complying, I thought. Maybe, I hoped. I'd let a secret out once, and now my brother was going to Europe and I was going to...wherever they were sending us. I didn't want to mess this up again.

"Huh. What does he care about our magic and a bomb?" Lola asked.

"The war. They want us to deliver bombs with magic," said Polly. "Can it be done?"

"In theory," said Stella, not looking at me. "They've used magic on balloons in Europe to help people escape."

Balloons. It was genius. Balloons would be easy to smuggle and carry when not inflated, naturally floated, and weren't suspect to soldiers or spies.

"Balloons. Like the things that pop?" Lola asked, raising an eyebrow.

"That's what they say," said Stella, all caution again with Lola's pushiness.

"Who says?" I asked.

"I just heard it," said Stella vaguely.

"You're from New York? Does your family know where you're going?" asked Lola, changing the topic when it was clear Stella would give up nothing more concrete.

"They came to the train station," I said with a nod. "They weren't allowed on the platform."

I didn't say it was because of my father's German accent that they couldn't cajole the guard. I didn't need to bring any more attention to my name than it had already gathered.

"At least they could see you off," said Polly sadly, sitting down on her trunk.

Maybe that was my cue to ask her where she was from, and why her family couldn't, but I couldn't quite form the words to talk to her directly. Something about holding on to her hand, and the way she had a doll's face, and how red I turned. Eventually, I'd have to get over the initial embarrassment of my awkwardness, but I couldn't yet.

"Does anyone know where we're going?" I asked, suddenly realizing I'd skipped some of the important logistical questions in favor of science. I could almost hear Wolf laughing at me, as if he could hear the question all the way down at the street.

"Knoxville," the three of them said together.

Lola tapped the ticket in my hand. "It's on the ticket. Not so smart now, are you, Professor?"

I rolled my eyes. "Please stop calling me that. Where's Knoxville?"

"Tennessee. Ever been there before?" asked Stella.

"I've never left New York City," I said honestly.

"You're in for a treat," said Polly with a dramatic sigh. She tilted her face up to the sky with a smile. "Let me tell you what fresh air feels like."

"I've been to the ocean!" I protested, a smile starting on my face too.

Stella snorted. "That is not fresh air. That is oxidized dead fish."

"That's not even *close* to being true," I told her. I did not explain the oxidization process to her, though, and I was secretly a little proud of my restraint. If it'd been my parents or Wolf, I wouldn't have resisted. Besides, Stella probably knew. No, Stella *definitely* knew. She knew how smart she was.

"That's what it smells like here. Dead fish. You're going to die from ecstasy when you breathe good country air," Polly said, the corner of her mouth tipping upward again.

I crossed my arms in faked outrage. "That seems like a terrible thing. To die just when you've breathed something that brought you joy."

"Isn't it just?" Lola teased.

Lola began to tell us about the boyfriend she was leaving behind in Princeton and how *dramatic* he was, even though she had been going to dump him before he shipped off to Europe. Behind her head and her flailing arms, Polly and I exchanged a secret smile.

I followed Stella up to the yellow line painted on the platform as the train grew closer, the smile blossoming on my face a small sign of the explosion of happiness in my chest. I'd survive the trip to Tennessee at least. And whatever came after this, I could handle it. I *would* handle it.

CHAPTER SEVEN

OAK RIDGE, TENNESSEE
AUGUST 20, 1943

ILSE

The military bus was quiet after the constant *clack-clack-clack* of the overnight train, and the weight of the unknown was piling up. I had a thousand questions, but none floated to the surface, crystal and clear. Instead, they clamored in my chest, indistinct like a New York City traffic jam. I didn't think they had traffic jams out here. There didn't seem to be enough people to block even a single intersection. We rolled out of Knoxville, past the train station and the downtown and the curious gazes of people on the streets. I supposed they wanted to know why a bus was leaving the train depot with only four girls on it, heading east into the mountains.

Two boys tried to race the bus on their bikes, shouting and waving, even as we drew past them. Polly smiled and waved back at them, but I just watched as they grew small in the distance. It was so *quiet* on the bus. I couldn't remember the last time I'd said something to any of the other girls, and yet I didn't feel like saying anything at all.

If Wolf was here, he'd be commenting on the roads, or the driver's skill, or what lay ahead of us, and I'd ask questions he'd tell me not to ask. We had a routine, Wolf and me. I knew exactly how it'd play out if he were here.

But he wasn't. He wasn't here, and I was all alone. I didn't know what to do. What to say. What if I messed up? What if I couldn't do the job Colonel Mann wanted me to do? What if Wolf was right, and we were two halves of a whole instead of two sides of the same coin? What if we couldn't do this? What if I couldn't do this? What if he died?

"Are you all right?" Polly asked next to me, her voice low. "You look like you might cry."

I swallowed hard, forcing a smile onto my face. "I'm fine."

I didn't want to lie to her, to add that to my list of awkwardness from the handshake that went on too long to this, but if I told her the truth, that would be even more awkward and then she might not look at me the same way. And I wanted her to keep looking at me.

I wished Wolf was here to tell me the difference between keeping secrets and lying.

At the end of the highway, we turned down a narrow road, and then down another one where the trees disappeared and a huge area of mud and dirt—brown and dusty—stretched as far as I could see, for miles. That type of mud came with erosion, when people just cut down everything that held together the earth. The army probably didn't care about that, not during times of war. We passed through a barbed-wire fence and a guard gate into a small village of tiny houses that all looked the same and a huge building that took up at least ten city blocks. Whatever we'd been brought here to work on, I was sure it was in that building. A scattering of other buildings filled the area, some large and some small between the houses, all marked with signs. The bus lurched over the poor roads and eventually came to a stop next to the main building.

Lola, Polly, and I started to stand, but the driver waved us to sit back down. Stella gave us a knowing look and went back to staring out the window. My legs were sticking to the seats, and I was desperate to stretch and shower, but we sat there waiting. I'd never been good at waiting.

Lola told a raunchy joke that made me blush furiously. Polly tapped her shoe against mine, and I jumped, startled, and stared at her. I'd forgotten we were sitting together for a moment, as distracted as I was by the view out the window and Lola's comment. Now that I remembered, my skin warmed where our arms nearly brushed against each other.

"She's wild," Polly whispered.

I glanced at Lola and relaxed. I wasn't the only one who'd never met anyone like Lola before. "These army boys won't know what hit them."

"Oh, these boys know," Lola said airily. I flushed at having been overheard, but she didn't seem to mind. The soldiers outside rose on their tiptoes and grinned, pointing at her through the bus windows as she stomped up and down the aisle, telling some story about a bar she'd gone to once. She was beautiful, dazzling, and a wild child.

No one looked at me, or at Stella, or at Polly.

I pushed away the needle of jealousy slipping through my skin. I wasn't here for attention. I was here because they wanted—no, needed—my help with magic, and because Wolf had been right. This was our duty, a way to serve. Not flirting. Not smiling and giggling. Work. I just needed to keep that in mind.

I leaned against the hot window. "Maybe that's why they recruited her. She keeps the rest of us from getting bored."

Polly giggled, and we shared another small smile that warmed my skin like the sun. Minutes ticked by until the door to the office opened and a balding man in a tan button-down shirt tucked into tan pants jogged down the steps. He strode toward the bus, and it wasn't until just before he reached the steps that I recognized him. Colonel Mann. He looked like he'd aged ten years and lost ten pounds in the days since I'd seen him. He seemed distinctly less threatening and less mysterious here, in a dusty, camel-colored uniform with grocery bags beneath his eyes.

He climbed the steps of the bus, and his eyes scanned over the four of us. If they lingered on me longer than on the other girls, I didn't notice. "Welcome, ladies. If you'll follow me."

We filed off the bus and stepped into the hot, oppressive summer heat. Leaving our bags behind at his direction, we followed him back into the office where fans at least cooled the sweat on our skin. The young men and women at desks looked up at us, curious, and we shuffled past their desks to a large meeting room, me leading the way, Stella on my heels, and Polly and Lola taking up the rear.

The door clicked shut behind Lola, and Colonel Mann gestured to the chairs. We sat down slowly, exchanging looks of confusion. The colonel locked his hands behind his back, staring at the floor and pacing in front of us. "I'll remind you now that everything you see here, everything you do here, and everything you hear here is top secret. It doesn't get repeated, not even inside these gates, and definitely not outside them. Am I understood?"

The four of us nodded, but it didn't matter. He never looked up. He just assumed we were following along. That faith in our discretion was probably misplaced. At least in me. I was already looking at the maps on the wall and trying to figure out what they showed and what they didn't show. Reactors weren't marked, but they had to be here somewhere.

"This is Oak Ridge, Tennessee, home of a special military project to aid the war effort. What you do in the lab, what information you might be given to do your work, and what you might learn must never be shared. If you do share information about your work, you will be declared an enemy of the state. And what happens from there, I cannot tell you. That's above my pay grade."

"Are we the only ones working on this?" Stella asked in the long, quiet pause that came after his quiet pronouncement. His threat. It was a good question, and it made her look good to him. I wished I'd thought of it.

Colonel Mann shook his head. "This project is multifaceted. That's all I can tell you."

I glanced around at the other girls, at Stella's carefully composed, thoughtful expression, at Polly's blank face, at Lola's slight frown. I probably had the most transparent expression. I felt like everyone could read my face like an advertisement at Times Square. We didn't have a choice, and I knew more than anyone, but I didn't hold all the cards. And I wasn't sure the colonel did either.

A minute later, a woman with big, blond curls and a smile that didn't reach her eyes stomped into the room. Colonel Mann gave her a strained smile. "Girls, this is Loretta Clark. She is in charge of civilian personnel here at Oak Ridge. She'll get you settled. I'll see you tomorrow at the lab, bright and early."

"Don't be late," added Loretta, squaring her shoulders as the colonel passed her on his way to the door. "We run on military time here."

I didn't know what she meant by that, but she didn't look like she was in the mood for my questions, so I kept my mouth shut for once in my life.

Loretta handed out identification cards to all four of us. Then to Lola, Polly, and me, she handed a map with a red *x* on our house and a red *x* on a building farther away—on the other side of the marked area—that I assumed was our lab. She handed Stella a different map, also with a red *x* on a house, but a different one than ours. My eyes flew up to Stella's face, but she kept it neutral and calm. I opened my mouth to ask, and she caught my eye, giving a short shake of her head.

Loretta clapped her hands. "Follow me. Stay in a line."

"Stella..." I began to say, but Stella shook her head again, mouthing *never mind that* at me. I bit down on the end of my question, even though it felt like it wanted to burst out of me.

Loretta glared over her shoulder, still marching away from us. Her voice hit some awful shrill note. "And keep your mouths *shut*."

"Did someone put a bee down her hose?" whispered Lola, slightly louder than necessarily, and Polly and I both had to duck our heads to stifle our giggles. They wouldn't *really* send Lola home. After all, she knew where this top secret location was now.

"Well, there's no use getting my knickers in a twist over her," Lola said, picking up her two small bags. "Let's go save America and end the war, girls!"

Polly picked up her bag from the ground next to the bus. "I didn't expect this to be such an...*adventure*."

"I think I have to adjust my definition of adventure," I said, lugging my trunk behind me. "I hadn't accounted for the factor of Lola."

"There's always one unknown variable," Stella said wisely.

There was more than one unknown in this experiment. I knew we were near Knoxville, where the train had arrived, and in the mountains, and they'd built this in a hurry, but I didn't know where we were exactly. Construction crews were working at a harried pace all over the hillside, and the site was nothing but wooden planks over muddy sections, followed by hard-packed dusty roads. I didn't know what we could do. I didn't know if we would succeed. I didn't know what would happen if we failed. I didn't know if I even wanted to succeed.

A group of men strolled by, shirts tucked into their pants, their hair long and slicked back, two of them with their heads bowed together. I caught a tail scrap of their conversation, and it snapped me clean from my thoughts. I blurted out, entirely without thinking, "The chain reaction of what?"

I clapped my hand over my mouth, wide-eyed, and stared at them as they jerked to a stop and spun to face me. Everyone's eyes were on me as Loretta stopped whatever mindless chatter she was uttering at the front of the group. I shouldn't have asked or spoken to anyone, but even worse, I knew the answer to my own question. Uranium. Of course it was uranium.

One of the young men—with small, beady eyes—smiled broadly and said, "What does a pretty little thing like you know about chain reactions?"

"Enough to know you oughtn't to be talking about them outside the walls of that building," I said sharply, lifting my chin and squaring my shoulders.

"Oh God," one of the others said, laughing, and for a second, I steeled myself for more jeering. But instead, he stepped forward and held out his hand. "You're Ilse Klein, aren't you?"

"German," muttered one of the other boys, glaring at me from under his fringe of dark hair.

Flushing, I determinedly ignored that comment and looked to the guy who'd named me. He had an easy grin on his face as though I should know him. When he shook my hand, it was as if we were colleagues and he wasn't a stranger. "And you are?"

"George Steele. I studied at the University of Chicago, but I've been working with Colonel Mann on your project," he said, nodding to the other girls. "I'll be working with you now when I'm not traveling to our other sites."

"Quitter," said one of the men, only half joking. "Stay until we fix the problem."

"What's the problem?" I asked, looking over George's shoulder at the man who'd spoken. "Maybe I can—"

George gave me a pitying look. "Can't talk about that."

"Right," I said, flushing. Besides, how could I possibly help? What did I know that they didn't?

He lowered his voice conspiratorially. "I'm sure glad to have you here. I read the paper you did with Steiner and Nibali and thought you might get recruited for that alone. When I found out what else you could do, I couldn't decide which team I wanted you on. Either way, it'll be good to have your expertise on this project."

Warmth flooded my cheeks. "Thank you. That means a lot."

I wanted to ask him if he had magic, but I didn't want to ask any more questions I shouldn't out here in the open. Colonel Mann's threat about secrets still hung over me.

"Did you just get here?" George asked, glancing from me to the other girls.

I nodded and started to ask if he knew any more details than I'd been given.

"If you please, Miss Klein," snapped Loretta from the front of the group. "You can flirt later. Right now, I need your full attention."

Flirting? With these men? They were colleagues. My face beet red, I stepped away from the lab group. George lifted his hand and said quickly, "See you later, Miss Klein."

"Ilse," I said.

"Ilse," he repeated and winked before sliding his hands into his pockets and spinning away from me to follow the other guys.

Lola and Polly looked at me, wide-eyed, as I joined the tour of the miniature town. Lola started to ask me a question, but Polly elbowed her hard, and I shot her an appreciative look. For a few minutes, I'd forgotten I was one of these girls, or that I'd been recruited not for my science but for my magic. But reality grounded me like a ball of lead settling in my stomach. I'd never get a chance to use the science I already knew here. I was here to do magic I barely understood.

CHAPTER EIGHT

ILSE

"I didn't expect it to be hot and humid," I said to Polly as we got on the bus that took us from our little house on the hill to our lab. They didn't particularly care about Shabbat here, and I felt too new to ask. It felt strange though, doing things on a Saturday. I resolved to keep this detail out of my phone calls with Mama and my letters to Wolf. "I thought the mountains would cool things down."

I didn't really know how I wanted her to react, but the pitying look Polly gave me wasn't my favorite. She brushed damp, blond curls off her forehead. "This isn't even that hot, Ilse. It's nearly September."

"It's even hotter than yesterday," I said. "I suppose that explains the humidity though."

She blinked at me. "It does?"

I was opening my mouth to explain when Lola swung into the seat in front of us, promptly twisting around to say, "I think we ought to switch rooms."

The bus pulled away from our station and lurched down the muddy road. I gripped the edge of the window as if that'd keep the bus upright and keep me safe if it tipped over. "Why should we switch rooms?"

The house had two rooms with two beds in each, a small living room, a dining area, and a kitchen. I'd accidentally pushed on the wall of the bedroom last night, and we could see it gap at the top where it met the ceiling. Polly and Lola had offered to room together, and I didn't mind that arrangement. I'd never shared a room with someone and couldn't imagine how awkward it'd be to listen to someone else fall asleep every night.

"I met someone at the grocery store this morning. I went to pick up a paper," Lola said matter-of-factly. "But he'd just picked up the last one! We talked about the war, and then he let me have the paper, even though he'd already paid for it. I invited him back tonight."

"To the *house*?" Polly sounded scandalized.

"What does that have to do with bedrooms?" I asked.

Lola patted the top of my head. "Oh, you sweet girl."

"I'll move into Ilse's room," said Polly hurriedly. "You won't mind, Ilse, will you?"

There was desperation to her voice that I didn't understand, but I said, "Of course not. It'll be fun," even though I didn't think it'd be much fun at all, even when I thought about how I'd have to change in the bathroom because the idea of changing with her in the same room made me turn the color of a tomato.

"Thank you," said Polly, squeezing my arm briefly in her warm hand.

Lola winked at me and slid back down onto her seat. By the time we picked up Stella from the neighborhood where all the African American workers lived, I had finally put together the pieces. Lola was bringing a man back to the house to *sleep* with him! In our house! With those thin walls! And they weren't even married.

I wanted to whisper something to Polly, but the bus was filling up and I didn't want to embarrass Lola in front of people we hadn't met yet, so I just kept my mouth shut. The backs of my thighs stuck to the seat from the sweat, and my shoulder burned where it bumped into the window. I had to peel myself off when I stood, grimacing. A dress had been, perhaps, a mistake. No, definitely a mistake. I hadn't known what to expect with the weather or with the dress code. I couldn't even tell where we'd be working.

Being a "professional" made me itch.

After breakfast in the dining hall, we were shown out the door and to the research facility beside the reactor, though they didn't call it a reactor. I just guessed, because why else would you call a large building with more guards than scientists by a coded site name like X-10?

Not that I had access to all the information, but judging by the math on the chalkboards in the labs we passed and the conversations I overheard, I was pretty confident that they hadn't managed to sustain a chain reaction. And without a chain reaction, we'd have no material. No material, no bomb. No bomb, no need for magic.

Part of me was still hoping we wouldn't have to be the ones to deliver the bomb. Wouldn't have to be the ones to kill anyone. But war felt so binary now that I was here, now that I had had to make a choice between not participating and participating. If I didn't help kill people, I was saving them. And if I was saving them, I wasn't saving my brother.

This was how it felt to be a contradiction. I wanted all of these things, and I wanted us all to get through the war safely. And statistically, that wasn't possible.

I really wished I'd never learned statistics.

As we entered the building where our lab would be, the secret of what was being built clawed at my innards. I looked sideways at Stella, but her face was the perfect model of composure. She didn't seem to struggle with keeping the secret at all. My mouth tasted like copper, and maybe I was starting to look panicked, because Colonel Mann appeared in the hallway and gestured to me to follow him. I waited for him to gesture to Stella too, but it was just me.

His shoulders were stiff, and he surveyed me with a cool, steady gaze. "Now, I am sure I can trust you not to spill the secrets you know and the others do not, Miss Klein."

Why *wasn't* Stella here? I almost asked him that, and then I ran through the possibilities in my mind. I stumbled and stopped on one. He didn't know that she knew. Somehow, Stella had figured out what they were building without the colonel telling her. I liked that theory better than the one where he trusted her more than me. I raised my chin. "What am I supposed to tell them we're doing, trying to deliver a birthday cake to the Führer?"

There was no Wolf to hiss under his breath when my tongue got away from me, and I liked that freedom. Colonel Mann's gaze narrowed. "That would be unwise and likely end up with a report on my desk or, worse, the general's."

I crossed my arms. "I wasn't trying to be facetious. What would you like me to say when they ask what we're doing?"

"Magic is based in physics and physical sciences. Find me an equation, and when appropriate, I'll give you the distance, the time, and the weight," he said crisply.

"Oh," I said, feigning surprise. "Is that all we need? Yes, you're completely right. This is such a known and well-studied matter that we know exactly how uranium acts upon magic and how magic acts upon uranium."

The colonel stepped smoothly and deliberately into my space, and I stumbled backward, hitting the wall. I pressed my palms against it, looking up at him, at the pores on his nose and the razor-sharp focus of his eyes. "Miss Klein, understand that I am the kindest person you'll encounter here. There are worse enemies to make in Oak Ridge." His gaze never wavered. "You are a brilliant scientist and equally brilliant at magic. I didn't bring you here for your smart mouth. I brought you here to do a job and to keep that mouth shut. Every time you flippantly mention what we're doing here, your brother is at risk. Do you understand?"

No mentioning uranium. Understood. I smiled at him, though it felt like more of a grimace. "From you or from Hitler, colonel?"

He stepped away from me as though he'd never been in my space. "Get to work and keep your mouth shut, and you won't find out."

I could just imagine Papa's and Mama's expressions at my impertinence, but I didn't apologize. I didn't have anything to apologize for.

Colonel Mann followed me back into the room where three chalkboards lined the interior walls and a set of windows looked over a small path between us and the reactor. There were two long tables and a handful of chairs. Stella, Lola, and Polly were all gathered around one table. Neatly stacked piles of paper sat next to pencils, needles, and syringes. A lab for blood magic.

The girls' conversations died down as they faced the colonel and me. I moved to join them, but he caught my arm and held me fast beside him. I grimaced, and Polly gave me a sympathetic smile. Stella's mouth was set in a tight, firm line. Did she think I ratted her out?

"Some guidelines," began Colonel Mann.

The door slammed open, and George Steele—the young man from yesterday—strolled in, a brown leather briefcase in one hand, a stopwatch in the other, sweat dotting his forehead, and an easy smile on his face. He winked at me before addressing the colonel. "Sorry I'm late, sir."

"You're always late, Steele," said Colonel Mann with a snort. "If you were enlisted, you'd be court-martialed."

"Let's all thank God I'm not," George said cheerfully. "Did I interrupt something?"

"Guidelines," said the colonel. "Take a seat, George."

I blinked, trying to figure out why the girls were sitting down and George was joining them, but I remained next to Colonel Mann.

Then he said, "This is a working group designed to explore and create a magical delivery system for bombs. Beyond that, I cannot tell you any details. Ilse Klein has the working knowledge you need to perform your task. You are being paid for magical discovery related to this task only. There will be no time for dillydallying. We're at war, and time is of the essence."

I did not ask, *Then why did it take you eighteen months to put this task force together?* I had already mouthed off to the colonel enough today. I could feel Wolf's elbow in my side as if he were right here with me.

"Any questions?"

"No," the three girls all said quietly, and I chimed in late. "No."

Stella gave me a look that said *Don't mess this up for all of us.* George didn't say anything.

"I'll expect weekly reports, Miss Klein," Colonel Mann said to me. "Get started."

The door closed behind him with a soft click, leaving us in silence. Stella looked resigned, frowning a bit at the desk in front of her. George looked baffled, as though he hadn't expected to be here, which surprised me. He seemed to know what was happening in every corner of Oak Ridge. Polly and Lola were looking at me expectantly as if it'd been entirely fair for the youngest person to be placed in charge of the entire group.

"So?" Lola looked at me and then around at the others before coming back to me. "What's next?"

I blinked. There hadn't been explicit instructions. Just "get to work." All we had was the equipment we needed to do our work, but Lola and Polly might not have known how to even do the work. I didn't even know what they knew and didn't know. Colonel Mann had told me what we'd need to know but had given me no values. We had nothing but my notebooks full of experiments and equations and what little was written about the supernatural power in our blood.

This, I realized, was why I was here. I knew just enough to get us started on the right path without the colonel needing to give us critical information. He knew that I'd been experimenting with magic already. And he knew that I knew from my science background that uranium and plutonium were heavy, toxic, and couldn't be dropped. I knew they were radioactive and corrosive and perhaps would act on magic differently. I knew that we'd have to use this magic to release this bomb against Germany or Japan, perhaps both, and those were different climates and elements. The distance was up to us. The farther, the better, but if we had the only model and it involved someone being on the ground—and sacrificing themselves—the army would take it, of that I had no doubt. And I wasn't sure I'd blame them.

"—know what's going on here," George snapped.

I shook my head, realizing there'd been a conversation while I spaced out. My heart pounded as I scrambled to fill in the blanks. Wolf would never have let me daydream while something important was happening. "What?"

"George," Stella said coolly, "thought that by virtue of him being a man, he would be put in charge. Even though, apparently, he's only going to be here part of the time when he's not acting as a liaison to the other groups."

I looked at him, and he scowled at Stella. "You shouldn't be here at all."

"Enough," I snapped before thinking. "That's enough."

Everyone went quiet, staring at me. I looked at George. "I didn't make the decision. If you have a problem with it, take it up with Colonel Mann."

George gave me a small, crooked smile. "'Surprised' is different than having a problem with it. I'm sure there's a reason for it, and I'm sure you'll do an adequate job, Ilse."

Something about his words rubbed me the wrong way, and I could see Lola leaning forward in her chair, words bubbling up on her face. I cut that off before it began. "Here's what we need to know. Are there limits to blood magic? If we write the equations directly on the bomb—"

"That seems like a bad idea," Lola interjected.

"Says the girl bringing home a man to the house tonight," muttered Polly.

"—will those equations act on the bomb, no matter what it's made of?" I waited to see if anyone caught the slip of my tongue, but no one blinked, not even Stella or George. Stella had turned to raise an eyebrow at Lola, who didn't even have the good sense to blush. "There must be a ratio for distance and weight. And what magic and how much blood get us there."

"Magic helped the British and the French escape Dunkirk," said George.

Dunkirk had been nearly three years ago, at the start of the war in Europe, and it'd been widely reported in our papers. I couldn't get the articles out of my mind, even after all this time. It'd been before Pearl Harbor, and the first time I'd read about something that made war sound so terrible.

Thousands of British and French troops had died and been captured, and British fishermen had gone back and forth, rescuing everyone else and bringing them back to the English coast. I hadn't heard anything about magic at Dunkirk, but I supposed that was the point: magic was secret, and those who escaped using magic kept it a secret. I hadn't even known magic was this widespread, much less in use, until a week ago.

But evacuation wasn't what we were doing now. We were delivering a bomb. A bomb that hadn't been invented yet, but that was beside the point.

"I'm not sure how much that helps us," I said quietly. "What we need to lift weighs considerably more and likely will be traveling a considerable distance."

"How much more does it weigh?" asked Polly.

I hesitated, unsure. I had no idea how much uranium they were putting in there and how exactly they'd design the material aspect of the atom bomb. I decided that it was better to overestimate than to underestimate. "A family of elephants."

There was a long moment of silence in the room, and then Lola burst out laughing. We all stared at her, stunned and a little confused. A small part of me wondered if Lola had gone mad, as wild as she'd been in the last twenty-four hours. But then she sat up and wiped at her face with the back of her hands. "I'm sorry, can you just imagine? A flying elephant? A family of elephants?"

The corner of my mouth twitched once, and then twice, and then Polly started to giggle, stifling it behind her hand. I met her eyes and grinned. "I don't know what you're talking about, Lola. It sounds perfectly sensible to me. That's how I always transport my elephants."

"You're all mad," Stella declared, but I saw humor hiding on her face too.

"I don't even know what an elephant weighs," George added.

"Six tons," said Polly, surprising me.

Lola gaped. "And how much is a ton?"

"Two thousand pounds." Stella lost the battle to keep a smile off her face.

Lola cursed, and we all tried not to laugh, failing miserably. Stella strode to a blackboard and picked up a piece of chalk. I watched her take charge of writing the variables on the chalkboard. She accounted for a few even I hadn't thought of.

She wrote, $Altitude = w$, and then turned back to me. "When you were experimenting, did you figure out if altitude is variable on sea level or ground level?"

I shook my head. "Not that I know of. How'd you know I was experimenting?"

"I was too," Stella said, turning back to the board. "And I saw your little red notebook in your bag. It was an educated guess."

I glanced at the schoolbag resting against a desk leg on the floor, and sure enough, the corner of my red cloth notebook poked out from beneath the flap. George tipped his chair and started to reach for it, and I jumped forward, grabbing it out of my bag before he could see it. I didn't want him to see all my scribbles, all my failures. If I was leading this group as Colonel Mann wanted, I needed to look credible.

"Easy," George said with a laugh, holding up his hands and letting his chair fall back to the floor. "I just wanted to see if I could help. Maybe you were close to the answer but just needed a new set of eyes on it."

"I think Ilse would know if she was close to the answer and needed us to look over her work to help her overcome a barrier," Stella said calmly from the board.

I sent her a grateful look. I looked to Polly and Lola. "I know that Stella and George have scientific backgrounds...What did you do before the war? Do you know anything about magic? Or what your blood can do?"

They both shook their heads, but Lola added quickly, "I worked with Dr. Einstein at Princeton. I know a lot of the lingo you scientists use, and I don't mind long hours. I'll take notes if you want. Th—" She stopped abruptly, as if she was interrupting another thought.

"And?" I prompted.

She hesitated. "There are rules for science, aren't there? What are the rules for magic? Are they the same?"

I ran my fingers over the cloth cover of the notebook. "I've noticed that magic acts and behaves much like a science. But I don't know all of the rules."

"Well," said George. "It isn't like we know all of the rules for science either."

"We know more than we know about magic," Stella pointed out.

"We find the limits as we go," argued George.

"Breaking rules of magic—even the unknown ones—has consequences," I said.

George nodded, his brow furrowing. "That's true. I don't think we should be limiting ourselves though. We ought to try whatever we can, applying all the science we know to magic and seeing if we can fill in the blanks. Science acts on the magic."

Stella shook her head. "Magic acts on science."

"It's possible for both to be true," I suggested.

"That violates rules of operation," argued George.

"Well, then," said Polly from her seat next to Lola. "It looks like we'll be the ones to break all the rules."

"Excellent," I said, joining Stella at the board and picking up a piece of chalk. "I've been practicing for this my whole life."

* * *

August 27, 1943

Dear Wolf,

You promised you'd write the moment you arrived in England! But it's been a week since I left, and I'm starting to grow irritated. Waiting has never been my forte, you know.

Luckily, I didn't have to wait here long before work began. I'm working with three other girls and a young man. They're all about your age. Will there ever be a time when I'm not the youngest? (This is a rhetorical question. Of course it would be statistically unlikely that I would forever be the youngest of any given group.)

Lola is very sweet, but she's a bit of a flirt, and I worry she won't keep focused on her work as long as George is in the room. I hope I shall never be like that, but sometimes I feel it might be inevitable. Time does come for us all, as Papa says.

Polly is very pretty and seems bright enough, but she's a bit of a follower. We are too small a team to have followers, I think. Do you agree? I value your insight, Wolf.

Stella is an African American girl from Spelman, and she's exceedingly bright and very confident. I do wish I had half her confidence. She's older than me too, so part of me wonders why she isn't leading the group—did I mention that Colonel Mann has me *leading* the group? Why is it me, Wolf? I'm the youngest. I shouldn't be leading them. I haven't the faintest clue what we need to do to move forward.

But I'm nearly done, so I ought to keep focused. I'm working on that, you know. I'm trying not to seem my age so much here, but it's very hard. Far harder than I would have guessed.

George probably would laugh at me if he read this letter. He has a very easy laugh. He was another candidate for leader, but Colonel Mann has given him the task of traveling to liaison with the other groups.

George is quite nice and hasn't questioned my age or my experience, not since the first day. At least, not to my face. Do you think he's doing it behind my back, Wolf? Do boys do that sort of thing?

I spend all day pretending to know what I'm doing until the questions start to pile up and it feels like there's this dam about to break inside my head. I'm afraid if I let it break though, they'll send me home. And then I'll have gotten you into this whole mess for nothing.

Oak Ridge, that's where we are. That's in Tennessee, and it's so beautiful out here. I'm writing this on our front porch, which overlooks a steep hill. There used to be trees here, but it's mostly mud on this side, and yet it's still pretty, the way the road winds down into the town, and I can see the top of the church they're building, and the library. Oak Ridge wouldn't impress Mama, but I'm so busy that I haven't even been to the library yet.

I hope England isn't too wet and do write me, Wolf. You promised.

Ilse

* * *

August 31, 1943

Ilse,

I am still on the boat. It takes two weeks to get to England. We won't get there for another few days, and I honestly can't wait. I spend most of my time being jeered by sailors and soldiers alike. I can't reveal what I'm really doing here, and most don't care for my diplomatic services cover story. To some of them, diplomacy is what they do. Drop bombs and shoot men. To the rest of them, "diplomacy" is why they have to fight in the first place. Because it failed. Suffice it to say, I am not well liked. And it bothers me more than it should.

None of this is an excuse for not writing, but sending—and receiving, dear sister—magic letters while on a ship just waiting for U-boats to torpedo it is far harder than you can imagine. Though I assume you haven't imagined it often. Do not share this part of the letter with Mama and Papa.

I apologize for not writing. Happy?

And I'm glad to hear you made it to Oak Ridge without incident. That really is in the middle of nowhere, isn't it? I borrowed a map from one of the officers, but I couldn't find it. I suppose that's the point.

I suspect the reason you were put in charge is twofold—first, no one will suspect your position because of your age. That protects you and the project. And second, you earned it. Are the other girls also capable of doing magic *and* high-level theoretical physics? It's not a terrible thing to show a little pride in yourself, Ilse.

That being said, I wonder if Stella is equally qualified for the job (seeing as she went to Spelman) but didn't get it because of her race. I know you know she isn't inferior to you, or lesser than you in any way, but that's not the way the government and thus the army sees it. And some people will put any white person in charge, even a Jew, to avoid promoting an African American. Remember—you two are allies in a hateful world. The people who hate her hate you too, and there is no basis in logic, science, or culture for that hatred. Don't let this cloud your work.

Magic makes equals of us all.

Your team sounds balanced, Ilse. If you value my opinion, that is my honest thought. The team sounds balanced between energies, personalities, and strengths.

As for George, if he is kind to your face, give him the benefit of the doubt. That goes for everyone you meet. I know that science comes easier than human motivations to you, so focus on the science and trust your instincts.

I was thinking, Ilse, about what you said before we parted ways. About asking about Max. And as soon as I meet my contact, I'm going to do that. You're right. It's important.

Don't forget to keep me apprised of any developments with magic I might be able to use over here. I feel like I'm flying blind.

Your brother,

Wolf

CHAPTER NINE

LONDON, ENGLAND
SEPTEMBER 3, 1943

WOLF

London hummed with an energy that I couldn't quite get to align with my own nervous buzz. The streets were congested, and I'd forgotten that cities, even those under siege from German bombardment, had a distinct way of not giving a damn and going about their business. People strode past bombed-out buildings, dressed to the nines, on their way to work, and people still shopped and chatted. Life went on. It made me miss home, and the silence of my cab made that ache grow, swelling until I couldn't breathe.

If Max were here, he'd make a joke and I'd laugh and the balloon in my chest would burst. But he wasn't here. He'd joined up, said goodbye, asked me to come see him off. And I hadn't. I couldn't. There'd been a distance between us the last few weeks that he'd been home, after something he'd said during the hurricane, something I couldn't unhear. It clawed at me at night when I tried to sleep. Even now. What happened when two people wanted something that was impossible?

So I hadn't said goodbye. I was never good at goodbyes. Saying goodbye to Ilse had left me red-eyed from the effort not to cry. We shouldn't say goodbyes. We should just leave and hope one day we'll get to say hello again. Disappearing was easier than figuring out the words. I felt them like pictures and sensations in my chest, a bow drawing across my heartstrings, low and mournful, but the words—the ones that came out of my mouth—I hadn't been able to find them. I still couldn't. Sometimes I'd try to imagine saying goodbye to him, pretend I could turn back time and live that moment again, and each time, I couldn't find the words.

The London pub was crowded, full of Americans like myself. Most of them were on leave, between flights and missions, desperate to talk about anything other than the steady rate of planes being shot down by the Germans and the steady advancement of the American forces into Italy. I felt out of place here, not in uniform and clearly on the outside. But they'd told me to have a nice night out before I reported for duty at the main OSS office in the morning, so here I was. A beer in hand, watching the Army Air Force Yankees as though I was looking through a pane of glass. One too many drinks, maybe. Who could blame me?

If anything, the alcohol swimming in my veins made me see everything a little clearer. Beneath the grins, the backslaps, the jostling at the bar, the flirting, and the dancing, everyone's eyes were a little pained, a little too full of ghosts, and everything felt a little too forced.

I spun a coin around in my hand, letting it roll through my fingers. It passed through the paper cuts from the letters I'd written Mama, Papa, and Ilse from the ship and posted this morning when I reached England safely. Every time my blood touched the edge of coin, I could feel the magic sing into my veins. *Magic,* Ilse had once told me, *wants to be used.* Except no one knew much about it. Everything we'd done so far felt crude and rudimentary, a high-risk game of guess-and-check without knowing any consequences of what we did.

"You look like you need another drink," said a cool, sweet voice next to me, and a girl swam into my vision, sliding onto the barstool next to me. She rapped her knuckles on the bar, and I raised my eyebrows at the demand in her motion. Her plain brown hair had long since lost its wave, barely staying in its clip at the back of her neck.

She was more handsome than pretty, with a square jaw and a firm set to her mouth. The bartender poured her two beers, and she slid one to me with a small smile.

I blinked and wrapped my hands around the cool glass. Mine had become warm from sitting so long. The last thing I needed was another drink. "Thanks, Miss...?"

She allowed the leading question. "Lillian Tasker. But most of my friends call me Lily."

"Wolf Klein," I said, shaking her hand.

"Where are you from?" she asked kindly.

I sipped at the beer. I didn't like the taste of it any more than the first one, but it seemed like the polite thing to do. "New York." There was an awkward lull, and I thought of what Ilse would have done, something that didn't let the conversation drop off the face of the earth. I cleared my throat. "You?"

"Inverness," she said, and as soon as she said it, I could hear the Scot in her accent. She must have spent a great deal of time down here to have lost most of it.

"ATA?" I guessed. The British Air Transport Auxiliary was almost entirely made up of women flying planes to where they needed to be, and I'd already heard they regularly drank American men under the table.

She smiled. "For a time. You're the one who looks out of place."

I looked back out at the dancing crowd. The idea of getting up and dancing made the room tilt a little. "I'd look out of place even if I was in uniform. I've never been in a pub before. I've never had a beer before either, if I'm telling you all my secrets."

"Oh good God," Lily muttered. "They've sent a lamb to the slaughter."

I straightened. "What?"

"I came to find out what our American recruit looked like," she said, looking me up and down with a hint of sadness. "I needed a wolf, but they sent me a lamb. I don't want to write your family a letter, lad."

I stared at her. "You're...OSS?"

"MI6," she said. "Assigned to your team though. This is a joint effort. Your OSS is a wee newborn kitten. Not unlike you."

I drained the rest of my beer. "I don't think we're supposed to talk about this here."

She swore, and I stopped, halfway off the barstool, to look at her. She softened a little. "I know you weren't expecting me tonight. I spotted you from across the room. It's coincidence, and I shouldn't have approached. But now I have. I swear I'm normally better at this."

"I hope so," I said quietly. "Otherwise you might be writing my family a letter."

She winced. "It's been a week. I'm sorry. You're wet behind the ears, but I assume they didn't pick your name out of a hat."

They might as well have, but I didn't tell her that.

"What happened this week?" I asked.

"I can't tell you that," she said. "Not here, anyway. And I can't promise I'll ever be able to tell you what I did before this mission."

A spy then, an operative. And a girl. Ilse would love the gender equality in espionage operations. Out on the dance floor, they started playing a familiar tune, "You Are My Sunshine," and I stepped away from the bar, offering my hand. "Tell me you're better at dancing than you are at approaching a mark."

"You're not a mark," she said.

"I could always sing it to you instead," I suggested.

"You wouldn't."

I picked up right on cue with the band, singing along with them.

The other night, dear, as I lay sleeping,
I dreamed I held you in my arms.

But when I awoke, dear, I was mistaken,
and I hung my head and cried.

She slipped her hand into mine, laughing. "Oh my God, you are a terrible singer. I'll dance if it'll get you to shut up."

I wanted to be normal. I wanted to be able to get out of my own body and my own mind for a few minutes every now and then. I couldn't before, but here, I was just another boy in the army, just another boy overseas, dancing with a girl on the eve of destruction.

Out on the dance floor, my hand settled on her lower back, and her lips touched the lobe of my ear. "My people skills are vastly overestimated."

"Then you're in the wrong line of work," I said to her softly. "Because isn't that all you do? People?"

Her smile was wild, toothy, and violent. Beautiful. "It is. And I'm very good at it. But I'm trying not to play you, Wolf Klein, because you aren't a mark. You're one of us. I'm sorry. I tend to be…"

Her voice trailed off, and I offered, "Rude?"

I spun her, and on the way back to me, she replied, "The more masks you wear, the harder it is to remember who you really are beneath them all."

I settled my hand on the small of her back again, feeling her muscles moving beneath my fingers. She wasn't soft like other girls I knew. She was hard, angular, more fox than bunny. "You can't be much older than me. How long you been doing this?"

"I'll be twenty-two on Christmas Day," she said. "I enlisted when I was nineteen, just after my husband died."

I sucked in a breath. "I'm sorry."

She nodded, accepting it. "I married my childhood sweetheart when he was called up. He died at Dunkirk."

I didn't know what to say. I was too drunk for this conversation.

I couldn't be sincere, because I didn't know anything, and I couldn't fake it, because I was drunk.

"What about you?" she asked, saving me from myself.

The band crooned.

You are my sunshine, my only sunshine,
You make me happy when skies are gray.
You'll never know, dear, how much I love you.
Please don't take my sunshine away.

"I was called up," I said, because that was the only way to describe it.

She tilted her chin up, her gaze shrewd. "For this line of work?"

"It's complicated," I said.

She laughed. "Isn't everything?"

I spun her around. "I wish it wasn't. I wish the world was more like this song."

"What do you mean?"

The world was dark and light, blackout curtains and big lamps, spinning people, and a loud band, the girl in my arms in a pretty blue dress, and the taste of stale beer drying my mouth and making my tongue stick.

I swallowed, dampening my throat. "It's a simple song for a simpler time."

"It's a sad song," she replied. "They're playing it quickly, but that doesn't change the words."

"I didn't say it was happy," I argued. "Just that it was simple."

We spun around while the accordion played, and I sang along, just to hear her laugh again. She groaned, told me she'd have me arrested for indecency ("and not the fun kind," she said, making me blush) because my singing voice was so horrendous. Maybe it was the beer, or maybe it was that we weren't talking about her husband anymore, or maybe it was something else entirely, but I grinned and sang louder on the next repeated chorus.

The song ended, and as everyone else dropped hands and applauded the band, Lily stepped closer to me. Her hips bumped against mine. "If you want the straight version of what we're doing, underneath all the propaganda and the lies and the secrets, the silos of information and the rules about who knows what pieces are on the table, I'll tell you. Come with me, Sunshine."

To the entire room, she looked like a woman propositioning a man. I supposed, in a way, she was.

And when I left with her, I looked like a man who had accepted.

I supposed, in a way, I had.

* * *

Lily linked her arm with mine, murmuring to me that we ought to pretend to be lovers, and I followed her lead, leaning in to her and smiling down at her as she giggled and laughed at a joke I hadn't told. We meandered along the high street for a block and then turned down a quieter lane, and then into an alley. She pulled me by the hand urgently, and for a brief moment, I thought that perhaps I hadn't made the right choice. Maybe she was going to kill me in the alley.

"I live with a handful of ATA girls here," she murmured, turning into the back garden of a simple house with blackout curtains drawn over the windows. "But I have a private room at the top of the stairs. I told them I snored."

I covered my snort with my hand and followed her as she carefully opened the door and we snuck in, both wincing when I stepped on a stair that creaked rather audibly through the house. She pushed me into her room and shut the door behind us. Moving quickly around the small, dark room, she lit a candle beside the bed and, with a shake of her wrist, extinguished the match. She sat on the edge of her bed and gestured for me to sit on a trunk.

"I'm sorry we're talking here," she said quietly. "But I know no one's listening. I keep close tabs on the other girls. They're as innocent as they get. Except one. But she's a spy for us, I'm pretty sure."

"You're pretty sure?"

She snorted. "I can't afford to worry about every possible point of penetration. I can only worry about this mission."

I stared at her. There was a strong possibility that I had been brought on board because I was used to being a counterweight to another person's narrow-focused intensity. "Shouldn't you be one hundred percent positive that another person is a spy for us or report it?"

"Really, I shouldn't suspect she's a spy at all," Lily said, leaning back on her hands with a smirk on her face. "She's not very good at espionage if I suspect her."

"*I* don't know very much about espionage," I said sharply.

"Good point. Why *were* you brought on board?" Lily said.

My mouth snapped shut. It was the perfect setup, and for all I knew, she was a German spy. I had no way of confirming her identity or knowing if she was cleared to know why I was on the team. I didn't know what to do, what to say, how to get myself out of a corner I'd let myself be backed into.

What would Ilse say? I thought.

"My charm and my devilish good looks," I quipped.

Lily lit a cigarette, her lips curving into a smile around the end of it. She offered it to me, and I shook my head. She inhaled deeply and blew out slowly. "That was clever. Your instincts are good."

"If I had instincts for this sort of thing, I wouldn't be in a bedroom with a girl smoking a cigarette and offering to tell me the truth," I pointed out.

She motioned at me with the cigarette. "Fair point, Sunshine. I'll tell you what I can. I work for an interallied project, consulting with both MI6 and the OSS—that is, the British Military Intelligence,

Section 6, and the American Office of Strategic Services—on uses of magic. We had a couple of different projects I oversaw, but they just moved me to a new one. It's called Malgo, and it's one arm of Operation Alsos."

She did know about magic then, but she didn't know about the bomb. Or, she thought I didn't. My head spun from overlapping circles of information, the inability to tell who knew what, and the task of trying to figure out where we could cross-compare information. I supposed that was the point.

"Our training will include parachuting and learning German, but you know it, don't you? That'll mostly be for me then."

"I speak it a little and understand it, but I can't always keep Yiddish and German straight," I admitted. "I'm not sure I can read it with any accuracy."

"That'll be fine. I've been working mostly in France, so my German could use work. Our goal is to be in and out of Germany within three weeks, but that depends on how much magic can do for us, and if there's more than you on the team."

I shot her a look. "So you knew why I was here. My magic."

She smiled again. "You're good at keeping secrets, but I'm better at retrieving them. You shouldn't have confirmed that just now."

"Lesson learned," I said and then hesitated. "Can I ask you a question?"

She sat up. "Sure."

"I'm Jewish," I said, swallowing hard. "You must know that."

"Yes," she said, sitting up. "So am I. My maiden name is Jacobs."

I leaned forward again, elbows on knees. "If we're caught, it's much worse for people like you and me. You've heard what I've heard, haven't you?"

"Then we must not get caught," she snapped and then looked away, stamping out her cigarette with unnecessary force. She took a deep breath and rested the remainder of the cigarette on the edge of the ashtray alongside a collection of other half-smoked cigarettes. I didn't think she really wanted to smoke as much as she needed something to do with her hands. Knitting didn't seem to suit her—or maybe she shouldn't have sharp objects in her hands.

After a beat of silence, Lily said, her voice steady again, "I'm sorry. I know. I know it's a concern that you and I will carry and our superiors might not understand."

She didn't want to go. But she would, out of a sense of duty. At least we were in the same boat.

I rubbed at my jaw with a tired hand and then stared down at my fingers covered in little cuts. I had a gift. The magic in my veins could change the laws of physics and chemistry, and maybe, change history. I hadn't asked for it, and without it, I was ordinary. Just a boy of average height and stocky build, with curly hair and a jaw set so firmly my mother said I was born sullen.

I looked up at Lily, at the shadows in her face cast by the candlelight, and listened to the sound of people outside drunkenly laughing their way home from the pub. "When did they tell you about what...what I could do?"

"Three days ago," she said with a small smile.

"You don't have questions?"

"I do. But that's not what tonight's about," she said. "That's for some other time."

"What's tonight about?" I asked. "You said yourself that you weren't supposed to make contact until tomorrow."

"I don't always follow the rules," said Lily. "It's one of the reasons they like me. They'll write me up and discipline me a thousand times, but I've stayed alive so much longer than others, and I've never been caught. You must be able to think on your feet and follow your instincts."

They should have brought Ilse over here instead of me. I couldn't do any of that. I liked to turn things over in my mind, chew on them awhile, examine every angle. Ilse asked questions, but she didn't think twice. She trusted her mind and followed where it led her. It should have led her to England instead of Tennessee.

"There's a note in your file," said Lily casually, playing with the hem of her skirt on her knees. She looked up at me, curiosity playing openly across her face. It didn't feel like an invented expression, something she picked out of a hat to elicit a certain reaction from me. She unclipped her hair, letting it fall around her shoulders and then swept it back up and reclipped it.

"What note?" I asked impatiently.

The corner of her mouth twitched. "That you dance on the other side of the ballroom."

I blinked. "I don't dance in ballrooms."

"It's an expression."

"Not one I get then," I said. "Just be straight with me."

"Do you prefer the company of men?"

My heart pounded. "That's in my file? What evidence do they have?"

"Is it true?"

"Does it matter?"

"I need to know who could seduce you, who might make you vulnerable. If the Germans send someone over here to infiltrate this program, who might get in with you? Where are your insecurities and weaknesses?"

"My vulnerability is being Jewish, and my weakness is my family. You could have just asked," I pointed out.

She shrugged. "You haven't answered the first question I asked you."

"There isn't any evidence," I said shortly, "so I think it's ridiculous that it's in my file or that you feel it's appropriate to ask me this."

"You can trust me, Wolf," Lily said.

"I *can't*," I snapped without thinking, shoving a hand into my hair. "It's *illegal*."

She held my gaze. "I know. And I do not care. I need to know for the safety of this team. I will not write this down or include it in any report. I think your gift protects you from the law in this case, because they need you, but I don't know what'd happen after the war so I'll keep your secret."

"It's not…" I groaned and closed my eyes, covering my face with my hands. "That's not even it."

"What is it?"

I hesitated and answered slowly, "That is not…how I experience—I don't feel what other people feel. When I said there was no evidence, I meant it. There's no evidence."

My face was hot, but Lily's expression didn't change from curiosity. "Not at all? You never think, 'Ah, now *there's* a person I'd want to take to bed?' You don't imagine it at all?"

One person. There's one person. Still, I shook my head. "No, not like that. I recognize when people are attractive, but I don't feel *desire* that way."

Except for him. The one exception to the way I was made. I used to think I was broken, but then the rebbe told me that I was made in God's image, and God was both perfect and imperfect, and I'd held on to that. It'd replaced a seed of resentment and self-hatred that'd begun to blossom in my chest. By the time I'd sorted out that the feeling I felt toward someone else was *desire*, something more charged in my veins than mere love and curiosity, he was gone.

But I wasn't going to offer Lily information she didn't need.

Perhaps I was better at espionage than I thought.

"Huh," she said and then shook her head, straightening her skirts and rising to her feet. "No matter. That'll make things easier, or at least more interesting. Do you know how to get back to your hotel from here?"

"I'll figure it out," I said, still reeling from her questions.

She opened her room door and whispered as I stepped into the hall, "The second-to-last step, remember."

"I'll remember," I promised.

She rubbed at her bottom lip, her lipstick color shining on her thumb, and she pressed it against the corner of my mouth and then on my shirt collar. "I'll see you tomorrow, soldier."

"Not a soldier," I said. She shut the door in my face.

CHAPTER TEN

OAK RIDGE, TENNESSEE
SEPTEMBER 3, 1943

ILSE

Where there was a will, there was a…growing irritation and the feeling that failure was bearing down on me like a train on the tracks. I'd never *failed* before. Not like this. Not against something I felt that I should know. I'd never run out of questions before either. But my mind was blank, my arm ached, it was hot, and I was cranky.

I glared at the blackboard, at the equations written on it, and the streaks of erased chalk that swam before my eyes. I *knew* I wasn't being patient, and I knew that science and magic didn't have timelines—but our project did. And we hadn't gotten anywhere. Maybe a week ago I'd been idealistic about the science and magic we'd be doing, but right now, I just wanted one win. I wanted to discover one aspect of magic that we could use for the delivery of the bomb. I was exhausted, and not just because I'd been the one to donate blood for experiments today. I'd nearly fainted from the heat and the needle in my arm, the bags filling up with dark-red blood that belonged in my body.

Then I thought about Wolf and the Nazi bomb, and I knew that I couldn't be precious about my blood. Not right now. It was, I admit, an unusual way to bleed for my country, but unusual times called for unusual measures.

"We could shrink the elephant," George suggested again.

"We have not proven we can alter the mass with magic," I retorted.

"We don't know that we can't," Stella said, taking George's side for once.

"That's a whole different experiment. We're losing the thread here," I said. I used to know all of the questions. Where were the questions? What would Wolf say here? Probably, *"I didn't know you ever ran out of questions."* I didn't know either, Wolf. My skin itched, and my shirt felt too tight. The buttons bothered my skin, and I wanted to scratch at myself. I squirmed, digging my fingernails into my palms, trying to clear my head so I could breathe and think again.

"Do you understand it's hard to have a fact-based conversation with someone who is hanging upside down on a desk?" Stella asked, her patience beginning to fray like a hem that was constantly stepped on.

I sat up with some effort, my feet poking off the end of the desk I had draped myself backward over. The blood swam in my head, and spots splashed across my vision. "We haven't proven we can alter mass with magic," I repeated and then flopped back down. Admittedly, I was sulking, a little bit, but I deserved a little sulk.

"Sit up," murmured Polly, sitting next to me on the desk. She raised an eyebrow, and I reluctantly sat up and slid back into the chair next to her. She looked over at George. "How would you propose altering mass?"

George's mouth opened, then shut. He slumped in his chair, looking frustrated, but said nothing. I supposed that should have made me feel better, but it didn't at all. The room felt stuffy, too hot for anything to think or move. I pulled at the collar of my shirt until Polly gently pulled my hand down.

I flushed at her dry, steady hand touching my clammy, trembling one. When I yanked my hand away, she cleared her throat, pink coloring her neck and cheeks. I supposed I'd been rude, but I couldn't apologize. That was the other thing. It felt like there was another question, one I ought to know, one that I had the words for and couldn't quite form yet. It hung out there, known and unknown at the same time. It felt just as awful as not knowing the right questions about magic, but I could ignore this one. For now.

"I don't know that we'd have to alter the mass, technically," Stella said, filling the awkward silence. "So if we're assuming that there's a subatomic level in which everything is connected, then we need to use magic to uncouple those atoms from the connected field."

I blinked, my mind whirling back into a proper headspace. "I'm following, I think. How do you propose controlling the magic?"

"I don't know yet," admitted Stella. "But I think we could do that. Then we could alter the density of objects, their space, their weight…but I'm not sure how long or far that'd last. We know magic equations wear off eventually."

"It'd be easier," Lola added lightly, "if we knew what this particular object *was*."

They all looked at me. I shook my head. "You know I can't share that information."

"She's ticklish," Lola said casually, having learned this the night before in our house. "Just so you know."

"That's torture!" I protested, giggling and curving away from Polly's hands that reached for my ribs.

George leaned forward, grinning, and Lola grabbed his shoulder, pushing him back into his seat. "Not you, cowboy."

He scowled at her. "I didn't mean anything by it."

George seemed to be the only man at Oak Ridge that Lola didn't flirt with. When I asked her if he'd said something uncouth to her, she had frowned and just said, "He's not my type." But from what I could tell, her type was male and breathing. Still, they spent most of each day snipping at each other, and I didn't know what to do about that.

Wolf would have known. But he was better at leading than I was.

Instead, I just changed the topic back. "Tickling won't make me give up the information. You know I can't tell. It's not like I'm keeping it for fun, you know."

"You understand it'd make our work easier, right?" Lola asked seriously.

My chest tightened. All of these questions for me, and none of my own for them. "I do. I also know I'd disappear and wouldn't be seen again. I know that it could get us killed. It's more—"

"—secret than our magic," said Lola. "We know."

What she didn't know was that George and Stella almost definitely also knew what was being built here. What they didn't know—and maybe what only I knew—was there might not be a bomb to deliver.

I hadn't seen the boys from those labs in days, and even before they disappeared, no one had seemed particular jubilant when I saw them around town. My guess was they hadn't yet achieved a sustained nuclear chain reaction. The girls at the other reactors worked all day and night, adjusting the levels and dials for the reactor. They didn't have any idea what they were doing—that much I could tell from snippets of conversations around town. They didn't know they were working with radioactive materials, or what would happen if anything went wrong.

I had questions about that. So many questions. But I wasn't here to do science. I was here to do magic. I couldn't ask the scientific questions. I squeezed my eyes shut painfully.

"You know science like you know magic, and you know magic like you know science. They aren't separate parts of you. Don't forget that." Wolf had been wrong. They were separate parts of me. I didn't know how to think at this level for magic. I didn't know how to lead. I didn't know how to be the prodigy when it came to magic.

What if I couldn't do this? What if I'd gotten us in trouble, but only Wolf would carry the burden of going to war for my mistakes?

When I opened my eyes, the room shrank down around me. Polly sat too close to me, with her pink cheeks and her fingers playing with the fringe of her hair around her ear, and George, watching me from across the room, and Lola and Stella returning to their work. Everything was too close. Too small. The pressure in my chest ballooned.

"I'm going to take a walk," I said, hoping the panic didn't shine through my voice.

"Don't faint," Lola said absentmindedly as she siphoned blood—*my* blood—into a small beaker sitting over an open flame. She'd learned a lot in the last week. Or maybe she'd absorbed more from being a secretary than she realized.

"Stop burning my blood," I said.

"We all have our pastimes," she said lightly. "Don't judge."

"Not judging!" I called, raising my hands innocently and backing toward the door. *Get out, get out, get out.* I thumped into the doorframe with my back and flushed as George and Lola laughed. Stella shook her head, not even looking up from her notebook. Polly just rolled her eyes at me, a smile tipping up the corner of her mouth. I really needed to stop noticing her smiles. The hallway was cooler than the room, though that wasn't hard; the windows in the lab turned it into a greenhouse. At least the hallway was dark, save for the hastily hung fluorescent lights above that barely cast light.

I walked quickly out of building, toward the exit that led to a small grove of trees. People liked to smoke out there, but this time of day, it'd be quiet and would offer me at least a break from the secrets of that room. The hot and humid air didn't feel much less claustrophobic, but it was enough. I wiped my palms down the front of my blouse.

"You can do this, Ilse Klein," I whispered to myself.

"Ilse," called George from behind me, the door banging shut in his wake.

I bit back the first question in my head, *Why are you following me?* and managed a pleasant smile. He grinned, his ever-present stopwatch in his hand as he clicked it down the hallway. "Mind if I join you?"

"I just needed some fresh air," I hedged.

He held his hands up. "I won't talk about anything from inside that room. Against the rules, and I can tell you need a break."

I relaxed a little bit. "Thank you."

It was one thing to be grateful for the lack of conversation—my brain felt like a nest full of bees was inside it—but I didn't know how to talk about what we did, about the only intersection of conversation I had with anyone here, without revealing secrets. State secrets. I could feel frustration bubbling up inside me as we began to walk down the path toward the training facility they'd built for the Site W staff visiting X-10. There was a cafeteria, somewhere we could get something cool to drink and a little bit to eat.

But I didn't trust myself to talk through my frustration and not ask questions I wasn't allowed to ask. There'd never been questions that'd been off-limits before in my life. And these weren't even questions that would help us. They weren't worth asking.

"The shade feels good," said George, the clicking of his stopwatch becoming background noise against the cicadas and the sound of the reactor in the background. "It's so goddamn hot in that lab."

"It'll be fall soon," I said. "Then we'll be complaining about the cold."

"Don't you wish you could just keep traveling to wherever the weather is ideal?" George asked. "Never stay anywhere long enough for it to be miserable?"

I laughed a little bit. "Is there such a place?"

"Italian coast," he said immediately. "I went there a few years ago with my father. Before the war."

I glanced around, looking to see if we were overheard, remembering that boy the first day who had heard my name and sneered at the German comment. If George had traveled to Italy, it might look like we were conspiring, like we had fascist sympathies together, and then if someone would ever accuse us—

"It was like Mussolini wasn't even in power," George said as if he could read my thoughts. "I'm sure it's different if you live there, but I loved my holiday."

I smiled. "Holiday. You speak like a European."

"I did go to boarding school over there," said George. "My father was a diplomat."

"And now you're at the University of Chicago," I guessed. "Is that how you got into such an elite program?"

"You think I needed his connections?" George asked, sounding wounded.

"Oh!" I stopped in my tracks. "I didn't mean...I'm sure you're smart enough...Enough's not the right word...I'm so sorry."

I stumbled over my words, and my voice trailed off when he laughed, throwing back his head. He nudged me with his elbow. "I'm teasing. My father helped me get into the program, yes, and I have no shame in saying that. Why not use the connections you have?"

Because, I thought, somewhere there's someone else who wanted into that program and didn't have a wealthy father. But who was I to think that? My father's money had saved me from an asylum when my magic manifested and had kept me and my brother safe in university for the last three years. We'd never wanted for anything, and neither had George. But maybe we were supposed to ask these questions. Maybe I didn't like the way that George just shrugged like it was simple when it wasn't.

He'd been recruited before the rest of us and seemed most comfortable here in Oak Ridge. I hadn't forgotten the look he gave me—and the look he gave Stella—when he found out that I'd been made the leader of the working group. Stella had been right. He'd expected a certain amount of power.

But since then, he hadn't given me any trouble. He contributed and thought and had managed not to say anything overtly terrible to Stella in the last week. Was it enough?

"You didn't want to join up?" The question slipped out before I could stop it.

He flinched a little. "This is service too."

I nodded, thinking of Wolf over in Europe, somewhere, doing God-knows-what. "That's what my brother would say."

"Your brother?"

"He's abroad," I confirmed, because it wasn't a lie.

George's face fell. "God. I'm so sorry, Ilse. Is he a scientist too? Does he have our gift? Maybe I can speak to Colonel Mann."

I didn't tell him that he didn't have that much sway over the colonel, even if he thought he did. I shook my head. "Wolf wanted to go."

Also not a lie.

Also not the full truth.

These half-truths were going to kill me at some point.

George looked stricken. "Wow. Well. Now I understand why you've really thrown yourself into the work here. You've done a good job."

I managed a smile. "We haven't made any progress."

His smile was small, gentle, and not at all pitying. "I know. But we're figuring out a system and a plan of attack. Besides, two weeks is a small amount of time."

I spread my hands wide. "Tasks are liquid."

It took him a beat, but he caught up. "They expand to fit the container."

"And the container is time." I nodded.

"You're clever, Ilse Klein," said George. He handed me a tray as we worked our way through the cafeteria. "So how does our gift affect the container?"

I blinked, looking around. A shiver ran through me. "Not here."

"No one's paying us any attention," he said.

Someone was always paying attention. The man in the park, tour guide Loretta, the cafeteria worker putting corn bread on a small plate and onto our plastic trays. I shook my head. "I said, not here."

"C'mon," he cajoled me.

"The last time I said something I shouldn't," I said, my voice pierced with shards of panic, "my brother was shipped overseas. So pardon me if I'm disinclined to break the rules again."

Heads turned toward me, and I knew I was bright red with anger and fear and embarrassment all muddled together, but I forced myself to walk to a table in the corner and set my tray down carefully. George hesitated and sat across from me. "I'm sorry."

"This is why I didn't want to talk about it here," I told him. "I don't know what we're doing. If we fail, people will die. My brother will die." I scrubbed at my face. "And if we succeed, other people will die. And we don't have a choice. So we need to make progress, George. And we need to obey their rules. There's no gray area here. I can't mess this up."

He reached across the table and wrapped his hand around mine. I stared at it, confused, but not pulling away. His voice was low, sincere. "I know. I understand. You're not going to mess this up. I didn't mean to be hasty or assume things. I'm on your side, Ilse."

I nodded and slid my hand from his. "I believe you."

"Good," he said softly.

When we returned to the lab, Lola looked up at us, a smile on her face slipping free. "What happened?"

"Nothing," I said. "We just got lunch. The food isn't bad."

Lola's frown deepened.

As I passed her, Stella said quietly, "You look like you're about to cry, Ilse."

I would not cry. Not here, not in the lab, and not in front of the others. I didn't even like crying in front of Wolf, and I knew he didn't think me lesser for it. I didn't want the team here to think I couldn't do this. I wanted it to be easier. I wanted being here, away from my family, not knowing if my brother was okay, doing something I didn't understand, to be easier. And that felt like such a stupid, simple thing to want. In a time when everyone was giving up what we wanted, I wanted something so unattainable, so silly, so frivolous.

Polly followed me to the blackboard as I picked up a piece of chalk and took a deep breath. I pressed the tip of the chalk into the board, but nothing came to my mind except my own words. *If we fail, people will die. If we succeed, people will also die.* And no matter what, my brother might die. I couldn't—didn't know *how* to—solve that with a piece of chalk and some math and blood siphoned from our veins.

"What do you need?" she asked, her voice soft.

"I don't know," I answered truthfully.

She touched my elbow, grounding me. "That's not an answer. What do you need?"

I closed my eyes. The question felt too big—like the question *How can we deliver a bomb with magic?* I couldn't wrap my mind around something so intangible, so abstract. I needed to find the concrete corners of it, like finding all the straight edges of a puzzle before beginning to work on a section. What we knew—blood was magical, clotted blood didn't work, physics and math equations written in our blood would act on objects—wasn't a great deal, but it was enough to form a picture. There were other things, theories and guesses. Rumors that I'd heard. What Stella said at the train station...how I'd thought to deliver the letters but hadn't yet tested the process.

"Balloons," I said quietly. "I need balloons."

* * *

September 5, 1943

Ilse,

I made it to England, and despite all the bombings, London's a lively city. I admire their persistence, the grim set of everyone's mouths as they carry on, even under strict rations. The pubs just cover up their windows, and everyone dances on. The idea that they're the last free country in all of Europe—Switzerland does not count—doesn't seem to weigh them down. Instead, it drives them forward.

I found my contact—she's another Jew, if you can believe it. It's odd. I thought maybe I'd be the only one, the Last Free Jew of Europe, but I'm not. And I've heard rumors all over the place about Jewish boys who fled Europe before the war and are now back fighting against Hitler. Their families probably aren't even alive, but they're back here, going out there every day.

Anyway, you asked me to write when I arrived, so I've written. I might not be able to write for a few days—we have to go learn how to jump out of airplanes.

Your brother,

Wolf

CHAPTER ELEVEN

WOLF

We rode out of London in the back of a Royal Air Force truck: two airmen back from leave, two Women's Land army girls, Lily, and myself. She said the third member of our team had alternate travel plans and would be meeting us in a day or two at Burtonwood, a small village about an hour north of London. The ride was quiet, save for the truck itself. Lily slept—or appeared to—her head resting against the side of the truck. The Women's Land army girls stared at her as though she was the most terrifying and intriguing thing they'd ever seen, and I understood the sentiment.

I watched the world pass by us from the back of the truck. I hadn't seen farmland like this except in photos. It rolled out from either side of the narrow road, peaceful and green. I found myself jolted out of a daydream by the roar of a low-flying plane, smoke trailing from its tail. I jolted forward on the bench as the airmen lurched simultaneously to the back of the truck, swearing and looking up into the sky.

"Ours," said one of them.

"It'll get home," said the other.

I sighed with relief and sank back against the bench. Lily didn't even crack an eye. The girls were whispering with each other now, distracted from Lily by the injured bird in the air.

Even out in the countryside, no one could escape war. The ration tickets, the city girls plowing the land, the POWs, the rallies to raise money for more Spitfires, the planes hobbling home pursued by enemy aircraft, the empty seats at kitchen tables. War was everywhere.

"I'm going to find our pilot," said Lily when we finally arrived at the base and checked into our rooms. They'd given Lily a bunk with a few of the ATA girls and found me an empty room with two bunks and a sink. "Wash up, and meet me out front in ten."

"I thought we were waiting for the other guy," I said, hoping she'd rethink this. I wanted to sleep. I wasn't ready to jump out of a plane. Not right now. Not yet.

Or ever, but that didn't seem to be an option on the table.

Lily shook her head. "We're not jumping out tonight. I want to get you comfortable with flying."

"I'll be fine," I told her. The less time I spent in a plane, the happier I'd be.

"It's a good thing you didn't join up, Sunshine," Lily said cheerfully. "You have serious issues with authority."

I scowled at her as she retreated.

After dumping my bag on the lower bunk, I changed into a new T-shirt and scrubbed my face at the sink. My head ached. I still hadn't caught up to the new time zone.

I rubbed my thumb and forefinger together, feeling where they'd gone rough from all the reading and writing I'd done. I'd sent Ilse another letter. At least the message system worked.

Stepping out into the midday sun, I squinted, holding my hand over my eyes to look for Lily. The airfield had rows and rows of planes lined up, with people walking back and forth between them. In the distance, I could see a plane on the tarmac with smoke on its tail. The pilot seemed to be standing next to it, so at least he hadn't been hurt.

"Oh, is that the plane we saw?" asked Lily from behind me.

"How could you possibly see it from the truck with your eyes closed?" I asked, turning around and stopping dead in my tracks. Lily was still smiling at me, one hand shading her eyes and the other hooked into a belt loop, looking like she'd walked off the cover of a pinup calendar. But I couldn't stare at her when she was standing next to him.

"Max," I said, and I hated the way my voice trembled.

He looked the same way he had the last time I saw him, one year ago before he signed up. Tanned from the sun, his sandy-blond hair a tousled wave, his deep-set green eyes invisible due to the way his face crinkled when he squinted into the sun. He wore the olive shirt and tan trousers of a pilot, silver wings affixed to his left breast pocket. If Lily looked like a pinup girl, he looked like the all-American boy on the posters about victory gardens and war ration cards.

He swallowed, wide-eyed, stiff-shouldered. His blue cap was crumpled in his fist at his side. "Wolf. What are you doing over here?"

"You two know each other?" Lily said with a snort. "Is America that small?"

I glanced at her. "Could you…give us a moment?"

"No," she said cheerfully. "I can't. This is war, boys. Second Lieutenant Egan will be taking us up today. All we're going to do is get you comfortable with short takeoffs and landings, the words we'll use up there, and opening the door. If you don't puke, I'll be happy. Let's go."

She spun on her heel and marched across the field, not bothering to see whether we'd followed her. I didn't move for a beat, and then I sucked in a breath. Max rocked back as if I'd hit him. I turned and followed Lily, who seemed to know where she was going.

* * *

The waves crashed against the pier, and Max stood on the railing, his arms pinwheeling in the air as he laughed. My heart hammered in my chest. He was going to fall, get swept out into the hurricane seas, and I wasn't a strong enough swimmer to jump in after him.

"Don't make me watch you drown," I yelled through the wind.

He bent over, grabbing the railing with one hand and took a swig from the bottle with his other hand. He tossed the bottle to me, and when I caught it, vodka sloshed all over me. The next wave washed it off, but I could still smell it mixing with the salt in the air.

He shouted into the air, but I couldn't catch his words.

"What?" I called to him.

He turned to look at me, his pupils blown from the booze. "This storm. This is how I feel when I look at you."

I stared at him for a beat, and then a huge wave slammed against us, soaking us, and I stumbled a few feet. He jumped off the railing, his hands locking around my elbows as he helped me stay on my feet. He swept my hair off my face with a hand and said, "You all right?"

"What do you mean?" I asked him. My voice didn't shake. It was just the wind.

His eyes were wide open, bright with the late-summer storm. "Come on. You're saying you didn't know."

"I don't know what you're talking about," I said, my heart hammering.

His eyes fell to my mouth, and then with some effort, he lifted his gaze back to my eyes. "God, you make a mess of me."

I staggered back a step, pushing away from him. The wind pulled at us, shoving me back against the railing and toward the sea. I couldn't stop looking at Max, but I wanted to look anywhere but at the raw yearning on his face.

"You're drunk," I shouted back over the storm. "Let's go home, Max."

Hope slipped off his face, running from his eyes down over his angular cheekbones and open mouth, falling to the pier and mixing with the ocean water. He swallowed, Adam's apple bobbing, and looked straight up into the rain. For a minute, I wondered if he'd even heard me. But then he dropped his head, shoulders slumping, and turned away from me and the sea.

* * *

"Wolf," said Max, falling into stride next to me. He kept his voice low, his face pointing straight ahead toward a plane. "What are you doing here?"

"I didn't know you were stationed here," I said, shaking from the effort to keep the hurt and the cold out of my voice. "If that helps."

"That's not what I asked," he said, his voice edged with pain. When I said nothing, he took two long strides and outpaced me to catch up with Lily. He said something to her and then pulled the side of the plane open. He climbed into the cockpit before I even climbed into the belly of the plane. I deserved that.

All I could hear were my memories, battering my mind. We'd never talked about what he'd said at the pier, but the next day he'd enlisted, and he'd shipped south to boot camp within a week. I hadn't seen him since that afternoon when he told me he was leaving.

"So you want to tell me what's going on?" Lily asked, showing me how to buckle myself in as the engines roared to life around us.

"Not really," I said.

"You were mistaken. That wasn't an optional question," Lily said.

I closed my eyes. "He's the oldest son of the general manager of one of my father's stores. We grew up together. We bonded over being expected to take over our fathers' jobs. He was my best friend."

"What happened?" she asked gently.

"The war," I said. But that wasn't the whole truth, and I could tell she didn't buy it.

He took us up, and we did a number of circles over the area as the plane tipped this way and that, touching down and taking off again. Max handled the plane with ease, and he looked so confident that I didn't feel afraid. Not for one moment. Even when Lily opened the door and my stomach turned at the image of the ground racing by us.

He looked over his shoulder at me, and despite myself, my mouth tilted up into a circle. Max's cheeks flooded with red, and he bit his lower lip before turning back. I looked down at my hands and took a deep breath.

I didn't know what I was doing.

I still had to do it.

When we landed for the last time and the plane came to a stop, Max unbuckled and climbed out of his seat, resting in the space between the cockpit and the belly of the plane. His question was directed at the two of us, but his eyes stayed trained on me. "What'd you think?"

"Terrifying," I said quietly. "Beautiful, but terrifying."

The corner of his mouth tipped up. "Yeah. That's the best sort of terrifying though, isn't it?"

"I can think of worse," Lily said, unbuckling without looking up at us.

Max turned away before I could see his whole smile, but I could feel it on my back while I followed Lily toward the hangars.

* * *

September 9, 1943

Dear Wolf,

Does your contact know about magic? What does she think? Can she do it? How are they going to use magic? Did you ask about Max? What's it like to jump out of an airplane?

I don't know how things are going here, other than they aren't. We're working on two different projects at the same time—but most importantly, using a balloon with magic written on it. That's right. A balloon. I hope you didn't throw out the ones I included in this envelope. Get more if you can. You write the equation on the balloon, just like you would on the letter, and tie the letter with the balloon string. It seems to protect the letter from weather, and it'll move faster. There are quite a number of uses for balloons...I'll let you know if anything here will help you too. Stella heard a rumor that they're using balloons to get people out of Hitler's camps. Of course, now I have to figure out how to get a balloon to lift something as heavy as what we need to lift.

Besides, Polly and Lola don't know what we're working with. That's put me in a terrible position, because I'm sure we'd make more progress if all of us knew what the magic we're writing is going to carry. But I *can't* tell, Wolf. And I'm not sure that Stella and George are supposed to know, but somehow they've worked it out, so it's just this thing that we dance around all the time.

Sometimes I think I might accidentally let it slip. I get to the edge of the secret, and then I have to stop myself.

How do people carry more than one secret inside them at the same time?

I hope you write. Do not jump out of the airplane before they tell you.

(Laugh, Wolf. It's good for you!)

I love you and miss you.

Forever,

Ilse

CHAPTER TWELVE

BURTONWOOD, ENGLAND
SEPTEMBER 12, 1943

WOLF

"We're going to jump today," Lily said by way of opening up the conversation. She plunked a cup of black coffee down in front of me. It smelled as acidic as the cup I'd already had. Coffee, milk, and sugar were all rationed, but somehow Lily seemed to know how to get extra cups of coffee. Not sugar, or milk, or anything to make the coffee drinkable. Just the coffee. How she hadn't burned a hole through her stomach already I didn't know. She reminded me of Ilse.

I poked at my eggs and boiled potatoes. "Shouldn't we fly more?"

We'd spent the last week flying with different pilots and in different planes, getting used to different types of takeoffs and weather. We'd studied German and French, and I'd demonstrated magic to Lily. She'd asked a thousand questions, and most of them were answered by the little notebook Ilse had given me. It'd been good practice. At home, Ilse had done most of the magic, and I'd done most of the avoiding. But I couldn't avoid using magic here any longer. Where I used to be unsure about the equations that Ilse had invented, I now wrote them on my bare arms and Lily's bare arms with ease.

Few of them worked—all of Ilse's magic in the notebook was experimental—until Lily saw the way Ilse sent me letters. Lily went into an office with Colonel Mann's second-in-command in England, Captain David Hutchinson, and emerged with a new plan. I'd use the same magic we used on letters to transport us around England and get us in and out of every site as fast as we could. On our first attempt, we'd used the equations on our skin. It'd gone...Well, it hadn't been terrible. It was an odd sensation. Lily wanted to move faster, but we moved at one speed no matter how we tried manipulating the equation. I had a new idea though, and I'd rather test that than jump out of a plane. It still made me queasy to be in one, even with the doors closed.

Lily stole one of my potatoes. "You're not a pilot. You need to make one good jump, that's it. How could you be fine with floating through the air but not with jumping out of a plane?"

"What's our exit strategy?" I asked, ignoring her nonsensical question.

Lily snorted over her coffee. "Win the war."

I rolled my eyes at her. "I'm serious, Lily."

Her returning smile was thin. "I am too, Wolf."

I nodded, still feeling exhausted and drained. "I've found a better way to travel using my gift. Balloons. With the equation written on them. My sister sent me a message by one to test it."

Lily perked up. "How is that different than writing on our skin?"

"If things go south," I said, then paused, thinking through the balloon theory. I could sense Ilse's doubt in her letter, but I understood immediately. Balloons were small, easy to hide when uninflated, and unlikely to attract much attention when inflated. They were soundless, so difficult to detect at night. Would they even show up on radar? Perhaps not. We could test that here. I imagined that if balloons could carry people using magic, there wouldn't be a weight limit like Ilse worried about. Of course, I could write a book about what I didn't know about magic.

I continued. "You let go. Once it's on your skin, you can't stop it. More control. Maybe we deliver the bombs with balloons too. I can ask my sister how to do that."

Lily nodded. "Do that. I like where you're going with this."

"Maybe we should try that and not jump today," I suggested casually.

But Lily was looking past me, a bright smile lighting up her face. She set her coffee down and rose in her seat, beginning to offer out her hand. A man stepped into my periphery, my age, maybe a little older at best, and shook it as he dropped a stopwatch back into his pocket. He was tall and clean-shaven, with dark hair swept back and held down with pomade and relaxed gray eyes.

"Lily Tasker," she said.

"Pleased to meet you, Miss Tasker," he said.

"Mrs.," she corrected him, her eyes tightening just a bit.

"Mrs.," he amended, his eyes dropping to her left hand and up again swiftly. "I'm Topher MacKenzie."

She dropped his hand. "This is Wolf Klein."

"Ah yes, I've heard of you," he said pleasantly, shaking my hand as I rose to greet him. "This is quite an unusual operative group, isn't it?"

"Oh, it's not *that* unusual. ATA girl hanging out with two bomber boys," Lily said lightly.

"I don't know anything about planes," I pointed out.

She gave me a look. "Today you do."

Right. How I was supposed to pretend to know anything about planes while carrying around a German-English dictionary was beyond me. I glanced at Topher, biting back a smile as he rolled his eyes at her. He sat down across from me and gestured at the second cup of coffee. "For me?"

"Sure," I said, because it was the right thing to say. I pushed it at him, and he snatched it, draining it in one gulp. He gave me a guilty smile. "It's been hell, traveling these days. Wars aren't conducive to sleeping."

I nodded a little, my eyes scanning around the room. I didn't want to believe I was looking for him, but who else could it be? No one. I wasn't sure last week if he wanted my apology, or wanted to apologize to me, and I wasn't sure if I'd apologized, or accepted his apology. Maybe it'd been both. Maybe we hadn't needed to apologize to each other at all. Maybe leaving without goodbyes was just the human thing to do.

"Come on, finish up. Time to go jump," Lily said.

It took two airmen to teach Topher and me how to get dressed in the paratrooper gear. If we were going to jump in this, we'd crash-land from gravity dragging us down. It all was heavy—the parachute, the pack lashed to our leg, the harness, the layers to keep us warm up in the plane. At first I felt like a failure. I'd been recruited to use magic to sabotage Hitler's bomb facilities, and I couldn't even walk across the room wearing the same gear I'd seen boys wear easily. But then Topher tipped over, falling backward on his ass, and I felt better.

I grinned, offering him a hand and hauling him to his feet. "It's a bit cumbersome."

He swept his hair back and glowered around the room. "That's an understatement. There are easier ways to travel."

I thought of the balloons. "There are. I'll give you a dollar if you tell that to Lily."

He snorted. "I'm not suicidal, brother."

I laughed.

The two men who helped us get dressed taught us the hand signals and the communication since it'd be hard to hear once we were up in the plane. They showed us the knife in a front vest pocket to cut away the main chute and use the reserve chute if the main chute didn't catch the wind and start breaking our fall. One of the men showed us how to tuck—with our arms across our chests and our legs pressed together, straight out in front of us with our toes to the sky—and how to release our pack a hundred and fifty feet above the ground so it wouldn't break our leg when we landed.

I had serious doubts about my ability to think through all of these steps *while plummeting to earth*, but I kept them to myself. I didn't want anyone to think I was less capable than I already suspected I was.

"Ready?" asked one of the airmen.

I snorted. "Does anyone ever say yes?"

He grinned at me, dimples flashing. "All the time. But they're daredevils. They'd be jumping out of planes even if there wasn't a war."

"Idiots," I muttered.

Topher grunted. "I can think of worse things they could do than jump out of planes."

"Rob banks?" I suggested, following the airmen out toward the plane. "This harness is uncomfortable."

"Yeah, it'll make you want to scratch your balls in relief when you get back," said the airman, flashing the dimples again. If he was trying something, he was out of luck. Especially with Max somewhere nearby.

"Rob banks," said Topher behind me, distracting me. "Hunt elephants. Tame tigers."

"Honestly, I don't understand why humans feel the need to mess with wild animals so much," I said. "I've only seen elephants in zoos, and that alone told me they weren't meant for the likes of me."

"Humans," said Topher wisely, "don't like to hear the word *no*. We're the toddlers of the animal world."

"Ain't that the truth," said the airman in front of us. He nodded to the open side door of a plane. "This is us."

I blinked in the changing light as I climbed up the stairs. Max hung out of the cockpit, his posture easy and relaxed as he chatted with Lily, already dressed in her gear, hair loose around her shoulders and helmet in her lap. I let out a long breath of relief. I hadn't realized how nervous I'd been while he'd been gone the last week on missions. He glanced at me, and the corner of his mouth tilted up. He said something to Lily that made her laugh.

"Old friends?" I asked loudly, sliding into a seat as Topher sat down next to me.

Lily glanced at us, eyes running up and down our outfits, amused. "Oh, they gave you the full treatment, I see."

I looked her up and down and realized she looked much less *bulky* than we did. We'd been pranked. I looked at our two airmen, and Dimples grinned at me again. "No hard feelings, spy boy."

I flinched, eyes flickering to Lily who was braiding her hair quickly. Our eyes met, and she shrugged. So they knew, I supposed, and she didn't care enough to deny it. The airmen sat down next to us, Dimples sitting by the door to act as jumpmaster. If anything went wrong in this practice jump, they'd find us. If they could. If we didn't go down in a fireball. Bile rose in my throat.

"MacKenzie, pinch Klein's cheeks," Lily said. "He's looking pale."

I smacked Topher away from me. "Oh, shut up."

"Ready?" asked Max, saving me from further embarrassment.

We nodded, and he disappeared in the cockpit again. We took off the same way we had the day before, but the sound was muffled through my helmet and there was some sense of calm from the weight of my equipment. Maybe it wasn't what I'd jump into Germany with, but if I landed on my side, at least I wouldn't break a rib today.

When the time came, I looked down at the squares of farming fields below us and rocked, my toes halfway out the door. Dimples shoved me. I yelped but remembered at the last minute to pull my legs together. The force of folding myself in half, against the pressure of the wind, pushed the air out of my chest. My chute caught, snapping open, and the burn of the harness made me gasp. But then the force stopped, the pain drifting into dullness, and I floated.

I breathed in.

I exhaled.

Sky above me, and all around me rolling farmlands, a distant field of airplanes, barracks. It was so quiet up here and so peaceful I nearly forgot to pay attention to where I was going.

"*Oy!*" yelled Lily as I drifted too close to her. I grabbed the steering line and yanked it hard, overcorrecting and tilting wildly off course. I pulled it back again, heart pounding, and leaning like that would help. The chute corrected slightly, and as we floated toward the ground, I tried to guess when to kick off the pack they'd strapped to my leg. I managed to kick it off just before leaning back, landing on the back of my heel and then on my butt. The chute caught in the wind again, yanking me forward until I twisted and found the release clasp. I stayed still, sucking in deep breaths, listening to the chute ripple and roll on the ground as the breeze caught it.

I'd done it. I'd jumped out of a plane. On purpose.

Lily was practically bouncing when she walked up to me, thumbs hooked on her harness. "Nicely done."

"We should just take balloons into Germany," I muttered.

"The advantage of parachuting in," she said, taking off her helmet again and undoing her braid, "is that we get farther before we get shot at. Higher chance of success."

I scowled. "You don't know this."

God help me, I sounded like Ilse, demanding proof for statistics that were actually rhetorical devices.

"Unless you have proof the balloons are better than dropping in exactly where we need to go, then I'm not interested," Lily said. "We're not experimenting with magic, Klein. I don't know anything about magic, but it's a tool, not a science. At least over here. Let your sister do her job. You do your job."

I bit my tongue and did not reply that part of my job was to tell Ilse what I needed. Topher appeared from the woods, limping a little but grinning, Dimples and Silent Airman right on his heels.

"Brilliant," said Topher.

"Daredevil," I muttered.

He laughed. "I didn't know I was until I started this game. Now I can't get enough."

Lily sighed. "Boys. Where's our ride?"

Dimple gestured to the horizon with the fields. "Should be the road right over there. They'll pick us up as soon as they get the call that we're safely away. Lieutenant Egan will have radioed that in."

"We'd best get over there," said Lily. "I don't fancy walking back to base."

"When do we leave?" I asked.

Lily gave me a sharp look. "We'll discuss later."

I looked at Dimples and Silent, who were suddenly investigating the straps of their packs. I shouldn't have said anything, but now that I've successfully completed a jump, all I wanted was to get the next one over with. I wanted to be in Europe. I was over waiting while somewhere Hitler was building a bomb that terrified my sister with the power and destruction it could wreak. But I kept my mouth shut and followed Lily across the field.

CHAPTER THIRTEEN

BURTONWOOD, ENGLAND
SEPTEMBER 12, 1943

WOLF

I avoided the mess hall at dinnertime, preferring to go hungry rather than deal with running into Max and risking my eagerness to get out of England playing out on my face. I sat in my room, bent over my German dictionary, silently mouthing the words, learning the spelling and grammar. It still twisted into Yiddish in my head, my father's two native tongues tangled behind my English. I needed to know this, though, so I kept studying. At some point, I had to take a leak and stood to discover my neck and eyes ached from bending over the little book in the low light.

I stepped out onto the base, looking around in the rosy glow of sunset. I was considering whether I'd walk up or down the street when I picked up a figure in my peripheral vision walking toward me, too close and too swiftly to be accidental. I swiveled toward him and barely had time to register the size of the man when he grabbed me by my jacket lapels and shoved me against the wall.

"Is this a game to you?" snapped Max, his pupils dilated so wide they almost swallowed the green. His breath smelled like cigarettes. He only smoked when he was stressed. *Me*, I realized. That was because of me.

"A game?" I repeated, sputtering and shoving him off me. "What's your problem?"

"You're avoiding me. You show up here after a *year*—" he began.

"You *left*," I snarled.

His glare could have lit me on fire. "I signed up. And you didn't even show up to say goodbye. You didn't write me. You did nothing. And then you stroll in here and stare at me with those eyes!"

"What's wrong with my eyes?" I protested.

He snorted. "Don't pretend like you don't know."

Some dark, monstrous part of me reared its head, feeding on the ache that grew in my chest at his proximity. "It doesn't matter now. Whatever…whatever that was, it doesn't matter now. We're at war."

It was the wrong thing to say. His face fell. "What do you mean?"

"It's *illegal*," I hissed. "What if they find out? What'd you say during the exam?"

"I lied!" Max's voice pitched high, wild. Desperate. "I lied, Wolf. It wasn't that hard. You should know something about that."

"I didn't lie to you." I scowled. "Calm down. Someone will hear you."

Max shoved his hands into his hair and made an angry noise of frustration. "I'm calm!"

I raised an eyebrow at him. "Oh yeah. You're the very picture of calm. If I looked up calm in the dictionary, it'd say, 'see also: Max Egan, right now.'"

"Dictionaries aren't radio shows," Max said, taking me too literally for once. "You're avoiding me. And you're always with that girl. What are you doing here, Wolf?"

"I can't tell you," I muttered. And it was the truth.

"Are you here to torture me?" Max asked, his voice dropping.

My heart clenched. "No, Max. I wouldn't do that."

He smiled as he looked away, the anger draining from his body as his hands fell from his hair. "Yeah. You would. You just wouldn't know you were doing it."

I grabbed Max and yanked him close. "What I signed up for is more classified than my *gift*. Think, Max! Use your goddamn brain and put a few things together."

He scowled at me and shoved off, running his hands through his hair, and then he spun, eyes wide and the color draining from his face.

He knew. He'd figured it out. I nodded. He blew out a hard breath and said, "Are they sending you over? France? Germany?"

I nodded again, my throat too tight for words. Max kicked at the wall and started to walk away from me. Dazed, I stared at him, but he didn't turn around. He just walked away from me, down the street going God knows where. A bar, if they had one on base. His plane. Maybe he'd fly away. I didn't even know where he'd go.

"Hey," I called, but my voice cracked and didn't carry down the street. I started to walk, my pace picking up into a jog. "*Hey!* Egan! Max. I'm talking to you."

He kept walking, though I could tell by the way his shoulders squared up that he'd heard me. He probably heard my footsteps too. I reached out and grabbed him by his arm, jerking him around to face me. He swung around, stepping too close into my space, seizing my jacket by the lapels. He nearly lifted me off the ground. I should have let him go, stepped out of his space, and shook him off. We were standing too close. Far too close.

I tried to tell him to let me go, but instead, I said, "Max."

"Not here," he growled and pulled me by my jacket down a small alley between two sets of buildings. He let me go, pushing me lightly against the wall. I stayed there, feeling the absence of his body.

"What do you want from me, Wolf?" He stared at me, a ferocious, predatory stare. I kept expecting him to back down, blink, and look away from all the unseen things crowding us in this small space. But he didn't.

"Don't walk away from me." My voice cracked.

He stepped closer to me, a pace away. I glanced up and down the alley, worried we were attracting attention, but no one was there. There wasn't enough space for all the emotions rattling around in my rib cage.

"You were just going to go," he rasped. "Parachute into *Germany* all by yourself *as a spy* without telling me. You want to talk about who walked first?"

"That's how you think this conversation should go?" I asked.

"Oh, *now* you want to have a conversation," he hissed, his shoulders drawing up. All of his muscles bunched, ready for a hit or to flee.

I didn't—couldn't—tear my eyes off him. "I couldn't tell you."

"I carry your other secret," snapped Max. He shoved a hand through his hair, a nervous gesture I realized. "Why not this one?"

He meant he'd known about my magic, even back in New York. He meant he wanted me to tell him that I was a spy now. As if that was the only secret standing between us. I opened my mouth to tell him Lily had forbidden it, but what came out was, "I was afraid."

His brows knit together. "Of me?"

"No. Yes." I closed my eyes. Dark skies. The smell of the sea. The look in his eyes. The words on his tongue. The twist of his mouth. "I've never had a friend like you, Max."

He snorted, disbelieving.

What secret was I trying not to tell again?

I opened my eyes. Max. A brick wall. "It's…" I had to find the words. I didn't know how I knew this. Maybe it was the vulnerability in his face, but I had to find the words for him or he really would walk away from me. And this morning I'd left, but maybe I'd been hoping he'd follow. Maybe I'd known he'd follow me. "…complicated."

He stared at me, his expression shifting from suspicion and hurt toward something akin to wariness and hope. Something I didn't understand but wanted to. Something that prickled at the back of my neck. He stepped closer to me, as close as we'd been when he'd grabbed my jacket on the street. "Yeah."

"You're not going to convince me not to go." My voice shook, cracked again, and we both stilled. I closed my eyes. "So please don't ask me."

I drew in a breath, the smell of his cigarettes tickling the back of my throat. I wanted to move, to push back, to seize control in the dance happening in the space between our chests, but I'd always been better at letting Max lead. The first time I'd broken from him had been standing on that pier, when he'd said the truth and I'd been too afraid. I ought to apologize, but I didn't have those words either.

Maybe I just needed to let him say goodbye properly this time. Maybe I just needed to know that he still felt the same way.

His hand glanced off my hip, bumping into my wrist and sending shock waves through me. I almost lurched forward, almost opened my eyes because I wanted to see him, see how close he was to me, but his fingers wrapped around my wrist and pushed my hand against the wall, pinning me there.

"Wolf," he said, and it wasn't a question and was a question, both in the same breath.

"Present, sir," I whispered.

"Asshole." His laugh was soft against my cheek, and then something brushed my forehead. His nose. Maybe his lips. This was the closest we'd ever been. And it wasn't close enough.

I couldn't move.

Couldn't breathe.

"Hey," he said, his other hand settling on my hip. "I need to know you're here."

"I'm here," I managed. Then I added, because he still hadn't moved, a hand on my hip, a hand on my wrist, his mouth at the corner of my mouth, "I *want* to be here."

He said my name again, and I must have said something in return, though my mind was too hazy to register what. Something that made his thumb press the pressure point between the tendons on my wrist, a warm warning hissing through my veins, vicious and bright.

His lips touched mine briefly, softer than the pain in my wrist between his grip and the wall, and harder than the breath I let out to mix with his in the miniscule space between our mouths.

Don't ruin this, I thought to myself. I didn't know what exactly was in danger here. Maybe everything. My new job. Lily's respect. My family. My life. My friendship with Max. Everything was at stake here.

I pressed my free hand against his chest and felt his growl straight up my arm. I mumbled his name against his mouth and then pulled away, saying louder, "Max."

He jerked away, dropping my wrist, and the world shifted from sharp edges and lines back into the smooth, softer focus of everyday life. He pressed himself against the wall across from me, horror and fear and shame running across his face. He dragged a hand over his face, the other covering his stomach as if he was going to be sick or expected me to hit him.

Everything about him suddenly seemed small, fragile, and I'd never seen him look like that before. Not in our entire lives, when he'd taught me to swing a bat and catch a ball, not when we'd played hide-and-seek in our fathers' stores, not when we started sneaking out at night and wandering the city and all its shady corners. He'd always been loud, big, brash, a goofball who took up space and loved the spotlight.

I reached out to him, my hand gripping his elbow. "I'm not mad."

They weren't quite the right words, but they were the first ones I found.

He closed his eyes and let his head tip back against the brick. "Why not?"

"I don't know," I said honestly. "I always thought...that I just didn't...want any of that." I stumbled over the words, but he didn't move, didn't even crack an eyelid at me. "I told you I wanted to be here."

Now he opened an eye at me, his brow furrowed with worry. "Did you mean it?"

What he really wanted to know was *do you still want to be here?*

"Yeah," I said, making myself smile at him. Only one of us could lose it over this at once, and right now, that was him. I had to be the confident one in this moment. "That doesn't mean we're all right now, you know. You can't just kiss me and make it better."

The corner of his mouth tipped up. "I don't know. It seemed to work pretty well."

I snorted and looked at the ground. "And you're not going to change my mind."

"That's not why I"—he paused and swallowed—"kissed you."

"Good," I said, dropping his elbow. "Makes me think you think I'm going to die over there."

"What if you do?" He stepped closer, touching my hip again. I wanted his skin against mine. I didn't think I could form those words, though, and this wasn't the time or the place.

"I'm sure you'll find someone to fill your time," I said dryly.

He shook his head. "I'm not talking about that, Wolf."

"I know," I said quietly. "But I'm not going over there to get killed, so maybe give me the benefit of the doubt."

"Who recruited you?"

"I can't tell you that."

He scowled at me. "It wasn't optional."

I couldn't help the smile. "So bossy. You aren't my commanding officer, Max."

He muttered something like, "Could be."

I wanted to touch him again. Too much. I stepped backward and shoved my hands into the pockets of my trousers. "Come on. I'll buy you a drink."

What I meant was, *Come on. We'll pretend like I'm staying. We'll pretend like you didn't leave. We'll pretend like we'll both make it through this war.*

And when he said yes, I knew he heard everything I hadn't said but wished I could.

CHAPTER FOURTEEN

OAK RIDGE, TENNESSEE
SEPTEMBER 18, 1943

ILSE

The thing about science was you could work all day—hours and hours without a break, bent over notebooks or standing at chalkboards, comparing notes and flipping through textbooks and arguing and shouting and proving things to each other with increasingly esoteric theories— and it still might not amount to any progress. You could do that day after day after day, for weeks or months or years, and still your progress would be minimal. And yet, that didn't mean the process wasn't important and you weren't making discoveries.

I kept telling myself that anyway, even if I didn't always believe it.

Stella wrote on the blackboards at the front of the room, *The discovery process is progress*, and every day, I sent her a silent thank-you for those words.

We did seem to make some progress. Polly had suggested rat poison, known for causing hemorrhaging, as a way to slow the clotting process. It worked, though we hadn't yet figured out a use for it, nor the exact ratio of poison to blood. The balloons seemed to be working, at least for Wolf. He had written me a letter that was positively *enthusiastic* about the balloons, but that might have been because he'd reunited with Max and that happiness bled into everything, including magical theory.

I could feel the mounting pressure to find things that were

useful both to him and to the bomb. I had to keep him safe. He'd been sent over to use magic, but how? Write in blood on explosives? It'd be easier if they could deliver explosives, or fire, or something, by magic.

Something sparked in the back of my mind. The way the fire moved in the park, from a botched equation, what Stella had said about lowering the ignition point…

"Ilse," said Polly, sliding into a seat next to me. "Have you eaten today?"

"Soon," I said, waving her off. The spark disappeared from the back of my mind. I tried not to be irritated at her and instead stood up, pacing across the room to Stella's blackboard.

She was the only one who seemed to be getting anywhere in practical application. We thought similarly, and as I looked over her work, I could pick up where she was going rather easily. But unlike me, she didn't seem afraid of failure or mistakes. And that seemed to be making all the difference.

"I'm following," I said, picking up a piece of chalk and tapping her equation. "Here's the lift equation, and this allows for temperature variation, so the balloon won't pop during pressure changes."

"Right," she said. "And this allows it to pop when the destination equation is complete."

"So you think magic knows where it is?" I asked.

Stella nodded. "If we're suggesting that a balloon can follow a trajectory between two sets of coordinates, that would suggest it knows where it is and when it's reached those coordinates."

"Well, I wouldn't use the word 'know.'" George stood up from his desk and joined us at the board. It was the first thing he'd said after showing up fifteen minutes late this morning, exhausted and cranky. He kept checking his stopwatch and the clock on the wall, but he was doing his work, so I couldn't complain. He scribbled something next to one of Stella's equations, making us both frown. "It's not *knowledge*. It's simply location detection."

"By coordinates that are invented by humans," said Stella coolly.

George looked past her to me. "Whether or not they're invented is beside the point. The point is that we're imposing certain laws onto the balloons, and knowledge is a step too far. Detections, yes. But if we say the balloons *know* where they are, we're suggesting that in the future, magical items might be capable of problem-solving."

"That's not at all what I said," said Stella with a frown.

"That isn't what she said," I echoed. "I was the one who used the word 'know' first. Stella matched my language. We're saying the same thing though."

"Are we?" asked George.

"Yes," I said firmly.

He held up his hands. "Semantics matter."

I didn't want to fight, and George seemed particularly testy today. "Let's call it location detection."

George nodded, satisfied over some invisible power struggle, and took his seat. Stella's chalk ground into the chalkboard for a minute, and she took a deep breath before going back to work. Sometimes I wished it was just us girls in the lab.

A rap at the door surprised us, and I glanced around the room quickly to see what we needed to hide. The blackboards were covered from top to bottom and left to right with equations, and papers with theories and unanswered questions were tacked up on the wall between blackboards. Lola was still experimenting with burning blood, and the room smelled sweet and coppery, like blood and sweat and frustration.

The door began to open, and I stood up, heart pounding. "Wait."

Colonel Mann stepped into the room. He saw me standing and raised an eyebrow. "Miss Klein."

I wrung my hands in front of myself. "Hello, colonel. My apologies. I thought perhaps…"

He looked around the room. "I should hope that you wouldn't have let anyone else in this room. You lock your notes at the end of each day, I am sure."

Now I will, I thought to myself as I nodded. Was lying to a colonel a crime? A felony? Would he know? Had he come and checked the drawers of our desks?

"I've come to ask about your progress." Colonel Mann closed the door behind himself with a click that sounded loud enough to be a gunshot in the deadly quiet room. Stella and Polly both flinched. I watched helplessly as the colonel walked up to one of our blackboards, surveying it. I didn't know how far we should be, or how much he knew about math and physics, or magic, and if he could understand our scribbles.

I realized after a beat that he'd been asking *me* for a progress report. I cleared my throat, trying to think how Wolf would spin this. *Focus on what you learned, and make it seem bigger than it is*, I could hear him advising in my head. He'd told me something similar when I'd been trying to convince my parents to let me study science, even though girls didn't study physics.

"We've decided on a delivery mechanism—balloons—and I… We're working on developing a delivery detection—"

"Location detection," George corrected.

All four of us girls leveled him with such a glare that I was surprised he didn't catch fire. Luckily, Colonel Mann didn't seem to notice as I carried on. "Location detection element to the magic for coordinates."

Would it be enough? Or would he put George in charge? I suddenly didn't want George in charge of the project. We *were* getting somewhere. Finally. My hand ached from writing, and my head pounded—from the heat or the lack of water or the mental exercise, I wasn't sure. But we were finally making progress. I could feel it.

"Hitler's made progress," said Colonel Mann, not facing us. "He's moving forward rapidly, and he's moved his laboratories from Berlin. They're harder to destroy now."

Wolf. My heart swelled in my throat. I couldn't breathe.

"We need answers," the colonel said, turning slowly. "We need to move faster. We can't afford for this element of the project to slow us down."

I almost asked him how the boys down the hall were doing and if any of the nuclear reactors had gone critical, barely stopping myself. Instead, I managed to say, "We understand."

"Good," he said, his eyes scanning over all of us. He looked at me. "I know you won't fail me."

And with a clipped, short walk, he left our lab, shutting the door with a firm click that echoed in our space. This time, we all flinched.

"No pressure," muttered Stella, still staring at the door.

"So where are we?" asked Lola, not flippant for once.

"Nowhere," muttered Polly.

Rattled, I sat next to her, aware of the way my skin felt too warm. "We're not nowhere. I mean, Stella has gotten somewhere. We have multiple written equations to test and a theorem that two balloons cannot necessarily lift double what a single balloon can lift. We haven't found exactly what a balloon can lift, which would help us resolve the relationship, but it is helpful. That's not nowhere."

The entire group, save for Stella, looked doubtfully at me.

"Did you just hear him, Ilse?" asked Lola. "We need to move faster. How are we supposed to do that?"

Stella was frowning at her blackboard. "It'd be really useful to know whether we could somehow diminish the mass of the object magically and have it calculated to fade and return to normal mass at a certain point."

"Those were words, weren't they?" Polly asked me.

"Here's something I never thought I'd say," Lola added. "I really think we're getting somewhere with burning magical blood. I'd like to keep working on that. I'm convinced it'll be helpful."

"Don't bleed yourself too much," George warned.

"We know," Lola said, rolling her eyes. George huffed.

My gaze skipped over to Polly, who looked as tired as I felt, or maybe worse. The corners of her eyes tipped down, her mouth a flat line instead of the soft, shy smile she usually wore, and her hair was frizzling at its ends from the humidity. She gave me a frustrated, sad smile. "Are you confident? Does this seem doable to you? Do you think they brought us in because they exhausted all their non-magical options? What if we can't handle it either? Will Hitler win the war?"

I blinked, startled at the rapid acceleration in her comments. "Oh. Well. That escalated, didn't it?"

I looked around and realized George, Lola, and Stella were surreptitiously watching the two of us, not curiously, but hopefully, as if they were thinking the same as Polly, and what they wanted to hear was whatever came next out of my mouth. Colonel Mann had rattled all of us. They felt the pressure as much as I did.

I didn't come here to be a leader. I didn't ask for this. All I wanted to do was science and magic and end the war. Preferably before it killed more people. I suddenly, desperately wanted balloons to travel instantaneously, for Wolf to come here with his calm and steady ways.

"The army wouldn't pin their hopes on one operation," Lola said confidently. "I've read the papers, and it just wouldn't make sense otherwise. They're always working a multipronged approach."

"They're always working a multipronged approach," George echoed. "They have to. Would you run an experiment with just one trial?"

"I'm not a scientist," Polly pointed out. "I was a nursing student. I just happened to be able to do magic. Lola and I aren't like you three."

"Think of it this way," Stella said. "If we were their last and only hope in the war, would you change how you approached this project?"

"No," I said immediately. "Because we should be treating it as if this was the last and only hope for the Allies in the war. That would mean we aren't leaving anything on the table. No reserves. No cards up our sleeves. You're either all in, or you're not. There isn't a half-way on this project, girls. We can't say, 'Well, I hope we're not the only ones,' without knowing, and then not give it our all. Whether we're part of a bigger picture or we're the last resort, we should always be giving everything our all."

"The process is progress," Stella agreed.

"We need to make more progress soon though. Colonel Mann's getting impatient, and if Hitler's accelerating, we might truly be running of time," George said, turning his stopwatch over in his hand. "We've been here for weeks, and we haven't actually tried using a balloon on a bomb yet."

"Tomorrow," I promised, finding a folder. "I suppose we should pack up for the day. Put all your notes in here, and I'll lock them in the drawer. Must keep the colonel happy. See you tomorrow?"

"It'll be good to keep track of what we've actually accomplished in our notes anyway," Stella said. "I'm going to catch the next bus. See you tomorrow."

I exhaled, wanting to tell her that it was ridiculous that she wasn't living with Lola, Polly, and me. It wasn't as though it was impossible for a space reason. There was an empty bed in Lola's room. Having Stella there might even stop Lola's bed from containing more than one person.

But maybe it wouldn't. I just said, "Be safe."

"Always am, Professor," Stella said with a smile.

I groaned, leaning my head into my hands. "I really don't want to be that know-it-all. If anything, we ought to be calling *you* the Professor. You're the one who's made all the progress."

Stella paused in sliding her notes into the folder and looked up at us. "Pardon?"

"You've made all the progress," I repeated, while Lola and Polly nodded. George studied the stopwatch in his hand. I gestured to her blackboard. "You're connecting the dots. We would be nowhere without you. At least we've gotten somewhere. Thank you."

Stella bit the bottom of her lip, looking at each of us, and then Lola said gently, "We're just saying thank you. That's all we mean by it."

Stella blew out a hard breath. "Thank you."

"Oh, it's too early to go home. Let's get dinner together. Stella, join us. We'll walk you home," Lola said just before it started to get awkward. She gallantly tossed her purse onto her shoulder and flipped her sweaty curls over her shoulder. They were slowly losing their shape like they did at the end of the day. Lola's natural hair was bone straight. "I'm positively *starved*," she added.

She always knew exactly what to say. And Stella always knew exactly what question to ask next. And Polly never let us lose focus. And George knew the science and boundaries of what we were trying from his travels to other sites. And I knew how to steer us in the right direction with the secrets I kept. We were, in fact, a rather good team, even if we weren't moving fast enough for Colonel Mann's approval.

And George wasn't running the team, as he'd thought he would be. We girls were. This was our time. We were determined to show it. And if it meant we used magic and science like a double-edged sword, as dangerous as the weapon we worked on, then so be it. This was war. And not all wars played out in the skies or in the forests and fields of Europe or on the waves of the Pacific Ocean. Some wars took place right here, at home, in the pages of books, in the equations on blackboards, and in the splitting of the atom.

* * *

September 18, 1943

Wolf,

I don't have much time, and my brain feels like it's been crushed beneath a rolling pin, so please pardon the brevity. On the other side of this letter are the equations for directing balloons to exact locations and for autoignition. If you use this, it'll lower the temperature of the material to the point where it melts or sparks. Will that help? We're working on invisibility and changing the equations so balloons can lift any weight—multiple people, supplies, etc. What else do you need from us?

Love,

Ilse

CHAPTER FIFTEEN

WOLF

After training, I returned to my room with a broken tooth, a fat lip, a black eye, a swelling cut on one cheek, and a decided limp. And every part of me felt electric.

I'd never used my body like this, learning to duck and dive and punch and grab and claw and stab my way out of any confrontation. If our cover was blown, we'd need to fight our way out, the instructor said. We didn't want to grab each other's balls and twist, but they taught us to do it. We didn't want to run away once we got the other person on the ground, but the instructor insisted we throw sportsmanship out the window, change our definition of honor and integrity, and know that we were more valuable alive, more capable of doing our duty and obligation to country, flag, and president, if we didn't die by courtesy rules.

I hadn't been sure I'd been made for fighting, but despite the injuries, I hadn't been half bad. I hadn't expected that. I hadn't expected to love training this much—the physicality of it and the way that being exhausted felt like waking up. But we'd practiced moving by balloon today, and even after losing blood, I hadn't minded the training run and the fighting. I thought about it the whole way back to my room. I opened the door and stepped in, closing and locking it behind me. I blinked, awareness coming to me in bits and pieces, and my hand closed around my sidearm. I spun around, pulling it out.

Max held open his hands where he stood in the dark space between the wardrobe and the edge of the second bed. "Hi."

I lowered the gun, mind spinning. "What are you doing in here?"

"What happened to your face?" he asked, stepping forward.

"I thought you were flying a mission," I said.

"Tonight," he said warily. "I wanted to see you before I went. What happened to your face, Wolf? Seriously. You're a spy, not a boxer."

I slipped the gun back into the inner pocket of my coat. "Stop saying that word so loudly. You're going to get me in trouble."

"I thought you'd be happy to see me," Max said, his hand reaching up to his hair.

I winced. "I am. I'm just surprised. Can't I be both?"

Max looked tired and pale. "I don't know. Can you?"

"*You* have only one emotion at once." I tried to tease him. "Some of us are more…"

My voice trailed off, and Max said lightly, "Complicated?"

"Yes," I murmured and swallowed. "Think the mess room has ice?"

"The infirmary does," he said. "Did you get jumped?"

"I have a gun. Do you think I'd get this beaten up if I got jumped right now?"

"You can't discharge that here. I'm not even sure you're allowed to have that here. Who gave you the gun?" Max stepped toward me, and I put my back against the door. He was still steps away, by the bed, but I hadn't been ready for this, hadn't put work away in a different part of my brain, and I needed steps between getting my ass kicked so I wouldn't die at the hands of the Gestapo and getting my heart kicked because I didn't know what I wanted from Max.

I frowned at him. "You know what I'm here for. You know I can't tell you anything."

"They think beating the crap out of you will get you ready for this?" Max scoffed.

"If they wanted to beat the crap out of me, I don't think I'd be walking," I retorted.

Max took two quick steps toward me. "You can get out of this."

I didn't think Colonel Mann, or Lily, would let me now. I knew too much. "But I won't."

Max's face twisted, pained. "Why not? Why this? You would have gotten out of the draft because you were in university. You didn't have to come."

"I had a deferment. But they found out about the gift, and this was what they offered me," I said. "And I wanted to come." Which was the truth, to a point. "Besides, why not use every tool at our disposal? Nothing else they've done for the last four years has stopped Hitler."

"You think you're going to be the man that takes down Hitler? Is that it?"

"So what if I did?" I snapped. The truth hit me like a wave. There was a part of me that hoped I'd survive long enough to be sent on that mission. There had to be a plan for his assassination somewhere, and if I could use my magic to help make it happen, or to do it myself, I would. "Who are you to say I can't?"

"No one," Max growled, only a step away from me now. "But you're asking me to sit by and watch you send yourself out to be slaughtered. Do you know what the life expectancy for a spy is? Six weeks, Wolf. Six weeks."

"How would you know that?" I snapped.

"I'm the pilot who drops them." He looked lost for a moment, swaying back slightly. "They rarely come home. The ones I bring over."

I didn't know what to say to that. "I'm not interested in dying, Max. If I was, I'd be dead already."

"That's not good enough," he insisted, stepping close against me now, hands turning into fists at his side. Not to hit me, I realized. To keep himself from reaching out to touch me.

"It has to be good enough," I said quietly. Then I raised my chin, meeting his gaze with as much steadiness and calm as I could muster inside me. "If you hadn't kissed me, would you still be asking this of me?"

He blinked, rocked back on his heels, and for a moment, I thought he'd surge forward and kiss me against this door the way he'd kissed me against the wall. I couldn't tell for a moment if I wanted him—or didn't want him—to do that. Then he said hoarsely, "Yes. How could you doubt that? Even if that had not happened, even if we were just friends, Wolf. A world without you...It'd be a darker one. I wouldn't want to live in it. I don't even want to consider it."

"It's war," I whispered, swallowing my own tears. "I can't make any promises. Please don't ask me to."

His right hand unfurled, and he lifted it cautiously to touch the bottom of my chin. I hadn't even realized I'd dropped my head. I let him lift my face again. His face was flushed, his pupils dilated. "I won't. Wolf, I won't."

I nodded, and he stepped back away from me. He wouldn't kiss me. Wouldn't touch me, maybe, at all. Wouldn't rock against me the way he did over a week ago, hard and desperate for something I didn't know if I wanted or needed. He'd let me go as best he could. I didn't know if I wanted that either. Everything inside me felt tight and tangled. There weren't words for what I wanted. Except him. I wanted him.

I wanted my lighthearted friend back, the one I'd known in New York, but I was starting to wonder if that'd always been a facade, and if the flash of the Max desperate and in pain and hopeful was the real one. A Max he'd hidden from me. I'd hidden nothing from him. I was trying to be an open book, while it felt as if his heart and soul and mind were in a lockbox. I wasn't even sure the key was on this side of the Atlantic Ocean.

I took a deep breath as he retreated to the spare bed. I needed ice for my face, and to rest. For hours, maybe. Until tomorrow. My body suddenly felt heavy, and the last forty-eight hours pulled at the edges of my brain, making everything go fuzzy. But another deep breath cleared the haze, and I threw myself on the bed. A groan escaped my lips.

I heard Max shift on the other bed, the thin mattress rustling. I couldn't bring myself to sit up though. "When do you have to leave?"

"I have a few hours," he said quietly.

"Where are you flying?"

He sighed. "I can't tell you any more than you can tell me."

For a long moment, we were quiet, two boys on separate beds, facing a war neither of us wanted to fight. My blackened eyes were closed, and the hurricane played out across the inside of my eyelids. The way he had stood up and faced the wild sea. The way he looked at me. I wanted him to look at me again like that.

I opened my eyes again and sat up slowly, wincing. He was stretched out on the other bed, one arm behind his head, his shirt rising slightly on his stomach so a pale stretch of skin showed. I could see a thin line of blondish hair trailing down below his belt, and my mouth felt dry. He flinched, watching me with concern. I must have looked worse than I felt.

"You should go to the infirmary," he said.

I tried to smile. "And say what? I have a secret job here that involves me getting beat up?"

He closed his eyes and sighed. "You're a pain in the ass, Wolf Klein."

"Yeah," I said without thinking. "But I'm *your* pain in the ass."

The corner of his mouth twitched up. "You don't even know what you're saying."

"So tell me."

He opened his eyes again. He studied me the way Ilse studied a math problem. As though I was something to be solved. As though there was an answer written in my bruises. "Come here."

I stood up and wobbled the two steps across the space to his bed, and he touched the edge of the bed with his free hand. I sat down. He scooted over, and I lay down next to him, letting my body sink into the mattress. It felt different, warmer where his body had been, and when I breathed in, I breathed in the smell of oil, gasoline, a sharp metallic scent. From the planes. From him. I didn't mind it.

He rolled onto his side with a soft grunt, and his fingers brushed against my cheekbone. I hissed but didn't move, just shifted my gaze over to him. His mouth was set in a soft frown, and his eyes followed his fingers that ran over the cut, the bruises, the fat lip, the black eye, the curls of dark hair stuck by sweat and blood to my forehead.

"I wish you'd stayed far away from this war," he said finally.

"Me too, but it doesn't matter," I said. "I would have found my way to you."

His eyes fell to mine. "You mean that?"

"Yes," I said. But I didn't know if it was true. I wanted to believe it was. Was that enough?

"You know, you're a lot like flying," Max said, his fingers resting on my chin. "Terrifying, and beautiful."

And he kissed me. Demanding. Inquisitive. Sensitive. Pressing. And I kissed him back, for hours, until he had to go. This time I said goodbye. This time, he promised to come back.

* * *

September 22, 1943

Dear Ilse,

The equations have been remarkably helpful. Have you made progress on invisibility? We could use that. But no fire.

And *shana tova*! May the year 5704 be the year that we end the war. Tell Mama and Papa I love them. My balloons may be delayed. I'll send you a letter as soon as I can. Keep your chin up, Ilse.

Love,

Wolf

COPY NO. _____

OSS AND MI6 JOINT COMMISSION ON SPECIAL PROJECTS

LILLIAN JACOBS TASKER

Leader of Special Projects, Team 2

Ref Maps: Attached

EXPECTED ENEMY MOVEMENTS AND STRENGTH

German troop strength: Wehrmacht 19th army; field army; approximately 150,000 across the area, under the command of General Georg von Sodenstern

Allied forces fly regular bombing routes over Germany; UK & Canadian by day, American by night. Proximity to military installations is dangerous. Bombing runs will not be suspended.

FIELD SUPPORT

No Resistance field support

CHAPTER SIXTEEN

OAK RIDGE, TENNESSEE
SEPTEMBER 26, 1943

ILSE

I chewed on the end of my pencil, something that would have gotten me scolded at home. Mama would say something about my teeth and how I'd ruin them, and Wolf would be asking me if that was healthy, a question he didn't actually want answered in detail, it turned out. There was no one to scold me here though, and the lab was empty and dark, save for the desk lamp I'd rescued from the trash bin. It'd required only a tiny bit of rewiring to function, and the bulb hadn't even been broken. And they scolded us about waste!

Invisibility. I needed to sort out invisibility for Wolf. I didn't even know where to start. But Wolf wouldn't have asked in his letter if he didn't need the answer. And now he was going to be out of reach. Did that mean he was in training? Or that he was going into Germany? I wish I knew. I wish he'd said.

I flipped open my notebook and picked up my pencil. I calculated how much blood might be needed, and thus how much of the rat poison would need to be added. Now that we could prevent clotting, we could store the blood in a jar and use it as ink, instead of drawing blood from a vein each time. Life-changing. I squinted down at the paper, double-checking the equation as I went. It was worth a try, but I'd still want to ask Stella if she thought it'd work.

"Be careful," came a smooth voice from the doorway. "Your face will stick like that."

I blinked and looked up in surprise. George, looking tired with dark circles under his eyes, leaned on the doorway, his arms crossed. There was a cut on one of his cheeks, and his hair looked dirty, greasy even, as if he hadn't showered in a few days. He was supposed to be gone for only three days to the Hill, one of the other sites for the project, but he'd been gone nearly a week.

I put down my pencil and sat primly in my chair. "Says the guy who looks like hell. Did you fall out of a moving car?"

His face screwed up, and then he winced, rubbing at his jaw, his fingers running over the cut. "Naw, I was part of the amateur boxing club before, so I thought I'd try out the Hill's club. And I've lost my edge, it turns out. You won't hold it against me, will you?"

I leaned back in my chair, amused. "No, but your face might."

He laughed and wandered into the room, moving between the desks, his fingers trailing over the edges. His dark eyes never left me though, a smile playing on his lips. "You don't think it gives me roguish charm?"

He was always like this after he came back from working with the other groups. A little too sharp, and a little too tired to be polite. I didn't know why he didn't just tell Colonel Mann he hated working with the other groups, but I supposed he might be here for the same reason I was. Because there wasn't another option.

I just rolled my eyes at him. "You don't need more charm."

"Oooh," he crowed. "So you think I'm charming, Ilse Klein."

I wished Lola was here. I didn't know what to say. What were the rules to this game? "Too much charm can be a bad thing, George Steele. All things in moderation."

He paused, considering my words seriously, and then he sat down on the edge of one table. His feet still touched the ground. When I sat on the tables, my feet dangled, childlike and girlish. I

wished I were as tall as Wolf or George right then. "Do you think?   .
Is there nothing you can have in excess?"

I tilted my head at him. "Nothing."

"You're too young to sound that sure," he countered.

I scowled before I could stop myself. "Oh, and here I was, liking
you so much."

His head reared back. "And now you don't?"

"I'm the head of a magical science program for the United States
government," I told him, feeling a tiny bit guilty for rubbing his face
in my position. But if he didn't want me to push back, he shouldn't
have pressed my buttons. "If I'm not too young for that, I'm not too
young to have opinions on a variety of other things."

"You can prove science. You can't prove to me that there's nothing you can have in excess," he argued.

"Not everything must be proved to be true," I snapped, my good
mood evaporating completely. "An excess of even good traits comes
back around. Stop thinking so linearly and begin to think of everything as being a circular or cyclical system."

His eyes glinted. "So you think there can be an excess of love?"

"Yes."

"And patriotism?"

"Yes," I said immediately.

"And devotion."

"Yes."

"Why?"

"Because we lose perspective. If we have an excess of one thing,
or even more than one thing, we fail to leave space for alternatives,
for balance."

"So humans are finite spaces?"

I gestured to my body. "Obviously."

"And intangible things—such as love, patriotism, devotion,

power—take up tangible space."

I considered this. "Yes. If only because they take physical effort, so energy, which is measurable inside the body."

"You are a delight, Ilse Klein," he said, crossing his arms. "Has anyone told you that?"

"Not in so many words," I admitted, but I didn't smile at being called a delight. I liked compliments, but this didn't feel like one.

He jutted his chin toward me. "What are you working on?"

"A letter to my brother." Secrets were so exhausting that where I could tell the truth, I wanted to tell it.

George's face fell a little bit. "Oh. Should I leave you then?"

I shrugged. "It's hard to know what to say."

"Besides," George added, "the censors will take out everything juicy."

My letter wouldn't be going through the censors, but even so, I laughed. "What would I have to share that was so juicy? I've done nothing but live in this lab since I got here."

He came off the desk so fast I jerked in surprise. "Oh! That's right. That's why I came here looking for you. There's a dance here on Tuesday. I was wondering if you'd like to go with me."

I raised my eyebrows. "A dance?"

"Not enough notice?" he guessed, deflating.

I felt bad about teasing him. "No, no, it's fine. I've just never been to a dance."

"Never?" He looked interested. "They don't dance in New York City?"

My parents wouldn't have let me dance, especially with some-one who wasn't Jewish and who wasn't a potential husband, and I was genuinely too busy with university to attend dances. Perhaps the university offered them, but I'd never heard any of the other physics students speaking of them.

I didn't want him to think me young again, though, so I said, "Thank you for asking me. Of course I'll go with you. Lab partners should stick together, shouldn't they?"

He shoved his hands in his pockets, fingers turning into fists, knuckles I could see through the fabric. He gave me a shy smile. "It'd be nice to get to know you somewhere other than the lab."

"Yes, it would," I said, watching him. He was acting so odd. "Are you sure you're feeling well, George? Maybe you should tell Colonel Mann you need a few days off."

"I'm as fit as a fiddle. Even better now. It's a date," he said, starting for the door. "Besides, a war doesn't take days off. I'm meeting a Site W team, so if you don't see me, that's what I'm doing. I won't be more than a few minutes late to the dance, I promise."

I nodded. "We'll miss you here. Let us know if they've made any progress, or if you hear anything more about the German project."

It was a lie. We'd do just fine without him. But it was the kind of lie we all told other people, the kind of lie that made society tick.

He flashed me a grin. "Absolutely. And, Ilse? It's Rosh Hashanah, right? Your New Year?"

I blinked at him. "Thursday."

He smiled, slowly and almost happily. Like he'd won something. "Happy new year."

"Thank you," I said, wondering how he'd known that. I didn't know what to say in response because *shana tova u'metukah* wasn't quite the response to someone who wasn't also celebrating the holiday.

"You should definitely wear that lipstick again on Tuesday," he said abruptly, and then he winked, shoving his hands into his pockets and backing toward the door.

I'd forgotten I'd put it on this morning, playing with Lola's makeup while she and Polly had gotten ready for church. My fingers touched my bottom lip while I watched George make his exit. Boys could be so distracted by the strangest things, and I didn't have time for distractions. I had a letter to write, a problem to solve.

"I thought he was on his way to meet the Site W team already," said Lola, sailing into the room. She glanced over her shoulder where George must have still been retreating.

"He came to ask me to a dance. Did he seem well to you? I'm worried that he's traveling too much," I said, looking up from my letter. "What are you doing here? I thought you were taking Sundays off."

"Came looking for you," she said, plopping down in the chair across from me. "He seems like he always does to me. A snake."

I blinked at her. "George?"

She watched me with a scrutiny I wasn't used to seeing on her face. "Yes. I don't like how he treats Stella. And I don't trust him. I think he's going to claim credit for every one of our successes. Especially your successes. He was expecting to be in charge, Ilse. I don't think you understand how jarring it must be for a man like him to be answering to a woman."

"I understand just fine," I said sharply, bristling.

Lola's eyebrows rose. "I wasn't trying to be condescending."

"But you were." In the back of my mind, I knew that she was right. I knew that I was just on edge after George's comments about my age. But I couldn't find the words to apologize.

"What's going on?" Polly asked from the doorway, her voice slow and cautious.

I glared at Lola. "Nothing."

"We're fine," said Lola, looking frustrated.

"I think," Polly said, her words carefully chosen, "we should focus just on work."

"It's Sunday," said Lola.

"I know," Polly said quickly. "You don't have to. I thought maybe if we were all here, in one space, we could try to get work done.

What were you working on, Ilse?"

I shifted uncomfortably in my seat. I hadn't told them about Wolf yet. Somehow, it hadn't come up yet. "My brother..." I hedged. "He's...He can do magic. And he's working on another part of the same project. He can't help us," I added quickly. "But I can help him. His practical skills with magic are excellent, but he's not as strong on theory."

"Is he single?" Lola joked, and for a moment, she grinned at me before she remembered our fight. The smile dropped off her face.

"As far as I know," I said, giving her a tiny smile, trying to make peace.

Polly exhaled, and then Stella walked in, dropping her bag by the door and reaching up to pull the pins from her cream skimmer hat. "Good Lord, it's too hot out there. What are all of you doing in here? It's Sunday. I thought I'd have the lab to myself."

"We're going to help Ilse's brother with magic," Polly told her.

Stella's eyebrows lifted, in surprise or in interest I wasn't sure. "I'm listening. Go on."

"I've been sending him letters by balloon," I said. "But he needs that invisibility equation. I know we keep putting it to the side because it's not the first thing we need to tackle the elephant problem, but—"

"He's overseas?" Stella asked when my voice trailed off.

I nodded. "I know we're not supposed to be working on that, but I can't *not* help him."

Stella leaned against a blackboard and nodded, looking thoughtfully into middle distance. The three of us watched her, watched her eyes moving back and forth as if she could see equations being written in the air in front of her, and then she closed her eyes for a long heartbeat. When she opened them, she stepped away from the chalkboard, the back of her dark-red dress all dusty.

"I have an idea," she said.

CHAPTER SEVENTEEN

WOLF

The bar was quiet, and it being 10:00 a.m. might have had something to do with it. We had just finished our last debriefing about the mission ahead of us, and our 6:00 p.m. departure was a long way off. I couldn't even remember walking here, because the entire way, I'd been replaying the instructions I'd given about how the balloons and magic would work, worried I'd left something out. Lily had shown us maps and gone over the order in which we'd reach our targets. The Nazis had just moved their scientific operations, and we had to strike while our intelligence was sure.

We'd checked our packs, cleaned our guns, and tucked little cyanide pills, called L-pills, into our breast pockets. In case we were caught. There was nothing left to do other than clear our minds before tonight's jump.

The beer wasn't working though, nor was the piano I'd tried to play in the corner. It was hideously out of tune, and I was glad Max wasn't there to witness me pouting. He would have run his thumb over my lower lip, his eyes darkening, and I would have wanted to kiss him, and none of that could happen. Not here in public, and not before our mission. I didn't want to muddy the waters right now.

I turned the beer around and around on the coaster, watching the condensation drip down the sides of the glass. I'd think that I'd rather drink my own piss than whatever they called this beer, but it was the last thing I'd buy in England with my own money. This was the last day that was all my own.

The doorbell chimed as it was shoved open, and Lily, dressed in an appallingly red dress with a wide black belt, sailed into the room, followed by Max and Topher. I should have picked a different bar.

"Thought I told you not to drink before missions," Lily said, sliding into the seat next to me at the bar. She lifted my beer and sniffed, making a face. "God, when we get back here, we're going to teach you how to drink good beer. Americans. You wouldn't know a good beer if it hit you in the face."

"Isn't beer German?" asked Max, kicking me under the table as he slid into the booth. I glared at him, and he quirked an eyebrow up until it disappeared beneath his hair. *Okay?* it asked. He must have tagged along because he was worried about me. Or Lily brought him for the same reason.

I shook my head, both to him and to Lily. "What's a guy got to do to get some damn privacy around here?"

"Die," said Lily simply. She tapped the edge of the glass with her finger. "Are you finishing this?"

"No," I said, but she was already drinking it before I finished the word. I sighed, relaxing despite the newfound noise in the space. It drowned out my thoughts. "You're all the worst."

"Definitely," Topher agreed easily, bringing a plate of fries— chips—back to the table. "Don't drink on an empty stomach." The waitress appeared behind him, carrying four small tumblers of whiskey very carefully.

"Potatoes," I said, leaning forward and plucking a fry from the basket. "My favorite."

Topher slapped my hand away. "These are mine. Get your own."

"I used up all my ration tickets already," I protested. "Besides, we're on the same team."

"We are not on the same team. This war has different stakes for me," said Topher, rolling his eyes.

"I'm Jewish," I said drolly. "You don't think I know what the stakes are in this war?"

"It's not like anyone's going to war to save us though," Lily pointed out.

Topher shook his head. "All I meant was that I'm British. You're American. The Nazis are likely to invade my homeland. Not yours."

"Technically," said Max, "aren't you Scottish? Think they'll make it all the way up there?"

"Technicality," said Topher.

"Scots always say that until someone accidentally calls them English," said Lily in a conspiratorial tone.

"Oy!" cried Topher.

"I'm Scottish!" Lily exclaimed. "I'm allowed to say that!"

She leaned over and stole one of his fries. I noticed she did not get swatted away. Instead, Topher's frown just deepened and he sighed dramatically. "Fine."

He shoved the fries to the center of the table, and the three of us descended on them as though we were starving. Lily took an enormous handful, stuffed two in her mouth, and took a swig of whiskey. Topher gaped at her.

"What happened to manners?" he managed to say.

"They're for people in a different line of work."

I grinned and shook my head at him. "You brought this on yourself. You deal with the consequences. You can have my whiskey though. That stuff is foul."

Topher grabbed a second glass and pulled it in front of himself, as if it was a barrier between him and Lily's intenseness. "That beer tastes like piss. At least the whiskey's good."

"Thank the Scots for that," said Lily cheerfully. I tried to reach for my beer in front of her, and she smacked my hand away. "I'm not finished with this yet."

"Bloody hell," said Max, reaching for a tumbler. "I need a drink to keep up with you lot."

Lily caught his wrist with her hand. "Don't get drunk, pilot. I want you to be sharp."

"You're our pilot?" I asked, my eyes snapping to him. "When did that happen?"

"A few days ago," he said, not meeting my gaze. His voice was, for once, not resentful and completely serious. "I'll be sharp, Lily."

Lily dropped his wrist, but I still stared at her handprint on his skin, trying to digest this information. He drummed his fingers on the table in front of me, catching my attention. "Wolf, it'll be fine. I do a lot of these missions. That's why they asked me."

I looked up at him, scanning him for any sign that he was lying, but his face was clear and solemn. I nodded, slowly, and then aware that Topher and Lily were watching us too keenly, I turned away from Max.

"I need this back." I snuck my beer from Lily and wiped her lipstick off the glass. I raised it toward him. "Cheers to that."

"To madness and deception," Lily said, lifting another whiskey glass to my beer.

"We're going to die," Topher said matter-of-factly as he raised his second glass.

"In a blaze of glory," agreed Max, joining in with an empty glass.

"After we finish our mission," I clarified.

"You are a spoilsport," Topher informed me.

"No, he's right. If we're going to die in a blaze of glory, it better be as we're blowing Hitler to the moon," Lily said cheerfully.

"Cheers!" cried Max, and the bar filled with the sound of our laughter and glasses clinking against glasses. My beer didn't taste any better, but my heart was full.

CHAPTER EIGHTEEN

OAK RIDGE, TENNESSEE
SEPTEMBER 27, 1943

ILSE

A crack of thunder jolted me away, and I snapped upright, breathing heavily. Lightning flashed outside, illuminating the rain running down the window. I rubbed at my face, trying to steady my breathing. Just a storm.

Yesterday, Stella and I had figured out the beginnings of balloon invisibility, enough to test. Enough to hope that maybe soon I'd have an option for Wolf. And some part of me was a tiny bit optimistic again. Stella seemed to have no limits on her ability to think outside the norms, and I was learning from her.

I could ask a thousand questions, but somehow, I wasn't always good at asking the right ones. At least not at the right times.

It wasn't me leading this group toward history. It was Stella. I examined the feeling of disappointment blossoming in my chest carefully and then consciously dismissed it.

Disappointment was a test of hope. That was all. A test, not a state of being.

In the bed next to me, Polly murmured, "You should take today off. You can't work every day."

I stared at the poorly painted ceilings and the gap where the ceiling met the wall. Already, water was trickling down the paint. I tried to think of something to say, something to make her smile so my heart would trip in my chest from that instead of the thunder. But all I came up with was, "There's more work to do."

I rolled over and ran my eyes over her face, the curve of her lips, the shadow of her cheekbone, and the way her hair stuck to her forehead in the morning. I loved how slowly she woke. The soft set to her mouth, the steady, slow blink threatening to turn back into sleep at every breath, the way her feet rustled beneath her sheets as if they wanted to go before the rest of her did.

"What do you miss?" I asked her.

She smiled, sunrise on her face. "Music. Sweet tea. I was living with my aunt, and she always had a record going, or the radio sometimes. She's wonderful. I miss her."

"Is that where you'll go after the war?" I didn't want her to stop talking.

"Maybe," she said and then cleared her throat. "I've thought about college."

"What would you study?" She'd been training to be a nurse before Mann recruited her.

She hesitated and said, "I don't know. Do I need to know? Wait, that's not true. I want to study literature."

I propped myself up on an elbow. "What kind of literature?"

"British," she answered immediately. "Austen. The Brontës. Have you ever considered that *Jane Eyre*'s as much of an adventure as *Robinson Crusoe*?"

"I've never read *Jane Eyre*," I admitted, feeling a little stupid. I made a plan to go to the library. Surely I could find time to read between work and sleep.

"Oh, you must," she said with a sigh, rolling onto her back. "You really must, Ilse. I'll ask my aunt to send me one of my copies. I can lend it to you."

I laughed. "*One of*? You have multiple copies?"

"You'll understand," she said. "When you read it, you'll understand."

I needed to get up, but I didn't want to leave bed, or this room, or this moment.

Then Polly ruined it by saying, "Do you like George, Ilse?"

I didn't know how to put it into words, so I said the first thing that came to my mind. "I don't know. He's not the worst. And I think he sees me like an equal."

She didn't say anything in response, even when I got up to take a shower and get ready for the day. Just as the door shut behind me, I heard her say, "So do I."

But it wasn't even true, and I knew it as I washed my hair and scrubbed my face and stared at my reflection in the bathroom mirror. Even if George saw me as an equal, he didn't treat me as one. He didn't *not* treat me as an equal, but ever since day two, when I was put in charge of the working group, he hadn't quite treated me the same way he had when we met beside the buses on my first day. Why had I said yes to the dance? Because he was the first person to ask me?

Because Polly couldn't ask me? I blinked, caught off guard by the force and ease of the thought. Of course she couldn't ask me. We were friends, and we were both girls. Except...

Except, I liked the way she blushed when our hands touched, and the shiver that went up my spine. And I noticed things about her—like her mouth, and the way she woke up, and her smile—the way I used to notice things about boys at home. I liked spending time with her. It was hard to leave the room she was in.

My chest felt very tight suddenly, full of unsure lines and blurry vision. My hands curled into fists at my sides. I thought about the confusing line of not knowing if I wished I were as beautiful as Polly or if I wanted to kiss Polly because she was beautiful. I wasn't even sure there was a difference. She never thought I was lesser because I was two years younger than her. But I didn't know if that was reason enough to think that maybe kissing her would be better than kissing boys.

But it couldn't be the *same* feeling as what I'd felt toward boys in the past. It had to be a similar feeling. Something that was adjacent, but different.

Unless it wasn't.

And I wouldn't be able to tell if it was the same feeling or a different feeling until I tested the theory.

I should talk to her, I decided. When I was clean and dressed, feeling much refreshed, I grabbed a cup of coffee in the kitchen, deciding how I'd phrase my realization. Lola raised her eyebrow at me and I stopped, mug in hand, glancing down and over myself self-consciously. My shirt was tucked into my pants, and my bra wasn't evident through the shirt buttons. My hair was tied up, and everything matched.

"What?"

"Polly looked very upset when she left." Lola sipped at her coffee, waiting for my explanation.

"Oh," I said quietly. She was gone already.

"Everything good between you two?" asked Lola kindly.

It didn't feel good, though I didn't want to spill everything to Lola. I wasn't sure I was ready to forgive her for yesterday. Besides, I didn't know how Polly felt, and I didn't want to get her in trouble. Polly was sweet and *good*. Something about her soul settled me, as if I could curl up with a cup of tea next to her on the couch and spill all of my secrets, all of my hopes and fears and dreams, and she'd carry them all for me in those big, honey eyes and that calm smile. Maybe that wasn't good for me. Maybe I wanted—no, needed—to learn how to be quiet in my own skin.

Then again, Polly didn't try to fix me. She just was.

I shook my head. "It's nothing."

It wasn't nothing though. Why did she care if I went to the dance with George? Why did *anyone* care who I went with? I wasn't a child. Not here. And I refused to be treated like one while I was leading this team.

"Hey," said Lola, snapping her fingers in front of my face. "You listening, Ilse?"

"Yes, sorry," I stammered, filling a cup of coffee and sipping at it. I still thought it smelled better than it tasted.

"Do you have a dress? For the dance?"

I had quite a few dresses Mama had packed in my trunk. None of which I wanted to wear. "Yes."

Lola smiled and leaned back, her eyes going dreamy as if she was already at the dance. "This is what we need. We'll get a chance to relax for once."

I did not say, *Nothing like a mass of people and music that's too loud for relaxation. What a brilliant thought, Lola.* But I still thought it. And it was a vicious thought that tasted like lemons when I'd thought it'd taste like honey.

Then a man came out of Lola's room, stuffing his shirt into his pants. He stopped when he saw me. I raised my eyebrows, turning to Lola slowly. "Oh yes. I see why you might want a chance to *relax*."

She swatted at me. "Get out of here."

"Me?" said the man.

"You too," we said together. He gave us a look of confusion and cautiously slid by us and out the front door.

Lola grinned. "Don't be all judgmental, Ilse Klein. You do math. I have flings."

"We're going to test invisibility today," I told her, rolling my eyes. "Don't be late."

It was still pouring when I stepped outside, and the day seemed to reflect my mood, or perhaps they fed each other in a feedback cycle I couldn't break. Mud splashed up my legs, past the top of the boots and onto my pants, and my coat was splattered up the back. I shoved my hands deeper into my pockets and tromped along the path, if one could call it that on rainy days.

* * *

Polly and Stella must have gone to breakfast first, because the lights were still off in our building. I flicked them on and unlocked our lab door. The room was quiet and still, and I wanted to stay here. I didn't want to face Polly yet or avoid Lola or worry about Wolf. I wanted to do my work and go home.

I ran my hands over the piles of paper on my desk again, frowning. I'd worked late the night before, but I hadn't worked so late that I couldn't remember stacking my paperwork and slipping it into its manila folder, right here on my desk. In our locked laboratory. That I'd locked last night and that I'd unlocked this morning, so I knew the other girls didn't beat me to work today. And George was meeting the Site W scientists. So where was that folder?

"We're not testing outside today, are we?" asked Lola, appearing in the doorway and pulling a scarf off her hair where she'd tried to protect her curls from the rain. Behind her, Polly stood, her eyes downcast, avoiding mine. It made my throat tight.

"No, I suppose we aren't," I said, distracted. "Give me a moment."

"Everything all right?" Lola asked.

"Yes," I said, but it didn't sound convincing even to my ears.

"If you're sure…" Lola began doubtfully.

"Lola," said Polly, "perhaps you could use the phone at the end of the hall and let the colonel know we aren't testing outside today?"

"Splendid," said Lola, and then it was just Polly in the doorway. I watched her warily out of the corner of my eye as I flipped through my papers again. Then she sighed. "I'm sorry, Ilse."

"Me too," I said, even though I wasn't sure why I was sorry. Or why she was sorry. Just that I was truly sorry. A weight lifted off my shoulders. "I'm sorry I was rude this morning."

"You always are, in the mornings," she said with a soft smile. "I'd been up for hours. I shouldn't have jumped down your throat."

"It's all right," I said awkwardly. I couldn't bring myself to say, *I think I need to test a theory, and my hypothesis is that I like you.* The words sat in my mind, but I couldn't make them come out of my mouth.

She nodded, and then her eyes fell to my hands on my desk. "Are you sure everything is all right? You seem on edge."

"I can't find my notes from yesterday," I said, frowning. "The desk isn't that disorganized."

Polly stepped into the room. "Do you want help looking?"

"Sure," I said, even though I didn't think she'd find the papers. I wanted her in here, helping me, talking to me. I wanted someone to tell me everything was going to be okay.

We began sorting through all the manila folders with notes by dates, and as we went, I realized there were other missing dates, a day earlier in September, a day from last week, and last night. Some of the folders seemed lighter than they should have. I didn't say anything to Polly, but by the way her shoulders tightened, flipping through a day when she had taken the notes, she was noticing the same thing.

"Maybe someone borrowed them," she said after a few minutes.

I nodded. "Maybe."

I didn't want to think about the alternative.

"Maybe George?" Polly suggested. "Give him a ring."

I'd have to ask Colonel Mann if I could call whatever site he was at—or have someone call him for me—and to do so, I'd have to explain that I had lost paperwork. I didn't want that conversation. If I'd lost paperwork, Colonel Mann would take me off this team. Or demote me. But he wouldn't promote Stella. Maybe he'd bring George back to lead us. And George didn't know how to lead our team. I didn't know the right questions to ask, but I knew who did. George wouldn't know the right questions either, but he wouldn't listen to Stella.

And besides, if I had lost paperwork for this project...What if someone had it? What if someone knew where Wolf was? My letters were in those folders too, copies and coordinates as I'd practiced writing different equations. Balloons had been tucked into every folder but the first two weeks.

Things I shouldn't have kept with magic and bombs, I'd kept with magic and bombs. The dots could be connected too easily.

I'd be in so much trouble. In my mind, I could hear Colonel Mann saying, *"If you do share information about your work, you will be declared an enemy of the state. And what happens from there, I cannot tell you. That's above my pay grade."*

"Ilse," said Polly, as though she could see the panic I was trying to hard to contain. "It'll be all right."

She put down a folder and picked up a notepad, flipping to a fresh sheet. She made a list of missing folders and their dates. To ask the other girls, she told me. Surely it was just Stella or Lola doing work late at night. They shouldn't do it outside the lab, but I wouldn't mind so much, as long as they had the notes.

I kept searching.

They had to be here.

Wolf.

Colonel Mann.

If I let Wolf down again...

"Ilse," said Polly.

"Hmm," I replied.

"Ilse," Polly repeated, and there was something about her voice that made me look up. Her arms were crossed, her gaze directed westward over the X-10 reactor and into the sky.

I stood and crossed to her quickly, following her finger as she pointed at something.

In the sky, a red balloon.

"Polly," I said, my eyes trained on the red balloon. "Have you ever seen anyone in this lab? Someone who wasn't one of us?"

"No." She looked at me. "It isn't yours? To your brother?"

I shook my head. "No."

"Should we tell someone?" she asked after a beat.

"No," I said slowly, my mind spinning. "I'm sure I just left those papers at home. My mistake for taking them home. That balloon looks like it escaped from a birthday party."

But I'd never taken any papers home. And that balloon was carrying a cylinder, the type used to carry paperwork and maps. Someone was stealing documents about magic and spiriting them out of the camp. Someone was stealing secrets.

"You're lying," said Polly after a beat.

I looked up at her sharply, too terrified to deny it. She chewed her lip. "We should tell Colonel Mann."

"We can't," I said. "We can't tell them. Not yet."

Someone was a spy.

And they'd stolen my secrets. The secrets about this project, the secrets about magic, and worst of all, the secrets about my brother and his mission. I had to find the spy, and those notes, before Colonel Mann found out this had ever happened.

CHAPTER NINETEEN

LONDON, ENGLAND; SOMEWHERE OVER FRANCE
SEPTEMBER 27, 1943

WOLF

"Ready?" asked Max, standing in the doorway of the cockpit where I'd grown so used to seeing him. The setting sun behind him lit up his blond hair, making his edges bright and fuzzy.

I closed my eyes and leaned back against the cold wall of the plane. The engines hummed through my body, and I didn't think I was ready. Ahead of us, we had only hope, prayers, and a little magic. I would bleed for the free world, hoping that some of the blood I'd shed somewhere behind enemy lines would land in the right place and buy the Allies the time they needed. How could I be ready for this?

"Yes," I said. The bar this morning, the morbid joviality seemed so far away.

"You're the worst liar," Max said cheerfully. "All this OSS training, and they couldn't train your face."

"Your face is a lie," I muttered.

He snorted. "And you can't even insult anyone."

"Shut up, Max," I said. It was a little harsh, but it worked. He shut up while Lily and Topher buckled themselves in across from me.

Max nodded to Lily. "You're all set?"

She looked to me for confirmation. I touched the straps of my bag to reassure myself and nodded. She looked at Topher, who had all the explosives for the mission, and he nodded too. Lily turned a bright, exhilarated smile toward Max. "Ready."

Max looked at me, a long, weighted gaze. *Come home*, the look said.

I couldn't manage a smile, but I did turn the corner of my mouth up just a bit. *I will. You too.*

He blinked and then nodded, disappearing again. Lily reached to the side and slid the door shut, encasing us in darkness. Blackout meant there were only a few lights on the runway, and none that I could see out the small window over my shoulder. The air was full, heavy, and silent, tasting like the metallic edges of my anxiety. Then the engines roared, and I couldn't hear anything anymore.

The plane hurtled down the runway, and then the nose tipped up into the air, and the plane lifted off the ground as if in slow motion, like a play plane in the hands of a child.

I blinked, and the world came back into focus. One mission at a time. One flight at a time. We just needed to do this and come home.

"So last night, this girl, Penny," Topher started, his voice a shout that we could barely hear across from him.

I groaned. "Seriously."

"Louder," yelled Max. "I don't want to miss out because I can't hear it over some goddamn flak."

"Jesus Christ," I muttered.

"Can you even say that?" joked Topher.

Lily snorted. "Just tell us the story, MacKenzie."

"So this chick, Penny, right? I met up with her, and I thought I'd try to get a *send-off* before our mission, but her friends always show up at the wrong moments. I hate when girls move in groups like that."

"How did she know about the mission?" I interrupted, frowning.

"I think you are allergic to fun, Sunshine," Lily told me, rolling her eyes. "Every time it gets near you, you get all blotchy and feverish. You should see a doctor about that."

"I'm serious," I protested.

She shrugged. "What are we going to do now? Delay because Topher might have stupidly told a girl that we were dropping into Germany? Piggish behavior never stopped a war before."

"Started some," I added, but my words were lost to the noise.

"All I said was I was leaving. She promised me a date when I'm back," Topher protested at a shout. He winked. "Just need to get her friends out of the way."

The plane rattled and shook, turning slightly, and Lily tilted her head, listening. "We've been spotted. They're shooting at us."

"Damn," muttered Topher. I couldn't hear him, but the words were easy enough to see on his lips. I closed my eyes again. I didn't want to get shot out of the sky. I didn't want to die before I even had my chance. My fingers itched for a pen, for a balloon, for the time to say things I didn't get to say.

A shoulder pressed into mine. I blinked, opening my eyes. Lily smiled at me as she buckled into the seat beside me, cheeks flushed with adrenaline. Then she leaned sideways, turning her face so her mouth was next to my ear. Her hand wrapped around mine as she began to sing, "The other night, dear, as I lay sleeping..."

The corner of my mouth tipped up. "You dreamed you held me in your arms? Lily, you don't know when to quit, do you?"

She shrugged, grinning and singing on. "But when I woke, dear, I was mistaken, and I hung my head and cried."

I took a deep breath and, over the rattle of the plane, joined in singing with her. I knew what she was doing, and I didn't care. It worked. We sang softly through the rest of the song, ending with grins and a little bit of laughter. Lily leaned her head on my shoulder. "We go in, we make a few things go boom, and we come home. Got it?"

"Got it," I repeated.

She lifted her head. "You owe me shots at the pub when we get back. I've had to listen to you sing that twice now."

"I'm not that bad," I protested.

"You're that bad," Topher yelled from across the plane.

"You can't hear anything!" I shouted, gesturing to my ear. The propellers, the engines, the antiaircraft tracer bullets zipping by striking the sides of the plane, the bigger artillery…it was all getting louder and louder. I couldn't hear myself think.

"Tasker!" Max called from the cockpit. Lily jolted at his tone and unbuckled, scrambling to the front of the plane. I couldn't hear her conversation with Max, but it went on for nearly ninety seconds.

"Like a goddamn movie," shouted Topher to me.

That was real. Far too real. But it was beautiful the way the clouds lit up from beneath, stuttering and exploding lights through the fog like spinning skirts or fireworks to music we couldn't hear over the roar of our own plane.

"We can do this," I whispered to myself. It was a little blood and a little magic and a little bit of seeing opportunities. I scanned the clouds through the foggy little window, hoping for anything that would tell us we were close to our drop site, but saw nothing but flak.

Lily waved her hand for our attention, her face grim, and shouted, "We're not going to make the drop zone. We're taking too much fire, and they've probably scrambled a few planes. Not enough clouds. He's going to get us as close as he can."

This wasn't the plan.

Lily smacked the side of my helmet. "Don't panic. Focus."

The jump light flicked on. Red. Lily yanked open the door just in time to see the wing of the plane get hit, exploding into bright yellow and orange flame. The plane jerked, tilting wildly to the right, toward the fireball of a wing, and Topher grabbed Lily by the arm before she fell out of the plane. He hauled her back to the seat, where I was already unbuckling.

"Max!" I yelled.

"Jump!" he yelled back.

I staggered to the front of the plane, leaning into the cockpit. "You won't make it home."

"Jump out of the plane, Klein," he ordered me, and everything in me wanted to obey. Every cell of my body screamed at me to jump out of the plane. I could see the veins in his arms popping as he held the plane as steady as he could for us, straining back against the plane's desire to plummet into the earth.

Another explosion slammed into the plane so hard that Max slammed forward, his face and head colliding with the controls. The plane screamed, heat and wind sliding through its body. Max was slumped forward, not moving.

"Let's go!" shouted Lily. She grabbed my pack. "Leave him!"

I knew what she meant. He wasn't part of the mission plan. He was disposable. To her, maybe, but not me. I staggered forward, grabbing Max by his arm and hauling him to his feet and out of the cockpit. I grabbed one of the nylon loops we hung onto, and he leaned on me, his hand closing around my parachute. I wrapped my arm around him. He was alive. He was dazed, his eyes wide and pupils dilated.

"Max," I yelled right into his face.

His eyes didn't focus. I turned and saw that Topher had jumped. Lily was reaching for us desperately. I nodded and slid my left arm through Max's pack straps. I wasn't going to leave without him.

"Go," snarled Lily, and she nearly shoved us toward the door.

"Max. We're jumping," I said to him. He nodded, but I didn't know if he understood me or not. I wrapped his hand around his chute cord and met his unfocused eyes as Lily pushed us, and we jumped.

CHAPTER TWENTY

WOLF

I cut the cords of my chute, staggering to my feet. I sucked in oxygen, holding my breath as I tried to hear past the roar in my ears, the pounding of my heart, the raggedness of my own breathing. The plane went down not far from here, exploding when it hit the ground. The Germans would be searching this area any minute, and I hadn't seen where Max went down. He'd pulled his chute on his own—thank *God*—but I'd lost track of him in the dark. My arm had been yanked from his pack straps by the force of our fall, and it ached with a pounding, visceral pain. I'd broken it, maybe. But more pressing was the need to find Max.

The last I'd seen him, he'd been blown a little east of me, and all of my instincts wanted to run that way, screaming his name at the top of my lungs. But that'd just get us both shot, and I remembered my training, Lily's words echoing in my head. *Don't panic. Focus.* I still had my pack. I still had blood in my body. If I couldn't find the others, I'd go to the first rendezvous point. And if they didn't join me there, I'd do all I could on my own. And if I couldn't do that, I'd find the Resistance, if there was any. I hadn't seen the map Lily had. I had no idea where I was, or how far from the original drop site we'd landed.

My hands shook, and around me, leaves blew up, a soft tornado around my ankles. The wind must have shifted, though the trees seemed still. The sound of guns still rang through the air, and planes roared in the distance. The smell of smoke stung the inside of my nose and the back of my throat. I slid my hand over the holster of my .45, fingers curling around the cold metal. If a gun was in my hands as I walked, I'd be shot on sight, definitely. If a gun wasn't in my hands as I walked, I'd be shot on sight, possibly.

I swallowed and pulled the gun from its holster. My head swam, tilting as if we were on a ship. Just now, just right now, it hit me that we'd been shot down in enemy territory. Planning a drop was different from being shot down. The night stretched out in front of me. My watch read just after midnight. I had some German and a little bit of French. Part of me whispered, *Find Max. Stay safe.* Perhaps we could survive out here in the countryside by pretending we were locals. Perhaps we didn't need to be captured, didn't need to join the Resistance. We could wait out this war.

Then I shook my head. *Focus*, I told myself. I wasn't here to wait out a war. I was here to end it.

I heard the sound of a truck, and headlights bobbed far away. It certainly wasn't one of ours. I moved quickly and quietly, deeper into the forest. My head throbbed and felt as if it weighed a hundred pounds on top of my neck, and my left arm scissored with pain every few steps, but I ignored it. When the truck rumbled past me, I hunkered down, gripping my pistol. *Don't shoot unless they're nearly on top of you.* I listened.

German voices. Good. That didn't necessarily mean we were in Germany, but it meant we were close enough to an outpost that I could orient myself, maybe, and figure out the way to Heidelberg. A great beam of light flooded the forest, passing back and forth, just shy of my hiding place.

I waited, holding my breath, but the truck packed up and moved on, and when I could no longer follow the distinct voices, I crawled out from my hiding spot. Lily, Topher, Max. I needed to find them, and then we could figure out where we were. And where we needed to be.

I followed the wind down from where I'd landed, looking for the telltale white parachutes in trees.

"Fire," called a soft, familiar voice.

"Smoke," I said, relieved.

Lily crawled out from underbrush ahead of me on her stomach and elbows, her pack high on her neck. She rolled and sat up, brushing dirt off herself. "You all right?"

"I'm alive," I said. "Where are Topher and Max?"

"We'll find them," Lily said. "Where'd you lose Max?"

"I don't know. His chute opened so fast that it jerked him away from me. I thought it'd break my arm," I said.

"Good thing you let go," Lily said. She checked my arm. "Seems to be all right. Look, if he's—"

"He's *alive*," I growled angrily. "I can feel it."

She held my gaze. "Then we'll find him. But he isn't the mission, Wolf. Don't forget that." She didn't let go of my arm until I nodded reluctantly. He's my mission, my responsibility, I thought, but it wouldn't have made a difference to Lily. She was looking around, orienting herself. "He probably came down south and east of you. Let's retrace your steps."

We stepped cautiously through the forest, single file, trying not to create trackable paths. I nearly stumbled into Lily when she stopped abruptly a few times, but we heard no one else for five, ten minutes, as we breathed in the pine and exhaled our anxiety.

Should I have left Max in the plane?

I could smell the fire and the burning fuel from here. He would have died in it. If he was dead now, at least I'd done something to save him. My throat felt tight, and when I swallowed, my vision spotted.

"You all right, Klein?" Lily asked again.

"Yeah," I managed.

She sounded doubtful. "We can camp overnight and look in the daylight."

"What if he's injured?"

"We need to find Topher too," she said, not unkindly.

"I should have taken some hair from everyone," I muttered.

"Other than sounding like a serial killer, what's the purpose of that?" she asked.

"That's how my sister and I send messages. A little bit of hair touching the blood, and the magic will find the person whose hair it is. We could just follow whatever I wrote the magic on," I said mournfully. "She called it a magical homing pigeon. I should have thought of that. Ilse would have thought of that."

"Ilse isn't here. You are, Wolf," Lily said firmly. "Focus."

I took a deep breath. *One step at a time. Like writing out the equation on a balloon*, I told myself.

Then Lily and I both heard a groan. I started toward the sound, but Lily gestured at me angrily. She held up one finger, and in the dim light of the moon, I could see her face. Determined. Wary.

She held up a hand. *Wait.*

Her sidearm out in one hand, a knife in the air, she crept forward in the dark. I watched the outline of her body get swallowed by the shadows and the woods. I sucked in a breath.

"Wolf," she called. "It's him."

I stumbled into a run after her, following the sound of her voice. I nearly tripped right over them. Max had landed—hard, it seemed, with blood trickling out the side of his mouth and both of his nostrils. But he'd cut himself free from his chute in the trees above us and fallen to the ground. He was sitting at the base of a tree.

"Woof," said Max, his voice slurred.

I fell forward, scooting on my knees until I reached him. My hands cradled his head, my thumbs running over the streaks of blood across his too-pale face. He felt fragile, clammy, and cold beneath my fingers. "Max. How's your head?"

"Hurts," he told me. His eyes fluttered closed.

"Don't go to sleep," I said sharply. "Sit up."

"Bossy," he murmured. "Dat's my job."

"I'm going to look for Topher," said Lily. "Clean him up and get him ready to move, okay?"

"You can find us again?" I asked.

"Yes," Lily said, the tension in her voice cracking to let amusement seep through. "I'm not leaving."

"I didn't think you would," I said quickly. "There was a German truck that passed me. Stay away from the road."

"I'll be back in a few minutes," Lily said after a pause.

When she left, Max said, his voice low, "What now?"

"We stay alive," I said grimly. "And we get out as soon as we can."

"Easy as pie," said Max, a smile in his voice, even though he spoke slower than normal.

"That's right," I said. "Easy as your momma's pie."

"Don't talk 'bout Momma," Max muttered.

Lily didn't come back for nearly an hour, and when she returned, Topher wasn't with her. My heart sank, and she squatted next to me, looking at sleeping Max with concern.

"Did you find a chute?" I asked her quietly.

She shook her head. "No. I didn't find anything. We'll proceed as normal to our first site in the morning, but we'll stay here tonight in case we hear him."

"What if he doesn't find us there?" I asked.

Lily looked up at me, her face drawn. "We continue as planned, Wolf. We'll figure it out, even without his pack."

We could get to where we needed to go, and we could steal what we needed to steal, but we couldn't destroy what we'd been told to destroy. The real value in sabotaging the German bomb was making things explode so the Germans couldn't easily rebuild after we'd stolen materials or papers, whatever we found. And exploding things was Topher's area of expertise with everything he needed in his pack. Lily didn't need him. Just his explosives. The truth and the callousness stung a little bit.

Max snored softly next to me, his nose swollen, his head rested gently on my shoulder. Lily sat down on my other side, shivering a little. I pulled my jacket around her shoulders, and she thanked me quietly.

I didn't think we'd get much sleep that night.

CHAPTER TWENTY-ONE

OAK RIDGE, TENNESSEE
SEPTEMBER 28, 1943

ILSE

There was a spy among us.

Somewhere in this crowded, ridiculously loud community hall filled with twirling skirts and bodies and people, there was a spy. There was someone else who could do *magic*. And they'd used that to steal secrets from *my* group, from *my* papers, *and my* mind, and who knew what they were doing with them. If they had sent the secrets out by balloon, one that was visible, they were no more advanced than us. If they'd stolen them, they couldn't be fighting for the United States. Who would send spies here?

Probably everyone.

I knew so little about what other people knew. Sometimes, at home, in the physics lab, we'd say that what held us back was not knowing the questions to ask. We didn't know what we didn't know. That was what this felt like. I had questions, but I didn't know if they were the right questions. I didn't know what I needed to know to find the spy before Colonel Mann realized they'd stolen secrets, before he learned we'd made very little progress—except in the magic for Wolf. Magic I wasn't supposed to be working on.

"If you keep glaring at everyone," murmured Polly, appearing next to me, flushed and with a drink in hand, "no one will dance with you."

"I'm not in the mood for dancing," I said crossly.

Polly's smile was upsettingly coy. "This is how I know you aren't the spy."

"What?" I straightened. That'd been an option?

She laughed a little and picked up my hand from my side. My skin tingled wherever she touched me, and I was sure I was redder than a tomato. She pressed the cool cup of punch into my hand. "You can't hide anything. Your face is an open book."

I studied her expression, unsure whether this was a compliment or an insult. There were things I wanted to keep hidden from her. At least for now, while I still didn't know what to do with my thoughts and feelings. "I can't help it."

"I know," she reassured me, and then she stepped closer. "There's nothing you can do, Ilse, but enjoy yourself for the night. It isn't up to us to find the spy. That's Colonel Mann's job."

I thought I'd convinced her not to tell the colonel until we tried to find the culprit first. It might be his job, but it felt like my responsibility. I sipped at the punch and nodded, turning my eyes away from her, her closeness, and gazed out at the dance floor. It felt strange without Stella there. We felt incomplete. And it bothered me that she wasn't allowed to come here—and that I'd still come. We were all doing the same work. We ought to be allowed to have the same fun.

Polly sighed, pulling me out of my own head. I looked at her shoes that she'd somehow kept clean of mud. "You could go dance. You don't have to stand here with me."

"I want to stand here with you," she said simply.

My eyes darted to her again. "Polly."

She looked down at her feet. "Ilse."

Say something, I ordered myself. But my throat was dry, despite the punch. It was just a theory. I didn't need to test every theory. We could still be friends. *Just* friends.

"Girls!" cried a familiar voice, and then Lola burst from the crowd and into view, flopping against the wall on my other side, breathless and red-faced. A soldier wandered out from the crowd, flushed and his hands shoved his pockets. He had eyes only for Lola, who snatched the punch from my hand and downed it in a single gulp.

"Oh, that was good," she said, bubbling with giddiness. "What a dreamboat he is."

I looked at him and thought that he was a perfectly mediocre example of a man. I almost told Lola that I thought he was quite the dish but remembered Polly's words about my face being an open book. I bit back the lie and asked, "But can he dance?"

"I'm only interested in one kind of dancing, Ilse Klein, and it's more horizontal than I'll let him get. At least tonight," Lola said airily. "I'll warn you if and when he's coming home."

"Lola!" Polly exclaimed, scandalized.

Lola grinned, winking at both of us. "Did he hear that?"

Oh, how I missed Stella and her dry wit. I looked over Lola's shoulder at the wide-eyed boy and the Adam's apple bobbing in his throat. "Yes, definitely."

"Perfect!" she exclaimed and pushed the empty punch cup back into my hand. "Toodles, girls!"

"Toodles," Polly and I echoed, amused.

"That poor boy," Polly murmured.

"I think he knows what he's getting into," I said. "How could you not?"

Polly cast me a sidelong look. "Very few people know what they're getting into until they're already in it."

"You can always get out," I argued.

Polly looked away again. "Sometimes someone doesn't want to, even if it wasn't what they were expecting."

I had a feeling we weren't talking about Lola anymore, but then someone appeared at my elbow, far too close, smelling like pine and cold air. I looked up at George, who looked even more tired and frustrated than he had the last time I'd seen him, in the lab a few days ago. He smiled down at me, the corners of his eyes crinkling a little bit.

"Why, fancy seeing you here, stranger."

Why did everyone keep interrupting Polly and me? But I managed a smile and a raised eyebrow. "You said you'd be a *little* late. The dance has been going for an hour."

I turned to look for Polly, hoping that she'd help me tease him, but she was gone, and I just caught the hem of her lavender skirt disappearing into the throng of people on the dance floor. I bit my lip. I should have said something when she was standing here. This bantering, this playing with George, didn't feel *more* natural than spending time with Polly, but it felt—easier. I had more practice talking to boys like this than girls, which was a flaw in this experiment I couldn't avoid much longer. The truth was, I didn't want to stand here with George while Polly was out there smiling at someone else. Holding hands with someone else.

I closed my eyes.

I shouldn't think of holding hands with her. I shouldn't want any of that.

But I did.

George elbowed me a little bit, jostling me back into the space with him. "So?"

I blinked up at him. "So what?"

He looked amused. "Do you want to dance?"

I said yes, because the dance floor was closer to Polly. I let him take me by the hand and lead me onto the floor. And the farther into the crowd we wove, the more my mind screamed at me to pull away, to find her, wherever she was. But I didn't. I let him put his hand on my waist, fold his hand around my hand, stand close enough that my chest brushed against his chest.

"Don't you wish this was the war? The whole of it?" he asked me.

I frowned at our hands. "This isn't war. This is a distraction from the war."

"So literal for someone with so many gifts," he said, his nose touching my hair.

I hadn't felt like a prodigy lately. I felt like someone being pulled in a million directions among all the people around me, between inventing magic for Wolf and inventing magic to drop a devastating weapon, between me and the person I didn't know but hoped could be me. Between knowing who I should like, and knowing who I did.

"Not literal," I said carefully. "Practical."

"Just let loose," George whispered into my hair.

I gripped his hand tighter, trying to let the music sway me. "That's not who I am."

"I could help you with that," he suggested.

I couldn't help the snort that slipped free. "Try that on another girl. It doesn't work on me."

"I want it to work on you," he said. "Don't you think we have a connection? From the moment we met, I felt it."

I risked a glance up at his face and saw only sincerity. I let him spin me around a few times, and when the music changed and he dipped me, a smile broke my face in half, and I wasn't even faking it. But still, he was just a man with a pretty face, and I'd so much of the world to see. And Lola thought he was a snake. And Stella didn't trust his science. And Polly had left when he showed up.

When he straightened me, his hand firmly splayed against my back, I said, "I've got things to do before I settle down."

He laughed. "I'm not asking you to marry me, Ilse."

The words stung when they hit home. I swallowed hard, keeping my eyes trained over his shoulder, catching sight of Lola's smile and spinning skirts, and Polly standing with a group of the girls I didn't recognize. I hadn't met a single person yet who saw me for all of me. Everyone could only see pieces of me. A pretty face, an available body, a bright mind, magic blood. I wanted to be all those things for someone. Not just one of them. All of them.

"We don't have to do everything," he said softly into my ear. "Don't be afraid."

My head started shaking before I realized it. "No. I don't want to."

There was a beat while I thought he might not take me at my word, but then he sighed and said, "I'm patient. I can wait."

I didn't have a response for that, but the tightness writhed in my chest and I didn't want to dance with him anymore. When the song ended, I stepped away from him, letting my sweaty palm fall from his. He looked a little confused, though he did his best to hide it.

"I need a drink and to rest," I said, hedging. When he started toward me, I held up a hand and added, "Alone."

He nodded, and I slipped toward the refreshment table and ladled myself a cup of punch. I didn't want it, but I couldn't exactly make another excuse now.

Lola slipped up beside me, her presence a warm comfort. She picked up one of the cookies, turning it over and examining it before nibbling at it. "How do you think they got enough butter to make these? Did they just hoard their ration tickets?"

"Most likely," I said, my heart still pounding. If I told Lola what George had said, would she believe me? Would she tell me I overreacted? Would she tell me to let him take me to bed? Was I too literal?

"Everything all right?" she asked, but something in her tone, kind and low, told me that she already knew it wasn't.

My throat was tight when I said softly, "I don't know."

She nodded a little, brushing cookie crumbs off her lips. "I can't think in here, not with a clear head. It's too noisy. It jumbles all my thoughts. Does that happen to you too?"

I blinked at her. "Yes. Yes, it does."

"Step outside," she advised. "Breathe in some fresh air. Find some quiet. Things will be clearer then."

The autumn night slid cold fingers over my sweat-slicked skin as soon as I stepped outside, and breathless, I leaned against the walls in the shadow. If I stayed out here long, I'd catch a cold, but for now, standing outside here—with the raucous party inside muted through the walls—felt like a piece of illicit freedom. Lola was right. Here, no one was watching me. George wasn't trying to touch me. He wasn't trying to get under my skirts. There were no questions about magic or blood or uranium or plutonium or distance or time or spies. Just me, and the night sky. I drew in another deep breath, relishing it. Everything cleared, clouds parting in the sky of my mind.

One of the things I loved the most about Tennessee was the night sky. In New York, I couldn't see the stars. I'd seen pictures and I'd see them sometimes in Central Park, but never like this. They filled the sky—not just the big constellations but as far as the eye could see. To the edges of the sky that fell into the trees and the edge of the sky that fell into the reactors, all three of them. The stars felt very close and very far away all at the same time.

"Miss Klein?" asked an unfamiliar voice.

I looked up, startled. A soldier in a beige uniform walked up to me out of the dark, an idling truck behind him. He wrung his hat in his hands. "Colonel Mann would like to see you, if you please."

"Now? It's so late," I said, panic rising in my throat. He knew about the missing papers. He thought I was a spy. He'd seen the balloon. A thousand possibilities, and all of them were awful. *My mind and my magic and science. They cannot take them from me.*

"He didn't say, miss. He'd just like to see you. Please get in the car." The boy looked at me with a flat expression. He gave away nothing.

I didn't have a choice. They'd arrest me for defying them if I refused, and that would look worse than simply complying. I took a deep rattling breath and climbed into the back seat. The boy sat next to me, stiff and upright. He didn't look familiar, but then, I rarely interacted with anyone beside the bus driver, George and the girls, and the scientists down the hall from our lab who always looked depressed.

No wonder Mama had been worried about my marriage prospects. The car jolted to a stop and snapped me out of my thoughts. The boy opened the door and offered me a hand, but I climbed out without taking it. If I was about to be fired from my job and sent home in disgrace, I'd walk into this office on my own volition. I was young, and I was confused, but I knew what type of person I wanted to be. And that person was a woman who stood on her own two feet. I didn't need a man or a woman at my side to hold open doors for me. I opened my own doors.

I stepped into Colonel Mann's office with the army boy hot on my heels. The office was dark, dimly lit by two lamps, casting the desk and the colonel into long shadows. He dismissed the boy with a wave. Colonel Mann looked tired, the shadows on his face cutting deep creases across his brow and jaw. He held a report in his hand, but he was watching me instead of reading it. I stood in front of him, hands behind my back, fingers crossed and heart in my throat. Would he take me as seriously, now that I wore a dress? Didn't he know me better than to think I was a spy? I kept my mouth shut, waiting for him to speak first.

"Miss Klein, please have a seat," he said.

"I'd rather stand," I said softly.

He looked up from his report. "You mistake me. That wasn't a request. That was an order. Take a seat, Miss Klein."

I took a seat, fighting to keep a scowl off my face. But when Colonel Mann looked up at me, full of sympathy and something else—pain or sadness—my heart dropped into my stomach. I leaned forward in my chair instinctively as he said, "Miss Klein, I'm sorry to share this terrible news with you. Wolf's plane was shot down over France last night. It isn't clear yet if anyone survived the crash."

The room spun, a wild mix of window and wood, lamplight and darkness refracting in long, sharp lines, and I whispered, "What?"

"Miss Klein. Ilse," said Colonel Mann, and I had a vague awareness that he was moving around his desk. My hands were not my hands, but he held them in his hands. "Ilse, put your head between your knees. Take a deep breath."

I tried to pull away. "You're lying!"

"I'm not lying, Ilse," he said, and I heard the tightness in his voice. The sadness. *He thinks Wolf's dead.*

A scream tore from my chest, something wordless and wild. I yanked my hands from his and slammed my fists against his chest. The door behind me opened and someone grabbed at me, but Colonel Mann said something like *Let her be, let her be.* And I slid to the floor, sobbing.

"Ilse," he said. "Keep up your hope. We're waiting for a signal from any survivors. As soon as I know anything, I'll share it with you. He's considered missing in action. And I am hopeful. Your brother's resourceful, Ilse. I wouldn't have sent him over there if I didn't have faith in his abilities to think his way out of a problem."

"I just sent him a balloon," I said on the floor, hands over my face.

I didn't mean to let it slip out, but the colonel seemed to take it in stride. "A balloon?"

"We just write little letters back and forth," I whispered. "You don't think he's dead?"

"No. I don't." And then in Colonel Mann's painfully honest way, he added, "The odds, I'll admit, are long."

"If he's not dead, he's in danger." He was in enemy territory. Maybe they'd lost other members of their team. Maybe he was all alone.

"Yes," the colonel said after a beat. "That I can't and won't deny."

I closed my eyes. My brother, who'd never wanted to be anything other than good and quiet, was a Jewish boy in enemy territory. I pressed my hands to my aching heart. "You should have sent me instead."

"But I didn't," he said calmly. "You are here. And he is there. And the best we can do is wait."

Unladylike, I wiped at my face with my sleeve and drew in a deep rattling breath. "If Wolf dies over there, I will never deliver your bomb."

Colonel Mann stiffened. "I don't think you're in your right mind right now, Ilse. Is there anyone we can call for you?"

I steadied my voice the way I fought to keep the room steady around me. "We are a package deal, Colonel."

"This is war, Miss Klein."

"And my brother is missing," I said softly, rising from the chair. "If you hear from him…"

"I will let you know," Colonel Mann said firmly. "If you contact him, tell him that he can reach out to Captain Hutchinson in England for assistance. Hutchinson has a handful of magic users operating elsewhere in Europe. That stays between you and me, Ilse, do you understand?"

I nodded.

He added, his voice still stiff, "If you hear from him before me, using whatever methods you have invented, I expect you'll show me the same courtesy."

I wanted to tell him that we'd have to see how I felt. Instead, I just nodded again, not trusting my voice, and left. I had been dancing, and my brother had been falling out of the sky. And there was nothing that I, with all of my knowledge and all of my questions and all of my theories and all of my gifts, could do.

* * *

September 28, 1943

Dear Wolf,

Please, please send me a letter. Please tell me you're okay. I'm terrified. Colonel Mann said that you were shot down. He knows I'm writing to you. He says there's someone named Hutchinson in London who's working there as his second-in-command. Send a balloon to him too. Do you need more balloons? I've included some, plus rat poison. *Be careful with this.* Use it to keep blood from clotting. If you have time, you can draw multiple syringes and keep them stored with the rat poison mixed in for whenever you need a balloon but don't have time to draw a fresh syringe.

I hope that makes sense. I'm worried sick.

Wolf, please be alive. I don't know what I'd do if you died.

Love,

Ilse

CHAPTER TWENTY-TWO

SOMEWHERE ON THE BORDER
OF FRANCE AND GERMANY
SEPTEMBER 28, 1943

WOLF

Fingers dug into my shoulder, and I woke with a grunt to feel a soft, small hand covering my mouth. My surroundings slid into focus, Lily's face close to mine, her pupils wide, her breath quick. She slowly let go of my mouth and then held up two fingers, pointing toward the road.

They'd found us.

She pointed east, into the woods and toward the hills, and I nodded. In the distance, I could hear German voices. Indistinct, but loud enough to make out words. Next to me, Max was a warm, heavy weight. I shifted him as Lily shouldered her pack and then grabbed mine from where I'd used it as a brace for Max. Max started to groan, and I clapped a hand over his mouth as Lily had done for me.

A pause in the German voices, then they picked up again. Through the trees, flashlights bobbed. The sound of bayonets sliding onto the ends of rifles.

Silence. We just needed a few moments of silence.

My heart battered my ribs, and I had to concentrate on making my breathing slow and steady. *Don't panic. Focus.* Max woke slowly, his motions fumbling and imprecise. His eyes didn't seem to focus, but that might have been the lighting. That was what I told myself anyway. I grasped him beneath the elbows and lifted him to his feet. He slumped forward against me, shuffling his feet. Branches snapped.

A low whistle came from behind us, the Germans signaling to move in our directions.

Lily hissed, "Go!"

I hoisted Max's arm around my shoulder. "Max. Pick up your feet."

My voice was hoarse from dropping that low, but he seemed to hear me and try, even if he wasn't very successful. We moved through the woods, ducking behind trees, following Lily as she moved swiftly, nimbly like a deer or a wood nymph. She acted like she'd been running in these woods her whole life—and carrying both our packs too. I couldn't keep up with her, not while holding Max, but I tried.

She yanked me down onto a low slope beside some trees and rocks in the foothills. "Hide him."

I lowered Max to the ground. He struggled, trying to get up, and I shoved him down by his shoulders. "Stop. Listen to me."

He made an unintelligible growl that sounded like a curse. I tried not to smile. Nazis were pursuing us, we didn't know where we are, and he could still make me smile. I pressed him back against the hill. "I'm going to put leaves and branches on you. Don't move. Max, they'll kill you. Don't move."

The voices picked up again. They were gaining on us. Lily lay on her stomach, gun in her hand, watching, waiting, while I quickly and quietly covered Max. He couldn't walk, much less fire a gun. I took his from his jacket holster and crawled over to where Lily was lying. I pushed the second gun at her. She was the better shot. She ought to have more ammo than I did.

She glanced at it and nodded. Her mouth was a thin, flat line in the growing light. Sunlight. It was sunrise. They'd come back to look for us at sunrise. "Killing people is hard, Wolf."

"That's not why. I don't have a problem with killing them. They're Nazis," I said.

Her jaw twitched. "I know. But it'll hit you more than you expect. Let me do it this time, okay? Just stay down."

I swallowed, then murmured. "Okay."

Voices, and footsteps. More than two flashlights, and then they clicked off, audibly. They were right on top of us. My heartbeat was thunder in my ears, and everything in my body screamed for me to curl up in a ball, close my eyes, surrender.

Don't panic. Focus.

My hand closed around the gun. Lily didn't move. Shadows, footsteps. I could hear each individual step. Then a cracking branch, leaves, the smell of pine, and a body leaned right over our little slope on the hill.

Lily pulled the trigger. I jumped, startled by how loud it was, how fast the Nazi dropped in front of us, his back arching and knees buckling as he hit the ground, blood blossoming on the front of his uniform. *Crack, crack, crack.* Gunfire exploded over our position, and we both ducked as the Nazis shouted at one another, advancing toward us.

Lily rose a bit, moving away from Max, and I followed suit, rising a little to see above the line of the ground. Seven men in gray uniforms, half of them with bayonets drawn and the other half without, converged through the thin light in the woods, firing at will.

My finger curled around the trigger, and I pulled. I missed, or so I assumed, because no one went down, and they kept advancing. Lily fired again, and again, and two Nazis dropped, both alive and yelling on the ground. The noise filled the hills, my ears.

I leveled my gun at the nearest Nazi and fired, and moved my gun to the next target. Again. Again. One went down. White-hot pain shot through my side and I yelped, falling to my knees and gasping as black and white spots of light danced across my vision.

A Nazi stood over me, leveling a gun at my head, and then his eyes went blank and he fell to the ground, blood seeping from an ear. Lily shot another one. I lifted my gun and shot again, hitting one in the arm. He spun to shoot at me, but another shot, somewhere high and behind me, took him out.

I sucked in a breath, adjusting my grip on the gun. Silence, save for the groans of the two Nazis Lily injured early, rolled over me.

"*Woo-heee!*" yelled a voice, and I twisted, expecting more Nazis, but it was Topher who appeared at the top of the opposite hill, rifle in hand, grinning like a damned fool. Lily let out a string of curses and knelt by me, reaching for the blood on my side before stopping herself.

I growled, "Don't touch it. Unless you'd like the advantage of flying."

Her lips twitched, and then she grinned, still shaking a little from the adrenaline. I yanked my shirt free from my belt and looked at the blood and wound on my side. One of my feet rose off the ground.

"The notebook," I said. "Chest pocket."

Lily pulled out the notebook for me, and I opened it, shaking and trying to find the page as fast as I could. There was a cancellation equation in here somewhere, but Ilse had called it something else. What did she call it? I found it. *Gravity equation.* I dipped my finger into the wound with a groan that made Lily look nervously at me.

"I don't think I'm going to die," I said, writing the equation sloppily on my skin, like finger painting.

"No, but I bet that hurts something awful," Lily said.

We both tensed when the sound of boots slapping against the ground and branches snapping interrupted the quiet, but relaxed when we saw Topher had made his way down from the top of the ridge. He squatted next to us, his grin taking up his whole face. "That was something else."

"Where have you been?" snapped Lily, breaking open the first aid kit and dabbing cautiously at my side with gauze.

"Finding you," Topher replied, then looked around, his grin slipping. "What happened to the pilot?"

"Max!" I called. I kept an eye on Topher who seemed like he might've hit his head too. He'd been a little foolhardy back in England, but now he was wild-eyed and hadn't stopped moving.

The pile of leaves and sticks started to move. Topher helped Max clear off his camouflage and lifted him to his feet. I could see words exchanged, but I couldn't hear much. Topher sat Max next to the tree and came toward Lily and me.

Lily patted a bandage into place. "You won't die."

"Good," I murmured. "That'd be so inconvenient."

She snorted. "Come on. Let's go pick some Nazi pockets."

Lily pocketed all the guns and ammo she could realistically carry with her, and then the three of us came to the two injured Nazis, one shot in the stomach and one shot in the chest, both still alive but barely so.

I grimaced, looking away. But Lily knelt right next to them. "*Wie lautet dein Name?*"

"Kurt," gasped the one with a stomach wound, his hand pressed to his abdomen. Blood leaked out from between his fingers.

Lily gave him a pitying smile. "Kurt, I am not going to kill you. *Verstehst du mich?*"

He nodded. Then she said softly, "What is the closest town?"

"Belfort," the boy whispered.

Lily looked at me. "Can you write him a way to Belfort?"

I stared at her. "I can't wipe his memory. He'll be able to tell them. They'll know."

"He's a boy," snapped Lily. "He has a mother."

"He's a *Nazi*," said Topher in disbelief.

"He is a boy," said Lily again, looking at the boy on the ground. "He's just a boy."

"He might not survive," I murmured. "Stomach wound."

"Can you write him a way to Belfort?" she asked again.

Silence ticked by in the next few seconds, and I turned over my options in my head. I didn't want to save a Nazi. I didn't want any part in saving any Nazi of any age. But he couldn't have been more than eighteen, and he looked so vulnerable there, surrounded by us as he tried to stop his own bleeding.

I swore softly. "I'll write it somewhere he can't see. You stop his bleeding though. I'm not wasting a balloon on a dead boy. Topher, find me the coordinates for Belfort."

Lily gave him her map and began to use our precious first aid supplies on a Nazi. I returned to Max and sat down next to him. His eyes still looked unfocused, and he held his head between both hands as if to steady himself, or hold it up.

"Dey dead?" he asked, his voice still low and slurred.

"Not all of them," I said grimly, unpacking my back for my balloon supplies.

He scowled. "Make dem dead."

"Not my call," I said, rolling up my sleeve and slipping a needle into my arm. I'd need blood for our balloons too. Might as well write them all at the same time. I drew enough blood for five balloons and laid them out. Topher pointed out Belfort on the map and read off the coordinates to me, as I carefully, painstakingly wrote with a small paintbrush the bloody equations to take the Nazi boy home to his mother.

"Waste your bloo'," said Max, closing his eyes and leaning back against the tree. "Turn off. Hurts."

"It's the sun," said Topher. "I can't turn it off. Sorry, mate."

I looked up in time to catch Max's grimace. "We could give you some morphine."

He thought about it for a minute, then started to shake his head. He winced, took a rattling breath, and then said quietly, "No."

"Don't give him morphine," Topher said. "Morphine thins the

blood, doesn't it? If he has a bleed on his brain, can't thin the blood more. That'll make it worse."

"What do you want me to do?" I asked Max. I looked at Topher. "What can we do? We can't exactly take him to a doctor."

Topher looked grim. "I don't know. He really shouldn't move. That's all I know. But it's not like we can't move him."

"Close your eyes," I told Max.

He closed his eyes, murmuring again. "Hurts."

"I know," I said. I capped the needle-brush and checked the equation, trying not to be furious that I was saving a Nazi when I could be figuring out how to get Max out of here. When I inflated the balloon, I tied a string to it and walked it back to Lily and the boy.

"Here," I said. "Don't let go. It'll take you to the center of town before it touches down. If you let go, you'll fall and it'll keep going."

Lily translated for me, and the boy stared, puzzled, but reached out, wrapping his hand around the string. He began to rise into the air, and at first, he panicked, kicking his feet, but his free arm came around his stomach, and he grimaced, hanging on with one hand. The balloon lifted him, and slowly he disappeared free of the trees.

Lily looked at the other man she'd wounded. I said bitterly, "Do you want a balloon for him too?"

"No," she said, and I was shocked by the coldness in her voice. "He's in command of this unit. See the decorations on his shoulders and the pins? He can drown in his own blood."

"They're both Nazis," I said, looking over the pins and medals. *Lannon*, read a small black label on the man's uniform. Commander Lannon. Private Kurt whatever his last name had been. To me, they were the same. People who chose to do evil and to dedicate their lives to die for their evil cause. And for all I cared, they could both die.

Lily looked at me. "One was a foolish boy. There's hope for him. He doesn't know any different. That man believes in the cause."

I shook my head. "You don't know that."

She looked up at the sky. "You wouldn't have sent him home."

I watched her face, trying to decide if there was a wrong answer. "No, I wouldn't have."

"I don't know what's right," she said after a pause, her face still upturned into the early-morning light. "But I'll sleep at night."

Then she turned and fired a single shot into the commanding officer's head. His groans stopped, his body fell limp, and she strode away. I followed her back to Topher and Max sitting at the base of the tree with the balloons.

I sat between them, brushing my hand over Max's shoulder. He didn't look up at me but made a soft noise that made me want to curl up against him, close my eyes, and forget the sound of bullets and screams.

"You're hurt," he muttered, making a full sentence for the first time.

"I'm fine," I told him. "Stop worrying about me. We have a bigger problem. I don't know how to make the balloons invisible yet, so there's a high possibility we'll be shot at if we use them by day. The plan was to travel only at night."

"We don't have a choice right now," said Lily.

"This doesn't sound safe. There's got to be another option," Topher said.

"Please share anything that comes to mind," I snapped, finding my little kit with syringes.

"Enough, Wolf. Nothing's safe, MacKenzie," Lily said sharply. "This is what we're using. We can consider alternatives when we're out of a valley full of dead Nazis."

I blew up a balloon and tied the white string around the opening, letting it run out a certain length before I cut it with a knife. "They're all set for our first rendezvous point. We'll check in there, regroup, and then use the cover of night to attack our first site."

Lily glanced at Max who was pale again, head lolled to the side. "How—?"

"I got it," I said sharply.

She held my gaze. "This isn't our mission, Klein. Don't put it at risk."

"This one is on me," I told her, not looking away. "I'll own it. And I'm not going to let it affect the mission."

"You sure?" she asked. When I nodded, she relaxed a fraction. I handed her the first balloon. She shouldered her pack and wrapped her hand around the string. "Fine. See you there."

She started to rise as I began to blow up the next balloon. Topher watched her, his face inscrutable. I tied off his balloon and held it in front of him. "Just like we said in training. Don't let go. Have your gun out, and fire back at anyone who shoots at you."

Topher nodded, tightening the straps of his pack. He took the balloon and rose slowly, his feet steadier than the boy we'd sent to Belfort. I watched him for a few more seconds than I'd watched Lily, but he seemed to be one of those people who took strangeness in stride. He didn't panic, so I went back to the balloons for Max and myself. I blew up both balloons and tied them together with one string. I looped them around a tree branch to hold them for a few minutes while I finished preparation. I took extra string and tied the straps of his pack to the straps of mine. I didn't tie us face-to-face—we'd be in the air for hours, and that seemed uncomfortable—but when I shouldered my pack and stood, it pulled Max to his feet too.

"Just leave me," he mumbled.

"Like hell," I snapped.

"Slow you down," he said, his voice rising, and I felt his hands fumbling at the knots.

I smacked his hand down, sidearm in my grip. "Stop it, Max. Did you ask to be our pilot?"

Silence.

"Did you ask to be our pilot?" I said louder.

"Yes," he murmured.

The forest was silent, breathing with us. Pine trees and shrub bushes around us, reaching toward a cloudy sky, sunlight sliding through tree trunks, warm and bright. If I stepped back, I wouldn't have thought we were in enemy territory. Too peaceful. Too serene.

"Did you ask to be our pilot because of me?" I asked him, even though I knew the answer.

"Yes," he grunted.

"Then I'm going to make sure you get home safe," I said, ferocious and furious. "Don't you try to talk me out of it."

He was quiet, so I untangled the balloon strings and we began to rise.

CHAPTER TWENTY-THREE

ILSE

At dawn, I slipped out of bed early, stuck my feet into my boots by the door, and shuffled out onto the porch. I knew that he wouldn't write back right away. He wouldn't even have my letter by now. But I couldn't help but scan the skies for his reply anyway. The dim light on the horizon didn't silhouette a balloon, and the air seemed unnaturally quiet.

I closed my eyes and whispered a quick prayer for my brother's safety.

I didn't pray often, but it was the end of the Jewish year, and Mama and Papa didn't know their son was missing, and I was the reason Wolf was overseas, and my brother was missing.

He'd been missing for two days now. I'd spent most of yesterday expecting Colonel Mann to find me, tell me they'd found Wolf, he was fine, it was someone else's plane that had gone down. But the sun had set and risen crisp and bright against the dew, the new year had begun, and my brother was still missing.

If the balloon found him, if the balloon found him, if the balloon found him, the letter contained the invisibility equations. The balloon had to find him. It would find him, wouldn't it?

Behind me, the screen door opened with a creak and slammed shut, making me jump. Polly settled on the porch railing next to me, a warm presence that made me blush before I even looked at her. We stood there for a while, looking down our street of cemesto houses toward Happy Valley where all the prefab houses were. Where Stella lived. It wasn't right that she lived down there, even though she was doing the same work as we were. I scowled.

Polly slid a cup of coffee in front of me. "Stop scowling. It's too early for one of your moods."

I didn't think my moods were that wild, so the comment stung a little, needling under my skin and drawing my blood to the surface. I closed my eyes and raised the mug to my mouth. Black, sharp, acidic. The way I liked my coffee. She added so much sugar in her own coffee that just thinking about it gave me a toothache.

"You're up early," she said.

I looked up at the sky and the early-morning light, at the balloon that didn't exist. I practiced the words in my mind before I spoke them aloud. But instead I said, "I couldn't sleep."

I didn't want to lie. It hurt, like a small, sharp pain in my heart. It wasn't any different than my inability to tell them what our magic would deliver, what they were building in the reactor next to our laboratory. It was a lie of omission, rather than a lie of falsehood or duplicity.

Polly leaned into my shoulder a little, her arm warm against mine. "Why not?"

My brother is missing.

I tucked my hair behind my ear, frowning out at the road as the first bus of the morning rumbled past us. "I..."

"You can tell me anything," Polly said. "You know that, right?"

But I couldn't. I couldn't tell her what we were building, or what Hitler was building, or where my brother was, or what his mission was. I wrapped my arms around myself and lied. "Yes."

"I don't know how you expect us to trust you, Ilse, when you can't even trust us," Polly said, her voice sharpening slightly.

"That's not fair," I protested. "This place *runs* on secrets, Polly. You know that."

"Some of us are sick of secrets," she said, her voice rising. "Secrets are toxic, Ilse. They'll eat you hollow. I don't know how you haven't seen that yet."

She spun on her heel and stomped back inside. The door slamming made me jump again, spilling hot coffee onto my skin. I hissed, rocking back in the wake of her disappearance.

Polly might as well have slapped me across the face. And here I'd been the one accused of having wild moods! I swallowed the last of the coffee and left the mug on the railing. I needed to get away.

Mama would have made me wear a coat, and maybe a scarf. Tennessee was cold in the early mornings, far earlier in the fall than I'd anticipated, but I didn't feel the chill as I walked down the road on the wooden planks to avoid the mud. I wandered into town, past the library, past the post office, smiling when people greeted me out of sheer survival instinct. Here, people would report you for not saying hello cheerfully one day. Disengagement could be a sign of a spy, after all. I supposed I hadn't given it much thought before.

But this morning, I felt paranoid. There was a spy, and my brother was missing. Were these things connected? Someone had stolen my papers, which had included draft letters to Wolf. I'd put my brother in a war zone. Had I accidentally given away his mission to someone who wanted to cause him harm? Was there a Nazi among us? Worse than a *spy* would be a *Nazi spy*.

I swallowed back my panic and spinning thoughts, and began to make my way across the valley toward the laboratory. Working would soothe my mind. That was what I needed: pure and simple math, a problem to solve, equations, a piece of chalk in my hand, magic in my blood. No matter what, I'd always have magic and science and my mind. No one could take those things away from me.

The laboratory was miles from our house. And it was cold, and damp, and my legs ached, but I kept walking. My brother was dead, or missing, or in a concentration camp, and it was my fault. I swallowed hard, my arms tight around my body, and kept walking. Even when I heard the low rumble of a car behind me on the road and the crunch of tires against cold gravel, I kept walking. One foot in front of the other.

"Miss Klein," said Colonel Mann from the car that pulled up slowly and cautiously beside me. "Ilse."

"I'm going to work," I said stubbornly.

The colonel said simply, "The Jewish congregation has the church this morning. Maybe it'll be helpful to be among your people today."

I didn't tell him that he was right because I thought I'd cry if I opened my mouth again. Instead, I simply climbed into the back seat of the car.

The new Church on the Hill was all white, with a slate-gray roof and a bell tower, and I hadn't been inside yet though it was all I heard about at the grocery store. They'd only dedicated it the week before, and it still smelled like fresh paint and sawdust inside.

A man wearing a kippah was standing at the door greeting people, and when I saw him in his black suit and white pressed shirt, I couldn't hold back the tears any longer. Colonel Mann's hand came down on my shoulder, and he said quietly to the man, "This young lady has heard some bad news about her brother in Europe. I thought she might find this useful."

"*Baruch HaShem*," said the man, his voice soft. "My name is Captain Walch. *Shana tova u'metukah*."

"*Shana tova*," I murmured back.

Colonel Mann turned his back to the man but didn't leave me right away. He looked out the doors at the warm morning and the mud and the reactors and the promise of what we hoped was coming.

I watched this play out on his face, because I wasn't ready to look at it myself. "I'm not a churchgoing man, Ilse. I don't know if I believe in God. But I do believe in keeping the faith, and all of the meanings in that phrase."

I swallowed hard. "Thank you."

And I was grateful. So grateful. Grateful that he had hope. Grateful that he'd come looking for me. Grateful that he brought me here, as if he knew I lacked hope and faith right now. As if he knew I was adrift.

He nodded and left me standing in the entryway, with Captain Walch smiling at me. It was a kind smile, one that reminded me of home. And as I started to walk through the doors, I found I wanted to be there. I wanted to be reminded of home, of something stable, something predictable, something that was reassuring.

I was one of only a few women there, but no one seemed put off by my presence or casual attire. I took a seat in one of the empty pews, picking up the prayer book. It was old but familiar.

"Welcome, everyone," said Captain Walch, walking to the front of the church. "This is our inaugural service in this new place of worship. Isn't it beautiful?"

We murmured our appreciation. I knotted my fingers on my lap. I'd never sat alone in a pew before now.

"It seems right," continued the captain, "that we begin our first service here on Rosh Hashanah. A new year. A celebration. The beginning of the Days of Awe when we reflect back on our year and pray to be inscribed in the Book of Life."

At home, when we went to synagogue, Wolf would sit next to me, flipping through the Tanakh, way ahead of the *parashat* of the week, and I loved to read the stories he found over his shoulder. His finger would run over the Hebrew, but my eyes read the English. Sometimes the stories he chose to stop and read seemed like clues to what he was thinking or feeling, but I never quite got close enough to unlocking the meaning.

I liked making my voice match his, singing harmonies together, elbowing each other during Yom Kippur services, jostling each other to touch the prayer book to the Torah as it was walked around and then kissing the spines of the books reverently. Once, I'd asked Wolf why we kissed the prayer books, why we kissed the Torah, why we touched the mezuzahs in the doorways of our house.

He'd said it was a way of reminding us of the true north of our faith.

I believed in God, but I didn't believe that God would interfere in our lives. We were on our own down here. But I wanted to believe that the stories Wolf read, the faith Wolf kept, the words he said every week were a true north for him, wherever he was.

In a way, my brother's faith was my true north. Sitting alone in the pew brought tears to my eyes, and I looked straight up at the ceiling, trying to make them disappear. It wasn't right to be here without him. Without knowing if he was alive or dead. Was it appropriate for me to rise for the Mourner's Kaddish? Or was that bad luck for Wolf? I wished I'd asked the captain before we began.

"I know that isn't the space we would have imagined for ourselves," Captain Walch said quietly, capturing my attention again. "And I know that as Jews, especially with the hatred and the violence and the death of our people, and our relatives in Europe, carving out a space of our own feels especially important right now. But this is our space. Wherever we as Jews are, that space is ours. Wherever we come together as Jews to affirm our Judaism, that space is our space. We," he said, his voice growing more powerful, "are a people who survives. We are here. We are alive. We are resilient. We are resourceful. We are empathetic. We are grieving. And we are hopeful."

My eyes fell from the ceiling to Captain Walch. I took a deep breath, and then another. His eyes flickered only briefly to me, no more than the time he spent looking at any of the others. I wasn't the only one here who might lose someone, who had already lost someone, who wasn't sure what she was doing or where this world was going.

I wasn't alone. I'd thought I was, but I wasn't. I never was.

He picked up a prayer book from the altar and said, "Let us begin."

And when his voice rose for the first prayer, mine joined in, unsure, but trusting.

I am here. I am alive. I am resilient. I am resourceful. I am empathetic. I am grieving. And I am hopeful.

CHAPTER TWENTY-FOUR

WOLF

Lily walked through the abandoned farmhouse again, suspicious. But the house was as empty as we'd found it. Topher, who had spotted it as he floated to our rendezvous spot and led us here on foot, called it *serendipitous*. Lily had said that serendipity was a trap. Her lips were pressed into a thin line. Whatever she suspected would be here, she hadn't found it yet. I was too tired and sore from the crash and the firefight and the floating to say anything.

We'd traveled to the first of four sites, and it'd been gone. Empty. Abandoned. Either the Germans knew we were coming, or the intelligence had been bad. I didn't think that was helping Lily's suspicions about the house near Haigerloch, the second site.

I tilted a tin filled with water from the tap to Max's lips. Some dribbled onto his tongue. Most dribbled out the corner of his mouth and rolled down his roughened chin. I'd never seen him anything but clean-shaven. I had to resist the urge to run my palm over the texture, to marvel at it and how it aged him.

I didn't touch him casually though, and not just because Topher was next to us, looking tired and stressed. Something about traveling by balloon had made Max's disorientation, speech, and thought patterns worse. He hadn't said a word since we got there, and he didn't seem to recognize me entirely. Topher thought it was the pressure change. Lily hadn't said anything, but she seemed increasingly worried every time she looked at us.

Not Max alone, but us, together.

I was trying not to think about it.

"Feels wrong," Lily muttered.

"Whoever owned it is long gone," Topher suggested. The agitation he'd shown in the woods had dissipated. He glanced at me. "Maybe they were Jewish. Does it matter?"

"It isn't dusty," Lily said.

I looked up, spilling water onto Max's lap. She was right. The house was clean, organized. Whoever left hadn't left too long ago, and there were no nail holes on the doorways of the rooms where mezuzahs would have gone. Whoever had lived here before and fled, they hadn't been Jewish.

"We should go soon," said Topher, eyeing the setting sun.

"Not yet," said Lily. "I'm trying to decide if they know we're here. If we're walking into a trap."

"Technically," I said in the silence that came after, "we'll be floating into a trap."

The corner of Lily's mouth turned up. "God. You're the worst, Wolf Klein. Fine. Let's go. Write us balloons to the lab outside Haigerloch."

I pulled out the map and spread it out on the table, finding Haigerloch to the north and east of our present location. "Yes, ma'am."

"I like the sound of that," Lily said. "Topher, take a cat nap. I'll take watch. We're going to need you to be sharp."

* * *

We landed in Haigerloch just after sunset, a dim sliver of light blue and orange mixing on the horizon. Darkness cloaked the houses around us, and we crept through the alleys and streets, avoiding anywhere we could be caught by headlights on passing trucks. Curfew was in full effect, and few people dotted the streets. Blackout curtains lined the windows, and not one streetlamp was lit.

I exhaled into the night, watching my breath puff up in front of me. Topher's face, caught in a line of light from a door that opened and shut quickly to throw ashes out, was pale and clammy. I understood the feeling. We couldn't afford to mess this one up. If we did, the Germans would move the prototype reactor to some other location, build it somewhere else, and take the science with them. It would take months, precious time in this war, for the intelligence services to find where they'd gone next.

And I sure as heck didn't want to come back here. I wanted to blow some stuff up and get the hell home. Or at least back to the farmhouse where we'd left Max.

We couldn't screw this up. I had to get home.

Lily consulted our map, and we followed her through the dark along the small river that wound its way around the edge of the town. The sound of the water made me thirsty and reminded me it'd been days since I'd showered, and would be days more until I could shower. I blocked the sound of running water from my mind and kept alert, scanning windows and doors, homes, alleys and the streets, looking for anyone who might be reporting us, following us, or looking too closely.

What I'd do if I noticed someone doing those things, I didn't know.

But I'd cross that bridge when I came to it, I supposed.

Dear Max, you didn't miss much. Just an elevated heart rate and the persistent fear that if a door slammed too loudly, you might piss your pants.

Lily looked down at her map, clicking on her flashlight briefly and then clicking it off, stopping in her tracks. "That can't be right."

Topher and I stopped too, looking at the white stone palace with her. It was a palace, or a church, or a church for a palace, three stories high with a bell tower and a wrought-iron fence around it. Whatever it was, and whoever lived there, didn't really matter. It didn't look like it contained a reactor. From everything Ilse had told me about reactors and nuclear fission, they'd need a substantial amount of space.

"Give me the map," I said.

"I assure you I'm reading it correctly," Lily said dryly, handing over the map.

I looked at it, tracing our route and coming to a stop, looking up at the palace. "I don't get it."

"Me neither," murmured Lily. "I was expecting a warehouse."

"You don't need that much space. Not for a prototype reactor," said Topher.

My head snapped toward him. "How'd you know what we were blowing up?"

He shrugged. "Easy to figure out. There were all sorts of warnings about how far away we ought to be at the time of blasts, so it had to be something radioactive."

I hadn't even known what radioactive was prior to Ilse explaining the bomb project to me, but Lily had said Topher had been around once or twice. Maybe he'd been working on sabotaging the German bomb for longer than me. Lily was still watching Topher, her unguarded expression playing out confusion and surprise like a film reel.

Topher began walking down the street winding around the palace. "You don't need much space for this equipment. It could be in a coat closet, for all we know."

"How are we supposed to find a coat closet?" I asked Lily.

He snorted. "It was an example." He wandered down the street, looking around at our surroundings. "All we need is somewhere safe, underground, where it wouldn't be easily bombed…Ah. The beer cellar."

"You think they put a *nuclear reactor* in a *beer cellar*?" hissed Lily.

"I agree," Topher said genially. "This seems a little *excessively* German."

"Now what?" I asked.

"We blow it up," muttered Lily, stalking toward the door and fiddling with something in her pack. Silver glinted in her hands as she bent over the lock, carefully sliding two thin bars into it.

"You don't know what's on the other side of that door," whispered Topher.

"Whatever it is, I'm shooting it." Lily grimaced as she turned the pick ever so slightly to the left and slid a second small piece of metal into the lock. Her eyes closed, her mouth parted in concentration.

"Don't shoot it first," Topher muttered. "They can tell us where they keep everything important."

"We find what we can and blow up the rest," said Lily tersely.

"How do we know what to find if you shoot the first person you see?" hissed Topher.

Lily froze, and I tensed for a brief moment, expecting her to whirl on Topher, when she whispered, "I got it."

She slipped her lockpicks back into her pocket, holding the door with one hand and pulling out her gun with the other. She lifted the pistol in front of her, steady and confident, a breeze out on the ocean that knew the waves would bend to her will. For a split second, I had a vision, a waking nightmare, of her flying backward with the force of being shot. Someone's inside that door, I thought, and I started to step forward. *Don't go first. We need you.* But we needed all of us.

Lily turned the handle. In a soft breath, she said, "Ready?"

She didn't wait for us to answer. She opened the door, and we stepped into the dark.

CHAPTER TWENTY-FIVE

WOLF

Topher's flashlight beam bounced around on the walls of the beer cellar, catching piles of paper, a tank of water, and strings with gray cubes hanging from the ceiling. The light caught the back of Lily's head and glinted off the gun in front of her, confident and sure as we moved through the space.

"No guards," I said to Lily. What I didn't say was *Did they know we were coming?* And the light splashed across her face just in time for me to get a clear view of her sidelong, knowing glance at me. That was exactly what she was thinking. We edged around the darkness but stayed close to the door. The last thing I wanted was to get pinned down inside a nuclear reactor with bullets flying. I didn't know much about science, but none of that sounded like a good time to me.

"Blow it up and get out," Lily murmured, half to me, half to herself. "You have our return balloons ready?"

I recognized her nerves. She didn't want to find any papers. She didn't care about Hitler's bomb, as long as we stopped it. She wasn't following our instructions, but my job was to follow Lily's.

"Just need to inflate and tie off," I said quietly. And then, perhaps stupidly, I added, "I feel bad blowing up a palace."

The look Lily gave me was withering. "Figure out where to stuff those feelings, Sunshine, so they stop showing up at the most inopportune times. Topher, find a good place to set up the explosives, and let's get the hell out of here. It shouldn't have been empty."

"What the hell?" murmured Topher, staring at the water tank and the cubes hanging on strings from a metal device.

"We're not here to make friends or go to school," Lily said coolly.

"Shouldn't we—" Topher began again.

"No," Lily said at the same time that I muttered, "For God's sake, Topher, listen to the lady."

"Don't call me a lady," Lily said, and I could feel the weight of her glare on me. "Just do what I say."

There was a pause, and then Topher and his flashlight bounced away from us, leaving Lily and me by the entrance, encased in darkness. Her elbow bumped into mine as she moved toward the doorway.

"We have time to look for the papers and notes," I told her.

"We don't have any time. We lost two days in the woods. We have to hit all three sites before the Nazis realize what's happening and move them again."

"Maybe it's quiet here because they don't think anyone is going to look here. It is a beer cellar, after all." I tried to reassure her the same way I reassured Ilse. Repeating facts as if they weren't insurmountable obstacles. "We blow this up, and then blow up Hechingen, then Oranienburg, and we're out."

She snorted softly in the dark. "It won't go that smoothly. Once this blows, we'll need to get in and out of Hechingen as fast as we can, and the same with Oranienburg. Intel says the Germans can't move a site in less than a week. They can't evacuate everything for Oranienburg, but they'll get the uranium out of there at least, unless we get to it first."

"Should we go there first?" I asked.

She shook her head. "Hechingen is higher priority. More scientists there."

"I know," she said after a beat. "I know this is a lot, Wolf. I know you're worried about Max. But in a week, we'll plan our way out. Just follow me."

My throat tightened and I nodded, but she couldn't see me in the dark. We stood there in silence for a few more heartbeats, me considering Lily's complicated version of empathy, and her contemplating who knows what.

Abruptly, she took a deep breath and said, "Will you go see what's taking Boy Wonder so long to blow some Nazi shit up?"

I didn't argue, even if she was just sending me because she wanted space. I walked back into the darkness, gun raised cautiously as I followed the bouncing beam of Topher's light through the room. He was bent over a desk, running wires to a pack of TNT and sharpening a fuse with the edge of his knife.

"Lily wants you to hurry up," I said, careful to keep my voice down. It echoed anyway through the cavern. "You don't need to be fancy. You just need to damage it enough so they can't use it."

"The thing about explosives," Topher said, bent over the device, "is you only get one chance to be sloppy. You know why?"

"No, why?"

"Because you die," Topher said. "If you're sloppy, you die. If your fuse isn't long enough, if you don't set up everything to give yourself enough time to get out, then you die. Hold my flashlight."

I held it over him, so he could use both hands to attach a small metal wire to the edge of the TNT. I moved the light out of the way of his hands so he could still see as he worked, and the edge of the beam caught on his pack sitting next to the table, a roll of papers sticking out of it.

He caught my eye briefly, his hands pausing. "One of us has to see the bigger picture."

I said nothing because he turned back to the explosives and his face turned into the picture of concentration. I'd ask him later, somewhere when he wasn't bent over a bomb he'd built and where Lily couldn't hear us. I didn't think she'd take lightly to being disobeyed, even if he was sticking to the mission. It'd delayed us unnecessarily.

His hands lifted free of the bomb. "Okay. Go."

"Now?"

"If I meant later, I would have said, 'Go at your own damn pace,' but I didn't, did I?" he snapped. "Go, let's go."

He grabbed the flashlight out of my hand and gestured for me to walk in front of him. The beam disappeared and appeared, making walking through the dark beer cellar a bizarre experience, like falling through the sky while being shot at, and my palms were clammy by the time we reached Lily. Behind me, Topher ran out a spool to the door where he bent down, cut it, and pressed it into the hinge of the door.

"Ready?" Lily asked me.

I nodded, my hand finding the balloons stuffed into my coat pocket. "Run and then jump?"

She nodded. "Lead the way. Light it up, Topher."

Topher struck a match, and the fuse caught. As soon as I saw the spark, I started to run, Lily hot on my heels, and after a few steps, I heard Topher's footsteps catch up with ours.

"*Halt!*" someone yelled in German.

"Do not stop," Lily panted next to me.

"Wasn't planning on it," I said.

A shot rang out, missing us wildly, and Topher appeared. He'd clicked off his flashlight, but I saw the flash of white as he grinned, holding up his stopwatch. *Countdown.*

Five.

Four.

Three.

We all sucked in a breath.

Two.

The wake of the explosion shot us off our feet, and we all hit the ground, rolling onto our packs. I inhaled dust and rocked, coughing and sputtering as I got onto my hands and knees, trying to make the world stop spinning and level out again.

Lily swore so colorfully that I started to laugh before I'd fully cleared my lungs of the road dust, and I fell back onto my back, coughing and laughing at the same time. If someone had told me six months ago that I'd be in Germany sabotaging Nazi science projects, I would have laughed at them. But I'd never been as dirty, gloriously happy, and determinedly hopeful as I was now.

"Let's do that again," I said to the sky.

"That's the plan," said Topher, cackling.

Lily sat up, brushing off her face and glaring at Topher. "Did you waste all of our explosives on that?"

"No, I just put it against the base of the wall, so it'd collapse. Two birds, one pack of TNT," Topher said, getting to his feet and offering her a hand. "They shouldn't have built it into bedrock. Though, I admit that was a particularly satisfactory explosion."

Lily accepted his hand, and I climbed to my feet too, brushing myself off. I pulled out the three balloons. "Let's get out of here."

I inflated the balloons, tied them off, and tied on the strings. I handed them out, and the balloons began to float, taking Topher and Lily away from the scene of the crime. In the distance, I could hear trucks starting up. We didn't have much time, but chances were that the Germans wouldn't know to look *up* for escapees. They'd keep their eyes on the road.

No one expected magic, sure, but they particularly didn't expect levitation or floating—I saw the genius in it now. And I'd never been more grateful for that than just then, clearing the tree line by the time a truck reached the spot where our tracks stopped. I watched, floating up, as the Nazis got out of their trucks, shining flashlights on the road, pointing at our tracks, and then began to comb the woods and sides of the road in the high grass. None of them saw the three red balloons taking us back to the farmhouse.

Just before sunrise, we landed north of the farmhouse, so no one would connect us to it, and the balloons disappeared. I rolled my shoulders and neck, stiff from traveling, and Lily yawned, covering her mouth.

"A bath," Topher said sleepily. "I'm taking a bath."

"It'll be cold," I said, remembering the tap water I'd given Max.

"Don't care," said Topher. "There are worse things than cold water."

"Are there?" I joked.

He didn't laugh.

"I'm sleeping," Lily murmured, walking with her eyes half closed as it was.

"I'll take first watch," I offered.

"Thanks, Sunshine," said Lily, bumping her shoulder into me and giving me a small smile. She must have known that all I wanted was to see how Max was doing. And I didn't know why, but I was glad she didn't say anything in front of Topher.

A balloon floated down out of the sky, and Topher was the first to point it out. I caught it as it drifted in front of me and untangled the letter from the string. The balloon dissolved, and I unfolded Ilse's letter, tucking the parcel beneath my arm.

A lump formed in my throat. "They've reported that we're dead."

I hadn't thought of that. My parents. Ilse. They thought I was dead because all the army knew was that I'd been shot out of the air.

"Reply immediately," Lily said. "That's the best we can do. What else?"

I held up the package. "Rat poison. To keep blood from clotting. Smart. And more balloons."

"She wouldn't have sent that if she had given up," Lily reassured me.

I nodded, taking a deep breath. I stuffed the rat poison, the balloons, and the letter into my pack. "I know. I know. I need to reply to this."

We paused so I could finish writing a letter to Ilse, and then I sent it off at sunrise. Lily proofread it for me and added her own questions, and Topher made sure I thanked her for the rat-poison idea.

"Creepy, but genius," he said appreciatively.

The balloon rose slowly into the hazy dawn light, and Lily nudged me. "Let's go."

We stumbled downhill in the rising sun, and as we turned around the old forest path and the farmhouse came into sight, Lily came to a stop. I blinked, frowning at her and the wide-eyed look on her face as she stared down the hill. Then I turned to see what she saw.

Nazi trucks, six of them, around the farmhouse, and soldiers milling everywhere. And then, while we watched, the door banged open and a Nazi shoved Max out of the house. Max staggered down the steps, his gait uneven, hands up over his head. The Nazi slammed the butt of his rifle between Max's shoulder blades, and Max crumpled to the ground.

I didn't think. I didn't say anything. I didn't shout his name. I just started to run. As fast as I could, as hard as I could, flying down the hill toward him, toward the dozens of Nazis standing around him, around Max, around *my* Max. One of the Nazis saw me approaching and raised his rifle.

I didn't stop running.

I saw him lift it to his eye.

I didn't stop running.

Max.

He lifted his head, and our eyes met across the field.

Don't, he mouthed.

Tough luck, I thought. I'm not leaving you behind.

Crack! Something jerked me sideways and I twisted, slamming into the ground. I gasped, kicking at the ground and trying to get my feet underneath me.

Max. Get up. You have to get to Max.

I rolled over, sky becoming grass becoming sky becoming grass, and a horizon reappeared. I staggered up, and out of the corner of my eye, I saw another person racing down from the woods, dark hair like a streak of midnight behind her. *Lily. Don't.* But I didn't have time to tell her that, didn't have time to wave her off, didn't have time to say anything to her.

I stumbled two steps, and then an order in German was shouted close to me.

Max. I have to get to Max.

A hand shoved me to my knees, and then flat on my face. Shouts and yelling of German in my ear, words I didn't know and couldn't translate right now. I struggled, and then the cool butt of a gun settled at the base of my neck. I sucked in a breath as someone tied my wrists together, sending pain lancing through my injured side, and hauled me to my feet.

Lily had her hands up, eyes wide, chattering in German as she knelt for the Nazis who approached her, guns raised. They didn't shoot her, but they tied her hands and hauled her to her feet too.

I'd gotten us both caught.

And almost definitely killed.

I lifted my head, tasting blood in my mouth. *Max.* Our eyes met again, and my knees buckled in relief. The corner of his mouth tilted up, and I could almost hear him saying, *You idiot. What the hell did you do this time?* But he was alive, and I was alive, and Lily was alive, and as long as we were all alive, there was a chance. A commander shouted at us and spat in our faces, but the three of us said nothing. We were hauled to one of the Nazi trucks and thrown unceremoniously into the back. I nearly bit through my tongue trying not to scream from pain.

The door slammed shut, and Lily sighed. "Nice job, Wolf."

"Woof," murmured Max, shifting and bending down, his breath soft on my forehead. I closed my eyes, feeling tears on my cheek, running through the blood and the dust. I turned my head slightly, pressing my face against his leg. He scooted closer, letting me curl between his legs. The blood from my shoulder soaked through my shirt and jacket, sticking to my skin. My mouth tasted like copper.

"Where's Topher?" I managed to say through the pain.

"Not here," Lily said. "Hopefully, he's smart enough to figure out where they're taking us."

Max isn't our mission, I remembered her telling me when we'd parachuted from the burning plane. I closed my eyes against the smell of blood. I'd made him our mission now. My mind reached for a thought, for a hope and an experiment, but the pain made my mind fuzz. Radio static filled my ears, and I concentrated on breathing slowly and carefully. We'd been captured by Nazis. Max had a head injury, Lily was a Jewish woman, and I was a Jewish man, and none of us were German. Every possibility I could think of ended with our deaths. Anonymous. Unknown. Unclaimed. Unsaved. Tortured.

At least we blew up the reactor, I thought numbly. I hadn't gotten a letter to Colonel Mann's contact in England. I could only hope Ilse would get my balloon and share it with the colonel.

We would fail. We wouldn't get to Hechingen or Oranienburg. We wouldn't finish the mission. The Germans could still get the bomb before the Allies did. How did this end? What world would come after this one?

"I'm sorry," I said to both of them. To myself, maybe.

The trucks started up, and Lily said quietly, "We know. We all made our choices, Wolf. Don't apologize for the ones you've made. You have a good heart."

But a good heart wouldn't keep me, or the people I loved, alive.

CHAPTER TWENTY-SIX

OAK RIDGE, TENNESSEE
OCTOBER 2, 1943

ILSE

I walked home from the lab after a long day, keeping my eyes on my feet and relishing the exhaustion in my body because it meant I was alive. Alive and hopeful and grateful and *here*. I kept humming prayers to myself. I looked briefly up at the sky, squinting for a balloon that wouldn't be there. Not yet. Not for days. I wouldn't know for days.

Hope, I reminded myself. *Have a little faith*, Colonel Mann had said. I would try. I owed Wolf at least that. My faith, my hope.

As I went up the hill, and houses appeared from the mud and the hillsides, my thoughts moved toward the other girls. I needed to tell them that Wolf was missing. I needed to tell Stella and Lola about the spy, if Polly hadn't already. She wouldn't, I reassured myself. Polly knew how to keep secrets. I could tell.

My fingers ran over my lips, curious. Wanting.

Everything in my life was provable by science.

And some part of me knew that attraction was chemical. That there was a *science* to attraction. One that I could study and quantify, if I wanted. But my blood was full of inexplicable magic, and when I thought about kissing Polly, it *sang* and I'd never felt something so magical in my entire life.

But that wasn't the kind of magic I needed right now. I needed the kind that could find a spy, and save my brother, and end this war.

I wanted answers, but I needed to pick my battles.

Spy. Brother. War. Kissing.

In my mind, Wolf whispered, *Good to see you've got your priorities straight, Ilse.*

My heart twisted painfully tight as I unlocked our front door and stepped into the house. The house smelled like the lemon cleaner Lola liked to use. I walked through the living room, running my fingers over the back of the sofa, the rocking chair by the fireplace we hadn't used yet—I wasn't sure I'd trust us with a fireplace—the dining room table with two empty, unused candlesticks. Lola and Polly had bought them after our first week here. It occurred to me now that they might have bought them as Shabbat candlesticks for me.

I didn't appreciate the other girls enough. They were still at the lab right now, and I was here.

That didn't need to stop me from doing my job.

"You can do this, Ilse Klein," I told myself. Alone in the house, my voice echoed. It wavered, but I felt reassured, the same way the rabbi's words had reassured me and Colonel Mann's words had reassured me.

I found a notebook in my room, curled up on the sofa, and began to write. Slowly at first, and then quickly. I could feel that quickening inside me, the knowledge that I was close to a breakthrough, as if I could see all the pieces to the puzzle in my head. I just needed to figure out how to click them together.

Vaguely, I was aware the room was growing darker and voices were gathering. My mind registered snippets in the background.

"I just think we should call the colonel if she's not home by nine." Lola. Decisive.

"We should look for her before then." Stella. Firm.

"She seemed off this morning." Polly. Frightened.

"Then maybe we should—"

"Shhh." Stella interrupting Lola.

The room lightened again. Bodies brushed by me, but my mind was mostly in the work, the equations stretching out and bending around the corners of papers in front of me. They grew, infinite in their possibilities, finite only as a result of my cramping hand and the edges of papers.

I could win the war.

I could find the spy.

I could bring my brother home.

I could get the girl.

Something heavy settled around my shoulders and I blinked, realizing that my face was so close to my hand that my nose brushed my knuckles. I straightened, stretched, and bent back over the work.

Sometime later, I looked up, blinking at the brightness and fullness of the room.

"Hi," I said warily.

Polly gave me a weary smile. "She emerges. Welcome back."

I rubbed at my eyes with ink-stained fingers, likely leaving streaks on my face, and I didn't mind. "What time is it?"

"After nine," said Stella. "Your coffee's gone cold. So's your dinner."

"Coffee?" I echoed. There was a mug on my desk, plain and simple, the way I liked it. When I looked up again, Polly caught my eye, blushed, and looked away, biting her lower lip.

Well, I'd solved one part of the espionage crisis through trial and error. Surely figuring out how to kiss a girl couldn't be much harder.

"I think I figured out how to track the spy," I said.

"Tell us tomorrow? You must be exhausted. And starving. I'll reheat you something," said Lola.

I frowned. "No, I don't…I shouldn't talk about it here. Shouldn't have even been writing it here."

"Paranoid," said Lola.

"No, she's right," said Stella. "Polly told us about the spy. If someone else here does magic, and it isn't one of the four of us, then we ought to be careful. But Ilse, they stole papers from the lab. Not from here. Is there anywhere safer than your house right now?"

"Oh," I said in sudden surprise. "You're here. I'm glad."

Stella gave me a pained smile. "I am. This house is nice."

"No one will notice if you stay," I offered.

She reached over, squeezing my hand briefly. "You are sweet. But they will. Lola, heat her up some food."

"I'll be fine," I protested.

"No," Stella said firmly. "No, you won't. Lola's right. You look peaky. Polly, make a new pot of coffee? Ilse, show me what you have."

Unlike me, Lola and Polly didn't argue. They both stood up quickly and disappeared into the kitchen while I met Stella's eyes steadily. "Nothing leaves this room."

"Of course."

I slid the notebook across to her lap. "I think I can track my own blood."

"Well, that's not a line you hear often," Polly said from the kitchen.

"Ilse always has the best party lines," said Lola, and it wasn't an unkind comment. I smiled down at my hands in surprise.

Stella frowned at the notebook, turning the pages slowly back and forth as she followed my math all over the place—into every corner and down every margin. "So you're trying to use surface tension for blood molecules to find each other. Instead of hair."

"It's easier to hide blood. Do you think it'll work?" I asked. "You understand surface tension much better than I do."

We'd been trying to use surface tension to increase the carrying capacity of the balloon to no effect, but that hadn't meant Stella's science was wrong. It was just not the magic we needed to use at the time.

She rubbed her forehead with the back of her hand, studying the equation, and then smiled. "Okay. We can do this. The theory is good. Let's work on it."

Three cups of coffee and a plate of reheated beans and chicken later, we still hadn't gotten any farther than my theory about using surface tension to have blood molecules find each other again. The surface tension equation seemed to undo the previous operations in the magical equations, which defeated the entire purpose.

"We should go to sleep," I said tiredly.

"Good," said Lola, yawning. "It's nearly midnight."

"I've got it. Multiple equations," said Stella, sitting up a little straighter. She turned to me, gesticulating wildly with her hands, urging me to catch on. And I did, right on her heels.

"Layered on each other," I said. "Instead of one long equation acting at once, layered equations each enacting their will on the object."

"What order?" asked Stella, tearing out a fresh sheet of paper.

"I would imagine that'd depend on our goal," I said, leaning over her. "I'll write."

"My handwriting's better," said Stella.

"She's right," said Lola. "Polly, we're going to need more coffee."

"It's your turn to make it," said Polly, settling down on the floor between Stella and me, resting her arm on my chair. "I want to watch them work."

"Make it a big pot of coffee," I called to Lola over my shoulder. To Stella, I said, "You're a genius."

She smiled. "I know."

* * *

October 2, 1943

Dear Ilse,

Our plane did crash, but we all survived. Topher, Lily, me, and Max. Max was our pilot. I don't have much time—I'm writing this in the middle of a field right now after we blew up one of our targets—but I wanted to reassure you that we received your letter and we're all right. I'll write Hutchinson a balloon when we're back at the safe house.

Lily says thank you for your letter, your concern, and the supplies. And Topher thinks the rat poison is genius.

I'm sorry I caused you pain.

I promise I'm coming home. If I can survive being shot down, I can survive the rest of this.

Love,

Wolf

CHAPTER TWENTY-SEVEN

OAK RIDGE, TENNESSEE
OCTOBER 3, 1943

ILSE

We were so engrossed with the science that we didn't hear them coming. Stella was bent over a balloon, dipping her paintbrush in a dish of her own blood, and I paced between her and our equations on the blackboard.

"So it's the blood following the blood," I repeated.

"It's finding itself," Stella said, not raising her head, her handwriting careful and deliberate. "It's the same method you and Wolf are using for your balloons, but instead of hair, there's blood."

"And we're doing that first because that's the first act the balloon needs to take," I murmured, tapping the chalk against my lip. The mention of my brother only caused a light twinge in the back of my mind; I was too absorbed with the science to pay it much attention.

"Don't do that," Stella said without looking up.

"Calcium," I told her, but I took the chalk away from my mouth anyway.

The corner of her mouth twitched. "It's not. Stop."

A door slammed down the hallway, and I could hear footsteps, hurried and a little bit frantic. When we'd arrived this morning, after barely any sleep, the scientists in the labs next to us had been here, looking drawn and red-eyed, like they'd been here all night. It didn't bode well for whatever was happening at the reactor. We'd heard two alarms last night. No one other than Stella and me knew enough to be alarmed.

I said under my breath to Stella, "I want to ask them what's wrong."

"You can't. Besides, you're smart, but they're smart too, Ilse. They probably have it under control," Stella told me not unkindly.

"Right," I said with a deep breath. That wasn't my problem. *Spy. Bomb. Brother. Girl.* I could solve only what was in front of me. We'd put a piece of paper with Stella's blood down the hallway. We'd start testing short distances. I was anxious, not writing the equation on my own. "It'd be nice if we could figure out how to track *without* our own blood."

"Magic's governed by laws, just like science," Stella said calmly. "We work within them, exploring them. You act like there aren't possibilities where there're confinements."

I scowled at her. "This better work."

The door slammed open, and a soldier burst in, his gun out, pointing first at Stella and then swiveling to me. Stella dropped her paintbrush, and out of the corner of my eye, I saw it slide through her equation. It burst into flame, and I reached to put out the fire. But then a second soldier with gun drawn stepped into the room, and they both pointed their guns at me.

At me.

Stella grabbed a rag from the chalkboard and slapped at the fire on the desk, the smell of burning blood stinging my eyes.

I couldn't take my eyes off the soldiers. I'd never seen a gun out of the holster before, much less pointed at anyone. Or me. My heart pounded. "Can...can I help you?"

Colonel Mann stepped into the room, his face impassive and flat. "Ilse Klein, you are under arrest for sabotage, espionage, and treason. Please kneel with your hands behind your head."

"What?" I asked, my whole body going cold. "It wasn't me! I'm *looking* for the spy!"

"On your knees!" shouted a soldier, and I flinched, tears filling my eyes.

Stella stared at me, wide-eyed, blood splattered everywhere, as I sank to my knees, sobbing, and touched the back of my head with my hands. The soldiers grabbed me roughly, twisting my arms behind my back as they slapped handcuffs a size too big against my skin. I bit back a yelp, and they hauled me to my feet, wrenching the handcuffs so I twisted in pain.

"I didn't do anything," I whispered through tears. "I am not a spy."

"The evidence concludes otherwise," Colonel Mann said quietly. He nodded to the soldiers. "Let's go."

"Stella," I whispered.

She shook her head a little—in disbelief or telling me she couldn't help me; I didn't know which—but they marched me out of the room, down the hallway, past the prying eyes of other scientists in other labs. Men massed in the doorways, watching me over glasses, pencils tapping against lips, their white button-down shirts and black slacks blurring together behind my tears.

Then a familiar face, pale with shock, stepped out from the crowd. George moved into the path of the soldiers, his stopwatch in his hand. "Ilse? Where are you taking her? What'd she do?"

"Mr. Steele, this is official business," Colonel Mann said crisply.

"When did you get back?" I whispered to him, but the soldier marching me jerked, and the handcuffs bit into my skin. I winced.

George backed down the hallway, staying ahead of us. His eyes met mine with a wildness I didn't quite understand, his fingers turning white around his stopwatch before he shoved it back into his jacket pocket. "Ilse, I know it wasn't you."

"*Thank you,*" I managed to mouth to him, before they pushed him to the side and shoved me out the front door.

They blindfolded me in the back of the car. Just yesterday I'd been in this car, and we'd been cordial. Friendly. Colonel Mann had been kind. That was gone. I hadn't realized it was so fleeting. *Trust him. Maybe this is just a ruse to trick the real spy.* I should have told him about the spy, should have told him what I suspected. *It isn't me.* I wanted to say it aloud, but my nose was running from crying, and my face was covered in snot I couldn't wipe away with my bound hands.

My bottom lip trembled, making my voice shake. "I-i-i-it was-s-s-n't m-m-me."

No one said anything to me. The car eventually came to a stop, and the engine turned off. I tensed up, hunching forward protectively, and the front doors opened, shut, and then mine opened. I felt the sun on my skin before I felt a strong hand wrap around my arm, dragging me out of the car. I stumbled to my feet and was shoved forward. I tripped up steps and stepped into a cool hallway.

Concentrate, Ilse, I told myself. *Pull yourself together. You're brilliant. Think your way out of this.*

My footsteps echoed, cold and almost a little wet. Stone. Tile sounded different. Warmer, almost. I was underground, I thought from the smell and the filtered quality of the air. Or I was in one of the reactors. I supposed that was a possibility. I'd never gone into a reactor before, but I imagined they smelled something like this.

They stopped me, and I heard a thick, heavy door open. The hinge creaked. I soaked up the only details I had and held them in my fists. I was pushed forward and guided to a chair. They sat me down, buckling the handcuffs to the chair and twisting my shoulders uncomfortably. The blindfold came off.

They had me in a small, dark, windowless room with only one fluorescent light swinging above me. Colonel Mann stood next to a man I'd never seen before. He was nearly a foot taller than the colonel, the tallest man I'd ever seen, and his beard was cropped close to his face. Still, I could see it was gray and flinty, like his eyes. Between us was a simple wooden table.

"Ilse Klein," he said coolly.

"I'd say your name, but I don't know it," I said without thinking. *This is no time for your mouth, Ilse Klein!* Wolf scolded me in my mind, and I shivered. He needed me. I had to get out of this. He might still be alive.

"Do you know why you're here?" asked the man, sitting down to stare at me with his flint-gray eyes.

"When they arrested me, they said espionage." I swallowed and added, "And treason. But that's not true, sir. I've done nothing. I'm *looking* for the spy."

"The spy," repeated Flint.

I hesitated, glancing at Colonel Mann. "I think there *is* a spy, sir...sirs. But it isn't me."

"Miss Klein, do you know what we do here?" Flint asked. "We're winning a war. This is not solely a war of weapons, but a war of ideology. New lines are being drawn in the world, and we need to make sure we're the ones holding the pen."

"What does that have to do with me?" I asked.

Flint stared at me impassively. "You wouldn't understand."

I nearly growled at him, at the implicit challenge in his words, but Colonel Mann cleared his throat, breaking my glare and catching my attention. He gave me a pointed look and asked, "Why do you think there's a spy?"

"She is the spy," said Flint, not breaking eye contact with me. "We have information that you've been sending state secrets away on balloons. You've been stealing information from the science labs, which you do not have clearance to enter. You've removed crucial information, which nearly led to a nuclear reactor meltdown last night."

I blinked at him. "That's what the alarms were? You stopped a meltdown."

Flint's teeth glinted between the thin lines of his lips. "No thanks to you. If treason and espionage in a time of war weren't enough to hang you, I'd add attempted murder of civilians to the list of charges."

A cold knot in my stomach untangled, spreading ice through me. Hanging. They were talking about hanging me. "I didn't commit treason. I didn't spy. There's someone else who is spying, sir. He caused the meltdown."

Flint's face didn't change. "You've sent state secrets using magic. Do you deny this?"

I didn't send out state secrets, but I had sent out secrets by magic to Wolf. I couldn't make the words come out. "I did not spy."

"What you learn here," said Colonel Mann quietly, almost sadly, "belongs to us. I told you this at the beginning."

I warned you, he meant.

"It's for my brother. The balloons and letters are to my brother. They're not secrets about here. He's asked me questions about magic he needs to do his job. I'm helping him," I protested. "There's nothing about"—I grasped for words—"what we do here."

"State secrets, a waste of federal resources, and an abdication of your duties," snapped Flint. "You've stolen secrets, you prevented scientists from doing their jobs, you nearly caused a meltdown, and you're sending magicked secrets to your brother! Is he in on it too?"

"As I mentioned to you before, sir, her brother is missing," said Colonel Mann stiffly.

Flint snorted. "Likely story. Have you sold these to your Soviet contacts?"

"I don't *know* anyone in the Soviet Union!" I cried. "Why would I know anyone in the Soviet Union?"

"You're Jewish," said Flint derisively. "The Bolsheviks were too."

I stared at him, and my mouth dropped open. I croaked, "We're

German. We're German Jews. Are you going to ask me if I sold secrets to Hitler?"

He shifted in his chair, but he didn't back down. "All the more reason for you to sell them to the Soviet Union. Are you looking to defeat
not only Hitler but democracy? Should we call you Comrade Klein?"

"No," I said, finding my voice again. "I sent my brother magic
equations to allow him to do his job. I did not send him anything
about what we're doing here. No more than Colonel Mann told us
when he recruited us two months ago, anyway."

The colonel's face flinched. Almost a scowl, almost panic, but
neither. Flint didn't look at him. "How do you know that it's your
brother asking you for advice? How do you verify it? You don't!
You've sent top secret military information to the enemy."

"I've sent my knowledge to my brother," I snapped back, leaning forward until the handcuffs cut into my wrists. "*You* sent my
brother into enemy territory woefully unprepared, and I'm fixing
that. My mind is not your property."

"It is for the duration of your stay." He spoke as if I were on vaca-
tion here, as though I could leave any time I wanted, and frustration
boiled up in my veins.

"You haven't answered my questions. How do you know those
requests are from your brother? How do you know that the secrets
you're sending aren't ending up in enemy hands?" Flint demanded.

"Because I know his handwriting and because his letters are coded to find me, the way mine are coded to find him," I spat out.

"Coded," repeated Flint.

I couldn't help the sneer that lifted my lips. "You wouldn't
understand."

Flint slapped me so hard my vision spotted and tears ran down
my cheeks as if he'd knocked them free of my eyes. Colonel Mann
lurched forward, slamming his hands down on the table between us.

"You said you wouldn't hurt her!"

"She's not hurt," snapped Flint.

Colonel Mann caught my chin, his eyes wide with concern, and turned my head, wincing at whatever he saw. His voice was cold when he turned back to Flint. "Do not touch her. If you are incapable of that, then you aren't qualified to conduct this interrogation and I will remove you."

"I wouldn't do that," said Flint, never blinking. "You could be implicated."

"If you touch her again," Colonel Mann repeated slowly, enunciating every word, "then I will remove you from this room and finish the interrogation myself." He let go of my chin and moved back to their side of the table.

"I'm only answering my brother's questions about magic so that he can do his job better," I said. "I'm not doing anything more than that. If I invent a magic equation for him, I write it in my notes here too. I'm not keeping anything from you."

"So far," said Flint, "the evidence disagrees with you."

My eyes widened as he pushed back his chair and stood up, gathering his things. Colonel Mann stood a beat after him, looking startled for the first time. Flint walked toward the door and rapped on it once firmly. I flinched, pulling at my handcuffs. Panic tied knots in my thinking, and I sucked in a shallow breath, my vision spotting.

A soldier opened the door, and Flint stepped through it. "Let's go, colonel."

The colonel looked torn as his gaze went from Flint in the dark hallway, out of view, to me. Then he said quietly, his voice just barely loud enough for me to hear, "We'll be back. Don't worry, Ilse."

But when the door shut behind him, I still screamed.

CHAPTER TWENTY-EIGHT

WOLF

The Gestapo put us in cells within a small cement building with thick walls and no windows. They'd asked us basic questions when we'd arrived midday, but then they'd left us chained to the wall without food or water, unable to relieve ourselves, for hours.

I leaned against the wall, taking a deep breath and trying to think my way out of the problem. I only knew the magic that Ilse had created or taught me. I didn't know how to create new equations and test them. And even if I could, how could I write an equation now?

Footsteps jolted me out of my thinking.

They walked past the first cell where I figured they were holding Lily. They walked past the second cell, which I suspected was Max's, since I'd heard nothing from it. I wondered if he was conscious. I wondered if he was alive. It was my fault he was over here, and now he was dead or dying in a Gestapo cell. The footsteps stopped at mine.

I cleared my mind of Max, Lily's heritage, my faith, our targets. I imagined my mind as glass, slippery smooth and opaque. Keys, and the door lock. The door swung open with a creak. I kept my head down but watched the black boots and gray trousers walk over to me. The man stood in front of me, and then two more sets of black boots and brown trousers walked into the cell. They shut the door behind them with a *thunk*.

I inhaled, exhaled. My mind was a glass room. Black, smooth, polished glass. Nothing to see. Nothing to glean. Nothing to extract. Nothing to shatter. Nothing to find. Nothing to hold.

The Gestapo snapped something in German, and the brown pants advanced, dragging me forward enough to straighten the chain holding me to the wall, my shoulders wrenched backward. Pain screamed through my body, but I pressed it below the surface. I inhaled. I exhaled. I faced the Nazi.

He snapped something else in German, and one of the brown pants held me while the other unbuttoned my trousers. Fear surged against the glass in my mind but I fought it, keeping my face impassive as they yanked down my trousers, then my underpants.

The Nazi stared at me and then lifted his eyes to my face. "*Jude.*"

"American," I repeated.

"*Jude,*" he said coolly. "*Beschnitten.*"

"Most Americans are," I said, hedging my bets.

His smile was thin. "*Nein. Nein, das andere ist nicht beschnitten.*"

I swallowed. Fear was hot against the glass, burning me up from the inside out. I needed just a little more time alone to figure out how to get out of here. But I could do it. I could. I could finish this mission. But I couldn't if I died here, executed in a small cement cell.

I lifted my chin. "American."

He slapped me across the face, and my neck cracked at the force. I inhaled deeply, the sting keeping the fear at bay.

"*Soll ich dich hier umbringen?*" he asked, his voice light and curious.

The brown pants forced me to my knees. I made myself look up, facing the Gestapo as he drew his sidearm and tripped the safety. His face was sallow, his hair thinning, and behind his cold eyes, I saw the irritation that he wouldn't have the satisfaction of knowing he had killed a Jew. He'd only *hope* he'd killed a Jew. And I wouldn't give him that satisfaction. I'd not denied it, just refused to confirm it. I would end up in a mass grave, unmarked, and I supposed that was how things went for Jews on this damn continent.

I lifted my chin. I would not die afraid.

"You can kill me where you like," I said, my words coming out sharper than I intended. "You will still lose this war."

He leveled the gun against my forehead.

I trembled. I couldn't deny that I trembled. But I forced myself still.

His finger curled around the trigger.

Click.

I flinched, but the gun wasn't loaded. Or that chamber wasn't.

I almost sank to the floor in relief. The Gestapo's expression never changed, and that terrified me into staying upright. *"Ich glaube,"* he said thoughtfully. *"Ich lasse denen dein Sterben mal zuschauen."* He nodded. *"Lässt ihn los!"*

They dropped me, and I stumbled back against the wall, too weak and terrified to do much of anything as they unlocked the door, spat on me, and exited my cell.

The crack of a gunshot in the hallway made me jump, followed by the sound of the guards' laughter echoing off the walls. I swallowed the bile that had risen to my mouth. They wanted Lily and Max to think they'd shot me. I wanted to vomit, to shout to Lily and Max and tell them I was alive, wanted to think through the magic of escaping. But I couldn't. My mind was fog, and my pants were still down around my knees. I slowly wiggled back into them; I was unable to zip them up but at least I was covered.

I inhaled the scent of my own piss and blood.

Then a strange rustling caught my attention, and I looked up.

In the opposite corner of the cell stood a man wearing a black button-down shirt, black trousers, and black boots. But his monochromatic attire wasn't the most unusual thing about him. Feathers, black feathers as if he'd stolen the wings of a dozen ravens, circled around his head between the bridge of his nose and the top of his forehead, slowly, occasionally obscuring his eyes, but rising and falling as if they were breathing. His hair was thinning on the top, dark brown in the back and closely cropped, but his beard was thick and dark, his mouth set solemnly in a line.

"I'm dead," I said.

"You aren't," said the raven man. "You are very much alive."

"What *are you*?" I asked, breathless, scooting backward into the corner. Was it English, or did I just understand whatever language he spoke? It was smooth, accentless. Not American. Not English. Not a second language, but not his first either.

"My name is Ashasher," he said, his voice cold and aloof. "I am here to offer you a deal, Wolf Klein."

"Do I look like I'm in the position to make deals?" I managed to say.

I might have been thirsty and hungry, but I wasn't an idiot.

He hadn't answered my question. He'd answered a different one.

"You look like a man who isn't in the position to refuse a deal," said Ashasher.

I closed my eyes. "This is a Nazi trick."

"I am not a Nazi. What I do is free people from the Nazis," said Ashasher.

I opened my eyes again. "You have my attention."

He pressed his lips together in a hard line. That must have been his smile. "I thought so. Wolf Klein, you can do magic. And so can I."

"I think you can do more than that," I said dryly.

He tilted his head. "I wasn't done."

I fell silent.

He continued. "There are hundreds of thousands of people imprisoned by the Nazis, hundreds of thousands or more, maybe, being killed daily all across Europe. I've been training people...There's a girl. She's just a girl who has been helping me in Poland. She is a visionary, and with her help, we now have twelve people trained to use magic on balloons to help people escape. But the process is slow, and we've helped people escape who weren't strong enough to hold on to a balloon. It did not end well, and it was a waste of an effort. There must be other ways of accomplishing this."

"You have the wrong Klein," I said coolly. "You'll need to find my sister. I don't invent magic. I just do it."

"I'm not asking you to invent *magic*. Magic cannot be *invented* any more than science can. It is *discovered*," Ashasher said impatiently. "I am capable of this. I need someone willing to handle"—he waved his hand a bit, as if he were looking for the word—"logistics. Someone who can make decisions. I cannot be everywhere at once."

"I'm in prison," I pointed out quietly.

"I can get you out."

My mind spun. Freedom, in exchange for me helping to free people from Hitler's concentration camps. I could do that. I *wanted* to do that. But that wasn't my mission. And it might all be for naught if Hitler got this bomb before I did. My heart swung wildly in my chest.

"What about my companions?" I asked.

Ashasher blinked at me. "They cannot do magic. I have no use for them."

"So you're only saving people who have a use to you?" I challenged him. "From camps too?"

He stared back at me, his face deliberately blank for just long enough that I growled, "You can't be serious. People deserve freedom, regardless of their *worth* to you."

"We have limited resources," Ashasher snapped. "I need people who can help me make this grow so we can save everyone we can possibly

226

save. Once I have a full team, then I can focus on saving whoever can hold a string. But it is a waste of my limited resources—"

"That's immoral."

"Is it?" He strode toward me. "Is triage immoral?"

"Triage," I spat back, "saves the person at risk of dying soonest, not the person who can help save other people."

"Maybe medicine has looked at that all wrong," Ashasher said softly.

"How can you look at large-scale tragedy and think so heartlessly?" I asked him.

"How can you look at large-scale tragedy and refuse to help me because you'll leave two people behind?" he countered.

I staggered to my feet. When Ashasher took a step backward, I smiled, satisfied. "Don't lecture me on morals when you are only here for people with magic in their blood."

"Think of what we could accomplish," he argued.

I shook my head. "Take Lily and Max too, or I won't go at all."

He appraised me in silence and then said, "You are a fool."

"Better a kind fool than a cruel genius," I replied.

He held up a hand and said, "Good luck, Wolf Klein."

When he snapped his fingers, there was the sound of rustling feathers and a tear in the air that zipped back up as if it'd never been there. He was gone. I stared at the spot for a long time, waiting for him to return, looking to see if he'd simply made himself invisible, and I supposed, in part, because I wasn't sure if I'd made the right decision.

CHAPTER TWENTY-NINE

OAK RIDGE, TENNESSEE
OCTOBER 4, 1943

ILSE

Some time later, after my arm had gone numb, the door unlocked. I lifted my head from the desk, my cheeks stiff with tears as Colonel Mann stepped into the small room, the light catching the shadows under his arm. He put a paper bag on the desk and then came around behind me. He unlocked the handcuffs, and my arms fell loose from the confinement. I bit back a cry of pain, curling my fingers into fists and stretching them out again. I could barely feel the bite of nails into my own palm.

The colonel walked back around and sat down across from me, unpacking the paper bag and handing me a thermos and a sandwich. I fumbled awkwardly at the sandwich with my numb hands and bit into it hungrily.

He unscrewed the top of the thermos for me and poured water into the little cup, sliding it across the table. His face was unreadable. I scarfed down the sandwich and the water, and he refilled the cup.

"You survived," he said gently. "You said you thought there *was* a spy."

For once I bit my lip and thought before I spoke. "Yes. I've noticed missing notes from my desk in our lab."

"Why didn't you tell me about the stolen papers?" he asked me.

I hesitated and decided on the truth. "I wanted to find the spy myself."

"Or you knew who it was," suggested Colonel Mann.

A little too vehemently, I shook my head. "No. I don't."

"What notes did they take?"

"Notes on the maximum weight experiments with balloons, distance, and variable terrain tests. Most recently, they've stolen notes on invisibility," I said to him.

"And you thought you could catch this person on your own?"

"I thought I could," I said. "I couldn't imagine that the notes they'd stolen were immediately threatening to Oak Ridge, or anyone. That was before I knew they were stealing notes from other labs. Did the reactor really almost melt down?"

"I don't know how close we were," said Colonel Mann, "but close enough that there was a question about evacuation."

I shuddered. "How did that happen?"

"When there were no records on how we stabilized uranium rods the last time it happened, we had to do the science from scratch," he said mildly. "As you know, science takes time."

"Do you think it was deliberate that they took those notes?" I asked.

Colonel Mann frowned. "You're asking if the meltdown was their goal or if that was a consequence of the espionage. I don't know. What do you think the risks are with the papers they took from you?"

"It depends," I told him. "They'd have to get into the hands of a very capable magic user."

"How long ago did you notice the missing paperwork?" he asked.

"A week ago," I murmured. "No earlier."

The colonel rubbed at his face and took a folded piece of paper from his pocket. "Ilse, your actions have consequences. You were arrested for espionage. You are the daughter of a German immigrant with socialist ties."

"Lots of people have socialist ties," I said stiffly.

"Your father was questioned in New York," Colonel Mann said quietly.

I thought I was going to vomit. "He has nothing to do with this!"

"Stolen papers. A German Jewish father with socialist leanings. You are just a child. You understand how it looks."

"It *looks* like I made a mistake, but you took it one step farther," I snarled. "My father is not part of this."

"He has been released," the colonel said, but the way he said it didn't reassure me. "He was at one of his stores when our people in New York brought him in for questioning. It made the papers."

This time, I did vomit. I bent over, wrapping my arms around my knees, shaking violently. Papa's business couldn't survive that. People would talk. His accent was trouble enough—this could ruin them. I thought about Mama and her strength and Papa and his gentleness, and I couldn't stop the tears running from my cheeks to my stockings.

"Sit up, Ilse," said Colonel Mann. "I'm going to explain to you what's going to happen now."

"If it was up to me, I would say you learned your lesson. But that's not enough for others involved, and I warned you when you came here that things would be out of my hands if you stepped outside the lines." He looked down at the letter. "You're going to discontinue all contact with anyone outside this facility, including your brother. Your magic belongs here at Oak Ridge. No phone calls. No letters. No magical correspondence."

"You can't ask me to do that," I whispered.

"I didn't ask you. I ordered you. If you fail to do so, you will be arrested on charges of treason, and this time, we won't clear you, Miss Klein."

Wolf. He needed those letters, and I needed to hear from him. We were in this together, no matter how many miles or oceans apart. If I couldn't write to him, if he wrote to me and I couldn't reply...if the magic was the difference between life and death behind enemy lines...if he was alive...

I swallowed and nodded. I had no choice. Yesterday, they'd spoken of hanging me. Today, I became a prisoner. I couldn't even talk to my father to find out if my parents were well after that ordeal. I had no choice.

Colonel Mann scrubbed at his face with the heel of his hand. "Ilse, you've put me in a really bad position here."

"I'm sorry," I said automatically.

His smile was small and dry. "You aren't, but that's okay. I didn't expect you to be. I don't understand why you kept this secret from me. But sometimes I forget how young you are."

I scowled a little bit, and he said gently, "It wasn't meant as an insult. You still see the trees. I'm overwhelmed by the forest."

"So am I still a spy?" I asked, unable to keep the bitterness out of my voice.

"No, Ilse," Colonel Mann said quietly. "But there is a spy, and there's an investigation. You'll need to be vigilant. A safe will be installed in your lab for your papers."

"Who was he?" I meant Flint, and the colonel knew it.

He shook his head. "Don't ask about him. It's better if you know as little as possible. I know that's hard for you. I know you want answers, and that's just the way you are. It makes you an exceptional scientist and a talented magician. But this one time, Ilse, please don't ask those questions. There are no good answers."

"Sir," I said, remembering something. "There's something I didn't tell you and the other man."

"Tell me," he said, leaning forward.

I hesitated. "I saw a balloon. Just one day. But it was a red balloon."

He stood up. "Like your balloons?"

"Yes. I didn't remember it earlier. But it wasn't mine, and I swear I didn't send secrets to Wolf. I mean, I sent him magic, but nothing that I'm keeping from you."

"If you saw it, then maybe it wasn't magic," he suggested.

"No," I said, swallowing a bit and giving him a sad smile. "It was before we figured out invisibility. I thought it wasn't magic, but it seems impossible to deny now."

Colonel Mann scowled at me. "I am not a fan of assumptions."

"Fine." I scowled at him. How could they be so fast to jump at the possibility of me being a spy but not consider other possibilities when presented? "Then let's revisit the possibility that the missing paperwork isn't going to someone with magic but rather has been stolen by someone who already has magic. Someone we don't know yet."

"I thought I knew everyone with magic," the colonel said with a frown.

"Foreign agent?" I said, testing the unusual words on my tongue.

He rubbed his head. "Unfortunately, possible. We've been so focused on the possibility of infiltration on the science teams that we didn't worry as much about the magic teams. I suppose we made a mistake there. Ilse, don't chase this down. Leave this to us. This is not your problem."

I held up my wrists, bruised and swollen from the handcuffs. "You made it my problem."

"I'm sorry," he said quietly. "I truly am."

CHAPTER THIRTY

WOLF

I stretched my neck, wincing and rolling my shoulders as best I could with my hands bound behind my back. Everything ached with a furious pulse, and my tongue felt thick, dry when it stuck to the roof of my mouth. I swallowed hard, trying to make my mouth wet enough to speak, and my dry, cracked lips split again. I tasted blood, copper and sweet, against my tongue and sucked on my lip hard. If it ran down my chin, I might rise off the floor, pulling at my chains. It'd out me to the Nazis, or they'd just shoot me. Neither situation was desirable.

I inhaled through my nose, trying to make the sensation go away, but I couldn't draw a full breath. Every inch of my body felt bruised and tight from spending two days half slouched over, chained to the wall.

But I'd told them nothing.

And they'd learned nothing.

If the others had done the same, if Max—God, Max—had, then maybe they'd back off. All I needed was a little time. I'd needed them to get one good round of interrogation and torture in before we escaped. We needed to be unimportant enough not to be pursued. Unimportant enough not to report up the chain of command right away. I didn't need the guards at the bomb research sites to be looking for three scraggly-looking prisoners with black eyes and bruised wrists.

I took a deep breath, my mouth softening. There might be enough blood in my spit to write magic on the door. Could I do that? Did I know an equation that would set me free?

I wondered if I'd made a mistake in turning down the raven man. Ashasher.

But then I thought about whether I could leave Lily and Max behind, and realized I couldn't. I didn't know how I'd feel in the future, if I'd feel guiltier for not helping Ashasher, or guiltier for leaving Max and Lily, but I couldn't do it. Right then, right now, leaving them behind was too much to consider.

Footsteps. Sharp, clipped, precise. I closed my eyes, listening to the approach.

The door opened, and the same Gestapo officer entered with two soldiers.

He pulled out his gun.

So he'd finally come to kill the Jew.

I wouldn't get to know what guilt would eat me the most.

An explosion boomed across the complex, shaking the floor and the walls. Dust and stone rained down around us. We all swayed— the two brown pants, the Gestapo, and me, and the Gestapo looked around, yelling wildly in German. He looked at me, wide-eyed, like I'd done this, but I hadn't. He shoved his sidearm back into the holster and yanked open the cell door, disappearing. The brown pants shoved me face-first onto the stone floor and then fled, slamming the door behind them and locking it.

I inhaled the dust on the floor for three breaths before shoving myself upright.

I was alive. An explosion that managed to pull all the guards far away from the prisoners without harming any of the cells? I knew someone who could control an explosion like that. Topher was here.

We had to leave now, while they were distracted. Another explosion from the side of the complex. Shouting in German, and the sound of trucks starting above us. So we *were* underground.

I spat onto the floor and scooted forward, dipping my swollen fingers into the bloody saliva. I bent my forefinger and wrote, the best I could, the equation to burn on the floor. I didn't think of it until the explosion, but now it made the most sense. The smell of smoke would be covered by the explosion, and I'd rather deal with burns later. The rope caught and loosened, turning into embers and flames that licked at my skin. I yanked my wrists free the moment I could, scrambling to my feet to stomp the fire out.

Stretching my arms in front of me and rolling my wrists, I folded my fingers into fists and unfolded them quickly. I zipped up my trousers.

They'd locked the door when they left because of the explosion, which was unfortunate. It would've been easier if they'd failed to think about that in the heat of the moment. I spat into my left hand again, working my tongue against a broken tooth to get my gums to bleed more. With a shaking, still-numb finger, I wrote an equation down the edge of the door.

Melt.

Metal couldn't catch fire, but it could melt. The blood and magic would lower the melting point to the air temperature. I finished the equation and it glowed, then faded until I couldn't see it anymore. It didn't matter because the metal at the edge began to melt instantly, dripping down, and I shoved at the door before it could seal to the cooler metal around it. The lock snapped, and the door swung open. I braced, fingers to the ground in a fighter's crouch, waiting for the guards.

But no one came.

I stepped into the hallway, holding my breath.

It was empty.

Another explosion. The third. Topher couldn't have much more TNT left.

I melted the lock on Lily's door, and she nearly stabbed me with a small piece of metal she held in her fist. She looked fine, save for a bruise blossoming like a purple flame over her left cheek. "I nearly killed you," she snapped.

"We have to go," I said in a low, sharp voice.

She raised an eyebrow. "To kill some Nazis? Because I am game."

"We don't have time for that right now," I said.

"I'll meet you at Max's cell," she said. "I'm getting our stuff."

"Leave it," I hissed.

"We need it," she said simply. "Meet you in two minutes."

Maybe by then Lily would have a plan. Because I sure as hell didn't.

I opened Max's cell and found him, a crumpled, still form in the back corner. They hadn't even bound his hands and feet. I stepped into the room, listening, aching to hear a heartbeat, the sound of breath, even rattled or harsh, or something. Something. Anything. But he lay still. I swallowed and took a step forward, and then another step forward. If he'd died here, we'd have to leave him. And I didn't want to do that. But if he wasn't dead, I'd carry him wherever we were going.

"Max," I croaked, squatting by his body. I touched his cheek. Cool. But not cold. My hand in front of his mouth caught the soft exhale of breath. My fingers found a faint pulse. I sagged against him, pressing a swift, soft kiss to his temple. I dragged him up onto my shoulder. He might have been taller than me, but he was all legs and arms, and I was built to survive famines and pogroms. Thank God for these Jewish peasant bones.

I carried him into the hallway, and Lily walked toward us, two packs in either hand. Our packs. With all our balloons, first aid kit, and maps. Somehow, she'd gotten them back. She gave me a smile as sharp as a razor blade gliding over skin.

Footsteps pounded down the hallway, and we froze, panicking, and then an unlikely person skidded around the turn.

"Topher!" we both said at once.

He blinked. "How did you get out?"

"How did you *find* us?" I asked.

"Never mind," Lily snapped. "We don't have time. We have to move."

"My bombs should hold them for a while," Topher said, sounding pleased with himself.

"Good," Lily said. "Let's go."

I adjusted Max against my side, heaving him higher up on my shoulder. The action drew Lily's concerned frown. My stomach clenched at the look on her face, the thoughtful, calculating, cold shift in her eyes.

"We don't know how much time we have. Max..." Her voice trailed off.

I spat blood on my hand and showed her my palm. "If you want my magic, he's coming with us."

We stared at each other for a long moment, and then Lily grimaced. "Fine. Let's go."

And we climbed out of the Gestapo headquarters, Max draped over my shoulder. The rubble was rough, large, sharp, and cut through our hands. It rolled out from beneath our feet, and I swore as I tried to keep my footing without dropping Max. Topher's bombs had done immense amounts of damage, and chaos reigned outside. Soldiers ran in every direction, and trucks screeched off toward a guard tower.

"Ah," said Topher, pleased. "I put a bayonet in the bushes over there with a helmet. Ought to catch their eyes."

"Smart," I told him.

He smiled. "We're not done here. Can't do the mission alone."

I just concentrated on not dropping Max, who groaned. I dug my fingers into the backs of his thighs where I held him. "Quiet, Egan."

He fell silent again, though I wasn't sure whether he was

conscious and responding to my command or had been unconscious and groaning in pain. I wondered what they'd done to him—if this was his original head injury, or if they'd beaten him and worsened it. My stomach twisted painfully, as if an invisible hand squeezed a fist around my intestines, and I stumbled, nearly dropping him.

Lily caught him and helped me heave him back onto my shoulder properly. She held my elbow and looked up at me, her eyes as steady as they always were. She squeezed my elbow. "You got him?"

"Yeah," I said.

"You're all right?" she asked.

"Not here," hissed Topher. "For God's sake, walk faster."

Lily didn't let go of my elbow. I forced myself to smile at her. "I'm all right."

"Okay, then," she murmured. "Come on, Sunshine. Let's get the hell out of here."

We crossed through the first set of gates and then had to pass through a large staging lot before coming to another gate by the road. The first gate we navigated without issue, but then the pattern of shouts and horns changed behind us. They'd realized Topher's dummy was just a dummy.

"Topher," I said, my voice taut with tension. "Lily."

"Shhh," Topher murmured.

"They're turning around. I can hear them," I said.

Topher paused, his gait altering slightly as he took in my words. "What do we do now?"

I watched Lily's thumb click off the safety on her gun. "Get ready."

We were fifty yards, maybe a little less, from the gate. I stopped, letting Max slide to the ground. I held him up, waiting for his feet to register they'd hit the ground, to press down and support his weight. They did, somewhat, but he slouched against me. My back screamed from carrying him.

"Max," I said quietly. "Can you hear me?" His head moved a little bit. I took a deep breath. "I need you to use your feet as much as you can. Let's go."

I shifted him to my left side so my right side was free, and we began shuffling and hobbling toward the gate, no longer trying to keep our footsteps light.

"Lily, go," I ordered her.

"Nice try," she began, and I cut her off with a snarl. "Figure out how to get us out of here. I'll get us to you."

"Don't make me regret this, Sunshine," Lily said after a beat. She moved swiftly, and though she must have become a mirage to the soldiers, she made it through the gate.

Out of the corner of my eye, I saw a soldier's head turn toward us. He looked puzzled, his posture unsure, as he tried to figure out what he was, or wasn't, seeing. We were out of time. In a second, he'd realize we weren't fellow soldiers but escaped prisoners.

"Topher," I said desperately. "Take Max."

"What are you going to do?" he asked, but he slid his arm around Max, muttering something that I didn't catch.

"Time to punch some goddamn Nazis," I said. "Go."

We were thirty feet from the gate, and we had nothing to lose. "Lily!" I yelled. "Cover!"

A shot cracked through the air, wildly, and I instinctively ducked as chaos erupted around us. I lunged forward for the first Nazi who lifted a gun, pointing it at Max and Topher, and slammed my fist into his face.

He dropped like a stone, and I snarled, "Tell your momma you got punched by a queer Jew, you lousy piece of—"

"Wolf!" yelled Lily.

I spun and slammed my fist into the next Nazi's gut as he swung wildly at my head. I shoved my knee up hard between his legs. People were shouting in German, guns going off, and somewhere beyond the gate, Lily was picking people off with alarming skill. I grappled with a Nazi, and then a shot echoed through the air and I gasped as blood splattered my face. The Nazi in my grip went limp, and I dropped him. Lily had blown a hole clean through his ear.

I wiped my face and ducked behind a truck, following Topher and Max toward Lily's location. Then a truck revved up near us, and I jerked in surprise. Lily grinned at us from behind the wheel of a Nazi truck, a rifle across her lap and a Luger in her left hand.

"Get in, losers," she called. "We're blowing up Nazis."

In the back of the truck, Max listed against my leg, a steady, comforting pressure. I wrote as furiously as Lily drove, her foot slammed down on the gas and her steering leaving a great deal to be desired.

"Stop swerving!" Topher yelled. "I'm making bombs!"

"It's not my fault German roads are so twisty!" Lily called back, her voice giddy.

One mile away, and with a full caravan of Nazis in hot pursuit, we released a half-dozen balloons and cheered as one by one, they exploded along the road, sending the Nazis and their trucks flying to the side and tilting off the edge of the road. Fire and smoke reached the sky above the trees. I breathed it in with a smile on my face.

CHAPTER THIRTY-ONE

OAK RIDGE, TENNESSEE
OCTOBER 5, 1943

ILSE

Stella was the first to hug me when I appeared at the lab the next day. "I'm sorry," she whispered. "But if I'd said anything…do you know what they'd do to me?"

It would have been so much worse for her, being African-American in segregated Oak Ridge. I hugged her back. "I know. Besides, you know everything I do. If I hadn't come back, at least you could have continued the work."

By the look on Stella's face, she knew I meant more than just delivering the elephant. She knew I was talking about finding the spy. She gave me a sly smile and said, "You never give up, do you?"

"No time for giving up," I said, forcing myself to be cheerful.

Polly looked hollow until she stepped into the lab and saw me. She flew at me, hugging me so hard she picked me clean off the ground. "You're back! They wouldn't say what happened! George was here. He said that he'd take over for you when he was back from his trip. I'm so glad you're back."

"Oh," I said with a soft laugh. Her heart pounded against her ribs, against my ribs, against my heart. I wrapped my arms around her and inhaled the sweet smell of the jasmine perfume she dabbed on her throat every morning. "I wouldn't let him take over."

Of course he had been waiting in the wings to take over. But I didn't get to say anything else to her because Lola ran into the room, squealing like a pig, and hugged Polly, who was hugging me, and we all fell, laughing, against one of the desks. I grinned into the mess of limbs, grateful for these girls in my life, for their belief in me and their courage to stand next to me despite what the military had said.

Stella said something, and I lifted my head free of Polly's shoulder. "What?"

Stella held up a piece of chalk. "This is touching, but we have work to do."

She was right. As usual.

I went to the chalkboard that didn't face any windows, where no one standing outside and monitoring us could see what I was writing. In the park at home, I hadn't been careful enough, and I'd been caught. My brother had been shot down and my father questioned, and I had been detained. I hadn't wanted to come here, and I didn't believe in building this bomb. But I'd convinced myself that I didn't mind doing the work because delivering a bomb was different than building it, and this was war. This was what I was obligated to do.

I'd been wrong. There was a spy, and far worse than us building the bomb would be our science and our magic ending up in the hands of Nazi Germany.

So, taking a deep breath, I committed treason.

I wrote on the board, *Our words might be being recorded. We can't speak this aloud. They accused me of spying. Someone reported the letters I've been writing my brother. I'm not the spy, but there is a spy. Someone stole papers from us, including letters from my brother, coordinates, and balloon magic. I fear that that information will end up in Hitler's hands. Colonel Mann and the powers that be here don't want me, or any of us, to investigate. They told me that the elephant mission is the only mission. But whatever we do with the elephant will just be putting more secrets into the hands of the enemies. What I want to do is pretend we're doing the elephant mission...and find this spy.*

When I turned around, they were all nodding in agreement, though Polly looked paler than Stella and Lola. I turned back to the blackboard and wrote, *So here's what I want. Stella and Polly, can you work on the elephant mission? Lola, will you help me figure out what Stella and I were working on the day I was arrested?*

They'd be suspicious if Stella and I were working together again, and they'd know that we were the two brightest. We had to divide and conquer.

I turned around and said loudly for any microphones they had in our walls, "So, do you think balloons can do this?"

"Yes," said Polly, nodding as she turned toward Stella.

Stella nodded. "I'll type a progress report about where we're at on the delivery possibility."

"Lola, you and I should look over Stella's notes," I said.

Lola studied the board and then looked at me. For a brief moment, I thought she'd say no, but then she grinned and said, "Let's do it."

Six hours into our work, we'd found an invisibility equation that worked. We wrote the equation into our notes—it was, after all, one of our goals and something needed to deliver the atomic bomb. If they decided to check our notes after my arrest, they'd see true work—but we were most thrilled about other uses for the magic. We locked all our notes in the new safe installed sometime after my release. I gave Stella the combination in case something happened to me again, but we did not write it down or speak it anywhere it could be overheard.

We went back to our little house on the hill, Stella included, and we told the guards it was just for dinner. Just before sunset, the girls gathered around as I wrote a balloon to Wolf. Stella checked my equation on the back of the letter, and then we all pulled on our coats and hats for the cool fall air and stepped into the little yard, where the trees and dusky light provided some privacy. I let go of the balloon, and though I trusted the magic and our science, I held my breath as it disappeared from view. Polly looped her arm through mine quickly in reassurance.

She looked at me, a shy smile on her face that reminded me of the day we met, and said, "I hope it works."

I squeezed her arm against my side, my heart slamming against my ribs. "Me too."

Stella and Lola went back inside after a long moment, but Polly stayed with me in the setting sunlight. She let go of my arm to walk a little farther into the yard, her boots crunching on the leaves. She tilted her open face to the sky, her arms around herself in her coat. Her hat sat on top of her curls, and her breath puffed visibly in front of her face.

I didn't know why she was still here, watching for an invisible balloon like I was, but I wanted her company. I was content to stand in the silence for a long time, but she finally spoke.

"I thought I'd hate autumn up here," she said. "But it's beautiful, isn't it? I can't explain it. Everything feels like it's on the precipice. It could be spring at any moment."

I laughed. "It's not even winter yet."

But from inside the secret spaces between my ribs, my heart sailed out and lodged in her chest. I wanted it back, but all I could think of were her hopeful words. *It could be spring at any moment.* It wouldn't be spring here for months. But she wanted to believe in that so much, and who was I to burst her bubble? She didn't seem lost in thoughts about the magic we hadn't yet invented, the war we hadn't yet won, or the spy we hadn't yet caught.

She turned to face me, the light silhouetting her golden curls and lanky arms. "Were you scared?"

"Yes," I said quietly. "I thought they were going to hang me."

She nodded, her fingers dancing across her throat. She blew out a long breath, and then I realized she was making small talk because she was nervous. I wanted to step close to her, to tell her I was nervous too, but I didn't.

"Where's George?" she asked.

I shrugged. "I wouldn't know. Sulking that I was released, I suppose? Ruined his plans for running our lab group."

"Do you miss him?"

I picked my words carefully, because I didn't think she was just asking if I missed him. I remembered her words from the other morning. *Do you like George?* "I keep hoping that if I try, it'll start to make sense."

Testing a theory.

"Ah," said Polly, her voice soft, sliding through the low light to me. "It never did for me."

"It's like an experiment," I explained, astonished at the steadiness of my voice. "It's a theory I'm trying to test."

She turned toward me again, the last of the sun's light catching the hem of her dress as it moved in a wave around her knees. "Well. What's the control, and what's the variable?"

You. You're the unknown variable, I wanted to tell her. *We thought it was Lola, but it was you.*

"How'd you end up here, Polly?" I asked her.

"I fell in love with a girl," she said, her voice hushed. "You're not supposed to fall in love with girls if you're a girl yourself. Not where I'm from. I didn't have a choice."

"We're not where you're from though," I said carefully.

She shivered. "The world isn't kind to girls like me, Ilse."

"Like us," I said quietly.

Her voice was hushed. "Ilse."

"I have a theory," I said. "A hypothesis. And I know the control.

I want to test the variable. And if I'm wrong, I'm sorry. I don't know how else to figure this out. I can't shake this question out of my mind."

"You should shake it out of your mind, Ilse," Polly said sadly. "This isn't a kind world."

"I don't care if the world's not kind to us. I don't want to kiss the world," I said.

She turned toward me. "Do you want to kiss me?"

"Yes," I whispered, licking my lips. She stepped toward me, and I started to babble. "I've only kissed one person, and that was just a boy at home, from shul. He was friends with my brother."

"Did you like it?" Polly asked, the corner of her mouth tilting up.

I shook my head. "It was fine enough, I suppose. I thought kissing might be one of those things I needed to practice before I liked it. Like skiing."

For a long moment, I thought Polly wouldn't do anything, that she'd stay at arm's length and we'd have to learn how to be friends at that distance. But then the war playing out across her face resolved, and she took a deep breath. She stepped close enough to touch, close enough that I could feel the breath rattling off her lips, but she didn't close the distance between us. Her mouth turned upward in a smile. "It's not skiing. It's a peach on a summer morning. It's coffee, hitting the spot. It's sunshine on your skin."

"So show me," I whispered.

She did.

Theory confirmed.

CHAPTER THIRTY-TWO

WOLF

The elation of freedom ended quickly. We abandoned the truck on the road and hiked into the woods around Hechingen, near our next target.

The nights were growing cold, but we didn't light a fire that night for fear of being found. And the chill hung heavily around our shoulders, a deepening weight that made us tired and cranky, liable to snap at each other. Which we did, and then we fell back into moody silences. Lily and Topher were the least roughed up of the four of us, so they distributed our food, found water from a stream, and filled our single tin cup again and again to keep us hydrated. We were bruised and battered and a little unsure of what came next.

Max had regained his consciousness, but not his strength. He spoke in fragmented sentences, or more often in one-word answers to yes-or-no questions. He slept most of the time. When we'd stripped him, looking for injuries, we'd found none. The Nazis had realized, it seemed, that he was truly injured and useless. Why they hadn't killed him was beyond me, but I wasn't going to second-guess the decision.

Sometimes, I saw Topher and Lily exchanging glances with each other, then looking at Max and murmuring, but I refused to acknowledge them. If they wanted me to let Max die here in the woods or to leave him behind, they would be disappointed. Dying in the hands of the Nazis was a cruel death. Dying of dehydration was a cruel death. If he was going to die, he'd die with me at his side. We were in this together.

In the morning, I woke before everyone else, cold and stiff. Max slept next to me, and I crouched next to him, flexing my hands and then touching his shoulder. "Max."

His eyes flickered open, unfocused and glassy. "Woof."

In a past life, I would have laughed, shoved him, pretended to bark. In another life, in another time, in another place. But right now, I just gave him my best attempt at a reassuring smile. "Hey. Time to get up, bud. Need to take a piss?"

He didn't nod, but he had a tight look on his face, the expression he made when he was going to nod, but couldn't because of the pain. I helped him to his feet and he leaned on me, warm but stiff. Unsteady. Unsure. We hobbled a few feet away from our small camp to a tree, and he fumbled with his trousers while I held him upright.

I looked up at the light-gray sky while he peed against the tree, waiting until I heard the sound of a zipper again. Max leaned against me. "Should've left me."

It was one of the only coherent things he'd said.

"I'm not leaving you," I said patiently and turned him back toward the camp. Through the trees, I caught sight of something drifting down from the sky. *Red. Balloon. Ilse.* I pushed at Max a little harder than I should have, my heart pounding. I dropped him roughly in his spot and marched through camp, eyes scanning and searching for where the balloon came down.

"Wolf," said Lily, appearing behind me. "We need to talk."

"Not now," I said shortly, scanning the woods. Hope sang through me, a light cutting through the heavy branches. "Ilse sent me a balloon. I saw it."

"Oh," Lily said in surprise, looking around. "Where?"

"Trying to find it," I said and then turned, seeing it halfway up in the tree. "There."

We both frowned up into the tree, and Lily sighed. "It's up there? How are you getting it? You're too hurt for that."

I held out a hand. "Give me your gun."

"If you kill me," Lily said, handing me her sidearm, "I'm going to be so pissed."

"If I kill you, I expect you to haunt me forever," I agreed. I raised the gun and fired it once, right into the balloon. The balloon popped, the magic breaking, and the string unraveled, dropping a thin envelope onto the ground.

I held the gun out for Lily, who took it with a smile twitching on her face. "You're getting to be a good shot."

"Better than getting worse," I said.

Footsteps pounded behind us, and Topher appeared, wild-eyed, as I picked up the envelope. "I heard a gun."

"That was me," I said, tearing open the seal and unfolding the letter. "I bet this balloon was trying to get to me for days while we were in prison. But I'm hoping..."

"Hoping what?" asked Topher, his hand in his pocket. I heard that infernal clicking from his stopwatch, but I didn't say anything about it. He'd helped me save Max, and we'd still be in the Gestapo prison if it wasn't for him.

Dear Wolf,

Things at Oak Ridge are complicated right now. I'll explain later, when this war is over, but I can't put it into a letter, even one that I'm sure is only landing in your hands.

On the back of this letter is the equation for invisibility. It doesn't last that long, but I hope that it's long enough for what you need. We're working on an extended equation.

Please write back when you can.

Love,

Ilse

"She gave us invisibility," I said, flipping over the letter. "But, it's going to take more blood than we anticipated. And it won't last that long."

"I owe your sister a drink after the war," Lily said after a beat. "Fine, let's do it. Let's not wait any longer."

Topher worked on explosives on one side of camp, and on my side, I drew blood from the inside of my forearm while Max watched. I filled the little jar Ilse had sent prior to our arrest and added the rat poison. Like she said, it didn't clot. I could write all the balloons without stopping to pull more fresh blood. It made things infinitely easier. Snow started falling, even through the trees, and my fingers felt thick and useless.

I glanced once at Max who was sitting upright, frowning at his shoes. "You doing all right?"

He looked up at me, still frowning. "Dangerous."

I looked over at the bombs Topher was building. "We'll be far away before anyone comes up here to look. I promise."

He growled, frustrated, and shook his head. His mouth worked, but whatever thought he had was trapped behind his injury, and he couldn't find the words for it. I watched him for a while out of the corner of my eye while I worked, feeling helpless. I didn't know what else we could do for him, other than keep him alive until we got home where a doctor could care for him. I was going to get him home, come hell or high water.

And we were already in hell.

Topher sat next to me, turning over the stopwatch in his hands. "We're behind schedule. We need to break in, get what we need, and get out."

"I make the calls," Lily said coolly from the other side of our campsite.

Topher winced. "Sorry. I didn't mean to imply…"

"But you did. Don't go to Wolf with your complaints about timing. Come to me. Wolf, does that invisibility work on people?"

I blinked. "I…don't see why not? Before balloons, we were going to use magic right on our skin, weren't we? Magic acts on objects. It doesn't particularly care that it's a balloon."

"That'll make it easier, won't it," Lily said, and it was a statement, not a question. "We can do it just like Haigerloch. Get in, poke around, set up the bombs, and get out."

I glanced at Max. "And come back here?"

"And come back here," Lily agreed. "Topher, mark the coordinates. Max, stay warm and out of sight."

I didn't want to leave him behind again. The last time we'd done that, three of us had ended up in prison.

"Wolf?" Lily asked.

I blinked, bringing the world back into focus. "Just need to inflate the balloons and let them go."

I'd have to leave Max behind this time. Again. And trust that this time he'd be okay.

"Let's do it then," Lily said, appearing next to Topher, who scowled at me.

I double-checked the equations I'd written against Ilse's notes and equations. My work had been imprecise and desperate in the Gestapo prison, written from memory. It'd worked, but there hadn't been any beauty or balance. Ilse's work was logical and flowed, even to my limited scientific knowledge.

I wrote the invisibility equation in blood on Topher, then Lily, and then, in a burst of inspiration, on Max.

He pushed me away at first, but I snapped his name, and he sagged in defeat. He faded from view, and I whispered, "I don't know how long it lasts. Don't leave this area. Please. I'm coming back for you."

"I know," I heard him say. "I know."

CHAPTER THIRTY-THREE

HECHINGEN, GERMANY
OCTOBER 6, 1943

WOLF

We walked into the lab at Hechingen, invisibility lasting long enough for us to slip past the guards and walk right up the stairs. Topher stuffed his pockets and Lily's bags with papers, and once we were outside the gate again, we released balloons with invisible bombs. As soon as they disappeared, we used balloons to float back to the woods. Midair, we watched the explosions, one by one, as they turned the sky red and orange.

They wouldn't be rebuilding that lab.

In the woods, I stumbled ahead of Lily and Topher, searching desperately for our little campsite. For Max. And for a brief moment I didn't see him, and my heart seized. *No, no, no, no.* And then I saw a small, dark figure curled at the base of a tree a few strides away.

I fell to my knees, pressing my forehead into his cold temple. "You're here."

"You came back," he mumbled, sounding cold but coherent. "It worked."

"So much confidence in me," I said with a smile. "Let's go. I've got you."

I pulled a shivering Max to his feet, and his arm around my waist felt like it belonged.

We didn't know where we were going next, now that Lily didn't trust the safe houses, so she led the way. Topher argued with her the whole way through the woods until she threatened to shoot him. Every time we traveled by balloon, he got antsy, nearly manic. I couldn't tell if it was a reaction to the magic, or if he hated to travel by balloon. We followed her higher into the woods, taking long, loping strides, trying to avoid snapping branches or leaving a trail, but it was almost impossible. Max kept up with us, losing his balance only a few times, and I steadied him with a hand on his elbow.

There was a roar above us, and then explosions rocked the ground and I stumbled, Max going to his knees. "Up," I whispered desperately, hauling him to his feet. "Max, keep going."

"Keep going," Lily murmured, falling back to take Max's other side up the hill. Above us, planes rumbled, accelerating. Away or toward? I couldn't tell. "Sounds like Spitfires in the air. Those're our planes. We're too close to the town."

We crested the hill and appeared on the other side of the town, a flat field stretching in front of us, a farmhouse and a barn in the distance. We could see a road leading down to a small town in the distance, but there'd be no way to get past the town safely without being seen, not in broad daylight.

"Heidelberg," Lily said breathlessly. "It must be."

"The barn," Topher said, pointing. He shifted, hand in his pocket, that infernal stopwatch clicking echoing in my head. "We'll hide in the barn."

"If the farmer finds us, he'll turn us in to the Gestapo. We should go back into the woods," I said.

"No, let's go to the barn. The animal smell will throw off dogs if they search the woods," said Lily. "We'll take the chance we aren't found for an hour or two, and then we'll move on."

It was midday, and no one appeared to be home in the farmhouse, so we crawled up into the hayloft, seating ourselves by the window to overlook the road, the hill, and the sky. I scanned everywhere, my side aching again, and swore softly under my breath. Max leaned against the wall, his arm thrown loosely over his stomach, and he smiled, closing his eyes. "Mouth, Woof."

"You like it," I shot back without thinking.

Lily gave us a look, casting a glance at Topher who pretended not to hear while he kept watch. Max didn't see any of that with his eyes closed and said, "Yeah."

I couldn't help the smile that curved up the corners of my mouth. I forced it away and stared out the window again. "We can't stay here. They'll search local outbuildings for us."

"It's just a rest," Lily said. "We've used a lot of your blood the last few days. We can afford a few hours, even a day. I don't think they can move everything at Oranienberg that fast. We can't just keep draining you like vampires."

Topher, standing by the doorway of the hayloft where they winched up hay and clicking that stopwatch, snorted without turning to look at us. "Some plan. We brought along a guy with magic and no ability to rebound."

His tone made me flinch. "What's your problem? We dropped the bombs. We've gotten to two out of three sites and nearly made up time."

"It'll all be a waste if they move Oranienberg before we get there," Topher said, turning away from the doorway, his face contorted with rage.

"Knock it off, boys," snapped Lily. "We don't have time for that nonsense."

"You're all so loud," murmured Max. "Stop shouting."

"You keep hauling around your boyfriend," Topher said to me, his voice rising. "Like we aren't going to notice you two...unnatural—"

"Are you jealous?" I said dryly, barely controlling my anger.

Topher lunged at me, and Max sat up, swinging wildly at him and slamming his fist into the side of Topher's jaw. I shoved between them, slamming Topher back against the wall of the barn. "Don't touch him."

Topher's grin was bloody and wild. "Oh, is that yours?"

"Get out," I growled, releasing his shirt and backing up, careful to stay between him and Max. "Just get out."

"Fine," Topher spat out, straightening his shirt and coat. He looked to Lily. "You're choosing this instead of coming with me?"

"You're all such *children*," Lily said, staring at him and then turning to me. "We're fighting a *war* here. Would you like to pull yourselves together?"

"I'm out," Topher growled. "I'll do the recon and meet you at the rendezvous point south of the city."

"Midnight. Don't be late. We have six jumps to do for our next site," said Lily, her voice betraying an uncertainty that I hadn't heard from her before. Something was bothering her, but I didn't ask her about it in front of Topher. I just wanted him gone.

"I won't," Topher muttered sullenly and climbed back down the ladder.

I watched him from the window. "He's so moody."

"Did you have to push his buttons?" Lily rolled her eyes.

I felt a tiny twinge of guilt but refused to acknowledge it. He'd been the asshole. "Think he'll get caught?"

Lily frowned. "He's smart. He'll keep out of the way. He knows this isn't about us. It's bigger than us. Not that it matters...We shouldn't stay much longer anyway."

I glanced at Max, who was rubbing his knuckles with a self-satisfied grin on his face. "So you're feeling better."

Max cracked open an eye, his grin growing wider. "Fun. Deserved it."

"You shouldn't have punched him, Max," I said. We were full of bad decisions in this hayloft. We'd done everything we shouldn't have done, apparently, and nothing we should have done, like keep our hands and words to ourselves.

Still, I was having a hard time summoning regret.

"Why not?" Max asked. "One reason."

I looked out the window again, letting him see a smile that Lily didn't get to see. "I wanted to do it."

Max snorted.

We stayed for a half hour more, until we stopped hearing planes, and then decided we needed to go before a farmer started pulling in animals for the evening. Lily and I had just climbed down the ladder and were spotting Max's descent when the barn door creaked open, and an old man's voice called out, "*Halt.*"

"Damn," said Lily calmly.

CHAPTER THIRTY-FOUR

WOLF

The man in the doorway was backlit by a halo of light, but I could see the gun he had leveled at us, the gray in his hair, and the steadiness in his stance. He was older, but not frail. We couldn't overpower him, especially from this distance with him holding a gun.

Lily said something in German, lifting her hands. Then, right before my eyes, she became a frightened schoolgirl. She backed away from me, her eyes wide and her tongue moving swiftly over the German, blaming everything—the barn, the shouting—on us boys. I had to hope this wasn't a game, and that Lily actually had a plan.

The man in the doorway didn't move, though he trained the gun to follow Lily across the room. Then he said in fluent, if accented English, "I am not an idiot. I heard you speaking English. Was the bomb in Hechingen yours?"

Lily didn't flinch, but I did. The man gestured at me with the gun as Max landed beside me and stumbled. "Are you Nazis?"

"If we were Nazis," I said, "would we be hiding in your barn?"

He smiled. "Maybe. They are not my greatest fans. Why don't you come inside?"

"Why?"

"Because you could use a good meal before you go wherever you're going."

I looked at Lily, and then she turned to him, morphing back into the confident team leader she'd been before the man's arrival. "How do we know we can trust you?"

"If you're blowing up things at Hechingen, you'll want to know what I know about Oranienburg."

My jaw might have dropped open when he named our next target, but if it didn't, it did when he slipped the gun back into the waistband of his trousers. "Come inside, Americans. And you, girl from everywhere."

Lily hesitated, but we didn't have much of a choice. We needed to know what he knew.

"Come on," I said, holding Max's elbow to keep him upright and hiking my pack higher on my shoulders. "Let's go."

Lily muttered, "This is *such a bad idea*."

But when we passed her, she fell in behind Max. We walked across from the barn to the farmhouse and up the back stairs, knocking off our boots obediently as the man did. He turned his back to us, but his hand always hovered near the gun at his hip. He didn't trust us either. We followed him inside the house, stepping into the kitchen where a woman with graying blond hair stood at the counter, cutting vegetables. She gave us wary looks, her mouth set into a flat line.

The man said something to her, and she said something in return that sounded sharp and disappointed. He shrugged, and she set down the knife, disappearing. Footsteps on stairs, and then footsteps overhead, told us she'd been dismissed from the kitchen. The door slamming above our heads told us that she didn't like it very much.

"Frau Schneider is a suspicious woman," the man said, looking up at the ceiling with such fondness I couldn't help my gaze sneaking over to Max. He was watching me. We both looked away, color rising in our cheeks.

"Dr. Schneider," said Lily with a soft breath. She laughed a little bit. "Of course."

He looked at her. "You know my work?"

"I don't," Lily admitted, sounding a little embarrassed. "School wasn't my strength. But I know you retired rather than serve the Nazis."

"I did," he said. "I am interested in atomic physics, but I am not interested in giving Hitler the atom bomb." He gestured outside with a hand. "Look what he can do without it."

I stared at him. "How are you still alive?"

"I live a quiet life," Dr. Schneider said, lighting a cigarette and offering them to us. Lily took one, but Max and I both declined. "I keep up on the research. I expect at some time that even that will become less possible. I think they hope I'll change my mind and join them."

"Dr. Friedrich Schneider," Lily said to us. "He won a Nobel Prize in 1914 for something to do with radiographs. Apologies, doctor."

"Sir," I said in awe. "My sister. She'd love to meet you."

"Then by all means," said Dr. Schneider, "send her over. I hear so seldom from students these days, especially from female students."

"After the war," I said.

He looked at me with a narrowed gaze. "What is a Jewish boy like you doing in Europe right now?"

"You already know," Lily cut in.

"Ah, yes, blowing up Hechingen's offices. I suppose you got what you needed from there last week when that team came through. I heard there were Americans in Strasbourg."

Lily shook her head. "We don't know anything about that."

He blew out a puff of smoke and smiled at her. "So you are going to stop the German bomb. There are causes in this world that are righteous, and that is one of them, children. You are so young. You'll be going to Oranienburg next."

I didn't want to admit to anything and said, "We have a list of targets."

He looked at me sharply. "The Oranienburg plant is bigger than you think it is, boy. You will not blow it up with little bombs thrown over fences."

So he didn't know about magic.

"What did you want to tell us about Oranienburg?"

"Where to bomb, so as not to cause a nuclear explosion," he said. He got up, shuffling over to a nearby desk where he found a piece of paper and began sketching with a pencil. "If you are caught, eat it, burn it, get rid of it. I do not wish for my wife to die in a camp because of choices I made."

I looked at him. "You know about the camps then."

He paused, looking up at me. "I do."

I looked at Lily, but she shook her head. "Keep going, Dr. Schneider."

He sketched us an entire map, chattering away about uranium sheets and cubes manufactured at this plant. He drew spots where we could bomb with maximum damage, but minimal risk of radiation poisoning.

"Why are you doing this?" I asked him when he handed me the map.

"Because in exchange," he said, "you will try to limit the deaths of civilians."

"I can't guarantee that, and you know it," interrupted Lily. I might have argued with her if we were talking about France, or the Netherlands, or Denmark, but we weren't.

He looked at her and then back to me. "I believe that the light of the future is brighter than the dark of the present," he said quietly. "I believe we can beat our swords into plowshares. If we do not survive, how will we ever tell anyone in the future how to resist the rise of the next Hitler?"

I folded the map and tucked it into my breast pocket. "I don't know if I can forgive Germany. Or its citizens."

"I didn't ask you for forgiveness," he said. "I wouldn't ask you for it."

"Good." I looked at Lily and then at Max. "I have one more favor to ask, Dr. Schneider."

CHAPTER THIRTY-FIVE

OAK RIDGE, TENNESSEE
OCTOBER 6, 1943

ILSE

The day after we unlocked invisibility, we struck gold again with the equation to track the spy. Working with magic was like science: one discovery led to another one. Once we learned to bend the light to create invisibility, we used a similar concept to leverage surface tension. Wolf had said to me that magic and science were the same for me, and I hadn't truly believed him. Now I did.

Lola and I left a single blood thumbprint on the edge of two papers with false magic and science about carrying a heavy object by balloon over an ocean without stopping. One had hers, one had mine, as to introduce redundancy and test two different methods of layering the equations over each other. The equations disappeared on the page with the same invisibility clause in the math as we had used on the balloons, and we wrote nothing with our thumbprints. Just enough to trace. Just enough for our blood to want to reunite with its sister cells, wherever they were.

We left the papers together in the top drawer of the desk without locking it, in a folder labeled *October 6 breakthrough wrt weight time distance* on the desk, locked the door, but didn't close it all the way.

And then the four of us went back to the house up on the hill. One of our neighbors tutted at the sight of Stella with us, frowning suspiciously as if one dinner at our house had been enough but this was too far. Stella held her head up as we walked together, but I could tell that she was afraid. I wanted to hold her hand as though we were small children trying to be brave together, but this wasn't something I could understand. Not in any place in the United States I'd ever been, and she got it everywhere she'd ever been.

"One day," I murmured to her as we walked together. "You'll have to come to New York. That isn't a problem there."

"It's sweet," she said when we were out of earshot of the guard, "that you Yanks think this doesn't happen up there."

I flushed, ashamed, and then changed the topic. "What do you think we'll find with the tracking equation?"

"A traitor," Stella said without missing a beat.

"Do you think he's American?" I asked, looking around us carefully.

She hesitated and then sighed. "I hope not. God, wouldn't that be something? An American selling secrets to the enemy."

"We don't know they're going to Germany," I pointed out. "I don't want to jump to conclusions."

"If the information is leaving the base, then it's going to the enemy," Stella said. She shook her head. "I didn't say it was right. I'm just saying how the army will see it. You see?"

"I know," I murmured. "I'm afraid I'll get blamed. Or *one* of us will get blamed. Even if it wasn't our fault."

"Colonel Mann interviewed us, the night you were gone," Stella said. "He seemed satisfied with our answers."

I looked over the hills and the setting sun. "I'm just afraid. I don't like being wrong about people. It's just…I'm not very good at people, so when I finally figure them out, I don't like to be surprised."

"Ah," Stella said gently. "I don't think it'll be someone you like, Ilse."

"I hope not," I said and remained quiet for the rest of our walk.

In the house, Polly made tea while Lola cooked and Stella and I set up on the living room table. I wrote the tracking equation in a mixture of our blood on a balloon, let it dry for a few seconds, and then inflated the balloon. For a long moment, we held our breath, but the balloon stayed there, hanging out by the ceiling directly above us.

"No one's picked up the papers yet," Polly guessed, setting mugs of tea down next to each of us. "Drink. This tea has an herb to help with iron in it."

"You think we might be anemic?" I joked, reaching for it.

Polly pursed her lips at me, not finding the joke funny. "You broke our schedule twice this week. You can't bleed yourself that much."

I also had my menses, but that I hadn't told her. I was, in fact, bleeding quite a bit, and writing a gravity equation on the inside of your arm several times a day grew wearing. "Yes, Mother."

She made a face. "Oh, don't."

I wanted to kiss her, or twine my fingers with hers, or play with her hair, or anything, just anything, to touch her and laugh with her and find out what her skin tasted like and how it felt to bury my face in the side of her neck, to smile into the curve of her throat, to find the curves of her body with my hand.

I realized I'd been staring at her mouth for far too long. I cleared my throat and looked away, brushing my wild curls behind my ear with a shaking hand. "So now we wait."

"We wait," agreed Stella.

We sat there, drinking tea and watching the balloon. It didn't move. We ate dinner on the sofa, our plates teetering on our laps, eyes locked on the balloon brushing the ceiling above the table. An hour passed. Another hour. The sun had long set. The balloon hadn't moved.

"What if it doesn't work?" asked Polly.

"We tested it," Stella and I said together.

"I know," Lola said after a beat, her voice gentle. "But Polly asked a good question. What step will you take next if this doesn't work?"

"I don't know," I said quietly.

"Ilse…" Polly began.

"No, this has to work," I said fiercely. "Because Wolf is at risk, and we're at risk, and someone was willing to let me be charged with espionage—and my father too—and I want to find out who that was."

"Ilse," Polly said again.

"It'll work," I repeated.

"It *is* working," Polly said softly, her knuckles turning white as she gripped her plate on her lap.

Stella's head and mine snapped around at the same time to stare at the balloon that began to bump furiously against the back door in the kitchen. I scrambled up—upending my plate everywhere, food scattering—and climbed over the back of the couch without a single thought as to what my mother would say.

"Get your coat," Stella said. "It's time to go."

CHAPTER THIRTY-SIX

HEIDELBERG, GERMANY
OCTOBER 7, 1943

WOLF

Three jumps. Six hours. Nearly six hundred kilometers. Today we'd be pushing my magic and ability to bleed myself to the edge. And then we'd have to get out, if not return the entire way, before we were caught. By now, the Nazis must have figured out that their bomb sites were being targeted. I stared into the blue dark. This wasn't my favorite hour, right after midnight, but we needed to start our jumps now so we'd be outside Oranienburg by sunrise.

Get in, and get out. That's all there is to it, I told myself.

"Do you know what would really put a damper on my life?" Lily asked.

"What?" I replied, checking my equations again with a click of the flashlight.

"If Topher was captured," Lily said. And then she added, "Or if we tried to ride invisible balloons through an Allied bombing campaign. Or if there was a thunderstorm and I was electrocuted on a balloon."

"I didn't realize we were making a list," I muttered.

"You're not invited to the pity party," Lily said pointedly. "Why did you ask Dr. Schneider to let Max stay? Why didn't you write Max a balloon home?"

"I don't know if he's strong enough to fly back," I said, fixing one equation carefully before it disappeared on the balloon. "I can't tell if I fixed that decimal point fast enough."

"If it's wrong, what happens?"

"I don't know."

"Wolf, I know you're tired. Check the equation again."

"Fine," I huffed. "And for the record, I don't really care if Topher gets caught. But the rest of it would be depressing, I admit."

I didn't actually not care whether he was caught. But it felt as if it could be true, somewhere that wasn't here, behind enemy lines. The things Topher had said about me. And Max. I didn't want to squish our names together like that, but there was no way not to squeeze them together. It wasn't that Topher wasn't right—it was the way he knew he was right and hated us because of it.

"Yes," Lily said with a sigh. "And some time when we're not in a war zone, I'll rip him a new one for what he said to you in Dr. Schneider's barn. Right now, I need you to double-check that equation."

I glared at her, but I checked the balloon again. The numbers and letters swam before my tired eyes, but the balloon matched the notebook and the coordinates were correct. I'd done my job.

"What happens if Max can't get extracted with us?"

I looked up at her. "I'll figure it out, Lily. That's my problem, not yours."

"It's not yours alone," she said finally, holding my gaze. "I agreed to him being our pilot. I knew that you cared about him more than was—"

I cut her off. "Lily—"

"I know," she said gently. "And I'm sorry I pushed to leave him behind. I know you care about him, and I do too."

"I care about you too," I said abruptly. I held a balloon out to her. "We're all going to get out of this, okay? We're all going to get home."

"Of course we are. You're avoiding the question though." She slipped on her glove and took the string from me. "So Max is just like anyone else? You care about me and Max the same way."

I glared at her. "No."

She smiled sadly. "I'm not like you, Wolf. I don't find it easy to love. But I was in love once, and I know what it looks like. And it's all over your face, even when you're scowling like right now. You care. Yes, everyone knows that. Your face, when Dr. Schneider mentioned the camps. But what you feel for Max is more."

"And if we don't finish this mission, I'll never get to tell him that, and this war won't end. I can't think about it until we're done here," I said, frustrated.

"What's there to think about? You kiss him, you take him to bed, he's yours," Lily said.

I rolled my eyes. "Right, and everything everyone says about men who like men is what, Lily?"

"Irrelevant," she said.

I sighed. "I don't want to talk about this."

Lily leaned forward, cupping my cheek in her small, soft, warm hand. "Don't let anyone else tell you who you are, Sunshine. Not me, not Topher, not anyone. What they say about you and Max is irrelevant. After the war, we're going to talk about this. We're going to find you a little cottage in the French countryside where no one gives a damn. Two bachelors with one bed."

I had to crack a smile at that. "In the French countryside, eh?"

"Or on the coast. Have you ever been to the coast of France? North, south, it doesn't matter. The coast is beautiful. There's something exquisite about French coastal towns. They live in a different world," she said, sighing dramatically.

"Okay," I agreed. "When we're done with this mess, you show us some French villages on the coast where no one will bother Max and me, and where he can get better."

"He's going to get better. Head trauma takes a long time, but he'll get better," Lily said.

"You're Captain Optimism this morning," I said, curiosity bleeding into my voice.

She snorted. "I'm always Captain Optimism. You're just too busy fawning over Max to notice."

"That's not true," I said, finishing Lily's balloon and handing it off to her. "You started today with a list of everything that could go wrong."

"True," she said. "Six jumps. Six hours. Ready for this?"

No. But I had to be.

Our next balloons were written, waiting to be inflated and tied with string to activate them, and tucked into my pack. Ahead of us was a uranium plant supplying the German nuclear bomb project and a map of how to blow up that plant without killing civilians. Then we were done. We just needed to get back here, pick up Max, and get back to England.

Easy as pie, as Max would say.

Lily checked her watch. "He should be here by now."

I didn't want to defend Topher, but evidence thus far had suggested that he always showed. Always in the nick of time, a little manic and a little frantic. At least he was good at his job. "Maybe he's collected some good...What do you call it?"

"Gossip," Lily said, looking away, up the road toward the town. We had agreed to meet by an abandoned fruit stand outside town. "Michael used to call it scuttlebutt. Navy term, I think."

"Do you think about him a lot?" It was the first she'd mentioned him since we met.

"Michael?" she asked, looking back at me. Her frown furrowed her forehead. "Only about every other heartbeat."

My heart ached. "Lily, I'm sorry."

She nodded and looked back up the road, as if she was going to see anything in the dark. "It's hard to fall in love early and lose so early too. I'm a twenty-two-year-old widow. We were married for six weeks. It wasn't enough."

"You deserved more," I told her.

I could just see the corner of her mouth turn up briefly. "We both did. I appreciate that you aren't telling me I'll fall in love again."

I shrugged. "I don't like making promises I can't keep."

She laughed. "God, it's too bad optimism isn't contagious. You could use a dose of it."

"I don't understand how you are so positive. Jews, we tend to be fatalistic," I said, peering over her shoulder at the sound of a truck. "Look at what happens to us."

"My family's Judaism wasn't particularly religious," Lily said. "My father is a jeweler. My mother raised us. We didn't celebrate holidays or go to synagogue. I don't think I've ever been to a synagogue, to be honest, and I can't speak a word of Hebrew."

"I don't know if I believe in God anymore," I admitted. Faith was more than God to me, and I didn't know how to explain that, but I tried. "But I miss going to synagogue. I like being a part of history. Something bigger than myself, surrounded by people who are also part of that history, sharing in something that's been passed down for thousands of years."

"If we get out of Germany," Lily said, "I'll come to synagogue with you."

"You would?" I asked, delighted.

Lily smiled again. "Yes. I think that would make my heart happy."

"I'd like that," I told her and then frowned as the noise grew closer. "Truck. Definitely coming this way."

We faded back into the grass, pulling the balloons close to our bodies and pressing ourselves down into the ditch. The truck sputtered past, backfired, and kept going without stopping. No footsteps.

I looked at Lily. "Do we go on without him?"

She closed her eyes and nodded. "We must."

CHAPTER THIRTY-SEVEN

OAK RIDGE, TENNESSEE
OCTOBER 6, 1943

ILSE

Stella and I stood at the edge of the woods. As soon as the blood trail proved not to be a fluke, I gave in to Polly's wishes and sent her and Lola to find Colonel Mann—or if not him, George. Just someone who would know what to do. Without them, it was unnaturally still around us, dark and foreboding. And cold. I hiked my backpack with my balloon kit up higher on my shoulders.

"Shall we?" asked Stella.

We had to. I nodded and held up the flashlight to the balloon drifting ahead of us.

We stepped off the road and into the woods. The woods were deep, and they went on forever, more endless than looking into space, and we bumped into each other, trees, stones, and rocks. Everything around us felt wild, new, like we were on the frontier of something dark and terrible. We followed the balloon forward, weaving through the forest at a snail's pace. Stella's face glowed, wide-eyed and frightened, in the flashlight's beam.

"We found it."

I hesitated and ran the flashlight at knee height across everything in front of us. It skimmed across tree trunks and darkness, and then we both screamed, catching ourselves with hands slapped over our mouths to stifle the noise, as the beam bounced over the edge of a wooden cabin.

I clicked off the flashlight and we squatted, breathing hard.

"I think I peed myself," I whispered.

"Me too," said Stella. "No lights."

"Do you think someone's in there?" I edged forward and then stood on legs that trembled violently. I wasn't even sure how I was going to walk. But I took one step, and then another. I clicked on the flashlight.

"Ilse," pleaded Stella. Then she cursed under her breath, said a prayer, and caught up with me. She gripped a stick like a weapon.

We found the stairs. We climbed them. Our breathing was so loud that if there was anyone inside the cabin, they surely heard us coming. And then on a silent count of three, I found the doorknob, turned it, and shoved it open. I leapt inside, holding the flashlight up and yelling, "*HRRAGHHHH!*" at the top of my lungs. Stella screamed.

The cabin was silent.

"Oh my God, oh my God, oh my God," Stella chanted.

I turned the flashlight around the room. It was empty. Quiet. My beam caught smoke curling up from a candle on a desk. It'd only been empty for a short time. "We just missed him."

"It could be a woman," said Stella with a shaking voice. "Ilse, what if they come back?"

"We need to take everything we can find." I said, walking around. "No, we need to leave it. Colonel Mann needs to see it. I can't decide."

"We're going to die," Stella said. "This is definitely how people die. Alone, in the woods, in someone else's cabin."

I moved around, pointing my flashlight at papers. "Let's find out who this person is."

We walked around in a circle. Vials of blood, needles, balloons, and equations I recognized scrawled on paper. Stella pointed out a few equations—some of the ones we'd been working on that had been stolen from the lab. I nodded, wide-eyed. This was where the spy was working.

Then my beam caught something underneath a notebook, and I reached forward, picking it up. I almost dropped it the moment I lifted it into the light.

George Steele

Chemist

X-10

All Pass

"Oh my God," I whispered.

I know it wasn't you, Ilse, he said in a memory echoing in my head. He hadn't known why I was being arrested. He *shouldn't* have known why I was being arrested that day. But he had. He had let it slip, and I hadn't even known it.

With shaking hands, I handed the ID to Stella and picked up the journal. I flipped through it, skimming it, but it was written in an alphanumeric code that I couldn't break quickly, or maybe at all without at least one of the keys. I flipped through, my eyes searching for anything familiar, catching on *nuclear* and *uranium*, and then stopping, along with my heart, as I flipped back to a page I had passed. At the top of the page, it said, *Wolf Klein.*

George had asked about my brother once, but this was filled with dates and entries for pages. He knew my brother, somehow. And not just from the notes he'd stolen from me.

"I need a balloon," I said shakily. "And a pen. And blood. Quickly. Please."

"It won't get there in time," Stella said.

"I don't care!" I screamed.

Stella grabbed my right arm, still aching from the handcuffs. "Ilse. I'm not saying you shouldn't care. Think this through. Can Colonel Mann get a message to him faster?"

"I don't know," I whispered. "But if George finds out that we know before we have time to warn Wolf, what happens?"

"How is George getting back and forth from…?" Stella looked at me and then added, "Europe. Let's pretend I don't know what they've sent your brother to do, and we'll just say Europe."

I wiped at the tears on my face. "I don't know."

"Look at the dates. Figure it out," Stella said, her voice a steady beacon in the chaos of my mind. "I'm going to look around for anything that looks odd."

"It's all odd," I whispered. *George! He'd recognized me on the first day!* I had been so taken in by him. I'd thought his fawning had been true admiration, from one scientist to another. Had he been playing me the whole time? Had he known what our mission was the entire time?

I began skimming dates and entries. He'd never been traveling to the other sites. How had Colonel Mann not known? Then I saw something even more curious. There was an entry on September 28. When he'd been here at the dance, he'd also recorded an event with Wolf. I didn't have the cipher for his journal, but the dates weren't in cipher. Likely an easy way for him to find certain information, but now it was his downfall. He was in Europe, and he was here on the same day. How had he done that?

He could travel faster than we knew how.

"He…There's a different way he moves," I said. "Look for equations that make no sense to you. Look for anything that doesn't look like it's based in a math you know."

"I know every math," said Stella, and it wasn't a boast. It was a simple truth.

"That's what I mean," I said, flipping through the journal. "He was here and in Germany on the same day. How?"

"Ilse," said Stella.

"I suppose he could be traveling faster than a plane but how could he do that without harming himself?" But then I thought about how different George had been the last time I'd seen him. Irritable and edgy, pushy and violent when he hadn't been before. Which was the real George? Or was the irritable George the one showing side effects of his traveling?

"*Ilse*," Stella said again, sharply this time. "I found something."

I moved over to where she stood, bent over a piece of paper with a formula on it I'd never seen before. We stared at it for a long moment, trying to make sense of it, and then Stella said, "We don't have time to test it. We have to hope this is right."

"You're right," I said quietly. I looked up into her dark eyes. "I'll write it."

Just in case it backfired.

Stella knew what I meant. She nodded slowly and handed me the piece of paper. "I'll get your kit."

She gathered materials for me while I wrote a letter to Wolf. I drew blood from my arm hastily, and Stella held off the vein while I dipped one of George's blood pens into the bloody inkwell and wrote on the balloon carefully. I wrote the strange equation, hoping that it was right. Then I tied the letter to the balloon string, blew it up, tied it off with string woven with Wolf's hair, and hurried to the door. Stella followed me with the light and watched as I let go of the balloon. Instead of it floating up, a line appeared in the air in front of us, as if someone had unzipped the universe. It swallowed the balloon without a sound and zipped back up.

"Dear Lord," murmured Stella, "What was that?"

"I don't know," I whispered. "I think that was how he was traveling."

"That wasn't natural," she said, still staring into the night where a balloon should have been floating away from us.

But an idea was taking hold. George was out there with my brother. If I could get there and get back quickly...I had to try. I raced back into the cabin.

CHAPTER THIRTY-EIGHT

WOLF

Our first jump took us to Koblenz, Germany. When we'd set up the jumps, we'd set up coordinate points near each city in case we became separated. They weren't immediately at the jumps, to avoid us being ambushed or compromised, so though we landed around 2:00 a.m. and were tired and aching from hanging on to the balloons, Lily and I walked to our coordinate point, in case Topher had somehow made it there by truck or train—or by hijacking a plane, for all I knew.

He wasn't there. He'd been grating on my nerves, but that didn't mean I wasn't worried. If he had been compromised, Dr. Schneider and Max were both in danger. If he'd been killed or captured, that also was a terrible fate. I wouldn't want to be in the hands of the Germans again. I thought I'd kill myself first. I still had my L-pill, and last I'd known, Topher still had his. I hoped he had the guts to use it.

"Just set up slower," advised Lily, looking anxiously around in the slowly warming light of day.

"Okay," I agreed, even though there was nothing I could do to move slower. Magic took the time that it took. And not that it was my call, but we couldn't put the whole mission at risk for Topher. I blew up the balloons, tied off the strings, and held on to all three of them. "Lily, if he's not coming…"

"He might have gone on to the next jump," she decided. She took his balloon, then hers. She began rising again, looking tired and worried.

I took off my glove and wrapped my bare hand around my balloon string, rising into the air. Beneath us, darkness stretched as far as I could see. There was a strange disorientation to floating through the night. In the distance, lights blinked and disappeared. Someone breaking blackout. And far to the west, I thought I could see the nightly flak of the Allied planes battling the Luftwaffe. But it could have been a storm, as far off as it was.

The sun rose to the east, a glimmer of soft blue that rose and stretched the way Sunday mornings used to be lazy ones at home before the war. Then as the light showed the wide expanse of German fields beneath me, I saw something that made my heart stumble and miss a beat. From the west, a glimmer of red hurtled toward me. *Ilse.* The balloon reached me in midair, as my arms were growing tired and aching, and I caught it, holding on to it while I floated swiftly toward our next stop, as far as the balloons could take people. I couldn't open the envelope while floating without letting go of my balloon, but I could see Ilse's handwriting on the outside. It wasn't her normal neat and tight handwriting. Something twisted in my stomach.

"What is it?" called Lily.

"Ilse," I replied as our balloons began to lose altitude. I stumbled as my feet hit the ground. Landing from the balloon was slower than from a parachute, but less graceful. I straightened, hoisting my pack higher on my shoulders, and then slid my fingers beneath the seal on the envelope, breaking it open.

Lily was walking ahead on the road.

I began to unfold the letter, following slowly. My eyes ran over the first lines of the letter.

Wolf,

    I don't know how you know him, but he knows you. There's a spy at Oak Ridge.

My heart clenched so tightly that it felt as if it had stopped beating. "Lily."

    I don't know what he calls himself with you. Sometimes he has a beard, sometimes he doesn't, but he has a stopwatch he's always clicking.

There was a *pop* in the air next to me, and I yanked my gun out, spinning around and dropping the letter to the ground. Ilse stumbled, breathless, out of the middle of the air onto the road next to me, her hands reaching out to grab me.

"Ilse?" I said, catching her with my free hand.

"Wolf," she gasped, her eyes wide and bloodshot, a trickle of red running from her nose to her upper lip. "He's a spy. He's a spy."

"There he is!" Lily cried with relief, breaking into a run ahead of us, off the road and toward an apple tree where Topher stood, an unused balloon at his side, tied to his pack.

A stopwatch in his hand.

Click, click, click.

Ilse gasped beside me.

Click.

I started to run, shoving Ilse to the side, out of danger. "Lily! Get away from him!"

Topher came off the tree, his expression changing from mild and pleasant to fierce and dark in one click of his stopwatch. He grabbed Lily by the wrist and twisted her, a blade appearing from nowhere in one of his hands to press against her throat. Though caught off guard, Lily reacted immediately. She slammed her elbow backward and her heel down onto his boot. The blade bit into her throat and she grunted, then swung her foot backward and upward, getting him in the crotch. He yelled and dropped away from her, swiping at her with the blade, and she spun away from him, her hand going to her hip.

He cocked her gun at her. "Looking for this, sweetheart?"

"Lily," I said, reaching for her. "Your neck."

"What the hell is going on?" she snapped, pressing a hand to her throat. Blood leaked through her fingers. She didn't shake at all. She didn't turn away from Topher, but her eyes slid from me, then widened slightly in surprise when she saw Ilse.

I held out my arm, catching Ilse as she threw herself forward. "You are a spy!"

Topher stared at her, his face caught between amusement and frustration. "I should have gotten rid of you."

Ilse growled in anger, and I kept a grip on her arm. "Topher, what's your real name?"

"I know him as George Steele," Ilse said.

Lily scowled at Topher. "What is this? Who are you? Who hired you?"

Topher flipped off the safety. "None of you will survive to tell anyone."

"Everyone knows," Ilse said, her breath and voice steady. "They know you're the one stealing secrets."

I said, "The game's up, Topher."

"The game isn't up," he said. "There's still Oranienburg."

There was a flash of light, and I lunged forward, but Lily's blade flew home, burying itself in Topher's gut. He gasped and jerked, a gunshot going off, echoing in the space around us. I shouted, and Lily began to crumple toward the ground. I caught her, cushioning her fall against my body. She gasped, eyes wide, dark-red blood blossoming over her front, just below her rib cage. He'd shot her right where she'd buried a knife in him.

Ilse cried out, "No!"

I pressed a hand to the wound. "It's all right, Lily. Lily, look at me. You're going to be all right."

Topher fumbled with the string of his balloon from his pack. I could have reached him, but Lily on my lap kept me from moving quickly. I gaped, helpless, as he took off one glove and grasped the string with one hand. Ilse charged at him, but it was too late. There was a strange twist to the air, as if the universe had cut a hole in the fabric of what I could see, sucked him in, and then zipped the hole shut again. He was gone. Just his pack remained.

Lily swore, and when I looked down, blood welled between my fingers.

"Lil," I said. "Stay with me."

I pressed my hand into her stomach, grimacing when she grunted in pain. I had to stop the bleeding. "Ilse, what's in his pack?"

"He's gone."

"Ilse," I said sharply. "I need whatever's in his pack. Whatever you can do to stop the bleeding."

Ilse dumped the pack upside down, and it jangled as everything spilled out onto the ground beneath the apple trees. I turned back to Lily. "We're going to get you fixed up. I'll take you back to England. Ilse can take you back to England. Right, Ilse?"

Ilse knelt beside me, bandages and a blanket tumbling from her arms. She touched Lily's face with trembling fingers. "Hi, I'm Ilse."

Lily's smile shook. "Hi, Ilse."

"Ilse, do something," I begged.

"Wolf," Lily said. "Stop."

I gripped her tightly, pulling her against my body. "No. No. Ilse, do what you did to come here. We can take her to a hospital."

Tears streamed down Ilse's face, and she shook her head. "I can't. She won't make it."

I screamed at her, my voice cracking and shattering around the words, "You can't, or you won't?"

"I'm so sorry," Ilse whispered, resting her hand against Lily's clammy cheek.

"I know." Lily smiled a little, lifting a bloody hand to my cheek. "You can't give up, Wolf."

"I'm not giving up, and neither are you," I snapped. "Ilse, get a balloon. Write it."

Ilse stared at me for a second, opening her mouth to protest, and then pulled a balloon from my pack and a set of needles. I'd never seen her hands shake before, but she couldn't make them still and steady.

"No," Lily said quietly. Her skin felt damp, cold and hot all at the same time. She gripped my hand. Her breathing was shallow. "Wolf. You have to get to Oranienburg. And then you have to get Max home. Do you hear me?"

"Are those orders?" I asked. I didn't even know I was crying until tears splashed down over our clasped hands, washing away the blood in spots, like rain on a dusty window.

Tears filled her eyes. "Those are your orders, Sunshine. No questions."

I turned my face to wipe it against my shoulder. "I don't want to let you go."

"I don't want to go," she whispered and then coughed, her body rising a little as she fought to breathe. "But we don't get to choose when it's our time."

"Ah, finally. There's that fatalism," I whispered back, tears falling steadily now. She blurred in my vision, becoming a patchwork of her blue shirt and pale skin and red blood and soft red-brown hair.

"Sing me a song?" she asked, gripping my hand tightly.

I swallowed hard and made myself smile. "Don't make fun of my singing voice."

She laughed a little and then coughed, pain making her body seize up, blood leaking into her lungs. It pooled in her mouth, slicking her tongue. I forced myself not to look away, not to miss a moment of this.

"I don't know too many songs," I whispered, brushing my hand against her cheek to push her hair out of her face, blood streaking under my thumb. "But I know one pretty well."

I sang "You Are My Sunshine" to her twice, while she died in my arms under the apple tree, my sister sitting next to us in the bloodied dirt, the scattered remains of betrayal in the long grass around us.

We buried her there, in the hollow ground where an apple tree had overturned in a storm, covering her with stones where the dirt couldn't cover her body. Ilse held my hand, and then when it was time to say goodbye, I wrote us new balloons.

CHAPTER THIRTY-NINE

ORANIENBURG, GERMANY
OCTOBER 7, 1943

ILSE

I'd never traveled by balloon, not like this. I'd stepped through the tear George's magic had made in the fabric of the world, but I hadn't hung on to a balloon string for miles, afraid to look down. When we started to descend, Wolf called instructions to me on how to hold my legs and land without breaking my ankle. I stumbled and fell over, letting go of the balloon, which disappeared instantly. Wolf landed on his feet, calmly letting go of the string without looking at the evaporating balloon. I might still know more magic and equations, but he'd surpassed me in comfort. This was his life—surviving and relying on magic.

I felt woefully unprepared, my hands still shaking and covered in Lily's blood. I couldn't forget the wild look in Wolf's eyes, the desperation in his voice when he'd begged me to do something. Was there something I could have done? Was there anything we could have done? I knew in my heart that there wasn't, but I couldn't meet Wolf's eyes. He looked like a different person. Thinner, harder, more of an edge to his voice, with wild eyes and a beard I'd never seen before. I had to remind myself, *This is my brother.*

"Where are we?" I managed to ask.

"Oranienburg," he said, his voice rough and hoarse. We stood on a grassy hill overlooking a main road. "There's a factory there. Two o'clock."

I twisted to look over my shoulder, and he said, "*My* two o'clock."

"Last time it was mine," I muttered. "You can't change it up on me."

There was a brief moment when we both almost smiled.

Then Wolf's face dropped, ruining the moment, and he faced the factory. "It's our last target."

"What do they make?"

He shot me a look. "I don't know. We don't need to know."

I swallowed. There was still an ocean between us, and I didn't know the magic, dark or not, to cross it.

"What do you need me to do?" I asked, trying to make my hands stop shaking.

"We used the equation for invisibility on ourselves once. It didn't last long though. Maybe an hour, tops. What are the chances you can figure out how to make it last longer?" Wolf asked quietly, crouching in the bushes and swinging his pack in front of him, pulling open the top flap.

I watched him dig for something. He seemed to know what he was looking for, even if he didn't share that information. "That's shorter than our experiments suggested it would last. Did you write the equation exactly how I sent it to you? Do you think it acts differently on skin than objects?"

"You're the scientist, Ilse," he muttered. He swore and opened a different part of the pack, digging deeper past his clothes, notebooks, needles, and balloons.

"I don't know," I said, trying to think. "Maybe it was diluted by your skin. Maybe the magic in your veins and capillaries really affected the magic. We tested it on Polly, but not on anyone else, and not while flying."

"Why *not*?" he growled.

"Wolf," I said, surprised by his tone and my gentleness. "We can do this."

He closed his eyes. "I've never had to do it without her."

"Do you want to get Max?" I asked, because I didn't know what else to say.

He opened his eyes, his brow furrowing. "No. He's safe where he is." He took a deep breath and nodded, exhaling slowly through his teeth. "Okay. Walk me through this."

I showed him how he'd draw the blood, set it in a glass tube, and use a match to heat the tube. When the blood started to congeal, he'd need to write with that, even if it was sticky and difficult. He tucked the pack of matches from his bag into the inside pocket of his coat, along with the syringes, a sealed glass vial full of blood we drew from me, the camera pen, and a fistful of uninflated balloons.

"Okay." He met my eyes. "I think it'll take me about an hour to get into the plant and find the office, take photos, and get out. I'll keep reapplying the invisibility equation with your blood and then jump back here. Two hours."

"Don't rush," I reminded him. "Don't set the burning balloons in a pattern that blocks your escape route."

"I'm worried, not stupid," Wolf said.

I snorted. "Oh, you're worried, Wolf? Wow, I had no idea."

He lightly smacked the side of my head, a smile playing on his face. "Shut up."

I pushed at his shoulder with a smile. "Okay. Go. We don't have all day."

"If I don't come back—" he began, zipping up his jacket.

"Don't talk like that," I snapped.

"Listen to me, Ilse. This is important," he said. He pulled out a map and, after a quick scan, drew a circle around one set of coordinates, a small, open area outside Heidelberg. "This is a safe place to go. Max is there, and you can tell the farmer who you are."

I took the map. "You're coming back."

"If you don't hear from me in four hours," he said. "Leave."

"Six," I tried.

"Four," he said after a long pause. I sighed, a little dramatically in an effort to get him to smile. He almost did. "And if I come back in four and a half and you're still here, I'll be so angry."

"But alive," I pointed out.

"Ah, Ilse," Wolf said, reaching over and fluffing my hair. "I missed you. Look for the explosions, but don't wait for me if I'm late. Things go wrong. I'll find my way out."

"Promise?" I asked him.

He let his hand fall from my head. "I promise."

"Go," I said.

And he took the first balloon from me and disappeared.

CHAPTER FORTY

ORANIENBURG, GERMANY
OCTOBER 7, 1943

WOLF

The Oranienburg plant was quiet. The kind of quiet that was un-natural. A stillness that settled in my bones and sent my heart out of rhythm. Had they known I was coming? Had Topher tipped them off? Were they lying in wait? I'd landed in the open, next to a fence and a large metal building, and I'd sprinted for the first door I saw, desperate not to be shot by a guard. But the building was empty. I hadn't expected that.

I walked down the long hallway, my footsteps echoing against the metal sides of the building and the blasted-out glass windows.

No, it wasn't quiet because they'd known I'd been coming. This had been abandoned for months, at the least.

I took a deep breath, reassured, and then the hum came through. Machinery. Workers. Footsteps. The factory was alive, just not the building I'd found. I walked down the stairs, my steps echoing through the space, announcing me to ghosts. At the door, cool even through my gloves, I took a deep breath, exhaling slowly.

"There's no way through but through," I said aloud. *Through* echoed in the space, drifting into syllables. *You, you, you.* I opened the door a crack, Lily's sidearm in my hand.

A truck rumbled by, and I nearly slammed the door shut but caught myself just in time. Training kicked in. Sudden movements, sudden changes were noticed. Infinitesimal changes were not. I waited until the truck rumbled away and then pressed the door open a little bit more. Daylight streamed through the crack—bright, white, crossing over my arm in the army greens and my black glove.

I waited for shouts.

A shot.

Some change in the pattern of movement outside the door.

Nothing.

I pushed the door open and slid out into the shadow and the shade, pressing myself against the wall. *Inside the building*, a voice that sounded like Lily's said inside my mind. *Get inside as fast as you can.* The informant had passed along a map of inside the building, but not of the entire factory grounds. I counted windows across the short south-facing side of the building across from the abandoned one. It seemed as though it ought to be the right one.

How will I get in? I scanned the guards, the doors, then the bays where trucks were leaving and coming. I'd be seen at any of those.

I shifted my pack on my back, trying to weigh my options. Then I remembered, *Magic. You use magic, you idiot.* If Ilse were here, she'd probably smack me upside the head. Lily would have given me the most suffering of all long-suffering sighs. Max would have snorted. Topher would have pretended he'd also forgotten I could use magic, while pretending he couldn't. All those times I bled myself to the brink, and we could have used his blood too.

I could kill him for that, not just his other crimes. I hoped I would get the chance.

I ducked back inside the abandoned plant and crouched by the door, pulling out the syringe. I held my breath, my eyes trained on the sliver of daylight by the door, waiting for shadows of patrols or someone who'd noticed me, but no one came while I drew blood and then wrote the equation for invisibility onto my skin.

I pushed open the door again, carefully, then pulled it shut, then shoved it open, as if the wind had caught it. They'd still see this moving, and I wanted to draw some attention. If they came this way, they wouldn't see me going into the building. Sure enough, there was a shout and a few guards pointed in my direction. I moved quickly around them, stepping quickly and lightly as not to leave footprints.

One more time. I needed to do this only one more time, and my mission—Lily's mission—would be complete. Our obligations to the war effort, to humanity, would be complete. Hitler couldn't get the bomb, and perhaps more selfishly, I needed to know that I had done everything in my power to prevent him from getting the bomb.

If I failed...

I would not fail.

I could not fail.

CHAPTER FORTY-ONE

ILSE

I should have gone with him. Waiting in the woods, blood drying on my skin as I made myself invisible to passersby, was almost painful. I had to raise my shirt and write on my stomach to find skin not tainted with Lily's blood. I kept thinking of everything that could have gone wrong—if Wolf was caught, if he was executed, if I had to go find him and I didn't know exactly where I was going, if I had to leave him behind, if I was caught, if they found me, unable to speak German—and it made my head pound inside my skull.

Cars passed back and forth on the road at fairly regular intervals, and each time, I retreated a little into the forest, despite the magic on my skin. But no one slowed or stopped me, even when I could feel the magic fading.

Then cars stopped coming by. None appeared for minutes. Then a quarter of an hour. Then thirty minutes. My panic grew, raising my heart rate and kicking my adrenaline into high gear. They'd caught Wolf. Something had gone wrong.

After forty minutes, I heard the sound of a truck, and it soothed me to know that traffic was resuming its normal pattern.

There was a soft pop in the air, and before I could react, a hand clapped around my mouth. I screamed into the sweaty palm as someone knelt next to me. A familiar voice said quietly, "Do not scream."

He started to let me go, but I spun on him, slamming my fist into the first part of George's body I could reach. He coughed, doubling over his injured stomach. He held up a gun, but his hand shook and I wasn't afraid of him. I was not afraid of him.

"Don't," he wheezed. "Ilse."

I fumbled with the gun Wolf had left me, but my hands shook and I dropped it. George lunged for it, snatching it out of the grass. I slammed my knee into the side of his head. He groaned and fell to the side, but lifted the pistol. There was a soft click, and I froze. He squinted at me. "God. That equation's good. This will go easier if you remove it."

"How can you see me?" I hissed.

"I come from a long line of people who know more magic than you can imagine exists. But I believe in you. You're brilliant. You'll figure it out eventually," he said.

"Or Stella will," I snipped at him.

He cracked a smile. "I'm pointing a pistol at you. Will you shut up?"

I lifted my chin. "No. You killed Lily."

George's face fell. "That…that was a mistake. I regret that."

"Why though? Why spy? Why have so many identities?"

"Because this war is immoral, and all I want is balance," he said, catching his breath. "I just want to bring balance to the world. You understand that, don't you? They're going to build this weapon, and the world hates imbalance. Someone else needs it, so that one nation-state cannot wield all the power."

"Or you could have helped me—us—stop anyone from building it," I whispered.

He smiled. "Maybe. You're an idealist. I'm not. I sold secrets to the Soviets, the same way I sold Soviet secrets to the United States. A different sort of war is coming, Ilse, but it only matters if we win this one."

"Why are you here?"

"I tracked you," he said. "Your hair trick is brilliant. Your papers were illuminating. I'm sorry that they hurt you for what I did."

He did not look very sorry, lying there on the forest floor, pointing a pistol at me.

"Where's my notebook, Ilse?" George asked quietly.

It was tucked into the waist of my pants right now, beneath my shirt and coat. I forced myself not to flinch. "In the cabin."

"It's not there. Nothing's there," he said in frustration.

In the distance, I heard the sound of a truck rumbling closer. I took a long step back when it drew George's attention. He glanced back at me, tightening his grip on the pistol as he got to his feet. "Who is that?"

"I don't know. You think anyone in Germany is going to help me?" I asked him, failing to keep the bitter sarcasm out of my voice.

"Not Wolf," he said. "He's at Oranienburg. And don't look at me like that. I won't hurt Wolf. I told you. Lily was a mistake."

One truck drew closer on the road, slow, with Germans sitting in the back, their guns slung over their shoulders lazily. I could see the muzzles of the rifles even over a distance. They were all facing behind them, like they were watching something. Was the truck broken? Why was it traveling so slowly? Occasionally, someone shouted in German, but I couldn't catch the word.

Then I saw them. Thin as the stripes on their uniforms, shuffling rather than marching, down the road, three rows of men. My eyes got so wide I thought they might fall out of my head as the rows kept going and going, as far as my eye could see as they came over the hill.

The men shuffled closer, and I sank into the woods, desperately trying to wipe tears from my face and think of something to do. I had to do something. I couldn't just sit here and do nothing, not while they marched—where? Where were they going? Why?

"Good God," said George softly next to me. He'd lowered the gun to his side. I could take it if I wanted, but my attention was trapped on the people on the road. "Good. *God.*"

"We have to do something," I whispered to him.

"We can't do anything," he said, his voice bitter and small. "It's Nazi Germany. It's a machine. We can only hope that the other machines stop them."

"You killed Lily, and you'll just refuse to help these people?" I hissed, spinning on him and shoving him with both hands. He grunted, stumbling back, pain flashing over his face. I stepped closer to him, lowering my voice. "You are a coward."

His face crumpled. "Ilse."

"If you aren't going to help, get out of my way." I sat down, unpacking the few supplies Wolf had left me. I rolled up my sleeve, finding my vein, and slipped a needle and syringe out of the case.

I slipped the needle into my vein, my hands shaking. "You're going to blow your vein," George said, crouching next to me and reaching for my arm. I pulled away from him, and he hesitated. "I'm sorry. Ilse, for everything."

"I do not forgive you," I whispered.

"Let me help," he said after a beat.

And I don't know why, but I did.

CHAPTER FORTY-TWO

ORANIENBURG, GERMANY
OCTOBER 7, 1943

WOLF

I understood why Lily had us coming in here during the dead of night on the original schedule. Moving around an active factory wasn't the easiest, even when invisible. They'd still feel me if I bumped into them, still see things I moved, and thus I could move only where they moved, open doors they opened, touch things that already were opened, until I reached the laboratory overlooking the refinement activities.

I crept into a laboratory, opening the file cabinets and drawers. Every one of them was empty. I looked around in confusion. I had to be in the wrong lab. But it was empty of people too, which seemed unusual given how busy the rest of the factory was. I slid past the desk and tables to the door on the other side of the laboratory. There was a meeting room on the other side, where men with solemn faces and downcast frowns were sitting around a table. A man in a Nazi uniform was speaking in clipped tones at the front of the room. I hesitated and then pressed the side of my face to the glass.

"Security breach," said the Nazi officer. "Unbelievable, unfathomable, and a true betrayal to the Fatherland."

Topher was here, I realized. He hadn't blown anything up, but he'd gotten here. He'd already taken all the secrets in Oranienburg.

Get out, my mind said. *There's nothing for you here.* My hands shook as I applied another equation for invisibility onto my arm. For a brief moment, I thought I'd screwed it up, and I wondered if my skin would catch fire. But the equation just warmed on my skin, and I was invisible again.

Get out, said Lily's voice in my mind.

Then the alarm went off.

I leapt to my feet, grabbing my bag from where it sat, visible, next to me, as lights and a warning bell flashed outside the door and I could hear people shouting instructions. The men inside the meeting room burst into action. The Nazi officer looked baffled. Whatever was happening wasn't normal.

Lockdown, I realized. Something had triggered a lockdown.

Bombing run? My skin ran cold.

I had to move fast, use this lockdown alarm as much as I could, and get to somewhere where I might survive a bomb. I pulled out the balloons, writing down the equations Ilse had shared with me, and then pulled out the small glass vial. I pulled blood quickly, sealed the vial, and then struck the match, holding it next to the glass. It grew warm quickly, and the blood curled, bubbled, and thickened. Before it turned into a clot, I shook out the match and tossed it to the side. I painted each balloon with the thickened blood and tied one, invisible, to a desk in the lab. The heat radiating off it was slow, but I could feel it.

I had to move fast. I couldn't care who saw the door open. I shoved it open and ran down the stairs, tying another balloon to the stairs, alongside other offices.

Get out.

On the floor of the factory, I examined the workers carefully, looking for any sign that they might be prisoners. But they all looked healthy, strong, and Aryan.

In my head, Lily said, *Pull the alarm. Get them out.* But the alarm was going out, and they seemed to be securing the material, their guttural German lighting a fire in my bones. They were help-ing a vile man, an evil man, kill tens of thousands of people, maybe hundreds of thousands, maybe more. And they were helping him build a weapon to do it at a grander scale.

I wasn't Lily. And maybe I wasn't a good person. But neither were they.

CHAPTER FORTY-THREE

ILSE

"Hurry," I murmured, as George wrote equation after equation on an inflated balloon.

"You can't rush magic any more than you can rush science," he said. We were using my blood because George looked half-dead, and because he'd hesitated long enough when I suggested using his blood too that it made my skin crawl. There was something haunted about his pale, gaunt face, about the way he talked about the magic he was using and creating.

"We can only free six," he said. "I can't pull more than that amount of blood from you without risking your ability to escape if needed."

"Six isn't enough," I argued.

He grimaced. "I know. I'm sorry."

But he offered no solutions, and when I racked my brain, I found none of my own.

Beyond the trees, one man dropped, fell to the ground, and the line bubbled. Two men stopped, trying to help him to his feet. He stumbled and fell again. A guard walking alongside them casually drew his pistol and shot the man on the ground. I clapped my hands over my mouth, muffling my scream as his body jolted and then remained still.

The line shifted and the men walked on, around his body.

They'd just shot him. Right there on the ground because he'd been too tired to go on.

"Please," I whispered. "Hurry."

"Do you have gloves?" George asked. I knew what he meant, had followed the math and codes he wrote in my blood on the red balloons. Without the blood of the prisoners, the balloon would accept the next person who touched it with their bare hand. If I touched it, I'd have to let go of the string, and then the balloon was gone. Wasted. If a guard touched it...everything was ruined. We'd be sending a Nazi to the same coordinates as five other Jews.

I had to take the chance. *We* had to take the chance.

We didn't have thousands, or hundreds, or even ten balloons. But we had six to spare, and we could save six people. I hoped we were saving them.

The first balloon floated free from the woods and bushes where we hid, as though it was attracted to the mass of people marching on the road. Maybe it was. Maybe magic needed people.

The first prisoner to see it smiled, lifting his gaunt, hunger-carved face toward it. He lifted a hand and grabbed the string. He disappeared from view. A murmur went up among the prisoners, and immediately they began looking around—to the sky for their friend, for another balloon—and filled in his space in the line so he wasn't missed. But a guard had noticed, and he shouted in German. The guards all began firing into the sky, but I held my breath. No balloon became visible. No body fell from the sky.

I looked sideways to George who gave me a weary smile. "Again."

We released the second balloon. This time, the guards began firing at it, but the balloon wavered, rocking in the air and floating on. A hundred shaking hands reached for it, and then two men held up a child—he was only a child, maybe eleven or twelve—and the boy's hand wrapped around the string.

I heard a man cry out, *"Zol Got mir helfen!"*

And the guards turned their guns on us in the bushes, where the two balloons had come from. They opened fire, descending on our hiding spot.

George grabbed my arm, hauling me to my feet as I tried to gather our supplies and move. He dragged me deeper into the woods, and we fell to our knees as he handed me the pistol and said, "Shoot back if you must."

It was cold and heavy in my hand, and I didn't want to kill anyone. But if I had to, I would. I peered through the brush, pointing the gun at a Nazi guard. George sighed and reached up, flicking off the safety for me. I forgot myself for a moment and gave him a comical, adrenaline-fueled grin.

He gave me a tired smile, bending over a balloon and closing off the equation. Two more balloons, released into the air.

Chaos broke out as the lines of marching skeletons broke apart and men tried to run for the woods. I grabbed the pack and moved, releasing the third balloon and carrying the last three, tripping over my own feet as I tried to tie the strings. I heard a man shout in pain as he was shot making a run for it.

I slid down the hill a bit, trying to stay beneath the edges of the grass to see who had grabbed the balloons.

Then one soldier appeared right on the edge of the embankment, his bayonet at the end of his rifle. He slammed it down, and it punched into the dirt not six inches from me. I lurched forward without thinking and shoved him, the pistol against his chin. He flew backward, losing his footing with a shout, and fell down, his rifle slipping out of his grasp. I fell on top of him with a squeak. I shoved backward off him and scrambled to my feet.

He shouted in German, struggling, but no one could see me. They just started running toward him. I kicked his ribs, hard, and he grunted, rolling onto his side, and then I slammed my foot down, first on his face and then on his crotch.

He screamed, and the guards came running as I ran back toward the forest. The guards all clustered around the fallen Nazi, leaving the prisoners unattended. A few more made achingly slow breaks for it, and then the group chose again, pushing forward a boy and an older man this time to take the balloon.

"Last balloon," I gasped, crouching next to George.

"*Shoot* the Nazis, Ilse," he snapped. "Don't shove them."

"It was the first thing I thought of!" I whispered back. "Write *faster*."

"You're impossible," he said through gritted teeth. "I am trying not to kill them."

"Better accidentally by balloon than by Nazi," I said.

He glanced at me. "You don't mean that."

I wasn't sure if he was right.

The lines of prisoners jostled, looking around in the sky, in the bushes, for the next balloon, calm in the face of shouts of German and the constant *rat-tat-tat* of guns. The world felt very small and very quiet as I looked down the hill at them. The boy was small and dirty, his eyes the largest part of his body, his feet bare and dark with blood. The man rested his hand on the boy's shoulder, and I had no doubt that they were father and son.

My heart climbed into my throat, and tears filled my eyes. "Pull more blood. We need a seventh balloon."

"I can't," George said gently, holding the string of the last balloon with a gloved hand. "And you don't have enough blood, and you've done a bit of magic today. You don't have the endurance. You won't be able to jump again if you need to, and I am not strong enough to help, Ilse."

They stood there in hope, and I wiped at my face with my sleeves. "We have to."

"Look away, if you want," George offered, his voice soft. "I can release this one."

"No," I said, staring straight at the father's eyes. I reached out for the balloon. "You should go."

"My notebook, Ilse," he said.

I shook my head. "I can't give that back to you. It has so much that's terrible in it."

"I know," he said. And he held the last and final balloon out of reach, picking up the pistol and pointing it at the balloon this time, instead of me. His eyes were soft and gray, not the dark brown I remembered at Oak Ridge. I wondered if he'd done that with magic too, and if that equation was in the notebook tucked against my waist. I remembered thinking he was handsome once upon a time. I remembered his whispered proposition at the dance and the way he'd made me feel. And I remembered his pale face in the hallway telling me he knew I wasn't the spy at Oak Ridge.

"The notebook, Ilse, for this final balloon."

"I hate you," I whispered, untucking my shirt and reaching for my waistband.

He gave me a tired smile. "I know. I deserve that. Tell Wolf that I'm sorry."

I handed him the notebook, and he lowered the pistol, handing me the last balloon for the prisoners on the road. I vibrated with an urgency, a hate, a panic. A Nazi guard held a gun to the father's head as he addressed my side of the road. He said something in German that I didn't understand, but the meaning was clear. If I released another balloon, this man would be shot.

George said quietly, "There's some magic that pulls you apart, Ilse. And the magic you used to get here, it'll do that to you. It'll make you not yourself. Don't use it. Let this be my gift to you."

"Get out," I whispered. "Get away before I kill you."

I couldn't tear my eyes from the father and son on the road, so I didn't see George disappear. I heard only the soft pop of his magic and the relief at the choice in front of me being my own.

The father looked at me as though he could see me—Wouldn't that be impossible? Isn't it impossible? Had the invisibility worn off completely?—and his voice carried across the distance. *"Bite helfn."*

Please help.

He wasn't asking me to save *his* life. He was asking me to save his son.

I released the balloon.

CHAPTER FORTY-FOUR

ORANIENBURG, GERMANY
OCTOBER 7, 1943

WOLF

Someone shouted as smoke curled through the air, singeing the inside of my nose.

I thought about dying by fire—the pain, the misery.

They deserved it. They deserved it tenfold. But I didn't want that weighing on me. I didn't deserve that for the rest of my days.

I propped open the door labeled VERBOTEN. An exit to be used if they wanted it.

The alarm wailed on, and I walked out, leaving the fates of those behind me in their own hands. They'd made their choices. I made mine. I'd promised my sister I'd return, and I wasn't about to break that promise.

I used a balloon to jump out of the factory, floating back to Ilse. The path swung north of how I floated in, which meant that Ilse had moved. My heart pounded, but I tried to reassure myself that I couldn't change anything until I got to her, and if she'd moved, it'd been for a good reason.

Should have sent her home, I thought, rising over trees and the main road with dark splotches on it. *Should have sent her home before this.* I hadn't been thinking, the fog of Lily's murder clouding my judgment. As I floated higher, rising over the trees and going north up the hill, out of the city, I saw a mass of people marching on the road, a truck guiding them. In the distance, I could see walls, a fence, guard towers. A concentration camp. My stomach clenched. *Soon.*

But all thoughts of what came next for me vanished when I landed on the road and the dark splotches I'd seen from the air came into focus. Bodies. Panic flooded me.

"*Ilse!*" I yelled at the top of my lungs.

"Wolf!" She scrambled from the woods, fully visible, wide-eyed and pale. She stumbled down the hill, tripping over the weeds and bushes, throwing her arms around me. "Oh my God, Wolf."

I held her, willing my heart to calm down as I looked past her at the bodies on the street. Lily would have known what to do. Lily would have known the right things to say. God, even Topher might have known what to say. I didn't know. I didn't know what to tell her about what she never should have seen.

I wished I didn't have to protect her. I wished there was nothing to protect her from. But this world wasn't that world, and she was here, pale and sobbing, and I was the only one to comfort her. "I'm here, Ilse. What happened?"

"They're just skeletons," she sobbed. "They're just skeletons, and they're making them march so far. They just shot one because he fell. I couldn't save them all. We tried, but we couldn't."

I thought I misheard her, but when she repeated it, I couldn't tell if my uncertainty was from pride or anger. I wanted to tell her I was sorry. Sorry she saw that. Sorry she knew. Sorry that it was happening. *Sorry, sorry, sorry.* But the word wasn't enough. There were no words. I wrapped my arms around her. "You're safe. That's what matters. Who's *we?*"

"I meant just me. I used our supplies," she said. She looked away. There were things she wasn't telling me, but this wasn't the time to pry.

"If you saved them, what'd you do with them?" I asked, looking around.

"I had to get them away, not just here and invisible," she said, wiping at her tears. "I sent them somewhere safe. I think. Six of them."

I exhaled. They might be dead now. "What's done is done." I kissed the top of her head. "You saved them. That was the right thing to do."

Ilse looked up the road at the other bodies strewn on the dirt. "Was it?"

"Yes," I said softly. "You did the right thing."

We couldn't bury the bodies, but we carried them off the road, laid them in a row beneath the trees. I rested pebbles on their eyes to keep them closed, and then Ilse held my hand while I chanted the Mourner's Kaddish for the two Jews, their yellow stars stitched to their prisoner's uniform. Three of the others were marked with red triangles, pointing downward, and the other two pointing up. I didn't know what that triangle meant, but whatever it meant, they were prisoners too. An enemy of the Nazis was a friend of mine, and I wished I'd known any words for their passing.

Ilse looked wrecked, so I wrote all our balloons back to Dr. Schneider's farm with my blood. I made her promise not to let go and then wrapped her bare hand around her balloon. She disappeared into the air. I wrote mine next, and we left behind the six bodies, the concentration camp, and the men still shuffling toward its gates.

CHAPTER FORTY-FIVE

WOLF

We stood on a hill and watched Allied planes bomb Leipzig. It was beautiful, in the way that destruction can sometimes be beautiful, in the way that force and violence had a way of bringing clarity in moments of cloudiness and uncertainty. And I hated myself for the sharpness that my mind took on, the edges where I'd once prided myself on softness and curves in a world that wanted men to be cutting instead of comforting.

But then I thought of Lily's body covered in her own blood, and her blood, dried on my hands and pants, flaked away, leaving bits of her all over Germany as Ilse and I took our second balloons from Leipzig back toward Heidelberg and Max. It wasn't until that balloon that I began to feel the pain and weariness creeping from my bone marrow out through my veins and arteries, my ligaments and my tendons, my muscles and my skin, until every movement became excruciating and painful. We walked slowly up the driveway at sunrise the next morning.

Ilse and I hadn't said anything to each other in hours, not since she'd let me write the balloons. But she was a constant presence next to me, unsure but steady, and I wanted to tell her I had missed her, that I was glad she came, that I was glad she hadn't gone straight back to Oak Ridge. I didn't have the words.

We walked up the porch of Schneider's house, and I knocked on the door.

Dr. Schneider answered the door, and his eyes widened. He looked at Ilse, then at me, and then past us. He was looking for her, but she wouldn't be coming again. He opened the door wider, silently, and gestured me inside the house. I walked in slowly, standing uselessly in the front hall. Ilse gently took the pack off my back, leaving it in the front hallway. She said something to Dr. Schneider, and he said something back to her, in German, I thought, but my mind had gone blank and slow, like a memory.

He led me upstairs to a bathroom and a tub with running water. He ran me a cold bath, but it was a bath nonetheless, and left folded clothes for me on a chair beside the sink.

When I stepped into the bath, the water turned red.

When I stepped out of the bath and let it drain, the tub was stained pink.

The first dress I'd ever seen Lily wear had been pink like this. I had thought of her like a lily then, but now I could only see her in blood.

I dressed slowly, numb to the pain I felt in the back of my head. There was a knock at the door, and I must have said something, because the door opened, and Max stepped into the bathroom. He stepped close to me, his hand coming up to my jaw, rubbing at the stubble there. I closed my eyes, leaning into his hand shamelessly.

"Wolf," he said softly. "Is it done?"

I nodded, just once, but it was enough. And I started to cry.

He led me gently into a bedroom, tucked me beneath the blankets, and sat there, his hand on my hair, until I fell asleep.

When I woke, I was alone in a room bathed in the warm light of sunrise. I sat up, momentarily confused about my whereabouts, and then I remembered. Lily. Dead. My sister. Here in Germany. Topher. George. Spies, and magic I didn't understand. I inhaled, and the smell of sausage and eggs filled my nose and mouth. My stomach growled. I climbed out of bed and cautiously stepped downstairs.

In the kitchen, Max was helping with the eggs and sausage, while Dr. Schneider read the paper at the table. And Ilse. She looked exhausted with dark circles under her eyes, her black curls tangled and unkempt.

Dr. Schneider appraised me over his glasses. "Did you sleep well?"

I managed to nod. "Thank you."

Max looked at me over his shoulder. "Hungry?"

Surreal. That was the word for this. It felt surreal. I pressed my hand to the inside of my left elbow where I'd draw the blood. I'd drawn too much, maybe. Maybe that was why I was weak and hallucinating.

"You need to eat," Ilse said quietly. "You're in shock."

"She's not here," I said hollowly.

I didn't miss the quick look between Max and Ilse. Ilse shook her head. "No, she's not."

I nodded slowly, feeling pieces of my heart shift to accommodate a world without Lily. I sank slowly into a chair next to Ilse, the same side where I sat next to her at home at breakfast, as if this was a normal day. As if there would ever be normal days again. I closed my eyes, and there was a bright-blue sky, and my hands covered in blood. I opened my eyes, setting my hands against the table to steady myself.

Max's hand came down on my shoulder, light but strong. He set a plate of eggs in front of me along with half a baked potato. "Eat."

I reached up, grabbing his hand and holding it tight. His fingers closed around mine, squeezed, and let go. I exhaled. *Don't panic. Focus.* I wiped my hands on my pants, still feeling Lily's blood, though my skin was clean and bright. And I ate the eggs. For once, Ilse didn't prattle on through a meal.

Max sat down, his chair angled toward me, and he propped up his foot on one of my chair rungs. His leg pressed against mine. "We need to talk about what comes next."

"Ilse needs to go home," I said. "So do you."

"And you," Max said gently.

"I need to talk to Ilse. Alone." I avoided his words. He grunted and pushed his chair back as I turned to Ilse. "How you got here... the spy's"—I paused, remembering Dr. Schneider at the table— "equations. Can you write Max a balloon home that way?"

Ilse glanced at Max who was halfway up the stairs. "It could exacerbate his head injury. Wolf, it's not...it's not right. What it does. It could hurt Max."

"I'm not leaving if you're not leaving," Max protested.

"You will," I said, ignoring the way he scowled at me. "You've made so much progress here because we haven't been moving around and you can sleep in a real bed and eat real food."

"You need a doctor," said Dr. Schneider, cleaning up dishes from the table. "You need to rest your brain. If you don't, you may never return to normal. We saw this a lot in the Great War."

"I meant what I said, Wolf," Max called back to me, climbing the rest of the stairs to give Ilse and me the privacy I requested.

"He could jump with multiple balloons," Ilse suggested. "Without the other equation."

In that case, I'd write all the balloons, and all Max would have to do was blow them up. One after another, blow up the balloons, tie them off, and keep going until he ran out of balloons.

If he was caught, he'd die.

If I messed up, he'd die.

If he messed up, he'd die.

If he used the spy's equation, it'd be faster, but it could do irreversible damage.

Then too, so would death.

There was such a narrow window in this world to live.

"Could you take Max home first?" I asked her. I wanted to hug her, the way I would have back in New York before this all began, before the war. But I couldn't make myself reach across that divide. "Could you travel with him and then go home?"

She swallowed. "If that's what you want."

"Send the other girls at Oak Ridge a balloon," I told her. "Today. Tell them you're safe. Send it as fast as you can."

She nodded. "Fine. Let's talk about you now."

The words were sharp and hard, allowing no room for a joke or a sarcastic brush-off, and I'd never heard Ilse sound this way. She'd never held my gaze like this either. "You look like hell, Wolf. You've lost weight. You haven't shaved in weeks. I'm not sure you could tie a knot around a balloon right now, much less write one."

"Ouch, Ilse," I muttered.

"You held it together to finish the mission," she said. "But it's catching up with you. You can't keep going like this."

"I'll figure it out."

She stared at me and then sighed. "Tell Max I'll take him to England tomorrow. And yes, I'll go home from there. Before we go, I need your help writing a report. Colonel Mann will want one."

"Thank you." I hesitated at the door, something pulling at my chest, but I didn't know what it was, so I opened the screen door and stepped back inside the house to an empty kitchen. Ilse stayed on the porch, watching the driveway again.

I went upstairs into the bedroom, where Max sat on the bed, frowning at a book. I closed the door behind me gently, and Max looked up at the click. I smiled weakly. "Hi."

He closed the book. "Hi."

The room felt suddenly too small.

I gestured to the book. An English Bible. "You can read again?"

He looked down at it. "Slowly. The words still look mixed up. Speaking's back, but I don't feel like my head or my eyes are yet."

"It's coming back," I said gently. "It'll come back."

He nodded, his fingers gliding over the gold words on the cover. "I know."

I sat down on the edge of his bed. I wanted to kiss him, but I couldn't right now. "Ilse will travel with you, back to England. That way it won't look like you've deserted. She'll connect you with Colonel Mann's person at our base."

Max's fingers stopped over the *B* on the book cover, and he peered up at me. "And you?"

I swallowed hard. "I'll come home. But I don't know when that'll be."

He watched me, eyes narrowing. "What comes next?"

I startled, and he caught my hand. "Here. In Germany. With the mission, Wolf. Just the mission."

I exhaled in relief, and he gave me a sad, gentle smile. What came after the mission was only slowly coming together in my mind.

"I can't tell you," I said.

"In case I'm caught," he said and sighed. "Wolf."

"You can say the *l* again," I said, aiming for lightness.

"Promise me you're coming back," he said softly, his eyes dropping again to the cover of his Bible.

"I promise."

"To me," he said, setting the Bible on the side table so he could scoot closer to me.

My throat was tight. "I promise I'm coming back to you."

He reached out, running the back of his hand down my rough, unshaven cheek. I closed my eyes, letting myself revel in the feeling of being touched. The world had changed so fundamentally, but I still didn't know how to ask for what I wanted. Him, touching me, like this in the quiet light of the midday sun, without the sound of bombs, without blood, without fear. His fingers curled around my chin and tipped it up, so I wasn't surprised when his mouth grazed mine, unsure, wondering, asking a thousand questions that remained between us.

"Please," I whispered.

His other hand slid around the back of my neck, and this time when he kissed me, it was purposeful, demanding, and hopeful, as though he could pass hope onto my tongue and steal my pain from my breath.

He brushed my mop of curls out of my face. "This is long."

"I know," I murmured. "I'd cut it, but it makes me look particularly Jewish, and I like the idea of looking particularly Jewish while killing Nazis."

He grinned. "So romantic."

"You like it," I challenged him.

He squeezed the back of my neck. "I do."

I kissed the corner of his mouth, then his mouth. I wanted to kiss him everywhere. We didn't have time for that. Not now. I wanted all the time in the world. "Promise me you'll be okay?"

He smiled, crooked, sincere, and beautiful. "I promise you."

CHAPTER FORTY-SIX

HEIDELBERG, GERMANY
OCTOBER 9, 1943

WOLF

I scrubbed at my face, as if that would keep me from crying. My throat was raw and tight, and if Ilse had asked me a thousand questions like she used to do, I didn't know if I could have kept myself together in one piece. But she didn't. She set a cup of tea next to me and folded herself into an armchair by the window. The blackout curtains and the low lamplight made her look older than sixteen. She gave me a faint smile, resting her dark hair against the edge of the golden velvet.

"You don't want to look for the spy," I said. I'd told her that he'd made it to Oranienburg before I'd gotten there. She hadn't seemed very surprised.

She shook her head. "What good would it do? The damage is done."

The secrets were stolen. His identity was revealed. Lily was dead. The damage was done. I nodded, studying her. "If you're sure."

"I'm sure," she said with a yawn.

Oranienburg felt like a mission forever unfinished. Someone had stolen the bomb information, and it hadn't been my team. I didn't know how to let go of that. I turned back to my notes, to Lily's notes, spread across the desk. Lily had taken detailed mission notes every day in a small notebook, and when she'd run out of room, on the backs of her previous notes and in every margin she could find.

There were doodles too, stick figures with crossed-out eyes—a head count, I thought. Only she could turn a body count into something both whimsical and sardonic.

The ache of missing her, someone I'd known only a month, settled deep in my chest. My body felt too small for the grief building inside me.

Don't panic. Focus, Sunshine. Her voice, warm and firm, in my mind.

I promise you, Max and I had told each other.

I had to finish the work. I had to finish the work so I could go home to him.

In the file folder next to me were the papers we'd stolen from Hechingen, and on the floor, a metal box containing samples from the beer cellar in Haigerloch and the notes I'd taken on Oranienburg. Ilse had said she'd take the box back to Oak Ridge. They had facilities there and people trained to handle that material. The look on her face when I told her we'd been carrying it around Europe for the last few weeks had made me feel sick to my stomach. How many people had we put in danger unknowingly? How much danger had I put *Max* in unknowingly?

On one of Lily's notes, she'd scribbled in a margin, *Honestly, just need a cup of tea.*

I smiled, picking up mine and sipping it. She was—had been—so *British* sometimes. She would have scowled at me for that, said something about Scotland, about Inverness or Macbeth or some war or another. I missed her no-nonsense way. The way she'd tell me to stop thinking and get to work. That we didn't have time to think or mourn.

That was the problem. I did have time.

I had far too much of it.

I put down the cup of tea and began writing, the pen moving tediously over the page as I crossed out and rewrote everything again and again.

Wolf Klein (Special Projects Officer); Max Egan (Pilot)

Classified Secret Top Secret

~~Status~~ Mission ~~Update~~ Report

~~Lily Tasker~~ Lillian Jacobs Tasker was ~~murdered~~ killed in action in Germany by double agent Topher MacKenzie—known as George Steele at Site X-10 in the United States of America. This final mission report is being written by Wolf Klein, Special Projects Officer and the remaining operative member of the team. Ilse Klein, a Special Projects officer (of sorts) from Site X-10 in the United States, joined me to complete the mission.

The final site of Oranienburg was infiltrated on October 7. However, the spy who infiltrated the project and murdered Lily Tasker had retrieved paperwork and data from Oranienburg prior to my infiltration. I destroyed the site with two balloon-delivered explosive devices. The team moved to a rendezvous spot outside Heidelberg.

The full team will not be returning to London as required by mission objectives. Along with surviving injured pilot, Max Egan, Ilse Klein will be returning by way of England to Site X-10, along with a copy of this mission report, and I will be completing my own mission. I understand that in doing this, I step outside the bounds of diplomatic protection (which was never offered to us in covert missions). I am not acting as an agent or operative of the United States but on my own accord. I will report to the OSP and OSS as soon as I return.

Ilse Klein was not aware of the details of the mission or this mission report prior to my writing it and sealing it for her to deliver.

Wolf Klein

I copied it with fewer mistakes onto a second sheet of paper and folded it up, signing over the seal. I sat back in the chair and looked over at Ilse. Her head had fallen to the side, her jaw dropped open, her eyes closed. She looked younger when she was sleeping, like the Ilse I remembered from New York, from the train station.

I didn't want to wake her—God knows when the last time she'd slept was. They'd be leaving at sunrise, and I wanted to do everything I could for them. I wrote the equations onto the balloon for the report going to England, carefully tucked the second copy into the inside pocket of my coat Ilse wore, and secured the bag I'd packed for her and Max.

"Wolf," Ilse said sleepily. "I can pack. Go spend time with Max."

"It's done," I said, looking at her over my shoulder. She rubbed at her eyes, her head still lolling against the chair. "You can rest a little longer if you need to."

She yawned, covering her mouth with her hand. "What time is it?"

"Two a.m.," I said, checking my watch.

"What?" Ilse said blankly, and then she blinked. "Oh. Yes. Eight p.m. my time. I've been gone how many days?"

"Two," I said. Only two days since Lily died. One day since we went to Oranienburg and returned. My life felt like a countdown clock. I knew what happened next. My skin itched for it.

"They'll be worried," she said with a frown. "Hopefully they don't think—"

I'd never heard Ilse cut off a thought before. I didn't even know she could self-censure. I waited for a moment and then realized she wasn't going to finish her sentence. "What?"

"Nothing," she said, considering me. "It'll be fine."

After a beat, she stretched, climbing out of the chair dramatically. One untied shoe dropped off her foot and landed heavily on the floor. I hissed her name, wincing and listening for Dr. Schneider or Max to wake up. Ilse made a face as she carefully picked up her shoe and slid it onto her foot again, lacing it tight.

"Foot's asleep," she whispered, sounding like a sister I recognized again. "You're sure about this? You could come with us, Wolf."

I ignored her question. "You'll have to use the spy's magic to get back to Oak Ridge. You'll be safe?"

She smiled a bit. "I don't have a choice, and I'm not sure it'll make it safer. But I don't think two uses will hurt me. We could try it with Max, if you want."

I shook my head. "No, I don't want to risk it. You'll make sure that he reaches Captain Hutchinson? Colonel Mann's commander there?"

I could feel Ilse teasing apart something, turning over the puzzle pieces. I didn't know how she'd react, and I didn't have the energy for it right now. "Promise me."

"I promise," she said. "If you tell me why you're staying."

"There's something I need to take care of first," I said quietly.

She nodded slowly and said, "Does it have to do with Lily?"

I shook my head. "Not at all."

But that wasn't the entire truth.

"Max?" Ilse asked.

I shook my head again. "No, not him either." I hesitated and said, "He's the reason I almost decided not to do it. But Ilse, I need to help."

She nodded slowly. "I understand."

I squeezed her hand. "Thank you." My throat tightened again. "Promise me."

"Promise you what?" Ilse blinked in surprise.

"That as far as you know, the science is stable and you'll be all right," I demanded. If Ilse died...if I lost her too...

"Oh, Wolf," she said, wrapping her arms around me. "I'm sorry. I'm sorry she's gone."

"Me too." I closed my eyes.

"I'll be safe," she whispered, and I believed her.

But my heart was breaking all the same. She didn't smell like home. She smelled like fire and sweat and blood. The smell of sabotage and war and magic. I hadn't thought I'd miss who we were before this war, but I did.

CHAPTER FORTY-SEVEN

ILSE

Dr. Schneider's house was the kind of place I could see myself falling in love with. It was musty and old and in poor repair, and every corner held a surprise. A stack of books about radiology—in English!—with Dr. Schneider's name on the corner. A notebook with scribbled notes in German I could somewhat read. The old man himself, balding, white hair, a distinguished mustache. He caught me off guard, watching me with his keen eyes.

We pretended not to know my brother and Max were upstairs together.

I fumbled through my German, asking questions about crystallography—how often would I get to share a house and have coffee made for me by a Nobel Prize–winning scientist?—and he handed me papers, crumpled at the edges and bent from travels, to read. He didn't ask me about the work I did. I suppose he thought it was just magic. But he didn't ask about magic either.

"Why not?" I asked him. "Why don't you ask me questions?"

"Ahhh," he murmured, folding his hands in front of his face. "That is a good question. I do not ask because I do not yet know what the good questions are."

I was desperate, I realized, to explain magic to someone who didn't know it. Didn't understand it. Because I'd run out of the questions to ask, and I had so many left inside me. I wanted to know what he thought of a dark science, a dark magic, like George's equations. I didn't know if I wanted to destroy them, and Wolf saw the world in such a binary way. Maybe always. Maybe especially right now.

"What if," I hedged. *What if there was a magic that was a science unto its own? What if there were things we should have left unknown?*

Dr. Schneider lifted an eyebrow. "Should I start the coffee?"

* * *

"I need Max's blood," I said to Wolf in the morning by way of a greeting. "To finish the balloons. Where is he?"

"Oh, he went for a walk this morning, down to the grocery store. Do you think his English will give him away?" Wolf made a face at me.

I glared at him. "Not funny."

"I know," he said with a laugh. "It's a joke, Ilse. He's upstairs resting. I'll draw his blood."

"It wasn't funny!" I yelled after him as he retreated upstairs.

"I'm sorry you left your sense of humor in America," he yelled back.

"I'm sorry I'm sending yours to England," I yelled.

"Oooh," I heard Max say. "That was a good one."

"Hey. Don't take her side, smart-ass," Wolf said right above me, clear as day through the thin floorboards.

Max laughed, and I smiled down at the work. I had missed that laugh. Wolf brought me Max's blood so I could code the balloons to him to render him invisible, and then we were ready. Truly, I wasn't ready, but it wasn't up to me. Wolf needed me to take care of Max, and I needed to return to Oak Ridge. There'd be questions.

I walked outside to the porch where Max and Wolf stood, talking quietly, close enough together that their heads kept bumping though they both stared at their shoes. When Max caught me approaching, he cleared his throat and stepped toward me with a smile.

"Did you ever think you'd be here, traveling with me by magic balloons out of Europe during the war?" he asked in his easy way. I'd always loved the way Max could seem so relaxed, even in the midst of chaos.

"No," I admitted, a smile finally breaking onto my face. "Let's try not to die. Wolf won't forgive me."

"I'm right here," Wolf muttered.

Max and I exchanged a small smile.

"And find Captain Hutchinson," added Wolf. "Just keep saying his name until you see him."

"We won't see each other until we land, but I promise I'll be there," I said, holding out the balloon to Max.

Max didn't take it at first. He spun and wrapped his arms around my brother. "You promised."

Wolf's face scrunched closed, as if he was in pain. "I know. So did you."

When Max released Wolf, he didn't hesitate. He reached out, wrapped his hand around the string, and disappeared.

Dr. Schneider came out to say goodbye to me, which I hadn't expected. I wondered what he thought, watching from a kitchen window and seeing people disappear before his very eyes. If he was curious or suspicious, it didn't show on his face.

He gripped my hand with the steady grip of someone who knew who he was. I envied his handshake.

"There will always be questions you wonder if you should have asked differently," he said. "And how that would affect the outcome. But the question you asked was the best question you knew to ask with the information you had available. That is not nothing, Ilse Klein."

I squeezed his hand. "Thank you."

I waited until he was back inside the house to say to Wolf, "I have to go. Otherwise Max will think I'm not coming."

His arms swallowed me in a hug, and I didn't want to let go. If I let go, if he let me go, it was like this was real. This leaving again. I thought we'd be reunited at the end of the war and we'd never leave again, but that wasn't how this would go. We'd always be leaving each other, again and again. It made the coming together again that much harder.

The breath he took trembled, as though he was going to cry. "You should go."

"I should," I agreed, but I didn't let go. Not for a few more heartbeats, and then he sighed, and I knew it was time.

"Thank you," Wolf said as I readied the balloon and began to tug off one of my gloves.

I looked up, surprised. "For what?"

"Coming here." His brown eyes under a tangle of curls, so much like my own, met my gaze, and I knew he felt it too, the pain of coming together, knowing that one of us would be leaving again.

I made myself give him a bright smile. "Of course. And whenever you need me, send me a balloon. I'll come right back."

He made a face, as if he was going to argue with me about what magic I could and couldn't use, but he stopped himself. Another coming together, and another leaving. "See you at the end of the war, Ilse."

"At the end of the war," I echoed, and wrapped my bare hand around the balloon string. I lifted off the ground, and beneath, my brother grew smaller and smaller. He stood there, his hands in his pocket, watching the sky until I could no longer see him.

CHAPTER FORTY-EIGHT

BURTONWOOD, ENGLAND
OCTOBER 10, 1943

ILSE

Outside of the RAF base where Max was stationed before this mission, he surveyed me with a suspicious gaze. We'd been arguing for the better part of an hour, and I had a terrible feeling I was about to lose this battle. I wasn't used to losing battles with Max. Before the war, at home, he liked to spoil me. But he'd always looked at me then as though I was a kid. That wasn't how he was looking at me now. He was looking at me as though I was his equal, and he wasn't letting me off the hook.

It was raining, because England wanted to welcome me for the first time in the best of ways. Max was standing over me, holding a rain slicker to protect the equation I was writing even as he disapproved.

"You look half-dead," he repeated.

"That happens," I said. "So do you. But I haven't drawn blood since Germany. I can jump straight back to Oak Ridge. I need to get back before they think that I'm part of George's plot."

I muttered under my breath, trying to remember the equation I'd written on the balloon only three days ago. I wished I hadn't given George back his notebook. "I don't need to go through that again."

"Again?" asked Max, worry darkening his tone.

I could feel the mistake in the air, and I wished I could pull it back. Wincing, I glanced up from the balloon. "You can't tell Wolf."

"I'm not in the business of keeping secrets from your brother," Max said.

I snorted. "Aren't you?"

"Anymore," he amended dryly. "What happened in...Where was it? Tennessee? Why are you in such a hurry to get back? What's the difference if you sleep one night in a bed and get a good meal?"

"George...Topher...God, do we even know what his real name was? He stole papers from me, and when they realized that and that I was sending balloons to Wolf, they arrested me on espionage charges," I said, carefully squeezing more blood down onto the brush at the end of the syringe. I figured if this wasn't right, the balloon would catch fire. And as cold and wet as I was, I wouldn't particularly mind that.

"So you've been missing for the same amount of time George-Topher has been missing, and you're worried that it looks bad," Max said. "You could have just said that instead of saying *I have to, Max.*"

"I didn't want you to judge me," I said, closing the equation and looking up at him. "Or tell Wolf."

Max gave me a pitying look. "Wolf wouldn't be angry with you. He'd be angry at *them* for arresting you. And it wasn't your fault. Topher tricked all of us. But Wolf's report will help. They won't think that."

"I can only hope," I said and got to my feet. "You'll be all right?"

Max frowned. "I'll be fine. I'm more worried about you. You could stay here, talk to Hutchinson. He'd talk to Colonel Mann for you."

I supposed I could just see Hutchinson, he could communicate with the colonel, and I wouldn't have to jump home tonight. But I wanted to go home tonight. I needed to go home tonight and make sure that the mess I'd left behind hadn't become someone else's mess.

I rocked back on my heels. I'd thought of Oak Ridge as home.

I shivered in the cold and from the thought. How had it become home?

"Ilse," Max said gently. "You don't have to go. You could go back to New York."

"No," I said softly. "Not yet. I have…I messed things up, Max. I made mistakes. And I have to make them right before I can go back to New York."

I'd tried to do too much on my own. I had worried so much about protecting the people I loved that I'd put them at risk even more. I wondered what would have happened if I'd gone straight to Colonel Mann and confessed that my papers had been stolen, and that I'd been writing about magic and my brother in those papers too. That I'd never been fully committed to delivering the blasted bomb as much as I'd been committed to finding magic that would keep Wolf safe, and in doing that I might have thrown both the bomb project and Wolf's mission into jeopardy. Was that fair to myself? Perhaps not.

"Ilse," Max said.

"What?" People were always saying my name multiple times.

"You're sure?" he asked.

"Yes," I said impatiently.

He hesitated and sighed. "Send me a balloon when you get there safely. Please."

I impulsively rose on my toes and pressed a kiss to his cheek. "Thank you. And what will you do?"

"Wait for your brother, of course," Max said as if it was the simplest and most wonderful thing in the world.

And maybe it was.

I'd go home. I'd end what I'd begun. I'd right a few wrongs, and I'd think about what I'd learned. That was the end of every experiment, wasn't it? The learning, the understanding, the conclusions.

I started to pull off my gloves again. "I'll see you soon, Max."

He shook his head slowly, grinning. "Stubborn as they come. If you get into trouble, get a letter to me, Ilse, and I'll help sort it out. Be safe."

I wished I had done that before. Just written a letter to someone and let them sort it out for me. But I hadn't. And I didn't know if I could the next time. I wanted to solve my own problems. I just wanted to know better, and not in hindsight, which problems were mine, and which were not.

"Thank you," I repeated.

I wrapped my hand around the string, and a tear opened in the air ahead of me, a curious black space with edges that curled and a glint of dim light, the sound of dishes in the background, a girl's laughter. And with one backward look at Max, I stepped through.

CHAPTER FORTY-NINE

ILSE

The house was quiet when I woke up, my head throbbing. I'd arrived and fainted dead away, probably from bleeding too much but maybe from the dark magic of George's equation, and spent most of the next day in bed. My tongue stuck to the roof of my mouth, and my limbs felt heavy as I rolled out of bed, stumbling to the bathroom. A shower didn't make me feel much more human, but it was a start.

Stella, Polly, and Lola sat around the table in the kitchen, murmuring quietly as Stella read the paper, Polly anxiously knit, and Lola stirred her coffee endlessly, the cream curdling on the top. They all looked up, falling silent, when I walked in.

"Need something to eat?" asked Stella, but Lola was already on her feet, ceding her chair and buttering bread for me.

"I know how to do it," I said quietly to the other girls. "To deliver the elephant."

Polly put down her knitting. "We don't need to talk about this right now."

"We do," Stella said firmly. She looked at me, her dark eyes knowing. "Do you really want to do it like that?"

"Like how?" asked Lola, setting a plate of toast with butter and jam in front of me, and then pushing a cup of black coffee at me.

"With the spy's magic," Stella said as I took a bite of the toast, my first food in far too many hours.

"I don't want to," I said between chewing, not caring if I was ladylike. "I think it's dangerous magic. It's wrong, and I can feel it in my bones. I think it pulls more than it should from someone."

"Maybe that's why you fainted," suggested Polly.

"If you don't want to," said Lola, without makeup for once, "then you shouldn't."

"But that's what we were supposed to do," I argued. Even I could hear how tepid my voice was.

Stella shook her head. "No, we were supposed to try. We did. We never found a way to carry that much weight that far, while invisible. We failed, and that isn't wrong. They can't say they didn't know it was a possibility."

She was right. It'd never been a sure thing, and the cold, hard knot in my stomach warmed, untangling as I considered backing out of the project. I'd never wanted to kill people, but I had wanted to be part of something bigger than myself. I'd lost sight of that moral compass somewhere along the way, chasing a spy and fearing for my brother and making friends with these girls. I'd forgotten to think about what my science and magic would do, and I didn't want to forget that. Not again.

I looked around at the other girls at the table. "I don't want to kill people. And I don't want to be a part of a project that uses dark magic to kill people. I'm only going to speak for myself here though. If you wish to stay, I won't blame you or judge you."

"You'd judge us a little bit," said Stella with a smile.

"I wouldn't!" I protested.

Polly shook her head. "You would, but we'd deserve it. I think our time at Oak Ridge has come to an end."

Lola caught my eye. "Do you want to tell Colonel Mann, or would you rather me?"

"I'll tell him," I said quietly, though it had been very kind of her to offer. "I got us into this big mess. It should be on me to get us out."

"We're all in it together," Stella said, looking around the table. "And just because we decided to end our project here doesn't mean you all get to be strangers."

"We're young," said Lola. "There are big things to come. Now, Ilse, finish eating. You need your strength back."

* * *

I walked to Colonel Mann's office with Polly, both of us quiet for most of the walk. I didn't know what I wanted. I wanted to kiss her. And ask her questions. She'd fallen in love with a girl before...Was she going home to that girl? Had she kissed that girl? Was it like with us? It was hard to think about what had happened when I was walking next to her, and I liked that feeling. I liked the feeling that the real world had melted away, and the letter in my hand was meaningless compared to what might happen between us.

But Polly broke the bubble. Just before we reached the office building, she stopped me with a hand on my elbow. "I'm glad you came back."

"Me too," I said, trying to give her a bright smile.

She didn't smile back. "Ilse, I shouldn't have...We shouldn't have...We can't. I'm sorry. But there's too much risk."

"There isn't," I said bravely. "No one looks sideways at two girls who are close and friendly."

"They do," she said softly. "That's how I ended up having to come here. I don't want that to happen again. Ilse, I want things from life. I want to go to school. I want to travel. I want to do all of those things without worrying about what someone thinks."

"So do that," I said, and even I could hear the naiveté in my own voice.

"I can't. And that's me," she said quickly. "That's me. I'm sorry.

I shouldn't have—"

"Did you want to?" I asked her, frowning up at Colonel Mann's office.

"Yes," she said softly. "Of course."

I made myself meet her eyes. "Then it wasn't wrong, and you don't have to apologize."

I had started to walk away because I thought I was about to cry when she called out my name. When I turned around, she was standing there in the autumn leaves, her arms wrapped around herself, looking fragile again, like she hadn't since that first day on the train platform.

"You'll write, won't you?" she asked.

I nodded because it would have been rude to say no. "Maybe it'll be different after the war."

She smiled a little bit. "Maybe. Write me."

I didn't say goodbye, and neither did she.

* * *

"We figured out the problem," said Colonel Mann as his secretary let me into his office. He looked as exhausted as I felt, with deep circles beneath his eyes.

"What problem?" I asked, gripping Wolf's letter and still trying to work the tightness out of my throat. I wouldn't cry in front of the colonel again. And I wouldn't cry over Polly. It was just a kiss. It was just one kiss and one infatuation. It felt as if someone had kicked a hole in my chest.

"X-10," he said. "With the uranium slugs. I expect it'll go critical any day now. I should be celebrating, but the whole thing could be blown. All those false reports George filed...I blame myself for not noticing. I can't help but think that we don't know who he was telling, so it doesn't matter anyway."

He'd never spoken so candidly to me before. I plopped down in a chair across from him. "Are we in a war with people that I don't know about?"

He smiled gently at me. "This war will end. There will be another one. Who knows what the lines of that war look like? George made sure the information got into someone's hands, probably the Soviets. They've begun their own program."

I knew the truth, but if I had told them what I knew, I'd have to reveal that I let the spy get away in exchange for six lives. Colonel Mann wouldn't understand—I wasn't even sure that Wolf would understand—so I stayed quiet. It was best to be honest about something else. "I hate war."

"So do I, even if you don't believe me. Did you have any of his papers? When we went through the cabin, it seemed like there were papers missing," the colonel said.

I shook my head. "I don't. I'm sorry."

The lie stuck to my tongue, but he didn't seem to notice. He nodded. "I asked Stella to work on the ones we found, so that'll need to be enough."

I saw an opening and seized it. "You should hire her, sir, to be your second-in-command. She's better at this."

"Better at what?" he asked.

"At this work than me," I admitted. "She's smarter than me, which no one sees because they only see the color of her skin. But she's smarter and a better leader. She'd serve you well."

The colonel narrowed his eyes at me and then nodded. "I'll take that under consideration. What else do you have for me?"

He flipped through a journal on his desk and began to take notes.

I unfolded Wolf's mission report and handing it over. I'd been surprised by what Wolf wrote in there, how careful he was to protect me from what he planned to do, but I hadn't been surprised by how little room he gave Colonel Mann to react. "George killed Lily Tasker."

The colonel's face fell. "Ah."

"You knew her?"

"I hand-picked her from MI6 to work with us on this mission. She was very good. Exceedingly competent, sharp, and responsible. She was irreplaceable. I am sorry for her loss. Wolf? Is he injured?"

"Wolf is fine," I said, though I didn't know if that was true or not. "Max Egan was injured. I took him to England by balloon, and he should be in contact with Captain Hutchinson by now."

Colonel Mann's eyes narrowed. "And where's Wolf going?"

I winced. "Don't shoot the messenger, sir. He's not coming home. Not yet. He'll come back at the end of the war. He says that when is up to us, sir. He wrote it all in that report."

The colonel grunted. "I thought it'd be you who rebelled on me. Figures it's your brother. You can never trust the quiet ones."

It wasn't that I hadn't rebelled. It just wasn't the same rebellion as Wolf's rebellion.

I didn't say that though. Instead, I said, "He's doing good work, sir."

"A rebellion is a rebellion," Colonel Mann said with a sigh.

I glanced out the windows of his office. A light rain was falling, mist crawling through the valley from the mountains. I'd miss it here. "What happened to our friend?"

Flint had interviewed the girls the night they'd reported the identity of the spy and had apparently been furious that I'd disappeared. But by the time I came back, he was gone. I didn't feel too bad about skipping one of his interrogations. The first one hadn't exactly been a walk in the park, and I wasn't keen on seeing him again, ever, if I could avoid it.

"He's chasing down some leads relating to the spy," said the colonel. "I don't expect him back, if that's what you're worried about. He didn't sound like he needed to interview anyone else here."

"Then you should relax, sir. The worry. It does terrible things to the lines on your face." I gestured to the frown lines on Colonel Mann's face, at the corners of his eyes and his forehead. "You're looking older by the minute."

The colonel ignored me and tapped his pencil on the desk. "Ilse."

I flinched. "Yes, sir."

"Are you going to tell me what really happened?"

I thought about the death march, about the prisoners we freed, about George pointing a pistol at me, about the man pleading for me to save his son. I shook my head. "I cannot tell you, sir. It's…complicated. I uncovered your spy. I need that to be enough."

For a long moment, I thought it wouldn't be. But then the colonel nodded, accepting my excuse. "You know that it's unlikely Wolf will come home from the war. And if he's captured now, I can't claim him. He's gone rogue."

I smiled a little bit. "At least one balloon maker gone rogue is doing good things with his talents."

Colonel Mann sighed. "I'm serious."

"So am I, colonel. I am choosing hope," I told him fiercely.

"This is war, Ilse," he told me unkindly.

"Hope doesn't appear in times of peace, sir."

He studied me as he lit a cigarette. "No, you're right. It doesn't."

I hesitated and then handed him the second piece of paper that I was carrying. "I don't want to use my magic to carry your bomb, sir. And neither do the other girls. We've seen enough violence in our lives, and we don't want to be a part of it. We wrote a letter, if you need to share it. We are objecting on the basis of our consciences."

He nodded and blew out smoke. "I thought you might say that after what happened. Ilse, you can never speak of what you did here or what we did here. The other gentleman is only the tip of the iceberg."

He was talking about Flint, and it made me flinch. I wouldn't spill secrets. I didn't want to end up in a black bag, in some remote prison, or at the bottom of the Hudson River.

He noticed the movement and seemed to take it as understanding because he continued. "The bomb project will go on, you understand. I'm not in charge of that, and I'd continue it, even if I was."

"It doesn't bother you, sir?" I asked him.

He turned the cigarette around in his fingers. "It does. But not as much as the idea of the war going on longer. We're a long way off from the bomb yet, and if you've recused yourself from the project, I can't speak about it anymore with you."

"I understand, sir," I said quietly, looking out his windows at the reactors. At the science I wouldn't get to know, at the genie that couldn't be put back into the bottle, and the project I'd never wrap my head around.

"Stop calling me sir. You never did that before," the colonel told me. "What will you do now, Ilse?"

"I don't know. I'd like to go home for a little bit. Finish school. And then I don't know what comes next. I guess I'll figure it out."

He put his feet up on his desk. "Are you going to be okay when I send you home? Without Wolf?"

"Yes," I said immediately and then after a beat added, my voice dropping, "Can we girls stay in touch with each other?"

He nodded. "I don't see any harm in that. But remember what I said."

I nodded and then added as an afterthought, "Promise me you won't ask me to do evil with magic again."

"I never asked you to do evil, Ilse, and it's been mostly for good. Don't let the recent events color your imagination."

We'd have to agree to disagree. "I will try, sir."

He stamped out his cigarette and stood. Walking around to the other side of his desk, he sat on the edge, his hands in his pockets. "You did good work here, Ilse."

I flushed. "Thank you, sir."

He gave me a smile that *almost* bordered on affectionate, at least for Colonel Mann. "Don't let this world chew you up, Ilse Klein."

I grinned. "No, sir, I don't intend to."

He was trying very hard not to smile broadly as he picked up the phone. "I'll get you a ticket home."

I stood up, grateful he hadn't scolded me, that he hadn't guilted me into staying and doing something I didn't want to do. "Thank you, sir."

He gestured with a hand. "Give me that letter, and go say your goodbyes. And, Ilse? Balloon makers?"

"I like it," I said.

He smiled. "Me too."

And with that, I was shooed out of his office for the last time.

I wandered through the town, smiling at people I knew and recognized, but mostly keeping to myself. I stopped by the phone booth outside the market and slipped a few coins from my pocket. My fingers dialed the number automatically, which was good because I couldn't see through my tears.

"Hello?"

"Mama?" I said, and then I started to cry. "I'm coming home."

CHAPTER FIFTY

WOLF

He came out of the woods like a myth, the dark clothes I remembered, silver buttons on a military-style coat, and a black cloak that reached to the tops of his black boots. He left no footprints in the snow. Around his head swirled black feathers like a hurricane made of ravens.

He terrified me.

But I stood my ground.

He smiled and said, "So you've come to help."

"I have conditions," I said, my hands curling into fists at my sides.

He cocked his head, the feathers moving with him. "I did not think you were in the position to demand conditions."

"You underestimated me," I said coolly. "You came to me when I was in prison and offered me a deal that I could not take because that would involve leaving people behind."

"People you loved."

"Yes," I said. "And you had the audacity to tell me I was making the wrong choice. And you left me there to be tortured."

"I did not tell you I was kind or benevolent."

"No, you didn't. And I never told you that of me either," I said.

He considered me for a long moment. "Very well. What are your conditions?"

"I'm establishing an organization to organize what magic is used when, where, and by whom."

"How incredibly American of you," he said dryly.

I did not let warmth drip into my voice. "You let people die because they do not conform to your black-and-white view of the world."

He stilled, and the feathers slowed. "You do not know me, Wolf Klein."

"We haven't had the pleasure of each other's company. But we will soon. I don't know how long it will take me, but I'll find allies among the balloon makers. And in return for you accepting that there are limitations to what we do, to who we hurt, to the reach we have as people who alter the natural way of things, I'll teach you magic that you and your balloon makers don't have yet."

The corner of his mouth tilted up. "You look at me and think there is magic I don't know."

I lifted my chin. "Yes. Or you wouldn't have asked me that."

He looked away, to the gray, snow-stilled sky and then back to me. "What limitations will you place on us?"

"I don't know yet," I admitted. "But there will be limitations. Magic that tears at the universe's fabric. Time. Space. We cannot make or destroy life, nor can we change matter. We can only change how the universe interacts with matter."

"You have a theory."

"No, but I have a sister with many theories."

"I should like to meet her."

"I hope you never do."

"I can leave Europe, you know."

"I think you'll stay where you are needed, and I hope you are never needed in the United States."

"I can respect that hope."

"I will not free Nazis."

He shook his head. "And here you criticize my black-and-white world view!"

I raised one eyebrow at him. "Would you like to go there? Right now? When you're desperate for my help?"

"Not everyone has a choice," said Ashasher.

"Everyone has a choice," I said. "And the choice not to choose is still a choice."

"The world may be more gray than either of us see it."

"Then we'll find out, won't we?"

"If I don't agree to your terms, you'll let people die."

"No, if you don't agree to my terms, I'll work on my own. I'm not like you. I would never let people die or suffer because one person failed to see the world as I do."

"You are colder than the last time I met you."

"I've seen a few things since then."

"I didn't expect you back so soon, Wolf Klein."

"Neither did I, Ashasher. What do you say?"

"What would you call your organization?"

"Zerberus."

Ashasher's smile almost parted his lips, and I thought I saw a glint of white teeth. "The dog who guards the gates of hell."

I thought of building my spine out of steel and squared my shoulders. "I want to define who we are now by what we will not do. If we do not make choices now, we are no better than those we fight."

"Ah, American idealism and exceptionalism."

"Perhaps. I come in here not with a savior complex, but with a desire to serve. And I cannot serve what currently exists."

"Me."

"Yes."

"Time has not treated me kindly. Perhaps the deal I offered you was cruel."

"Perhaps."

"I can accept your offer."

I reached out my hand, and his cold one took mine. We shook once and dropped hands. I looked around us at the desolate forest. "Where is the girl? You said she was the first to save a boy using the balloon magic."

"Working," said Ashasher. "She's picked a name. Aurora."

"Dawn. Pretty. And you thought I was the idealistic one." I shoved my hands into my pockets, feeling for my pen, a vial of blood, and a handful of balloons and string. "Let's go."

CHAPTER FIFTY-ONE

WOLF

I closed my eyes, and I saw fire. When I opened my eyes, I saw sky.

The war was over. Others were taking over the task I'd assigned myself for the last two years. And now I returned to something left unfinished. I'd left the OSS—a mutually agreed-upon solution for my decision to go AWOL—but I had a full pension and the ability to do what I wanted. And what I wanted was to be here, in this little village between Liverpool and Manchester, on the western coast of England where the United States had taken over an RAF air base.

The driver showed the soldiers at the gate his pass, and I handed over my pass too without looking. If my eyes scanned the passing soldiers, I couldn't be blamed.

We pulled through the gates, and I pocketed my ID again, opening the door and sliding out before the driver had even stopped. I slammed the door behind me and stood in the middle of the court-yard. We'd stood together on this field once, together. Learning to jump. Learning to fly. Learning to die.

He wouldn't recognize me. I was thinner. Wiry and edged. There was a look in my eyes so sharp that I nearly made myself jump when I went to the mirror. I hadn't looked myself in the eye in weeks.

"Hey," I said to a passing soldier.

He glanced at me, at my civvy clothes, and frowned. "Yeah?"

"I'm just back from France," I said. "I'm looking for a buddy of mine. He was sent here after he was injured. Max Egan."

The soldier's eyebrow shot up. "Ah. Mad Max."

I fought to keep my voice level. "He was shot out of the sky and survived Gestapo interrogation and weeks behind enemy lines. He's not mad."

"Whoa," said the soldier, snorting. "Relax. That's just what we call him. Yeah, he'll be at the end of the runway. He watches the planes there. He'll be easy to find."

Hutchinson had done his job. He'd kept Max safe. And Max had stayed. I thanked the soldier and started to walk.

At the end of the runway, a lone figure sat on a stool, silhouetted and thin and slumped over a pair of binoculars. *Don't run*, I told myself. *Everyone is watching you.* But everyone would be watching us for the rest of our lives. And right then, I didn't really care. I started to run, my feet pounding against the pavement, the air burning in my lungs like fire. I felt as powerful and wide and brilliant as the sky when I opened my eyes.

"Max!" I shouted, his name lost to the wind.

He looked up at me as though he could sense me even from this distance, as though he knew it was me. As though what he'd been doing out there on that stool with those binoculars was waiting for me.

I'd flown by balloon a thousand times, but the thought that he might have been waiting for me, that he needed me, looked for me as though I was here searching for him, lifted me off the ground, and I was bursting, wild and hot.

I loved him. I loved him. I loved him. I wanted to love him forever. I wanted to wake up next to him and fall asleep next to him, wanted to feel his skin against my skin, wanted to feel his fingers in my hair. I loved who I was with him, that the Wolf who had to save everyone didn't need to save everyone anymore, didn't need to hold up the world, could just be someone who loved and was loved.

Somewhere between France and Germany, after we jumped but before we got home, somewhere along the way, I'd realized something. I would stand in the storm with him. No matter how long it lasted or the damage it wrought, I would stand in the storm with him.

A few paces away, I stumbled to an uneven walk, my muscles seizing up, my chest heaving with the effort. I knew I should stop, breathe in this moment, but I couldn't stop moving. He stared at me, open-mouthed, wide-eyed, as I staggered in to him. I pressed my face into the crook of his neck, my hot tears burning tracks on our skin, and his arms folded around me, strong, capable, and sure.

"Wolf," he croaked. "You came back."

"I'm back," I said. "Please don't let me leave again."

He laughed a little, a rushed, breathless sound. "Okay."

His hand came up to the back of my head, pressing me against him. "Where have you been?"

"Everywhere."

"What did you see?"

My fingers found his shirtfront, and I gripped it tightly. "The worst things. I—I can't get them out of my head, Max."

"Shhh," he murmured, sounding like the Max I'd known before we parachuted into Germany. "You're not there anymore. You're here. I'm here. You don't have to see that again."

I pulled away slightly, but his hand on the back of my head prevented me from stepping back. He was in control again. He arched an eyebrow at me, and I said, "I want to go back to Europe. To France. To lead an organization handling all of the magic users we pulled together during the war and how we use magic."

Max nodded slowly, his thumb running in a short, caressing arc against my shaved head. "Okay."

"Come with me," I whispered. "I don't want to do it alone."

His brow furrowed, his eyes running over mine and then dropping to my mouth. "Do you mean that?"

"Yes," I said quietly. "I don't want to leave you alone on a pier in a hurricane again. I don't want you to look at me as though I'm the person who broke your heart. I want to wake up next to you and feel like the rest of the world doesn't exist. I don't know what this looks like, but I want it to look like you and me."

His hand slid to the back of my neck, around to the side, and to my jaw. He ran his knuckles along the line of my jaw, his eyes focused on mine. "Do you know what you're getting yourself into, Wolf?"

"Of course I know what I'm getting into," I started to growl.

His fingers gripped my chin, and I shut up. He said quietly, "I get headaches. They're debilitating. They last for days sometimes. There's nothing to do but let me ride it out in the dark. Light hurts. Noise hurts. You'll feel helpless."

I swallowed. "Isn't there—"

"No." He cut me off. "If there's a treatment option, I'll find it. But you need to accept me like this. Not the person you hope I'll be in the future. Wolf, look at me." I met his eyes, and something in my gaze made the corner of his mouth tip up. "You can't fix Europe and me. And I don't want to be fixed. I don't need to be fixed, and I can't be fixed by you. So you'll either take it, or leave it."

I scowled at him. "I didn't come all this way to leave you behind again."

"And I didn't wait all this time for you to leave again," he said. "So do the right thing. Say okay, you want me just as I am now, and then kiss me."

"Bossy," I murmured, rising up to brush my lips against his.

"Always," he said, then pressed a finger between our lips. "You haven't said it yet."

"Okay," I said impatiently, my lips against his calloused fingers.

"I want you, just as you are. I don't understand why we're stating such obvious things when we could be doing anything else. For instance, we could be—"

His mouth closed around mine, and I surrendered.

EPILOGUE

ILSE

The northern coast of France had been the ideal place for an invasion, for anyone who wasn't trying to kill Hitler and, I supposed, men who weren't Roosevelt and Churchill. When I took walks along the coast, I wondered how different it would look if all the Allied invading forces had driven over these beaches, these hills, through these towns. I wondered if they would have made it that far. I wondered if I would be standing in a free Europe.

But they hadn't picked Calais. They'd picked Normandy. And somehow, through a spy network, through parts and wings and branches of the OSS and MI6 operations that Wolf had been a part but not me, they'd tricked Hitler long enough for the invasion to succeed. Some part of me was jealous—I'd wanted to be a part of winning the war; that's why I had started down this path—but I was proud of the people I trained on balloon magic. Proud of the work we'd done in the past few months, of reuniting displaced families and helping people emigrate to Israel, of finding lost soldiers and bringing them home.

They'd picked Hiroshima, Japan, for the bomb, for what we had called elephants. They'd picked Nagasaki, Japan. There'd been more elephants. I hadn't even known that part of it. Maybe they'd built it after I left. And maybe Japan wouldn't have surrendered without the bombs. Maybe. But now we'd never know. I didn't know how to feel about that. Relieved, I supposed, that my balloons had never helped deliver the bombs that killed those people. But now, it was like I hadn't helped the war effort at all. I hadn't won this war (Wolf had done that), and I hadn't won the other war (the scientists, not the balloon makers, had done that).

I had mixed feelings on my role in the war. But I was glad it was over.

"Are you going to stare out that window all day, or are you going to get some work done?" Wolf asked as he passed me in the foyer of the house we rented in Calais, where we ran a small group of balloon makers trying to organize other balloon makers. Wolf led the charge with a Danish man named Nils and a French-Polish woman named Anya. They called themselves the Zerberus, and they organized balloon makers under one set of standards and ethos, setting up local councils wherever balloon makers were needed.

The idea was splendid. It just wasn't my idea.

"I'll get work done when I want to get work done," I told him, intentionally adding a bit of sass to my voice, but he took the steps two at a time, ignoring me.

Brothers didn't change just because a war had happened.

But Wolf had changed. He was quieter, and he took more in, instead of letting it slide right over him like he'd done before. Sometimes I saw him looking up at the sky, his expression tortured and pained, and sometimes he leaned in to Max at the sink while they did dishes together, as though he'd fall if not for Max's steady strength.

Anya, with her dark hair and her sharp, knowing eyes, said to me, "You better get to work. He's in a mood today."

I wanted to stick out my tongue at her, but I was trying to be as grown-up as I ought to be at my age. So I didn't. I started up the stairs, pausing on the second floor at Wolf and Max's office. The door was half-open, and Rafi, our puppy, was just visible on the floor where he chewed on a bone. He was a German shorthaired pointer crossed with a Brittany. The farmer from whom we bought him had affectionately said he was a bastard of the war. Maybe he was. He didn't know it. He seemed to make life better for Max, who was plagued with constant headaches, insomnia, and spasms of pain through his body that no medicine seemed to control.

Max and Wolf had desks across from each other in front of the bay windows where they collected information, assigned balloon makers to different chapters, and wrote magical bylaws. Something had happened between them during the war, and their relationship was rebuilding, slowly and beautifully. Wolf glared at papers on his desk, one hand shoved deep into his hair. Max reached over, running his knuckles down Wolf's cheek. Tension shifted, leaking out of Wolf's body as he sank into the touch. He looked up, eyes soft.

"You could take a holiday," Max said, his voice low.

"And go home? Would you come?" When Max didn't say anything, Wolf tensed again, snorting. "Then no, I will not be taking a holiday."

"We'll go home for Thanksgiving," Max promised. His fingers brushed the small curls of dark hair framing Wolf's face. "Wolf."

"Yeah." Wolf's eyes closed.

"Okay," Max said softly.

A twinge crisscrossed my chest, but I ignored it.

On the third floor worked a core group of balloon makers. And that's where *I* lived. With the rule breakers and the experimenters. We found the limits of the magic in our blood, wrote them down, and pushed past them, just to see what would happen. We were discovering magic that shouldn't be—*couldn't be*—used, even under the direst of circumstances. We were discovering magic that some people could do, and others could not. We were developing a curriculum to be used by all balloon makers, no matter where they were in the world, so that balloon magic was safe and no one was at disproportional risk from magic.

I loved the work, but I was restless. My French was minimal, my German minimal, and my devotion to the cause negligible compared to the others. I liked experimenting, but I didn't want to be writing down the rules. I wanted to be breaking them.

I knocked on the door and heard Nils call for me to enter, so I slipped through and shut the door behind me. The room had nothing but blackboards and a simple wooden table with four different legs. It'd been cobbled together from surviving pieces of furniture we'd found in the house when we'd rented it. We needed at least one surface to write down notes and to make the ink. We'd recently discovered that we didn't need a great quantity of blood to write magic. Instead of writing with straight blood, we could dilute it in a one-to-sixteen ratio with ink without losing efficacy.

Wolf and Anya were still debating the ramifications of creating a standard blood-to-ink ratio. Meanwhile, Nils experimented with different types of ink.

It was frustrating. Sometimes all I wanted to do was to play with magic, to see what we could and couldn't do with it. But every time I suggested something like that, Wolf corrected me. He said our focus was on creating safe balloon magic for the balloon makers, and that was the only type of experimentation Nils and I could be doing right now. To Wolf, everything else was a waste of time.

So Nils and I played a game of doing mundane things—like finding out how high balloons could go with magic, and if magic could make balloons bulletproof—while talking about what *else* we'd like to study.

Nils had been one of the Dutch Jews I'd saved from the death march to Sachsenhausen, the concentration camp near Oranienburg.

When he'd walked into the house the day after I arrived, I hadn't even recognized him. He was handsome and filled out and didn't look like the skeleton who had taken the first balloon. When he found out who I was, it'd been a tearful reunion.

Now Nils looked up from where he stood at a blackboard, his hand poised in midair. Chemical properties of different inks. He looked tired. He'd been up most of the night with a balloon maker who had gotten a blood infection from a dirty needle.

The balloon maker was still alive, for now.

"Have you been here all night? You should go to sleep," I told him, eyeing him and the coffee cup next to him. "Ink will still be ink tomorrow."

He shook his head. "I want to isolate the chemical responsible for ink-and-magic efficacy so we can standardize it across brands and industries."

"Stop being so smart," I complained, but jokingly, and he knew it.

He smiled. "You're in a better mood. What are you up to today?"

"Writing the standards for equations. We can't assume everyone who will be writing magical equations has had the education from which you and I benefited," I said, picking up a piece of chalk. I liked to map things out on a blackboard before I began.

A soft knock at the door and I sighed. "What?"

"A letter," said Anya. "For you. From America."

Probably my parents. But if it'd been our parents, Anya would have given it to Wolf first, and she wouldn't have come upstairs to deliver it. She would have waited until we took a midday break. I frowned and opened the door, taking the letter from her. I broke the seal and unfolded it.

Dear Ilse,
     You are a hard woman to find.

Colonel Mann told me what you were doing in France, and as admirable as it is, it isn't what you should be doing. You aren't a cog in the machine. You aren't there to create bureaucracy for someone else. You ought to be pushing the boundaries of what we can do with what's in our blood. I'm offering you the opportunity to do just that. I've received government funding with no strings attached—yes, truly—to open a lab to find out what we can do. It'll be a working group, but one of our making and without the requirement that we serve the army at their request.

Lola has already joined me, along with two other girls the colonel helped me track down: Dahlia and Rachel, who are absolutely wonderful. And you know what high praise that is from me. We also have three young men back from the war: Howard, Neal, and Ivan.

I know about you and Polly. I don't mind, Ilse, and if it helps, she's in the area. She wanted to do something else with her life, but she's studying at a women's college only about a half hour away from where I've set up the lab. I asked her if she wanted me to mention that to you, and she said, and I quote, "*Please.*" Do with that what you will. I think you should come home for scientific discovery, but I'll bribe you with whatever I can to get you in my lab.

I'm in charge though. That's the only condition.

This is one ocean liner ticket. It's for October 10. I hope that gives you enough time.

I'll see you by the end of October.

Sincerely,

Stella Montgomery

Director of the American Magical Exploratory Group (AMEG)

Slowly, I walked past Anya, down the stairs, and into Wolf's office doorway. I was vaguely aware of Wolf peeling away from Max and walking toward me. He plucked the letter out of my hands and read it quickly. Then he looked at me for a long moment, and I met his gaze honestly. He nodded, folding the letter, and handed it back to me.

"Max, we're going to borrow Rafi."

"Everything okay?" Max asked.

"Yes. We're going to go for a walk," said Wolf, whistling for the puppy and shutting the door behind him. He put a hand on my shoulder. "Come on. Let's go to the beach."

The beach was cold today, windy and overcast and mostly vacant. Rafi bounded ahead of us over the sand and stone, joyful and exuberant. Wolf was silent for a long time and then said, "It's been two years since Lily died."

I looked over at him. "Do you miss her?"

He nodded, looking like the answer surprised him. "Every day. It's the kind of grief that catches me off guard. I see her in unexpected places."

"I'm sorry, Wolf," I whispered, and the words sounded small and helpless. He'd returned to her grave after the war and had moved her body back to England, to her family's plot, so she could be buried next to her husband.

He smiled a little, tilting his face toward the sea. "You would have liked her. She would have liked you a great deal, though I think you might talk too much for her."

"I talk too much for most people," I said with a grin.

He changed the topic abruptly. "Are you unhappy here?"

"I shouldn't be," I said, surprised into honesty. "Besides, I've only been here for a few months."

"I didn't ask if you should be unhappy, and I don't know that time's got anything to do with this," he said quietly. "I asked you to help, and you did, and I'm grateful for that. But I know this isn't what you thought you'd be doing."

"I didn't know *what* I thought I'd be doing," I admitted. "I think that's the problem. I've been floundering ever since I left Oak Ridge. I didn't help with the bomb. I didn't help here. I went home. I wanted to help. This should feel good."

"And it doesn't. That's fine," he said gently. "Ilse, you're not letting me down."

Tears pricked my eyes. "Are you sure?"

"Of course I'm sure. You're not letting me down. Go home. Go experiment with magic. Don't blow yourself up."

I laughed a little and wiped at my eyes. "That easy?"

"That easy," he said and snapped his fingers.

"How many times am I going to go home, only to leave it again?" I asked him.

Wolf sighed, rubbed at his cheek and the stubble growing there. "I don't know. Maybe forever. Maybe just once more. It's not wrong to miss home, Ilse, or to keep looking for it."

"I miss *you*," I said after a while.

"I know," he said. "I'm sorry. I'm sorry everything changed so much."

I folded my arms around myself. "I hate it, but I'm relieved too, and then I feel guilty about feeling relieved."

He laughed and said, "God, every time I think we aren't that alike, you say something like that."

"We're upsettingly alike," I told him. I elbowed him. "You read the letter. Polly?"

He gave me a sideways look. "Yeah."

"I like her the same way I like some boys," I said, hoping the color in my cheeks could be blamed on the wind. "But then I went home."

"Ah, we are a little alike, aren't we?" said Wolf, and his words weren't half as sad as I'd expected. "Except, for me, I think it took me longer to see Max than it took for him to see me. Do you think Polly sees you?"

"I think so," I said slowly. "But I think she was mad at me. For leaving. For not understanding what she'd gone through before Oak Ridge. I don't know. I don't know how to talk to her."

He put his fingers to his mouth and whistled, calling Rafi back to us from where he'd gotten too far ahead, barking at the waves. "Max and I are complicated. But if he's mad at me, I apologize, if I should. Honestly. And then I listen. And he forgives me. And I do the same for him. Talking's easy. It just takes time and practice."

"Think that'll work with her?"

"Probably. But if it doesn't, Ilse, there will be others."

I made a face at him. "You don't know that."

"I don't," he acknowledged, grinning, and reaching down to rub Rafi's wet head as he returned to us, panting. "But I can trust that it'll still be true."

"I'm not good at that," I said, watching as he threw a stick for Rafi.

"No, you aren't," he agreed. "But it's something you can learn. And I've never seen you back down from a challenge."

"Max."

"What about him?"

"Do you love him?" I asked.

He looked at me. "Yes."

I looked at the ocean. "What's it feel like? Being in love?"

He snorted, as if surprised by the question. "It's a hard feeling to describe."

"Try."

"Okay. You know the first moment you did magic?"

"Yes."

"How did that feel?"

"Terrifying. And incredible. At once. Like I could take over the world, but also like I wanted to cry."

"That's what it feels like to be in love. It's very mundane, most of the time. But there are moments where I am terrified and thrilled at the same time."

I nodded and said quietly, "I think that I learned things about myself from Polly, but I'm not sure that I love her the way you love Max."

"That's okay, you know," Wolf said, throwing a stick into the waves. The dog plunged into the sea, barking and getting a mouthful of seawater. "Love that doesn't work out is still love. It's still worth something."

I took a deep breath, frowning at the ocean. "I don't like not having a purpose."

"I know," he said gently.

And I figured he did. He hadn't known what he was doing before the war, not in the same way I had. I'd lost my way, and he'd found his. I didn't want to be jealous of him, but I couldn't help having a small fragmented part of me that was furiously angry I had fallen behind him like this.

"It isn't easy," he said finally. "Keeping that feeling to yourself. But I figure we're better equipped than most, because we've already done it once with magic. But there's a part of me that wishes I could marry Max in front of a big group of people, that I could stand there and have witnesses hear me tell him how much I love him."

"Do it now," I said, gesturing at the empty beach and the sea. "There's no one else here."

Wolf looked scandalized. "Ilse."

"Ilse," I mimicked him. "Here. I'll demonstrate."

I took a deep breath and faced the ocean. Cupping my hands around my mouth, I shouted at the sea, "I love Max Egan!"

Nothing happened, other than the waves crashing against the beach and the sound of Rafi chewing a stick behind us. I turned to Wolf, satisfied and smiling. "See?"

He shook his head. "You're ridiculous. Fine." He cupped his hands around his mouth and shouted, "I love Max Egan."

I burst into laughter. "Louder!"

"I LOVE MAX EGAN," shouted Wolf, and the sea crashed against the shore.

I cracked up. "I got you to yell at the ocean."

"Oh, shut up," Wolf groused, but he was smiling when he swatted at me. He caught me by the shoulder and I squealed, trying to squirm away until I saw his face. "Ilse, will it make you happy?"

I held his gaze. "I don't know. But I want to try."

That seemed enough for him. He slung his arm around my shoulders. "Good. Write to me."

"I will," I said. "Tell Max you love him."

"I do," he said, and then he added, "I will."

I was going home, and Wolf was already there. We walked along the sea, our feet growing red from the cold water, but we didn't mind. We'd faced monsters and magic we didn't understand, found people we loved, and lost others we'd never forget, and we'd done it all without losing each other. Somehow, miraculously, against all odds, against prevailing winds and thoughts, we'd made it through the war.

AUTHOR'S NOTE

Mixing magic and history is much like a science experiment. It takes just the right amount of each ingredient to make it work. In *The Spy with the Red Balloon*, I wove together many different threads of history along with the emergence of the magic system seen in *The Girl with the Red Balloon*.

The Manhattan Project was a real project. It was the code name for the top secret scientific and engineering experiment to design and create the world's first atomic bomb. It was so secret that Vice President Harry Truman had no idea it existed. When Roosevelt died, Truman was sworn in as president—and promptly briefed about the Manhattan Project and the atomic bombs it'd created.

The project had several sites, including Chicago, Illinois; Los Alamos, New Mexico (referred to as the Hill in this book); Hanford, Washington; and, as depicted in the book, Oak Ridge, Tennessee. In 1943, Oak Ridge was called Clinton Engineer Works. The town was planned and designed to support the research and engineering needs of the three reactors: Y-12, X-10, and K-25. Ilse worked beside the X-10 reactor, otherwise known as the graphite reactor. On my website, you can see photos of this reactor that I took on my trip to Oak Ridge in November 2016.

As the draft pulled men from America's workforce, women filled the jobs. Oak Ridge was home to nearly 75,000 workers, a majority of whom were women. Many worked on the reactors as technicians or as scientists. Though there was not an all-women scientific team at Oak Ridge, many women scientists did work on the Manhattan Project at each of its sites, and they should not be forgotten by history.

As mentioned in the book, Oak Ridge was a segregated town. The African American community that built Oak Ridge, lived there, and supported the Manhattan Project has an unsung history but a vital one. Jim Crow politics kept African American scientists like J. Ernest Wilkins Jr., PhD, from working at Oak Ridge. Stella is a figment of my imagination, but she also represents my hope that we will honor African American contributions to World War II, including the Manhattan Project, with more research, visibility, and discussion.

For readers interested in the decision that Ilse, Stella, Polly, and Lola make at the end of *Spy*, I encourage you to read up on the Szilard petition to President Truman. Many of the scientists and engineers who worked on the Manhattan Project signed the petition urging President Truman not to use the atomic bomb against Japan, believing that such use was no longer warranted.

The Manhattan Project reached abroad too. The project sought to slow down or halt the progress of Hitler's atomic bomb with Operation Alsos, largely operating in 1944 instead of the 1943 of the story. While Wolf's mission is not taken directly from one of Operation Alsos's operations, Alsos served as a model. Haigerloch, Hechingen, and Oranienburg were real German nuclear weapons sites, right down to the unusual prototype reactor in the beer cellar of the church of a castle. You can read more about that in the article about the Atomkeller Museum on the Atlas Obscura website, or you can visit it yourself in Germany.

You can find a complete list of the books that assisted my research for this book on my website, www.katherinelockebooks.com.

ACKNOWLEDGMENTS

I am extraordinarily grateful to be writing the acknowledgments of *Spy*. This is truly a dream come true, and I hope that this is still the beginning. And as they say, teamwork makes the dream work.

Thank you to my agent, Louise Fury, who always has my back. This journey would not be the same without you, and I appreciate your wisdom, honesty, and humor every step of the way. Thank you to everyone at The Bent Agency for all your support and kindness. You're the real magicians here.

Thank you to my editor, Annie Nybo, who took on *Spy* (and me!) with such grace and determination. I knew I was in good hands as soon as I saw we shared an alma mater (yay Allegheny College!) but your guidance went above and beyond. Your vision and feel for story are unparalleled. And thank you to Wendy McClure for your guidance and patience along the way!

Everyone at Albert Whitman has been a treat to work with—thank you to Alexandra Messina-Schultheis, Laurel Symonds, Tracie Schneider, Annette Hobbs Magier, Lauren Michalczyk, and everyone else who are the unsung heroes of publishing. And as always, thank you to Cynthia Fliege and Nina Simoneaux for creating such beautiful covers for my books. I am the luckiest.

Thank you to all the librarians, teachers, and booksellers who championed, hand-sold, book-talked, and supported *The Girl with the Red Balloon*. I am here because of you, and I am so grateful for the work you do to get books into the hands of readers. You're the real heroes of this story.

To my MTWBWY crew, Christina June, Rebekah Campbell, Becka Paula, and Leigh Smith, thank you for all your support, love, and critique over the years. You are the best of the best. Thank you to Kat Howard for reading an early draft of this book and helping me untangle the biggest knots. Thank you to Dahlia Adler, Paul Krueger, Kate Johnston, Stephen Mazzeo, Lindsay Smith, Ashley Poston, Kaitlyn Sage Peterson, Jules Walker, Alex London, Fran Wilde, Nita Tyndall, Blair Thornburgh, Tara Sonin, Kosoko Jackson, S. Jae-Jones, Miriam Weinberg, Candice Montgomery, Justina Ireland, Heidi Heilig, Laura Silverman, Rabbi Yair Robinson, Marisa Robinson, Ian Ramsey-North, Kim-Thao Nguyen, and so many others who have been amazing friends throughout this journey. Thank you to Fight Me Club for always having my back and for teaching me so much. And the GIFs. Always the GIFs.

The book couldn't have been written without the kindness of strangers, museums, historians, citizens, and sensitivity readers. Thank you to Bradley, my host in Oak Ridge, who let me stay in his beautifully restored 1940s house built for the Manhattan Project, and to the Museum of Science and Energy for fantastic information and a wonderful tour. Thank you to Didem Uca for translating the German in this book. And thank you to Gene Schlesinger for knowing a shocking amount about the history of NYC transportation systems. Any mistakes regarding Oak Ridge, its facilities, its history, German translations, or train schedules are mine.

And thank you to Candice Montgomery for reading an early draft of *Spy*. Stella represents a huge contingent of often forgotten African American workers and scientists who worked on the Manhattan Project. It was incredibly important to me that I include her, and I am grateful for Candice's guidance in doing so.

Any mistakes made in Stella's representation or characterization are mine and mine alone.

My family has been incredibly patient and supportive—understanding when I work over holidays or disappear into the revision cave and cheering for every milestone I reach. Mom, Dad, thank you for everything. Jacob and Hannah, you are the best siblings I have. Thanks for reading silently in the back of the car with me for all of our childhoods. Thank you to Michelle, my favorite sister-in-law, for all of your support and for making sure Jacob knows when it's my birthday. Thank you to Emma, Sophie, Elissa, Julia, babies Emi, Rose, and Jane, and the whole Cousin Chat experience for keeping me going. And thank you to my extended family for all your love and support for all my books. I appreciate you all so much.

This book was written and revised during a period of heightened nuclear posturing and attacks on American democracy. For everyone who has contacted their representatives, marched, protested, boycotted, and stood up (physically or emotionally), I am grateful for you. Your spirit and heart keeps me going. Don't panic. Focus.

KATHERINE LOCKE

lives and writes in Philadelphia, where she's ruled by her feline overlords and her addiction to chai lattes. She writes about that which she cannot do: ballet, time travel, and magic. She not-so-secretly believes most stories are fairy tales in disguise. *The Girl with the Red Balloon* was her young adult debut. Visit her at www.katherinelockebooks.com.